I0819664

THE GIRL WITH A THOUSAND FACES

ALSO BY SUNYI DEAN

The Book Eaters

THE GIRL WITH A THOUSAND FACES

SUNYI DEAN

TOR PUBLISHING GROUP
NEW YORK

This is a work of fiction. All of the names, characters, organizations, places, and events portrayed in this work are either products of the author's imagination or used fictitiously.

THE GIRL WITH A THOUSAND FACES

A Tor Book
Published by Tom Doherty Associates / Tor Publishing Group
120 Broadway
New York, NY 10271

www.torpublishinggroup.com

EU Representative: Macmillan Publishers Ireland Ltd, 1st Floor, The Liffey Trust Centre, 117–126 Sheriff Street Upper, Dublin 1, D01 YC43

The Library of Congress Cataloging-in-Publication Data is available upon request.

ISBN 978-1-250-81021-2 (hardcover)
ISBN 978-1-250-46077-6 (international, sold outside the U.S., subject to rights availability)
ISBN 978-1-250-81022-9 (ebook)

First Edition: 2026

Printed in the United States of America

10 9 8 7 6 5 4 3 2 1

My grandmother, Poon Kingfar, was never taught to read or write. Born over one hundred years ago in rural Shanghai, she was a quiet hero who survived two world wars, great deprivation, and the Japanese occupation of Hong Kong. She worked to ensure that her children and grandchildren had the chance to learn, travel, and gain education—opportunities that she herself never had.

This book is dedicated to every woman who could not tell their own story, because the world did not give them a voice.

Pronunciation Guide

Bao: Like the bun. He is named after food.

Cha chaan teng: tsah TSAHN taang

Chan, Mercy: Chann, MER-see. The Canto/English version of Chen Mei Chi.

Chen, Mei Chi: Chinn, Mei-Chee. Chen is a Hakka dialect surname, which is often translated as "Chan" in the Cantonese dialect.

Chiu, Wing Yun: CHEW, wing-yuhnn

Dai pai dong: die pie dohng. A type of open-air stall in Hong Kong, selling street food.

Guanyin: GWAN-yeen/KWAN-yeen. The more widely known Mandarin name of the Goddess of Mercy.

Gweilo: GWAI-low/KWAI-low. Literally "ghost man," although it is sometimes translated as "foreign devil" or "white ghost," because that arguably better portrays the context in which it was coined. Although derogatory in origin, its contextual meaning has softened considerably in modern times.

Kowloon: Kow-LOON. A large district in Hong Kong, within which Kowloon Walled City is located.

Kwun Yam: KWUN-yumm/Gwun-yumm. The Cantonese translation for Guanyin, the Goddess of Mercy. Similar to Kit Ling, the "k" consonant is slightly devoiced.

Leung Lau Yik: Lung Lao-Yick

Maogui: MAO gwey. Literally, "cat-ghost."

Ng Chungpo: Ing CHUNG-poe

Poon Li Fan: Poon Lee-FAHN

Qun Kwa: Choon KWAH. Literally, "skirt + jacket." Refers to a type of two-piece wedding suit, traditionally worn by brides in Southern China.

Shek Ham Chau: Shek Hahm Chow. The literal meaning is Stone Shrine Island, but it has broadly been interpreted as Stone Temple Island.

Sung Daiyu: Sung DIE-Yuu. Traditionally, Chinese women keep their own name when getting married, but Daiyu chose to buck that by adopting her new husband's surname, Sung, in an effort to erase her own past.

Sung Ho Tung: Sung Hoe-Tung

Sung Siu Yin: Sung SIEU (to rhyme with lieu) Yehn

Tsang, Kit Ling: Szaang GEET-Ling/KEET-Ling. Similar to Kwun Yam, the first consonant of "k" is devoiced, and sounds more like "g" to native speakers of English.

For more detailed information on my decisions regarding naming conventions, spelling conventions, and other details, please see the Author's Note in the back of the book.

THE GIRL WITH A THOUSAND FACES

PROLOGUE

Do you like ghost stories, little sister?

Sit down, get comfortable. You haven't heard this one before.

PART ONE

1

MADAM GHOST TALKER

August 20, 1975

Late afternoon, and the Walled City was a fleshy soup. Human pedestrians slicked past each other in narrow alleys, bodies filmed with sweat. Sad-faced ghosts peered out from corners or hovered on filthy eaves. Steam rose from mildewed gutters, suffusing both living and dead alike.

In among the shifting crowd, Mercy Chan paused at a crossroads, peering down the different alleys and struggling to recall the directions that her boss had given her not an hour before. The district was a maze, even for those who knew it well.

Should have written the directions down, she thought sourly. It was too hot to remember things that weren't written down.

Every part of Kowloon was layered in shade, but the lack of sunlight brought no relief. The lower levels in particular were full of machineries and factories; they built up heat, like an oven. Mercy was trying not to bake in that dark oven. She tugged at the soggy neck of her plain linen shirt, peeling it from her skin in an attempt to create a little air circulation. But there was no air to circulate, only humidity.

She was supposed to be wearing a triad jacket—white and green, Cobra Lily's colors, patterned in a snakeskin brocade—but she *could not* be bothered with long sleeves in this heat. Besides, Bao didn't like her jacket, wouldn't sit on her shoulder when she wore it. Even less incentive to ever put it on.

Since she'd chosen a regular sleeveless vest, the ghost cat had deigned to accompany her, compacting himself into a white, fluffy-looking bundle of fur. He nestled between the crook of her neck and shoulder, emanating a tiny radius of chilly air. A long tail curled over her upper arm in languid rest. It was a good, safe comfort to know he was there.

Bao opened one bright-red eye, stretched out a claw, and raked her collarbone lightly.

"Stop that!" Clearly, she'd stood in one place too long for his liking. "If you get bored so easily, why do you come with me?"

The ghost cat yawned.

"Some use you are," she said, affectionate. "Be a good little hunter and find this rogue spirit for me, since you're in such a hurry."

Nose twitching, he leaped from her shoulder and began drifting serenely above the sweat-soaked masses. A few people flinched, but most ignored him, recognizing that he was no threat. Main streets like this one were guarded carefully by triad exorcists, and the only ghosts who traveled along it openly were those—like Bao—who had special exemption.

Mercy, who could not float eerily through the air, began shoving her way through the crowd after him. The sooner she got this done, the sooner she could get back to the fan-cooled bliss of her own flat. And have a damn bath.

Kowloon was as much vertical as it was horizontal. She was currently about three levels up on the east side, walking through a warren of noodle-thin "roads" made of metal sheets laid across pipes and struts. Five-foot-nothing and she still had to duck in places beneath low-hanging signs or protruding construction.

Directly beneath her sandaled feet was another street, or possibly the interior of someone's house. She could hear people moving about on all sides: above, below, around her, for several streets up and down and extending to the sides, pierced with loud clangs from the metalworking shops on the ground level.

Bao appeared to be heading for a particular flat one level up. She could just see it from here. The windows were boarded but an unearthly light seeped from the cracks, visible in the city's perpetual semidarkness.

"Good job," she said.

Bao flicked his tail and darted ahead of her. He led her off the main road, up a rickety staircase and down a short alleyway that was devoid of light. Garbage crusted the gutters while rusted, irregularly spaced doorframes sank into the surrounding concrete. Her job never took her to friendly places.

He floated across a narrow gap between buildings; Mercy jumped it with practiced ease. At the end of the alleyway was a pair of doors, almost next to each other. Judging by the number etched into its frame and the eerie light seeping through the cracks, the left door was the one she wanted.

Unfortunately, someone had secured it shut with a chain and a padlock.

"No easy way through there," she said to the cat. "Perhaps the neighbors can be of help."

Bao leaped up to sit on her shoulder and curled into an indifferent lump, as if to reply, *I did my bit; the rest is your problem now*. Which was perfectly true.

She approached the unlocked door. Nobody answered her knock, so she simply pushed it open.

Dilapidation greeted her. A stove, a couch, a folding table, two plastic stools, and a broken TV all crowded for space against one wall, while a narrow pallet took up the opposite side. There was no toilet, no closet, just a few unwashed dishes, and clothes of dubious hygiene in a pile. Like most homes, this one sat in semidarkness; electricity was expensive in Kowloon, and unreliable.

On the far side, two men sat hunched over a small dining table, talking intently in low voices. They looked to be in their early twenties—young enough to be her sons, if she'd had children. One of them bore a rat tattoo winding around his neck, cheaply done and the ink bleeding across lines. The other wore a series of thin gold bracelets on his wrist. Both looked up as she entered.

"Cobra Lily sent me," Mercy said, when they continued to stare at her in silence. "I hear the place next to yours has an exceptional ghost problem."

"We are the ones who called on Cobra Lily." Rat Tattoo rubbed his nose and added guardedly, "You are the exorcist?" His disbelieving gaze took in this early-fifties woman, stocky frame draped in a washed-worn shirt and battered shorts. The broken flip-flops on her feet and the fuzzy cat on her shoulder. The smattering of cheap tattoos on her skin.

"Ghost talker," she corrected, cheerfully. "Not exorcist."

His scowl deepened. "Even worse! We pay our dues, we pay them on time, and Cobra Lily sends some . . . middle-aged shopkeeper? What are you going to do, gossip it to death?"

Bao chose that moment to open those red, red eyes.

There was an intake of breath from both men, the shared recognition of a ghost cat. Maogui were no laughing matter.

For the first time, Rat Tattoo seemed to notice the branching lightning scar that ran from Mercy's shoulder to her wrist, and his forehead creased in uneasy alarm. His hand drifted to the watermelon chopper that hung from his belt.

"Don't you dare draw that knife! And I am here for what I can do, not for how I look," Mercy said sharply. Middle-aged shopkeeper, indeed! Young people had no respect these days. "Do you want my help, or not? Hungry Ghost Festival is just around the corner."

The men exchanged glances, clearly absorbing her warning. Ghosts were already a pain at the best of times, but during Ghost Month—and on the nights surrounding the festival in particular—they could be especially dangerous. The veil to the underworld was thinnest, and the dead at their strongest, on those inauspicious days.

"Fine, but you'd better be competent, little auntie," Rat Tattoo said, releasing his chopper grudgingly. He had a strong Mandarin accent, although his

Cantonese was very good. "The old lady died a few days ago. She won't go away, nor will she let anyone inside for long, and she is violent if disturbed. That's why we asked Cobra Lily for an exorcist."

Mercy kept her face still and neutral. Almost everyone who died in the Walled City returned as a ghost, these days. Nothing unusual there; this city was a pit trap for spirits, its energy saturated with years of violence.

But those who died peacefully did not usually linger very long. Even those who died brutally could often be placated by offerings or apologies. Either these men were missing information, or they were hoarding facts.

"How did you know her?" she said. "Are you just neighbors?"

Unease flashed across Rat Tattoo's face. "She was Ng Chungpo's grandmother." He gestured at his bracelet-wearing friend. "He lives here, next to her."

Chungpo remained silent and drummed his fingers on the tabletop. For someone who had recently lost a grandmother, he didn't seem very upset. Bored, even.

"I see," Mercy said, when it became clear the bereaved man had no interest in replying. "How long has she been a concern? Was it you who chained everything shut?"

Her gaze kept straying to Chungpo's bracelets; they did not seem like the kind of thing a streetwise young man would wear in these parts. She could imagine them having belonged to his dead grandmother, though.

"Few days." Chungpo spoke at last, picking sullenly at his lip. "She keeps crying and ranting. Won't talk to anyone. We only boarded up the door because we were afraid."

Rat Tattoo leaned forward. "Will you banish her?"

"I will certainly speak to her," Mercy said, carefully. "Can you let me into her place?"

Five minutes later, they stood crowded around as Chungpo jammed a key forcefully into the lock. Loose chain links slithered to the ground in a messy coil.

"Now what?" Rat Tattoo ran his thumb repeatedly over tobacco-stained teeth. "Do we stay here, or—"

"No. Come with me." Mercy pressed a hand to the peeling wood and gently nudged it open, stepping inside.

With a mutter of swearing, the two young men edged reluctantly after her. A waft of cooler air rolled over them, pleasant relief from the sticky heat outside. Bao leaped down from her shoulder to stand next to her, tail lashing.

This flat was a more cheerful replica of the one she'd just left. A sofa bed in tolerable condition, the walls scrubbed clean, and Buddhist paraphernalia lining rickety wooden shelves. The old lady had been devout; there was a shrine to the wealth god, some small statues, a bowl of fruit left out for hungry spirits. A few ancient newspaper clippings were pinned to the wall, headlines shouting about the end of the war; they were decades old, yellow with age.

On the far side of the room, an elderly woman bent over a charcoal cooker, stirring something in a wok. A dark button-down shirt draped loose over her stooped shoulders, spine humped with age and poor nutrition. She did not look up at their entrance.

The ghost herself.

Quite corporeal, too. If not for the slightly translucent quality of her flesh, the old lady might almost have passed for a living woman. That solidity, and the degree of the coldness in here, suggested a spirit of notable strength.

Or notable anger.

"This is her," Chungpo said. "My dear old Ahma." A hint of irony underpinned the affectionate term.

"No shit." Mercy cleared her throat then said, more loudly and more politely, "Good afternoon, grandmother."

Silence.

"What are you doing?" Rat Tattoo said, in a low hiss. "You are supposed to banish her!"

"She doesn't talk to anyone," Chungpo added. "She won't talk to you, either."

"Shut up, stupid eggs," Mercy told them, then raised her voice again. "Grandmother? Can you hear me? Please answer, if you can."

The men were right to be cynical. Despite having unfinished business, ghosts were not always willing to communicate, and it sounded like they had already tried that here. But ghosts *did* answer to Mercy. Always. She had a way of speaking, of putting force into her words, that seemed to draw their attention.

As usual, it worked. The elderly woman paused in her stirring and partly turned her head.

"Is that you?" Her face was still hidden by a fall of shoulder-length hair, black strands shot thickly with gray. "Aiyah, you were gone so long!"

Another waiting woman, Mercy thought resignedly. There were many kinds of waiting-women ghosts, from wives pining for dead or unfaithful husbands, to mothers wasting away as they hoped for the return of a child, to young girls with broken hearts, and so on. She felt sorry for them, but also annoyed by them. Bad enough to spend your life waiting on other people; even worse to spend the afterlife doing it, too.

Still, it was the kind of opening she needed.

"Sorry, grandmother." Mercy took a cautious step forward. "I am just a guest in your home. The person you were waiting for is . . . Actually, who *are* you waiting for?"

Feverescent eyes peered through a veil of monochrome hair. "My grandson. My handsome, clever grandson!"

"Oh? Did he go somewhere?"

"Out." The ghost seemed to dim briefly, like a faltering candle. "My grandson went . . . out . . . when I got sick. He said he would get a doctor and come right back."

Chungpo wiped his hands, as if his palms were sweating.

"But he did not come back, did he." Mercy was swept with a sense of resignation; she suspected where this was going. "Did he leave you here? Alone, and sick?"

"He is coming back." The ghost shivered. "Very soon. Very soon!"

Cheeks reddening, Chungpo edged back into the shadows.

"Why haven't you banished her?" Rat Tattoo cut in. Even in this cold room, he was flushed and red, too. "End her suffering! What kind of exorcist are you, anyway?"

"I'm a ghost talker, not an exorcist," Mercy said, sharply. "Interrupt me again and I'll bind your spirit to a bedpan."

She couldn't really do it, but Rat Tattoo didn't know that. He blanched and fell silent.

To the old woman, she said, "Listen, grandmother. If your grandson was going to come back, why did he lock and bar the doors?"

"I . . . don't know." The ghost finally tilted her head up, and there was nothing horrific or scary about her features. Only a pained sadness in the sunken face. "He took my money when he left. Said it was to pay the doctor."

Chungpo swore under his breath.

"Fuck a crab," Mercy said, and sighed. "Grandmother, you are dead. I don't know if the sickness killed you or starvation did, but either way, the only 'help' your grandson gave was to hurry you along and make sure you could not escape death. He waited till you were bedbound, stole your money and your jewelry, and locked you in here to die." She looked at Chungpo. "Am I right?"

The man glared. Gold bracelets clacked on his wrists as his fists curled.

"No!" The ghost began to cry with black tears, smoke trickling from her nostrils. "No, he would never!" Long cooking chopsticks dropped from fragile hands and dispersed into ethereal mist. Her body flickered like a television with a bad signal.

Rat Tattoo grabbed Mercy's shoulder with some force. "If you are accusing us of—"

Bao hissed, fur standing on end. He was only a small ghost, but the sudden noise was enough to make the man release his grip in shock.

"You must have known, in those final moments, what your grandson had done," Mercy said, stepping sideways to avoid Rat Tattoo's grasp, still keeping steady eye contact with the elderly lady. "Or you would not be lingering here now, attacking anyone who tries to move you out of this house."

"No, he would not . . . he . . ." Pallid lips writhed in sudden anger. "How could he leave me like that? His own grandmother. I took *days* to die!"

"Ghosts always have unfinished business," Mercy said, softening her tone. "Ghosts always want something. What is it you want, grandmother? You can tell me."

It was true. The dead who returned were not quite who they used to be. Dying damaged the different parts of the soul, and what lingered on was the hurt, the betrayal, the grief. The dead came back because they had unfinished business, always, and ignoring that context was deeply shortsighted. In Mercy's professional opinion, anyway.

"I want . . ." The ghost shuddered, grew taller and broader. The stick-thin shoulders filled out, broadening with muscle. Ghostly etherealness solidified into weighty spirit-flesh. Her eyes went wide, the red light behind them bright as a beacon. She opened her mouth, jaw unhinging as smoke poured out. "I want justice!"

"Thought so." Mercy dived for cover behind the rickety sofa-bed.

Rat Tattoo, quick on the uptake, dived to the opposite corner.

Only Chungpo remained, frozen and terrified, crouching in a corner. "Ahma—"

The ghost shrieked and vomited a stream of fire. Everything in front of her melted or caught alight. Mercy, already too hot, felt a fresh raft of sweat break across her skin.

Chungpo screamed and launched himself through the single window, narrowly avoiding a fiery death. He burst through the cheap glass and landed on the eaves just outside. Mercy could no longer see him, but she could hear the frantic slap of his feet as he desperately leaped to another balcony with a crash.

"What did you do!" Rat Tattoo yelled, still cowering. "What the hell, what the hell, what the—"

"*Chungpo!*" the ghost moaned, loudly enough that the picture frames rattled. "*My murderous, ungrateful brat!*"

"Go after him, get your justice!" Mercy called out, hands cupped over her mouth. "You can do it, grandmother!"

The ghost vomited another jet of fire and took off, lithe and fast in death as she had not been in life. She flew through the same window, speeding after Chungpo. Moments later, screams and yells echoed from the streets beyond as terrified pedestrians fled from the spectacle of a red-eyed, fire-breathing old woman.

Even that did not last very long. Chungpo howled, the sound entangled with the roar of his grandmother's flames. His cries cut off abruptly as death took him. The noise of fire faded to a trickle; her vengeance was satisfied.

The sudden stillness was breathtaking. Bao sat in the center of the quiet room, cleaning perfectly white paws. If he was calm, that meant the danger had passed; the old lady was at rest.

"Job done." Mercy stood and dusted the ash from her hands, trying vainly to fan some air on her face. It was hot as a metal furnace in here, not helped by the sofa still being on fire. "We did good, little cat."

"Are you crazy?" Rat Tattoo grabbed her arm, whipping her round so hard it gave her a crick in the neck. "That ghost killed him because of what you said!"

Mercy punched his throat with her free arm. Rat Tattoo wheeled backward, gagging, and tried to draw his watermelon chopper.

In a blink, Bao rippled and grew larger, tiny body burgeoning to the size of a leopard. A bone-white, fluffy-as-a-cloud leopard. He leaped at the startled young man, knocking him to the ground. Enormous, claw-tipped paws pressed stocky shoulders to the floor, heavy with unexpected weight.

Rat Tattoo lay flat, breathing hard from the punch to his throat. Still clutching the chopper.

Mercy drew her own knife and knelt over him, the blade tip pressed to the underside of Rat Tattoo's chin. "Stop opening your mouth, small son. Stupid things come out every time you do."

He stared at her, eyes round like teacups. He had rather delicate skin for such a hard man.

"Did you know that some ghosts can change how corporeal they are? Easier for them to do if there is less light." Mercy prized the watermelon chopper from his hand, examining the blade; it was dull and cheap, notched in four places.

"That is why ghosts in Kowloon are so strong, compared to the ghosts in the rest of Hong Kong. It is always dark here."

She tossed the cleaver through the ruined wall of the burning flat, into the alleyway beyond. "Bao is particularly strong, because I have been feeding him for years. Not only can he change his size and corporeality, but his bite will fuck you up—whether it is night or day, whether you're a living human or a dead spirit."

Bao growled in agreement.

"You murdered Chungpo," Rat Tattoo said, tightly. "Cobra Lily will not be impressed!"

Mercy laughed. "My boss, whose name is too good for your mouth, doesn't take kindly to anyone in Kowloon who kills women. Especially one's own grandmother. Chungpo was already dead no matter what I did, you wooden chicken. I just saved Cobra Lily the hassle of doing it herself. Believe me, she will be happy."

Rat Tattoo's eyes swam with insults, but for once, his mouth was silent. He was learning.

"Be glad I don't mark you down for accessory to his murder. You are not innocent either, are you?" she said, pointedly. "Covering for your friend, lying to—"

Catch him.

The urge. It struck her with blinding force, her hands spasming with that sudden rush of violent desire.

Hold him.

Her knife wobbled against his skin; he swallowed.

Drag him to water and keep him down until his blood is salt and his eyes are food for the fishes—

Mercy breathed in deep, then breathed out slowly again, struggling for control. She mentally counted to ten until the irrational moment passed. That darkness in her, whatever it was, which gave her such unpleasant ideas and whispered to her at night, had no place here.

She didn't know why those thoughts plagued her relentlessly, only that they did. It was simply a part of herself that she had learned to live with.

Rat Tattoo had not missed the flux of emotions passing across her face, or the dangerous twitching of her hands. He went completely still, like a frightened mouse.

"Whatever, I'm done." Mercy stood up and put her knife away, trying to conceal the tremor in her limbs. "Bao, let's go!"

Bao withdrew from the prone man, his form shimmering and compacting down. By the time he reached Mercy's side, he was again the size of a small kitten.

Rat Tattoo scrambled upright, face red from anger and shame. "Fuck you, dog-faced bitch! Fuck your mother, fuck your father and your uncle and your bastard demon cat! May your whole family fall down in the street and get run over!"

"Too late for curses," she said, stepping through the burned door. "I have no family."

His swearing echoed after her all the way down the alley and halfway down the next block. But he didn't actually follow her, and she didn't look back.

2

PICTURE A GIRL

Thirty-three years ago . . .

Picture a girl, floating in a storm-churned ocean.

Her arms hang limp, eyes lidded and unresponsive. She has a worker's build, strong all over, hands blooming with calluses. Dark hair fans out in the water, forming a cloud around her face. A thin bracelet with a tiger charm encircles one wrist.

The current stirs and swirls. She does not.

Dead things surround her. A few drowned men drift in the water, limbs rigid and possessions scattered. The broken remnants of freshly sunken boats lie half buried on the ocean floor. History is eroding down here, rusting in the mud.

Beneath the water, her eyes open.

So does her mouth. She is drowning, floundering. Splayed hands paddle, sturdy legs kicking her upward. The instinct to live is strong.

She breaks the ocean surface with a gargling shriek. How long was she underwater? How did she get here? Questions without answers. She needs to get out of the ocean before she dies. The shore isn't far, visible as a hump of indistinct trees. She swims.

And swims. Against the surf, against the tide. It drags her out and she rides the waves, knowing instinctively how to work with the ocean's pull. This surprises her, to find how well she navigates water. She must be experienced at swimming.

Soon enough, the girl slogs onto the beach in the dead of night, feeling raw for reasons she can't explain, yet knowing she has done a terrible . . . what? What is it? Something she does not want to remember and can't think about. Not yet.

There is water inside of her, a lot of it. She spends a while vomiting it up, chest aching. But at the end of that ache is air, sweet and clear.

More water pours from her eyes. Not ocean water, though it tastes of salt. She is crying and can't stop. *You can't cry under the sea without drowning.* Who said that to her? Someone now lost. The crying only ends when her dehydrated body runs out of tears.

Thoughts and memories contradict each other inside her head and she can't sift through the confusion. Slumped up against an abandoned fishing boat, entirely alone, she dares risk thinking about the memories which frighten her.

Names, first. She must have one, is sure she did once. She can't recall it, though, which is scary. It is then that she notices the injuries along her forearms. In the stress of everything happening, those details have only just registered.

Firstly, there is the scar. On her left side runs a branching mark, from shoulder to wrist. It looks like a lightning bolt etched into her skin and it is violently red, still raw to the touch.

Secondly, there are the words. On her right arm, someone has scratched characters in a red weal along the skin. Just a simple name: Chen Mei Chi.

She traces the scratched characters, puzzled. No idea why she'd have her own name etched into her skin like a wound. Or who made that wound in the first place, or why she can't remember more.

She examines the gold tiger charm on its plain bracelet chain. The sort of thing given to mark the zodiac of one's birth year. But what year is it currently? That's the real question. If she knew that, she might know her own age.

As for the rest, she has little enough to go on. She was swimming . . . where? A green place, on the ocean. An island, yes. Mei Chi can picture it, just, though the details slip away when she tries to focus on them.

A raging storm.

A girl who loved the sea.

A statue, standing in darkness.

The *something* she did, which she should not have done.

That is it. The full extent of her fractured memories.

Exhaustion is conquering her, and she can't keep awake much longer. It feels as if she has been swimming for decades without rest. Maybe tomorrow will bring more answers. She lifts up the overturned boat and crawls beneath it, curling up.

Confused and exhausted, Mei Chi slides into an uneasy sleep.

Her first night is a difficult one. Initially, her dreams are a jumble of drowning-related things and screaming faces of sailors. Regular nightmare stuff.

Then, without warning, she wakes abruptly. Something is wrong. Instead of sand, she lies on a bed of lotus blossoms and curling vines, as if she has appeared in the middle of a forest. It is stuffy and hot in here.

Lifting up the boat, she finds the beach is a bleak landscape; the vines exist only under the boat. The beach is now a place where the desert meets the sea, ash-white shore on one side (no trees, nothing for miles) and black water on the other. The sand rattles like bones and the waves are turgid, barely moving, as if the water is too heavy for currents.

A woman stands ankle-deep in the surf, hair blowing in a wind that Mei Chi cannot feel. Her skin is the color of light jade, her nails unnaturally long and sharp-edged. She wears rags, the fabric drenched; rivulets of water run down her arms and drip from her limbs. Strands of kelp wrap around her ankles, and her feet are caked in sand grains. The scent of brine overpowers.

The woman is speaking now. Or rather, she is screaming—the same phrase, over and over. It's oddly difficult to hear because the air is thick, distorting and muting all noise.

"I can't hear you," Mei Chi says. Her words are distorted, too. She walks closer to the green-hued woman. Movement is difficult; it's like trying to wade in thick jelly.

"SEA . . . SISTER!" The woman cups her hands around a wind-chapped mouth to holler. "SEA! SISTER!" Her eyes are impossible to see, hidden by her hair.

"Sea Sister?" Mei Chi says, with an uneasy spark of recognition. She should know the answer to her own question. The fact that she doesn't sends a thrill of panicked anxiety down her spine. "Who is Sea Sister?"

The green-hued woman throws back her head. The hair streams back from her face and her eyes are solid orbs, glistening and dark, like a sea lion's. Inhuman, yet oddly beautiful.

Then she lunges for Mei Chi, who yelps and leaps backward.

There is no ground behind her, though. Only blackness. She steps into that blackness and falls forever and a day, while the green-hued woman shrieks from an ever-growing distance.

In the shadow of an overturned boat, Mei Chi wakes with a gasp. Just a dream.

Even so, she bursts into tears. Outside, the rainstorm has taken a turn for the worse, battering the hull. The noise is tremendous. Eventually, she drifts to sleep again, and this time the night lets her rest.

In the morning, her already scant memories feel even more shaky and uncertain, like something she merely imagined. Mei Chi (if that is her name) eases out of the overturned boat into a brand-new day. The beach is quiet, which strikes her as odd. There should be fishermen going about their business; this boat should be in use.

Fishermen. So. She knows about their habits, their life. That only amplifies her frustration with what is unknown. It's as if seeing things she should know helps trigger the memories, but she can't summon them of her own volition.

It's too hard to think; the distractions are mounting. She is hungry, but has no food. She is thirsty, but the ocean isn't drinkable. Find those things first. Once she is safe and warm, that will be a good time to examine the half-remembered echoes which fill her with inexplicable fear.

The scratched name on her arm stings as she walks; she pulls down her tattered sleeve to cover it, and tries not to think too hard about anything for now.

There is an overgrown trail, leading away from the beach and through clusters of trees. Mei Chi follows it until she emerges through leafy foliage at a small village. A few houses, some chickens. If anyone is awake, they are still inside.

Well, except one. A man is crouched down, trying to fix a broken fence. Next to him are barrels which look to be full of rainwater; Mei Chi's thirst intensifies.

She hobbles over. The man stiffens at her approach, turning to regard her with a wary expression.

"Good morning, uncle." Her voice is raspy and creaky; she tries to clear her throat in vain.

The man glowers. "What do you want?" He uses no honorific for her, she notices.

"Do you have any water?" she asks, inching closer. Looking pointedly at the barrels. "I am lost, and very thirsty."

"Lost? What do you mean? Did you come from the city?"

"No," she says, unsure which city he means. She adds, on impulse, "But I am trying to get there. Do you know which way I should walk?" A city sounds more promising than jumping back into the ocean.

His lip curls. "Are you mad, or just stupid?"

She recoils. "What do you mean?"

"Hong Kong surrendered to the Japanese months ago," he says, half snarling. "They called it Black Christmas. You must know that."

She shakes her head emphatically. "I . . . have been living on the islands."

She intends it as a half lie to cover her ignorance, but it feels oddly like the truth in her mouth.

"The islands?! That's very lucky. Did you sail through that storm, then?"

"I think so," she says, in a small voice. "The boat turned over. I managed to swim to shore."

"Lucky you, twice over. Anyway, Hong Kong belongs to the Japanese troops, now." He spits on the ground. "You must be insane or a simpleton to think of going there." His eyes narrow. "Or maybe, you work for the Japanese. Is that what you are? One of their collaborators?"

"I am not anything like that!" She begins to cry. "I am just lost and confused!"

Far from being moved by her plight, he seems alarmed by her neediness, her vulnerability. "We cannot help you, we cannot help you! Go away, little miss!" And he shoves her bodily down the road.

She resists, just trying to keep her balance. He shoves her again and something dark within her flares in sudden fury.

Catch him.

She snatches his wrists.

Hold him.

"Let go of me, kid!" he says, full of revulsion and anger.

Drag him to the water and—

One moment her fingers are tight around his wrists and the next she is hauling him to a nearby rain barrel, oddly strong despite being shorter and smaller than this grown man.

—keep him down until his blood is salt and his eyes are food for the fishes—

He's yelling and thrashing and still, somehow, she wrestles him down and shoves his head into the barrel. The villager screams horribly with his head underwater, bubbles churning as he expends the air from his lungs.

—and there is nothing left of him but empty skin.

"Stop her!" People are bursting out of nearby houses, shouting and pointing as they sprint to her victim's rescue.

Mei Chi gasps and releases the man, backing away so fast she stumbles and nearly falls. What is she doing? Why did she do that? There are no good answers to that question. She simply felt a terrible urge, heard those awful intrusive thoughts, and acted on them.

"Demon!" The man has pulled his head out of the water barrel, face bright red and streaming with water. "Demon bitch!"

Villagers are converging, furious and frightened. Mei Chi can't blame them. She's furious and frightened, too. At herself, as much as them.

There are thick woods, not far from here. Perhaps she can find safety there. Mei Chi flees, cringing at the villagers' shouting.

3

WATER FETCHER

August 20, 1975

Catch him.

People milled in the streets, trying to smother the small fires started by the elderly ghost.

Hold him.

Rat Tattoo's yelling echoed, faintly audible above the racket. And Mercy veered away from the crowds, the noise, hands curled into fists, breathing through her nose.

Drag him to the water—

The refrain echoed through her head, cacophonously loud. Tight pain speared behind her eyes, as if her blood pressure were rising sharply.

—and keep him down until his blood is salt and his eyes are food for the fishes—

She held her face still as a stone statue and kept walking, conscious of Rat Tattoo still in the background somewhere. Conscious, too, of the local residents still flustered and cross.

The moment she turned a fresh corner, Mercy broke into a jog. She didn't like running at the best of times and was soon out of breath, but she knew from experience that when *the urge* crept up on her, she should avoid other people. She needed space.

Space, of course, was the one thing that was not easy to find in Kowloon. The city was small in area, the foundations hemmed in by fort walls built long ago.

It compensated by being complex in structure. Dozens of paths and alleys crisscrossed at all levels. Of these, the Snakeskin triad guarded only the eight main roads which ran at ground level, and slapped wards on the bigger alleys or streets in upper areas. It made sense to do this; the eight main roads were the most important to keep free of ghosts. Most of the ground-level areas were steeped in perpetual shadow.

People still traversed the smaller roads and alleys, because they had to. They either lived there, worked there, could not afford the tolls too often, or all three. But those streets were less crowded, and that was what Mercy wanted right now.

Three streets over and two stories down, she finally came to a quiet little courtyard on the ground level, squashed on all sides by other buildings. No sunlight at all. The only other person around was a young girl, perhaps twelve or thirteen, who was drawing filthy water from a crude well. It was too much to expect total privacy in Kowloon; this would have to do.

Mercy slumped against the nearest wall in a crouch, heels of her hands pressed to her eye sockets, waiting for her breath to settle and the headache to subside. Bao pressed close against her neck, oozing chilly comfort. She counted up to fifteen, then down again in reverse.

After so many years, Mercy had more or less accepted the intrusive thoughts she could not explain, because she could at least control them. Even when they overwhelmed her, it was never enough to drive her to unfortunate acts—apart from that very first time, as a girl at Silverstrand Beach.

Didn't mean she wasn't scared by it every time, though.

"Hey? Hey, auntie!"

Mercy looked up, trying to suppress a flash of irritation at being disturbed. Bao, who had immediately fallen into a nap, opened one resentful eye.

The young girl was gesturing at them, a hopeful expression on her face.

Mercy sighed. "What is it, little niece?"

She grinned. "You're Madam Chan, right? The ghost talker who works for Cobra Lily?"

"Heard of me, have you?"

"I watched you talk to a ghost on my street," she said, excitedly. "It wouldn't speak to anyone except you."

"I'm lucky." Mercy hated this line of conversation, because she never knew what to say when it came up, or how to explain why ghosts responded to her. Maybe other people just didn't use the right tone of voice. "I have a knack."

"It ate a man's head after you talked to it," the girl said, chewing a ragged nail.

"*She* ate her husband's head, and it was no worse than what he'd done to her while she was alive," Mercy said, shortly. The head-eating thing was specific enough for her to recall the case. She added, with a hint of guilt, "Sorry you had to see that."

"Naw, it was fun. You were clever, too." She lifted the bucket, holding it up. "Need a drink of water, Madam Ghost Talker?"

Gray liquid slopped over the rim of the metallic pail. It had an oily sheen and smelled like rotten cabbage. Bao actually bared his teeth, as if threatened.

Mercy eyed first the girl, and then the bucket, with a raised eyebrow. Next to the well was a basket of cheap bottles that she had partly filled up.

Water fetchers were a common enough sight. There were wells all over the district, though you couldn't pay Mercy to drink from any of them. Any water that came from the ground in Kowloon was heavily contaminated by open sewage and industrial waste. Still, some folk had a use for it, and savvy kids could make a few pennies collecting and delivering.

"Not right now, sorry," Mercy said finally, rubbing throbbing temples. Thankfully, *the urge* had abated, for now, which was a welcome relief. She needed to get home and report to Cobra Lily.

The girl's face fell. She muttered something rude under her breath and turned back to her work. Even with a rope, her slight form had to lean over and into the crude well, just to lower her pail.

Mercy watched, struck by immediate remorse. She herself had not been much older when she'd first come to the Walled City, alone and friendless, struggling to stay safe and find work to feed herself.

Things were better these days than they used to be, with the war long done and modernity creeping in, but kids here still had a hard life. Harder than most people's, all things considered. A few pennies meant nothing to her, these days, but would mean a lot to this girl.

She stood slowly, brushing dust off her legs. "Hey kid, I changed my mind. How much for a couple of bottles?"

The girl did not reply. Perhaps she hadn't heard—her back was toward Mercy, her body leaned over the well. Head out of sight.

Bao stood up abruptly, suddenly alert when he hadn't been before.

"Hey, little niece . . ." Mercy began, then trailed off.

The girl wasn't moving. Her narrow frame was slumped and completely limp.

Mercy swore under her breath and darted forward, closing the distance between them. She grasped fistfuls of threadbare shirt and hauled the kid upward and back.

Sour-smelling liquid sloshed her shirt and the ground around them. Bao hissed, leaping off her shoulder and backing away to avoid getting wet. Even as a ghost, he disliked the sensation.

Dirty, oily water surged up and over the lip of the well, as if a pipe had burst or flooded from below. It pooled on the concrete, having nowhere to sink into, and showed no signs of abating.

The girl, meanwhile, collapsed in Mercy's arms. She was soaked from the chest up, and Mercy realized with appalled horror that the kid's head had been hanging upside down in water. That small face was white as death: chest not moving, lungs not breathing. She needed to get the kid breathing—

Pale lids flew open, sharp gaze fixing instantly to Mercy's own. She should have been relieved, but instead the sight made her stomach sink. There was something watchful and alien behind those eyes. No trace of the hard-bitten child she'd spoken to only moments before.

"Shit," Mercy said, wearily. "I'm too late."

"Don't worry, Madam Ghost Talker." The girl broke into a slow, cold smile. "This body has been dead for days."

From a few feet away, Bao hissed, ghost fur standing on end. He was telling her what she already could see for herself: the kid was possessed.

Water continued to glug from the well, slowly filling the small, sunken courtyard. It lapped at her sandal-clad feet, threatening to rise to her ankles.

None of this was good. A normal person might have dropped the kid and fled, but Mercy was too experienced for that. If it wanted to attack, it would have already. For whatever reason, this ghost wished to speak.

And talking to ghosts was the one thing Mercy Chan truly had a gift for. Best she deal with this problem, before it did harm to someone less adept.

She held the thin frame steady and said, with a calm she did not feel, "Who are you, then? What do you want?"

"I am a messenger." The girl's smile twisted into a snarl. "The demon who killed me wanted me to ask you a question."

A bizarre answer. Most ghosts were confused, to one extent or another. Returning as an undead spirit meant portions of the soul were missing or fractured, and that in turn meant a ghost's self-awareness and ability to reason were also damaged.

But this spirit did not sound confused. It sounded extremely confident.

"Who was this demon that killed you?" she asked, skin prickling with goose bumps. "Why doesn't this demon speak to me itself?"

"How should I know?" Small flies landed on the girl's face, crawling across the unblinking eyes, across the teeth bared in a fixed grin. "I am just a good little ghost, doing as I am told."

"I see." Mercy's mouth was suddenly dry. "What was the question this demon wanted you to ask?"

The dead girl blinked first one eye, and then the other. "Do you remember the island, Chen Mei Chi?"

Her headache from before came crashing back, like a rain of stones on the inside of her skull. A strange, terrible pressure was building up behind her temples, so powerful it left her dizzy and staggering.

"No!" she gasped, as much to rebuke the pain as to answer reflexively.

"Lies! Lies, lies, *lies*!" The dead girl launched up at her, mouth twisted into a snarl.

Mercy didn't even have to react. Bao tackled the girl from the side, lion sized and roaring.

Supernatural or not, the girl had a slight frame that buckled under the ghost cat's hefty corporeality. She crashed sideways to the ground under a heap of maogui flesh.

And before Mercy could even think the word "stop," let alone shout it, Bao put his jaws around the dead kid's head and bit down.

There was a sound like a watermelon bursting, followed by silence. The headless body toppled into the well.

Mercy probably should have tried to catch the body and haul it out, rather than allow yet another contaminant into the water system below. Instead, she was too busy swallowing sick, repulsed by the pop of blood and brains that squished from between Bao's teeth. She loved her pet, but in moments like these, she remembered why most people ran from ghost cats, or tried to banish them.

Around them, the gray water receded rapidly, seeming to either sink into the ground or retreat back into the well from which it had surged. The mangled head was gone, swallowed cheerfully into Bao's gullet.

"What the hell was that about?" Mercy said out loud, hands still shaking from the encounter. She'd faced down death before, and seen far more gruesome ghosts than this one. Yet the intensity of the experience had unnerved her deeply. "Demons leaving messages? Ghosts with a personal angle? I don't like this."

Bao looked at her, tail lashing. Far from bored or indifferent, he seemed curiously alert and intense; he had still not shrunk back down to his kitten size. As if he still sensed a threat.

From elsewhere in the neighborhood, a clatter of noise echoed: voices talking, laughing, arguing. Even quiet spaces like this did not stay quiet long, in Kowloon. Other people would be here soon.

"Let's put some warding talismans down," she said, rising to her feet. "After that, we're heading home. There are no answers here, and I still need a bath."

4

A GOOD BATH

August 20, 1975

The bath was heaven for the entire fifteen minutes Mercy sat in it. She scrubbed until all trace of salt and grime and burned furniture and brain matter was gone. Eventually, she felt almost human again.

Being clean was a luxury she would never take for granted. In the old days, before Cobra Lily had plucked her from obscurity and squalor, Mercy hadn't ever bathed. Mostly because she hadn't owned a tub. She'd made do with a quick rag-rinse over a sink in the evenings.

These days, with triad money and filtered rainwater coming through newly built pipes, Mercy could bask in the satisfaction of actually feeling clean. Lying here, half floating, she could almost forget about the day's madness.

"Almost" being the key word.

I am a messenger.

Her shoulders twitched.

The demon who killed me wanted me to ask you a question.

Mercy took a deep breath through her nose.

Do you remember the island, Chen Mei Chi?

Mercy sat up and turned off the faucet. In all her years, no ghost had ever posed such a personal, shocking question. She did not remember the specifics of an island, but the dreams and waking visions were a clear indication of some lost, unremembered past.

The question could mean nothing. Over the years, she had gathered a modest reputation among ghosts and living humans alike in this district. Outside of Kowloon, no one really knew her, but quite a few people within these walls did. Many knew a few snippets of her past, or had heard rumors of her missing memory. That a ghost would reference it in conversation was a little odd, but not wildly so.

The mention of a "demon" was disquieting, though. Demons could refer to different things, from actual denizens of the underworld, to malignant gods, to particularly vicious ghosts. Without more context, it was hard to say which the water fetcher had been thinking of. Regardless, it was never a good thing to have one in the neighborhood.

Or, perhaps she was overthinking it. It was Ghost Month, after all, and that always came with a barrage of particularly strange encounters. The ghosts were stronger, more connected to the world of the living, and often seemed to know or say things that they should not normally.

Either way, she couldn't sit here all day. Time to report to her boss. Mercy pulled the plug and climbed out.

The second she stepped from the tub, the heat came right back and draped over her like a moist blanket. Hot. Heavy. Suffocatingly damp. She toweled off a mix of cool water and fresh sweat, threw on some clothes, and parted the jangling bead curtain with one hand.

Her flat was well shaded, boasting freestanding fans in two corners and a slow-turning one on the ceiling. Warding fu talismans hung over doors and on windows, to keep out errant ghosts. Afternoon sunlight streamed through slatted blinds, hazy with dust motes. Thirteen stories up was high enough to snag some sky, although it did get a little noisy with all the passing planes.

In the center of the room, Bao lounged on an embroidered silk cushion. One red eye opened briefly at her entrance.

"You should not even need sleep, you are already dead," Mercy said, accusingly. "Yet here you are, napping again. I think you must be the laziest cat ever, even in spirit form."

Predictably, there was no answer to her unjust insult. But just looking at him soothed her mood in a way that the bath had not, and she relaxed. She stroked his nose and left him snoozing.

It would be luxurious in here if she cleared the clutter, but Mercy liked owning things. She couldn't remember her childhood, knew little of herself before she'd arrived in the Walled City as a traumatized and penniless young woman, but her adult life had been defined and shaped by poverty. And poverty meant never getting to own shit that you didn't need.

So these days, she put paintings and calligraphy stencils on her walls, bought nested wooden tables inlaid with lacquer and stacked them with elaborate books she never opened. She crammed faux silk flowers into ceramic vases, hung an eclectic collection of woks from the rafters, admired her rarely used yixing tea sets, piled up folding fans and sewing boxes and newspaper articles with odd stories; she collected cat toys and Taoist coins and jade bracelets.

Most of her possessions had mysteriously "fallen" out of various shipping containers over the years and landed in Cobra Lily's territory, before finding their way into her flat. Mercy carried no guilt over any of this. Rich people had enough rich things; they could spare her a few bits. And it made her feel safe, having it all. As if she were insulated from the world's troubles.

She slipped on her tiger charm bracelet—the only thing she'd owned when she arrived in the district—and sat down on her mahogany bed, a big carved thing all the way from England. The sheets were a messy tangle, because Mercy had never understood the point of making beds. Why bother when you were only going to sleep in it later?

She ran a comb through her short hair, then walked through the front door of her flat. Outside, in a broad shared hallway, she turned right and took the stairs to the topmost level—where her boss lived, in the flat above her own. One deep breath to calm her nerves, and she stepped through lacquered wood doors and into Cobra Lily's living space.

"Living space" was the wrong description. It might have been intended for that originally, but Cobra Lily had repurposed it. Everything precious or valuable was stored elsewhere. This space, with its bare wooden floors and high ceiling and mirrored walls, was for training.

The leader of the Snakeskin triad occupied the center of the room, sword in one hand, lean form draped in a loose robe as she moved languidly through a series of poses and stances. Her movements came from no single recognizable school, but a blend of techniques picked up through the years.

Mercy watched in respectful silence, waiting for her boss to finish practice.

Cobra Lily carried an undeniably powerful presence. She was a handsome woman in her mid-fifties—only a sliver older than Mercy herself—with fine lines softening the corners of her eyes. Sleek, dark hair was shot through with silver, giving a dramatic flair to her profile. Snake-patterned tattoos ran up her arms, across her back and collarbone, and all the way under her chin; they seemed to writhe in the shifting light as she moved. The years had not bowed Cobra Lily, only honed her sharp edges and forged steel in her spine.

"There you are," the triad queen called out. "Feeling any cooler, Chan?"

"For about half a second, but I'm already too hot again." Mercy walked over on damp feet, toes sticking to the wood slightly. "Having fun, boss?"

"I am." Cobra Lily spun, arced her blade, swept it down. "Join me, sometime."

"Hah! In another life, maybe." After years of hard work and staying one step ahead of hunger, Mercy took great satisfaction in being comfortably chubby and deliberately lazy. It was a luxury to be both. "Besides, I'm happy with my knives." They were easier to throw and easier to hide than any sword.

"You limit yourself." Another spin, the blade curving across with perfect control. "I think you could be a truly wonderful fighter, if you wanted."

"So you have been telling me for years." Mercy thought of Rat Tattoo lying on the ground earlier, her blade pressed to his throat, and the whisper inside her head to *catch him hold him drag him*; she winced. "I prefer not to encourage violence in myself. More than I already do."

"Stubborn as an old turtle," Cobra Lily said, laughing, and came to a stop. Not remotely out of breath from all that exertion, despite the thin sheen of perspiration on her skin. "Did the job go well?"

"Another waiting woman. You were right, someone in the family had killed her."

Mercy nearly mentioned the water fetcher, then decided it wasn't worth the trouble. She dealt with ghosts all the time, every single day, because it was her job to do so. Reporting each encounter to her boss was unnecessary and tedious, particularly during Ghost Month.

"I see." Cobra Lily brushed past to reach the weapons rack. The sword clanked as it slotted into place. "Was it the husband?"

"No, no. Her husband was already long deceased. It was the grandson. Soon as she got sick, he locked her in, took her money, and left her to die." Mercy paused. "He's been taken care of. By the grandmother."

"Ouch. Very rude for a young man! Still, that makes me glad I sent you to handle it, and not someone more . . . traditional."

Mercy smiled. "One day your intuition will let you down. And then I'll be stuck dealing with a ghost I cannot handle."

"Nonsense. Who is better than you at speaking to ghosts? What can you not handle?"

"Anything that needs actual exorcism, for a start. Talking only solves certain problems."

"As a businesswoman, I disagree. Talking both causes and solves most problems," her boss said, dryly. "If we had simply exorcised the ghost, then a murderer would have walked free, and perhaps killed again."

"True. It is important to know the story behind a death."

"Exactly," Cobra Lily said, with a languid wave of her hand. "Besides, it is so much fun when you do it your way."

Mercy thought of the bystanders who had fled screaming from the elderly woman's indiscriminate fire breath, and twinged with guilt. "I'm not sure fun is the right word, boss."

"It was justice, and justice is fun when it happens to other people," Cobra Lily said, with a hint of impatience. She didn't like being disagreed with. "Humans have no natural empathy. We must be taught it, and we can only learn it through suffering the same pain we inflict on others. Like that young man! No sympathy for his grandmother when he left her to die. I bet he could summon up some now."

Except he was dead, Mercy thought. Not able to summon up anything, anymore.

Still, he had deserved his fate, as his grandmother had deserved justice, and if his grandmother hadn't killed him, then Cobra Lily's laws would have. Either way, he lost his life. At least this way, the elderly lady had the chance to exact her own vengeance.

And that was justice.

Wasn't it?

"I suppose," Mercy agreed, doubtfully. "You know best, boss."

"I do, yes. Speaking of which, are you ready for today?"

"Today?" All thoughts of her own silly worries vanished instantly. "What's happening today?"

One slim eyebrow arched in disapproval. "You've forgotten?"

"Of course not," Mercy lied. She reached for a handy excuse, and found one. "I'm just distracted. On the walk home, after dealing with that grandmother ghost, I had a strange encounter."

"Oh? What with?"

"Well, I . . ." Mercy froze in shock, train of thought instantly lost.

Soft tendrils of vine were creeping across the weapons rack, spreading and growing in little green twists. Leaves unfurled in rapid succession, buds fruiting on stems and erupting into flowers. The sight filled her guts with icy fright.

Cobra Lily's mocking smile wavered. "What's wrong?"

Mercy backed away from the vine-riddled rack, then yelped as her feet stepped into cold water. She looked down.

Water flooded across the floor, puddles and rivulets trickling across wooden slats and pooling on the mats. She wanted to gasp but her chest had constricted tight. Around her, the noise of a stream grew louder, even though the water had no source; it seemed to well up from gaps and nooks and joins.

"No," she said, thickly, managing to squeeze the words out. "It is just a dream, it isn't real—"

Vines burst across the walls in rapid, frantic growth. Branches tangled with the spinning ceiling fan, grinding it to a halt, squeezing the wood until it cracked; pieces of it rained down. Bamboo shoots erupted from the ground; giant taro erupted, the leaves and roots rending the walls.

Every single moment we are undergoing birth and death.

The words were soft yet clear as a bell. Mercy felt the hairs on her arms and the back of her neck stand up straight, her teeth chattering with a sudden chill.

Mercy looked up. Already knowing what she would see.

In the center of the room stood a woman with pallid skin, her nails unnaturally long and sharp-edged. She wore rags, the fabric drenched and sodden. Rivulets of water trickled down her arms and dripped from her limbs, as if she'd just stepped from the ocean. Strands of kelp wrapped around her ankles, and her feet were caked in sand. The scent of brine overpowered.

"Sea Sister," Mercy whispered.

The green-skinned woman lifted her head. Gleaming pearlescent eyes peered from a luminous face. She seemed to draw all sound and light in the room; even the vines and lotus flowers had paused in their frenzied creeping.

Thin lips moved and she spoke again, without breath or sound.

Stay with me. Stay with me, forever.

Sea Sister held out a hand and Mercy swore, stumbling to get away. She tripped over her own feet and landed hard on elbows and knees.

A keening reverberated in the room. A sensation like the world was straightening, correcting, uncoiling; as if a universal string had been twisted taut, then suddenly released. Terrible light on all sides. She gasped out loud, shut her eyes against the brightness.

"Chan? Chan!" Cobra Lily was shaking her by the shoulder. "What the hell is happening? Are you sick?"

"I . . ." Mercy opened her eyes. She sat on dry linoleum. The vines had vanished and so had the water. The creature she thought of as Sea Sister was also gone. The ceiling fan spun with nonchalant indifference. "Fine. Good. All fine." Her heart hammered erratically.

Cobra Lily helped her stand. "That's a strange definition of fine."

"It was a dream." Mercy leaned against the nearest wall. "The same one that I get, sometimes. Memories, old things." From a life she could not recall.

"Dreams happen when you sleep," her boss said, sharp as razor wire. "We are wide-awake. You even said so yourself."

". . . I know."

"For the second time this month!"

"I know."

"Stubborn as an old turtle!" Cobra Lily said again, exasperated this time. "If this were happening to someone else, I would assume they were experiencing a haunting. It has all the classic signs."

"It can't be." Mercy trailed her fingers over her skin, her clothes, seeking comfort in the solidity of familiar things. Wanting to check her own tangibility. "It is not a ghost. No spiritual traces. The experts you hired found nothing—"

"Maybe we are not looking hard enough. Or in the right way. Maybe my experts were bad."

"—and you never see it either, boss," Mercy continued, firmly. "It is bad memories, waking dreams for a wounded mind. The war has left lots of people with scars on their spirit."

"The war ended over thirty years ago," Cobra Lily said, brows drawn together. "If this is something left from the war, then why don't you see . . . oh, I don't know. Battles, dead bodies, ships, burning . . . angry soldiers . . . any of that?"

"No idea." Mercy ran her hand through her short hair. "I am not even sure it's malignant, as dreams go. Just vines. Water. Jungle flowers and tiny plants." A green-skinned monster, spouting cliché Buddhist quotes.

Cobra Lily glowered. "Losing your sense of reality cannot be a good thing, however benevolent the visions."

"Please don't worry, boss." Mercy offered a shaky bow. "It's just the effect of Ghost Month. Strange winds and negative energies. I will be fine."

Catch them. Hold them. Drag them to the water and keep them down until their blood is salt and their eyes are food for the fishes—

Head still bowed, Mercy ground her teeth and fought down the grotesque whisper. In truth, the problem was getting worse. Nightly dreams she was used to, and did not mind. Ever since washing up on the shores of Hong Kong's mainland, missing her past and her memories and having nothing but a name, she had been plagued by odd dreams.

But these waking visions, or whatever one was supposed to call them, were very new and extremely disconcerting. The incidents had gotten steadily more frequent over the past year, and harder to hide. Especially from Cobra Lily, who was so often around.

Same for the whispers to *catch, hold, drag*; she could always ignore them, but she could not shut them out. She dared not say anything about that in case people started thinking that she was some kind of crazed killer.

"In that case, promise me you will do something about it if this doesn't clear up when Ghost Month ends," Cobra Lily said, clapping her shoulder. "We will find more doctors, or speak to a specialist, if you wish. What if you embarrass me in public?"

Of course. Her boss was always concerned about losing face.

"I am the best ghost talker around, and you are the most powerful person in Kowloon." Mercy laughed shakily. "If we cannot solve my problems, no one else will, either."

"How do you know, if you do not let them try?" Cobra Lily sighed. "I do hate to see you like this. Having all these . . ." She paused, left the word hanging.

Hallucinations, Mercy finished silently. Too heavy a term to speak out loud, as if admitting to what was happening was also an admission of weakness.

"You are right," she said, more to change the subject than out of true agreement. "I should seek help." She straightened up. "But for now, we have that, um . . . wait, what are we doing this afternoon?"

"I *knew* you'd forgotten," Cobra Lily said, instantly aggrieved and distracted. Just as Mercy had hoped. "The demolition consultation? Fate of our city, that's all. Nothing much, hey!"

A pit formed in Mercy's stomach. "Oh. Yes. Very serious." It wasn't so much that she'd forgotten as she'd been trying not to think about it. Trying a little too hard, clearly.

The local Hong Kong authorities, which included both British and Chinese officials, had an intense dislike of the Walled City. They considered it an eyesore, a filthy embarrassment that signified the shame and trauma of past war years, and they desperately wanted to demolish the whole place. Didn't help that the general Hong Kong public felt much the same.

Every so often, someone went through the administrative motions of trying to organize the destruction of the neighborhood, but still, it usually stalled. The operation would be huge and expensive, and the Walled City residents did not want their home destroyed. Buying them out would cost the government a lot of money, and that was just the first of many costs.

This was one of those times; another proposal had been put forward. The city was once again under legislative threat. Only, it was moving forward a lot further and faster than other attempts.

"I specifically wanted you at this meeting," said the triad queen, eyeing her carefully. "Are you well enough to attend, or should I request a postponement?"

The words were kind, but beneath them lurked a more sinister question: about Mercy's usefulness, her poise, her propensity to help or embarrass the leader of a triad. It was a dicey thing, sometimes, to be one of Cobra Lily's favored employees.

"I feel focused and fine," Mercy lied, offering another bow. "I'll be right by your side, boss."

"Good." Cobra Lily's features relaxed into a cool smile. "Then I will pour us a drink, and we will review the documents one more time."

5
OCCUPIED TERRITORY

Thirty-three years ago . . .

A few of the villagers chase, but Mei Chi has a head start and they don't really want to catch her. Just scare her off. She is soon able to reach the woods. They can't follow her so easily there, or perhaps aren't willing to venture among the trees after her. If she really were a demon, that would be foolish of them.

When her lungs and legs burn too much to keep going, she stumbles to a halt and bursts into tears.

She shouts at the trees for a while, demanding to know what is wrong with her. They don't answer. Nothing makes sense. She thinks about sleeping, doesn't dare, is afraid to have more nightmares.

Slowly, Mei Chi gets to her feet. It is past noon, now. She cannot stay here forever. Numb, exhausted, dehydrated, hips and feet aching, she limps barefoot through the woods, seeking a way out, some kind of path.

She gets lucky, again. Eventually, she emerges from the woods at a paved crossroads. One path is unmarked; the other has signs pointing toward the city. Mei Chi looks northward, where the unpaved path winds into denser trees and stubby hills. She does not know how to live out there. She has vague memories of a farm, and maybe fishing, but they are truly vague, and anyway that is untamed land. Not a tilled and managed farm.

She looks southward, where buildings rise in the distance.

Hong Kong belongs to the Japanese, or so the village man told her. She has a sense of what that means, understands the vague concept of war, even if "Japan" as such doesn't conjure up any associations. War sounds bad, but surely the city will be calmer now it has surrendered.

Not like she has any better options, either.

She sets off walking, keeping her gaze on the buildings ahead.

Mei Chi soon figures out why the man warned her against going to Hong Kong.

It takes at most an hour and a half to walk to the city boundary, winding through the rural New Territories. She doesn't know at the time how lucky she is not to encounter soldiers.

The corpses are the first thing she sees here. Corpses in the streets and alleys, corpses on the boardwalks and slumping against doorframes. Corpses piled on corpses in great stinking mounds of flesh.

War has left its mark.

Oddly, the sight of death doesn't bother her, and she isn't sure if that's a bad thing or not. But it does make her cautious, because where there are bodies, there are also killers and weapons.

Many of the bodies have a warding fu talisman stuck on them, deterring any ghosts from arising. In some cases, multiple bodies are arranged in a large pile or pit, with one enormous fu talisman on the lot. Occasionally she spies captured monks standing over mass graves, being forced to pray and ward to the point of exhaustion.

The Japanese have been efficient in their takeover. They do not want the dead interfering with occupation; such ghosts would wreak terrible vengeance. It is almost admirable, this level of organization.

She picks her way around corpses and ashen-faced pedestrians, none of whom meet her eye, and sticks to the shadows. Soldiers are everywhere, now. Men in uniform practice drills in courtyards, congregating outside the bigger buildings like the hospitals and government offices. If any civilians catch their attention, it is a toss of the die whether they murder, beat, ignore, or drag someone away.

Mei Chi, after watching in horror as a pair of soldiers batter an old man to death for no discernible reason, decides to exercise extreme caution. She flits from alley to alley, avoiding the main roads.

She is still hungry and thirsty, and has no money. Not that it matters, since no shops are open. Money is likely worthless, too. She manages to find a shop front that has been bombed to rubble. Most of the foodstuffs are destroyed or looted. She searches anyway, picking through slag and brick dust to find a jug of juice, a few dried mushrooms and—immense treasure!—two small jars of salted fish.

She drains the juice, finishes the mushrooms, and is midway through the first jar of fish when she spies an elderly lady, small and wiry, peering at her through one of the shattered windows.

Unlike the man at the village, the elderly lady smiles, open and warm. She gestures at Mei Chi and says, "Any to share for a hungry old woman?"

Mei Chi hesitates. She's hungry herself, and one jar wasn't enough food. But the elderly lady is even leaner than she, and twice as frail.

Reluctantly, she nods and holds up the last jar. "Yours if you want it, grandmother."

"Thank you. Such a kind heart." The elderly woman steps inside with delicate agility and crouches next to her, two souls taking shelter in a destroyed building. "I am not so fast as I used to be. I cannot outrun the young people who are looking for food." She pops the lid, pulls out the scrap of fish. "My name is Poon Li Fan. How are you called?"

"Chen Mei Chi," she says, after a moment. "I think."

"You think?"

"My memory is not working well. I woke up on the beach some miles away and walked here by myself. No family, no money. I remember some things, but very little."

"Ah." Li Fan nods around a mouthful of fish. "Sometimes people have injuries to their head which does this. More common in war. I am sure it will come back to you."

"A man told me the Japanese took over months ago," Mei Chi says, trying to shove away the memory of holding that man's head underwater in a fit of fury. "Why is it still so bad here, in the city?"

"Occupation is different from war," Li Fan says. "The soldiers control the city, but cannot feed it. Many people are starving, and the government is paralyzed. Everything is chaos. Has been for months, will be for years."

Outside the shop, gunfire ricochets and a person screams. Mei Chi folds tight into a corner and doesn't move again until the street is fully quiet. Li Fan does the same, pausing her chewing to huddle in perfect stillness.

When it is safe again, Mei Chi says, "What should I do while I wait for my memory to heal?" She thinks, *What if my memory never heals?* but doesn't dare ask that, in case saying it aloud somehow makes it happen.

"Survive," Li Fan says, bluntly. "That is all anybody is trying to do right now. Stay alive, think about today only. Cannot remember the past? Fine, never mind. You are not living in the past, you are living right now." She points in the direction of the street. "The present out there is our danger. The past cannot kill you because it is done with."

"But how?" Mei Chi says, desperate. "How do I survive when I do not know anything and the world is so dangerous?"

"There is Kowloon Walled City," Li Fan says, with a sidelong glance. "All of Hong Kong is dangerous right now, but the Japanese will not go in there."

"The Walled City?" Mei Chi echoes. She doesn't know of the place, but then who can say what her memory has forgotten.

"It may have a bad reputation, but do not judge it too harshly," Li Fan says, mistaking the reason for her question. "Kowloon is crowded and dirty, but so is the rest of Hong Kong right now. At least no one will shoot you just for walking around." She sighs. "I am going there myself, if you want to come with me. I was already heading there but had to stop and eat."

Mei Chi thinks about it. Why not, she has no better idea for where to go or what to do.

"Is it far?" she asks.

"Not at all. It is just a district like any other. Come, I will show you." Li Fan gets up and leads her to a different window, pointing in the distance. "See that cluster of buildings? We walk toward it, then circle around to the left. A few blocks behind that, and just out of sight, is the Walled City."

"How do we get through the wall that surrounds it?"

Li Fan beams. She is so friendly, so genuine despite the harshness of their surroundings. "There is not much wall these days, little miss. Not anymore. It used to be an old fort, but now it is just like a neighborhood."

"I see."

"The Japanese have been rebuilding the wall, to keep the ghosts inside, but it is early days, and at the moment there are more gaps than bricks," Li Fan continues. "If you reach the edge of it, you can just stroll in and—"

A bullet careens through the window. The back of Li Fan's head blossoms like a bouquet of squirming gray and pink roses, like a gift nobody ever wants, and lands all over Mei Chi's arms and face. All she can smell is blood and brains.

Time cracks like a dropped egg.

Skips in her memory.

Men in green khakis with tall boots and long guns, all firing.

A soldier surges up and over the nearest rubble, and her fists move of their own accord.

Catch him.

Her knuckles slam into his eye socket and he sprawls flat from the force of it. She is strong, despite her size.

Hold him.

No. There's no water, no time, too many. She savagely ignores the intrusive thoughts and runs, instead. Runs, and runs, and runs.

Mei Chi knows only fleeing and dodging for several streets. Out of the building, covered in red gore that isn't hers. Open air feels exposed and unsafe. Back to alleys. Bare feet pounding, eyes dry. No crying, she's too dehydrated for tears. Glass and rubble underfoot, cutting her toes. Keep going. Her stupid brain thinking: *I should have eaten that last jar of fish, after all.*

Something else catches the soldiers' attention—men brawling or fighting, a distraction, doesn't matter. Most of them peel away. Two keep pursuit, calling out lewd taunts that strike a chill in Mei Chi's heart. She needs a direction, she can't flee aimlessly like this.

Keep running, or the past will catch up and kill you, she thinks. Keep running, or you'll die in the present.

Ahead, she spots the cluster of buildings that Li Fan—who did not deserve such an end—pointed out earlier. Fine, that will do. Anywhere that isn't here is all she wants. Circle around to the left, just a few blocks away.

She can see it. A sunken mess of low-rise buildings, decaying and decrepit. The shape of the old fort still visible, some of the walls crumbling and some of them partially rebuilt. Slums fester within, the shadows and leaning frames beckoning Mei Chi with their promise of no soldiers, no bullets through brains.

So close. She casts a glance over one shoulder. The two men who were still chasing her have stopped, looking disgruntled. They know where she is headed, and don't care to follow.

For the moment, Mei Chi is too relieved to worry about what that means.

She crosses the boundary, leaping feetfirst into darkness.

6

THE COUNCILWOMAN

August 20, 1975

In the distance, Kowloon receded like an outgoing tide.

The rooftops of gray-and-beige buildings, just visible over the tall dust-colored wall which encircled them, were melting into the clinging smog. A haze of pollution softened harsh lines and tiny figures. Electric lights glinted dimly in shadowed buildings, as if winking goodbye.

Crammed in the backseat of a red Toyota, with Cobra Lily on one side and a grimy window on the other, Mercy watched her home disappear. The sight filled her with a rising panic. The fact that three other triad cars were following close behind them did nothing to soften her anxiety.

She wished, yet again, that Bao could come with her. But the ghost cat had to stay behind for this trip; no spirits allowed in civic buildings. Anyway, he'd only have hated it out here. Bright sunlight made him weak, kept him the size of a kitten.

"Remind me again, Chan." Cobra Lily shook out a cigarette and lit it, the waft of tobacco and tar overpowering in that small space. "When was the last time you took a trip outside of Kowloon?"

"Never, boss."

"What, really?"

"Came here, stayed here, never left."

"That's a long time to be in such a small neighborhood!" Cobra Lily laughed her tiger laugh. "Well, I'm sure you'll be glad for a change of scenery. I do love coming to the city, when I can."

Mercy looked out the window and didn't reply.

She'd spent the past thirty-plus years living shoulder-to-shoulder with her fellow denizens among the claustrophobic high-rise buildings, circled by its wartime wall and walking its multi-layered streets whose gutters flowed like a blocked nose. Where children played along narrow, sewage-stained sidewalks lined with tiny shops and smoky eateries selling cigarettes or fish balls, while hidden opium dens folded between mazed passages within bigger buildings—a total firetrap—and everyone paid the triad dues to travel safely at night. Where the wet markets ran slick with guts and blood, chicken feathers tangled in canopies of wires amidst the steady drip of leaking pipes, and fu talismans of warding were nailed on every door to keep out hostile spirits.

That, to her, was home. A familiar, safe place, with its warren of narrow alleys and hot damp concrete on all sides.

The other face of Hong Kong, that she was now being driven through, looked very different. Out here: strips of prickly trees, half-built boulevards, endless construction, big asphalt roads. High-rise buildings, yes, but the streets were wide enough for cars and pedestrians to travel easily. Space to breathe, move, think, stretch a limb or two, sometimes catch the sun.

Same as in Kowloon, preparations were underway out here for Hungry Ghost Festival. The temples surged with crowds, all keen to come for prayers and fu talismans. Street markets displayed charms, fans, incense, and paper gifts to burn for the underworld. Almost no one was wearing red, and *no one* was wearing black. Such colors attracted spirits, this time of year.

It was all very pretty, and far less derelict than what she was used to in Kowloon. If only that sky didn't make her feel so overwhelmed and exposed.

Mercy leaned her head against the window and swallowed against a rising sense of nausea. Either she was getting carsick or homesick, and both were pathetic reactions. She needed to get her shit together, and not embarrass her boss. It was crucial they make a good impression.

In truth, Mercy had always intended to move back out to the main city. All the opportunities, as they say, were in the bigger half. But in the early years, the raging war and its desolate aftermath made it safer to stay put in Kowloon. Later, poverty and lack of means kept her pinned. Inertia and habit did the rest.

These days, her skin had filled up with triad tattoos, while her bank account had filled up with triad money. She enjoyed the intimacy of knowing her neighborhood thoroughly, of having a hard-won place and purpose. The district had grown, and she had grown with it. Now, at fifty-three years of age, Mercy knew only Kowloon.

The cars entered the Cross Harbor Tunnel, and darkness surrounded them. Mercy tried not to flinch. The idea of being *under* the ocean appalled her a little, especially since these tunnels had only been open a few years. You couldn't really be sure how safe they were, she felt.

"May I ask a question?" she said, as much to distract herself as anything. "I know it is a serious matter, boss, but this has been tried before. The government never seems to get anywhere. Demolition doesn't ever happen, and Kowloon endures. Why the concern this time?"

"That is true, it has been tried many times before." Cobra Lily picked at some invisible thread on her sleeve. "But this application, with all its costs and careful graphs, is the furthest I've seen anyone go."

"I don't understand. What's changed?"

"The anti-ghost laws."

Mercy nodded slowly.

Hong Kong had increasingly cracked down with anti-ghost laws in recent years. It was a bad look for a world-class city to have so many spirits visible on the streets. Westerners did not like to see hordes of dead, and Hong Kong was trying to attract Western investment, along with Western tourists.

For the most part, Hong Kong had cleaned away its unwanted spirits. But Kowloon Walled City was still rife with the unsettled ghosts, still carrying the spiritual trauma of World War II etched into its concrete walls and gutters. It remained a catchment for the unhappy dead. And thus the appetite to demolish Kowloon was growing.

Cobra Lily coughed a cloud of smoke. "One of the ongoing complaints that these dogfuckers keep leveling against Kowloon involves the ghosts that roam our streets. The ghosts *they* shoved in here, both during the war and after."

"I understand," Mercy said.

"Good." The triad queen handed the remains of her cigarette to the enforcer next to her; he chucked it casually out of the rolled-down window. "We must make a good impression today, if our arguments are to carry any weight. People think many things about me, but my attachment to Kowloon is genuine."

Mercy did not doubt that for a minute. All of Cobra Lily's power and money was tied up in Kowloon. She owned many of the buildings, and was one of the biggest landlords. If the place was razed, paved over, and swallowed up into the rest of Hong Kong, that would be the end of this triad. They'd both be out of a job, and Mercy's boss would likely land in a jail cell.

"I look forward to this encounter," Cobra Lily said, opening up a small folder of appeal documents. "They will not be prepared for me!"

Mercy was about to say something in response, but then their car emerged from the tunnel and the ocean came into sight. She'd managed to avoid glimpsing the harbor till now, but there was no avoiding the view any longer.

To one side, the city continued to shoulder upward, bustling and heaving. To the other, Mercy now stared at a vast expanse of green water, glittering in the mid-afternoon sun. Ferries and junk boats and small vessels and big ships cluttered the waves, vying for space in crowded lanes.

Suddenly, her mouth was dry like an oven, her hands clammy. It was hard to breathe or blink.

Looking at the sea did that to her, even just in photos or from a distance. Up close, the reality was far worse. It reminded her, with terrible clarity, of waking in a storm-wracked ocean, having no memories or possessions other than the clothes on her back and the bracelet around her wrist. Painfully aware that she was drowning—

"—but I anticipate we will have resistance to these claims in particular," Cobra Lily said, tapping a particular page. "Chan? Chan, stop daydreaming."

"Sorry, boss." She dragged her gaze from the mesmerizing, sickening ocean view. "I'm just not used to being out here."

Cobra Lily compressed her lips. "Clearly not."

The rush of scenery slowed as the car pulled up onto the pavement, right in front of the Murray Building in Central District. It was rectangular and white, with arches along the bottom level. The windows slanted at an odd angle. She'd read once that it was designed to minimize hot sunlight streaming in.

The accompanying cars pulled up, too: one in front, two behind. Behind them, the street chugged with sluggish morning traffic, horns screeching in dismay at their awkward parking.

"We're here," the enforcer said, then got out and held the door for them both.

Cobra Lily stepped to the pavement with effortless elegance, pristinely dressed and collar turned up despite the heat. Mercy, already sweating down the back of her neck and through her shirt, clambered out of the car with considerably less grace. They strode into the Murray Building in a tight-knit formation.

They made an impressive group overall—Cobra Lily herself, in a white silk jacket patterned with black snakes, flanked by enforcers in sharp black suits and sunglasses. Mercy, still sweating in their midst, was much less impressive, and her jacket was somehow already crumpled. At least no one could see her very well, when surrounded by so many men.

"Excuse me," said a voice in Cantonese-accented English.

A woman wearing a crisp gray dress suit, cut in the American style, was striding toward them across the air-conditioned lobby. She looked to be about late twenties in age, her face a confusing combination of youthful skin and cynical eyes. Very young, for an executive member, yet very confident.

She was not alone, either. Two nervous staffers followed at her heels. Behind them trailed a group of building security guards, armed with blackjacks.

"What is this?" Cobra Lily pointedly did not reply in English. "Are you speaking to me?"

The gray suited-woman inclined her head; not quite a real bow, but not quite disrespectful, either. "I'm Miss Tsang Kit Ling, a senior member of Hong Kong's Executive Council, and I'm overseeing the demolition application for Kowloon Walled City," she continued, still in English. "Thank you for bringing in your written concerns. I'll take a copy and make sure the Council reviews it."

Cobra Lily bristled, her hands tightening around the bundle of documents. "I was invited to speak to the Council directly, as a landlord with a vested interest. Are you now disallowing me entry?"

"Ms. Wong," Kit Ling said, finally switching back to Cantonese, "I don't know if you are aware, but this building is more than just a civic government office. There are highly dangerous spirits contained in the lower levels, with significant security procedures in place. I cannot allow regular citizens, let alone a known triad leader, to simply walk around with her violent thugs. We are, of course, willing to read any documentation you provide, but this is as far as you'll go."

There was a collective mutter of shock from the enforcers, and Cobra Lily herself had gone pale with fury the moment Kit Ling said *Ms. Wong*. No one in Kowloon knew the triad queen's real name. Or if they did, they were smart enough not to use it publicly.

Mercy stepped in front of her boss. "We are not thugs," she said, as much to save face as to prevent Cobra Lily from starting a massacre. "The Snakeskins manage crime when your police force does not dare enter Kowloon. We run schools. We look after the elderly. We protect women. Even the girls who work in opium dens. Yes, there are drugs, but you have that, too, out here! As for the ghosts, we have long managed their infestation, without government support. The Walled City is our home, and you do not have the right to destroy it, when you have done nothing to help it!"

"Well-spoken," Kit Ling said, turning toward Mercy. "And who are . . ."

Her words died away as their eyes locked. The councilwoman stood frozen, lips parted and eyes so wide the whites were visible. As if she'd seen a ghost.

Mercy stared back, feeling a strange buzz that ran from her belly to her fingertips. She would swear, on her life, that she'd never glimpsed this person before. Yet that did nothing to dispel the niggling feeling of familiarity.

"This is Mercy Chan," Cobra Lily said, poise recovered, her gesture imperious.

"A trusted aide, and best of my exorcists. It is with her work that we successfully contain the ghost problem in Kowloon."

"I see." Kit Ling's nostrils flared. "Who gave you that scar?"

"Huh?" Mercy glanced down at the red scar that peeped out from the sleeve of her shirt, livid streaks running from wrist to shoulder and along the collarbone. "Nobody gave it to me."

"Nonsense," Kit Ling said flatly. "That's not a birthmark, it's a scar. How did you get it?"

"Not that it is any of your business, Miss Tsang," Mercy said, stiffly, "but I have had this scar for as long as I can remember. A doctor told me it is probably from a lightning strike."

Of all the things she had expected from today's confrontation, being quizzed about her scar was not one of them.

"What is this rude questioning?" Cobra Lily said, almost swelling with indignation at being first insulted, then so rudely ignored. "We are here to—"

"I know why you are here, and I want to be sure your exorcist is a reliable person," Kit Ling retorted, without even turning around. "What do you mean, *as long as I can remember*?"

Everyone in the room was staring at Mercy: the guards and enforcers in suspicious confusion; the staffers with nervous attention; Cobra Lily, with furious indignation at being left out. And Kit Ling, with a powerful, single-minded intensity, as if the whole world rested on the answer.

Mercy found herself saying, "I don't remember my life before 1942. I arrived in Kowloon in the middle of the war, without family or memories." She added, "That's a little before your time, Miss Tsang, unless you are much older than you look."

A muscle twitched in Kit Ling's cheek. "A little, yes. I was born in 1945."

"Then why does it matter? Am I offensive to look at?"

"No. But your face, and that scar, are extremely familiar to me. I could have sworn . . ." A strained pause. "Are you sure, completely sure, we have not met before?"

"Never that I remember," Mercy said, coolly. "In another life, maybe."

"In . . . another life." A light tremor ran through the other woman. For a second, Mercy had a strong sense that the councilwoman was about to lunge forward and grab her.

But Kit Ling only put on a polite smile, as if their conversation had been entirely ordinary, and said mildly, "My mistake. You are quite right, I am too young to remember the war years." She angled her gray-suited form back toward Cobra Lily. "Please accept my apologies for my confusion, Ms. Wong. As I was saying . . . your whole entourage cannot come into the building. Perhaps I can suggest a compromise? You are welcome to come to my office, where we can speak in private."

Mercy blinked furiously, still reeling from the strange confrontation that had been so hastily abandoned.

"Alone?" Cobra Lily's eyebrows rose. "I don't go places *alone*."

"This is an official government building." Kit Ling spread her hands to include the air-conditioned luxury around them, in all its beige concrete glory. "You are safe here, as any citizen would be. Our concern is for our own safety, not yours." She added, "And you won't be alone. Ms. Chan may come with you."

"Boss," Mercy said, in low tones, "I don't think—"

"I don't pay you to think," the triad queen snapped.

Mercy held her tongue diplomatically. Her boss was nettled and embarrassed by the whole encounter, which she understood, but she still didn't appreciate having to bear the brunt of someone else's loss of face.

"I'm glad we could come to a compromise." Kit Ling inclined her head in another borderline disdainful bow. "Your assistants can wait in the lobby."

Assistants? Don't you mean "violent thugs"? Mercy thought, but she was old enough and wise enough not to say so out loud.

Kit Ling gestured and stepped aside, allowing Cobra Lily to walk ahead of her. The triad queen led the way, folder of documents tucked under one arm, though she could not have possibly known where they were going.

Mercy followed after them, a sinking feeling in her belly.

The journey was short, and anticlimactic. Kit Ling simply guided them up a floor via some stairs, and into a gray, overly tidy office. The colors were so muted that Mercy felt for a moment as if she'd stepped into a black-and-white television broadcast.

"Please sit," Kit Ling said, and took her own seat behind the desk.

There was only one chair. Cobra Lily perched on it while Mercy, naturally, stood at ease behind her.

"I will get straight to the point," Kit Ling said. "Kowloon has a ghost problem, and it is very serious. I am aware of your neighborhood's unfortunate history and how Japan treated it, but we live in the present now, and cannot always look back at the past."

"We have many ghosts, yes," Cobra Lily said, coolly. Her index finger tapped rapidly against the armrest: a sign of fury, in her. "Which, as I said downstairs, my organization is adept at managing."

Technically, it was Mercy that had said that, but she didn't quibble with her boss's version of events.

"Are you, though?" Kit Ling lifted out a thick binder and began laying papers, one at a time, across her desk. "Please ask your exorcist to examine these reports."

Mercy glanced at Cobra Lily, who gave her a nod, before stepping forward and peering over. The documents detailed a slew of deaths, with fuzzy photographs clipped to the top. Names, times, dates, and locations; all of them in Kowloon.

"These are reports of dead bodies," Mercy said, after a moment. "Strangling victims, it would seem."

"Multiple strangling victims over the past year," Kit Ling corrected. "I don't have enough space to lay them all out, but rest assured we have gathered records on dozens. And many more civilians who have been reported missing, lately." She waved the thick binder like a flag. "We believe they've all been killed by some sort of demon. It seems to attack when people are alone, often bathing."

The demon who killed me wanted me to ask you a question.

Just a coincidence, Mercy told herself, yet a shiver ran through her. The inclusion of water was another uneasy clue she couldn't ignore. What the hell was going on in her district? Maybe she'd been too quick to dismiss the encounter with the water fetcher.

Cobra Lily said firmly, "That can't be. We would have noticed—"

"Or maybe, you are not as on top of the ghost problem as you believe," the councilwoman said. "How many other 'problems' are slipping by unnoticed? Can you be sure you are tracking everything?"

Cobra Lily stared, apparently speechless.

Mercy found herself saying, "We hear your criticisms, Miss Tsang. But how will demolishing Kowloon solve any of those problems?"

"That's easy. With the walls down, the fengshui of the neighborhood can be realigned. Streets can be straightened, widened, and cleaned. Buildings can be rebuilt to have proper space and light, sewer and electrical systems integrated with the rest of Hong Kong. And appropriate warding can be constructed. Ghosts will have nowhere to hide."

"It is better to talk to ghosts than to banish them, surely!"

"Not when they reach a certain threshold, I'm afraid. Government guidelines are quite clear."

"But it is our home. Our property." Mercy spread her hands. "We have a right to our existence."

"Small comfort to those who die for your desire to have triad jurisprudence," Kit Ling said crisply. "Look through the data and see for yourself." The councilwoman held out the hefty binder. "No, I insist, we have other copies. In the meantime, the demolition application will take a full week or more to process, before we begin the next stage. Come back to me with proof you have handled this drowning ghost, and dealt with the corruption in your ranks. If you do that, I will allow you to file an appeal."

". . . I see." Cobra Lily rose slowly, adjusting the creases out of her clothes. "Chan, take the councilwoman's 'reports,' please." She flung down her own useless documents, brought so carefully all the way from Kowloon, then swept out of the room with a stiff spine and a face like granite.

Mercy picked up Kit Ling's binder. "Goodbye," she said, so awkwardly that it sounded ruder than silence would have been.

"Don't worry," Kit Ling said with an unpleasant smile. "We'll meet again."

⁂

Cobra Lily stormed out of the government offices, her expression like a thundercloud. Mercy hurried after her, the binder of death records clutched ineffectually in her arms. Neither of them spoke.

The enforcers stood up as Cobra Lily arrived back in the foyer, clearly alarmed and off-balance. The triad queen walked past without saying a word. Mercy caught their collective gazes and gestured surreptitiously for everyone to follow.

Ten minutes later, they were piled back into the same cars they'd arrived in, heading home in deafening silence. Cobra Lily sat like a carved statue, hands in lap and lips pressed together. Still not speaking, which was a very bad sign.

"Were you lying?" Cobra Lily's curt, cold question cut across Mercy's ruminations, pulling her abruptly from the depths of memory to the surface of the present.

"I'm . . . sorry, boss?" Wrong response; it sounded weak and feeble to stammer. But Mercy really was caught off guard.

Cobra Lily hissed an intake of breath. "About having met her, Chan. Did you know that Council bitch?"

"I've never seen her before. I would swear that by any grave, temple, or god," Mercy said, and meant it. "Honestly, boss, I think she was making it up to try and put us off-balance."

Cobra Lily said nothing, jaw clenched tight. Outside the car window, the city slid by in a blur of concrete and electric lights.

"The woman was barely thirty," Mercy said. "Kit Ling was born at the end of the war, years after I was already in Kowloon. How could we have met? Unless she knows something I don't."

"She certainly knows more than you," came the clipped reply. "How the fuck did you miss all those deaths? A mass-murdering ghost, demon, whatever it is, right under our noses? Your ignorance and failure have humiliated me."

"We don't even know if what she said was true." Mercy was acutely aware of how unwise it was to argue with her boss, yet her mouth wouldn't shut. "A folder of dead strangers. It could mean nothing. I need time to look through this first—"

"Time?" Cobra Lily hissed, eyes narrowing. "We have *one week* to find a monster which has eluded us for an entire year, and deal with it. Even then, the fate of Kowloon may still be sealed. You were in charge of handling ghosts for me, and this is entirely your failure!"

Mercy swallowed a comeback that would have got her shot, and instead bowed her head with a humility she didn't feel. "Boss, I can fix this."

"Can you? *Can you?*" Cobra Lily's voice rose, far too loud for the small space in their little vehicle. "You cannot even fix yourself. Hallucinations and panic attacks. A faulty memory that never healed. Now a prolific and dangerous ghost is found to be operating under your nose. I should have seen it sooner. You are a disaster, Mercy Chan, and your chaos threatens everything I have built!"

Mercy said nothing, holding her peace. It was best to let Cobra Lily's fires burn themselves out.

After a few moments, her boss took a ragged breath and said, "Do you have any ideas or leads, at least?"

A good sign, if Cobra Lily was still asking for her advice.

"I do, actually," Mercy said, because something had been niggling in her brain. "Ghosts like this don't come from nowhere. If it is a ghost, sneaking into people's bathrooms and drowning them, then I suspect someone dug the spirit up and inflicted it on Kowloon. Kit Ling herself, maybe? Just to give her an excuse to demolish the neighborhood."

"I suppose that is possible," Cobra Lily said, with grudging approval. "Where would she have found such a creature, though?"

Mercy tugged on a lip. "Kit Ling herself said there are many ghosts locked in specially built vaults beneath the Murray Building, which is what makes me suspicious. Sentient and nasty ones, who were used in the war. By her own admission, she has access to them."

"That was years ago, Chan. Surely they'd have faded by now!"

"It only takes one," Mercy said, shrugging. "A strong ghost will endure for as long as it remains angry. I've heard of stranger things."

When her boss still frowned uncertainly, Mercy added, "Let me ask around. I have old friends who might know something. I'll report to you tomorrow evening with what I've found."

"You'd better," her boss said, curtly.

The rest of their trip home passed in frigid silence.

7

THE MAN WHO KNOWS EVERYONE

Thirty-three years ago . . .

Kowloon Walled City is an experience.

Half an hour after Mei Chi arrives at the Walled City, someone tries to rob her, only to give up in disgust when they realize she has nothing at all to steal. Her bracelet is so small, so cheap, it doesn't even register to a thief.

Later, two men try to drag her into an alley, pawing at her dress. The fact that she is covered in Li Fan's blood doesn't deter them. The first one she kicks so hard between the legs that he faints, the refrain *Catch him* running through her head. The other man rips out a fistful of her hair before she manages to escape.

After that, she lurks in open spaces, afraid of the side alleys and quiet streets. Afraid of every man or stranger.

A bad day, certainly.

Then nighttime comes, and that is worse.

At first, Mei Chi feels cautious relief at seeing the streets empty. Children dart indoors, called inside by uneasy parents. Adults run from work or errands, fleeing home. Even pickpockets and tough men and phoenix girls are nowhere to be seen, having disappeared to houses where they peer out anxiously from spirit-warded windows.

Before long, the only people left on the Walled City streets are the drunk, the opiate-fuddled, and the homeless. Alone in the quiet, she finds a doorway to crouch in, dirty and still famished, desperate enough to drink from a rancid puddle on the concrete steps. It tastes the way sewage smells, and upsets her belly.

By the time she looks up again, it is fully dark.

In these early days, the Walled City is merely a squatter's ground. Much of it is old fort buildings; once regal, now grotesque and old. Shacks and ramshackle shelters are beginning to fill the free spaces, but it has not yet knifed upward in looming, unstable towers. And so the transition from day to night is starkly noticeable, because the sky is actually visible.

As the sun drowns itself under the horizon, the first ghost comes creeping out, an odd frog-like man who breathes fire. Mei Chi has an understanding of ghosts but no memory of seeing one; her limbs freeze rigid, and she cannot even run for fear.

There is no refrain running through her head, no urge to commit inexplicable violence; she is prey, here. Not predator. The ghost rampages down the street, chattering inanely to itself while she huddles in the doorway, petrified with quiet terror.

Soon enough, the narrow sidewalks fill with the riotous dead: Ghosts with bony faces and iron needles for hair, ghosts with multiple heads, ghosts with stinking, bulbous growths that ooze pus or acid. Ghosts with pinprick mouths and distended bellies, whistling hideously as they beg for food they cannot eat. Ghosts who have taken on animal traits, with claws or gills or spikes. Ghosts who look normal, yet their flesh is lighter than mist. Ghosts who are pools of inhuman darkness, ghosts with exploded bodies or bleeding eyes, ghosts who swing from lampposts by their own viscera, ghosts whose heads detach or whose necks unwind like ribbons, ghosts heaving with diseases and scabs, beautiful ghosts with white hair and red dresses who scream like air raid sirens. Ghosts who look like little old ladies or fragile young children until you touch them on the shoulder and they turn around, ravenous of tooth and shrieking with demonic fury.

Ghosts, ghosts, *ghosts* everywhere.

Spirits flow and tumble and streak through alleys, over railings, up concrete steps, in gutters and in sewers, from rooftops and electrical lines, clawing or baying at warded windows and protected doorways, coming after the unlucky living to cause torment or even death.

It is malice, but undirected malice; the wild, flailing trauma of many thousands of lives cut short through mass-scale violence. When the ghosts cannot find humans to torment, they turn on each other, bigger ones shredding smaller ones.

For these are the years of war and devastation, when the distressed dead far outnumber the peaceful dead, and threaten to outnumber the fearful living. Even in Hong Kong, which has seen less death than other big Chinese cities, the slaughter is leaving its mark. And the Japanese occupiers naturally do not want vengeful spirits hanging around. They banish what they can, but there are too many for even them to exorcise; the rest are effectively chased away by wards and protective fu talismans.

With nowhere else to dwell, the ghosts flee to the Walled City, the place where laws and good intentions come to die and unlucky girls get lost in the shuffle. Kowloon is awash with supernatural violence; all of Hong Kong's collective spiritual pain is compacted into a single, decrepit district.

Before long, an ashen-faced ghost with half its head missing spots Mei Chi, alone and frightened and very much lost in the shuffle, and comes lumbering over.

She can't even move. There's nowhere to go; the street is full of more monstrous spirits. She has no weapons or tricks or anyone to save her. The ghost hisses something unintelligible, the mouth partly missing, jaw hanging by threads; another victim of war, blown or shot into the spirit world, filled with fury and injustice.

Mei Chi bursts into tears. "*Go away!*"

The ghost stops. It stares at her in vague confusion, tongue lolling uncertainly. Mei Chi stares back, dumbfounded. For reasons she doesn't understand, the ghost has listened. Sort of. It is still hostile, yet it hesitates.

That hesitation saves her life—just long enough. A ferocious white beast leaps from the shadows and tackles the ghost to the ground. No, not a beast. A maogui; a *ghost cat*, huge and corporeal. Lion sized, albeit white and fluffy.

She watches in astonishment as the maogui savages the other ghost, shredding its semi-ephemeral limbs. The mangled spirit gabbles in distress and flees.

The cat turns round and Mei Chi squeaks in terror, sure that she is next.

But to her astonishment, the ghost cat begins to shrink. In moments it is the size of a kitten, small and white in appearance. It snuggles on her lap as if it has known her all her life, and goes to sleep.

It has saved her.

Maogui are not known for doing that.

She sits, stunned and sweating with relief. Dares not move in case the ghost cat changes its mind and eats her alive. It does not.

"Thank you," she whispers.

The cat opens one eye, blinks at her, shuts it again. Back to sleep. Hardly daring to breathe, Mei Chi tries a tentative stroke along its spine; the ghost cat purrs.

Maogui are widely considered bad luck, but she isn't going to shoo away a guardian spirit. Especially one that is undeniably adorable when in kitten form, a wisp of soft fluff in a landscape of toothy, gory horror.

"Ghosts should not be so cute. You look like a perfect steamed bao." Her stomach rumbles. "Or else I am just really hungry." Even mentioning bao is enough to make her mouth water.

The cat flicks a ghostly tail.

"Where did you come from?" she says. "Why did you help me?"

No answer. He simply nestles into her lap as if he has always belonged. Mei

Chi is sure she heard somewhere that ghosts are difficult to talk to, but the cat seems to understand her perfectly. She curls around it, seeking and giving comfort.

Several more times that night, various spirits approach. And almost all of them either walk past her as if she doesn't exist, or retreat from her uneasily when she tells them to leave. For the few who are stubborn or particularly aggressive, Bao attacks.

By morning, she has not only survived, but also realized that her survival could be a way of making money. Between her ability to speak to ghosts and Bao's protectiveness when they don't listen, she can surely be useful to someone.

The difficulty is finding the right client.

She starts knocking on doors, approaching strangers. How else could one ask for a job? Few people talk to her, most can't help her. They have no need of messages or packages sent at night. After the thirtieth attempt, though, she finds an elderly woman running a shoe shop who suggests seeking out a man called Lau Yik. No family name, and his address is a cha chaan teng eatery, only a few streets over.

"Who is he?" Mei Chi asks. "What does he do?"

"He is the man who knows everyone. I think he will find a use for your ghost-talking." The shopkeeper refuses to say anything more about it, and shoos her away.

Bloodstained, barefoot, starving, and broke, Mei Chi stumbles into a room full of smoking, dour men, asking to meet Lau Yik. And claiming she can navigate the streets of Kowloon at night, no less.

One of them comes forward. He is lean and slight of build, with intelligent eyes and greasy hair. "Who the hell are you?"

"Just a refugee," she says, tiredly. "Please, I was told you could give me work. I can walk the streets safely at night."

He frowns. "Do you even know what we do here?"

"I don't care," she says. "I only want to eat, to live. To survive the occupation."

"We all want that," he says, annoyed. "We are part of the resistance, girl. Do you understand what that means?"

"People who fight the soldiers." She adds, because she is afraid he will think she is a collaborator, "The Japanese chased me into this district. They make everything unsafe."

He spits. "I want the Japanese out of my city, like we all do, and I work toward that goal with many others. I admit it is difficult to organize at night, but trusting my messages to a homeless beggar is ludicrous."

"I can do it," she insists, standing before him in her tattered clothes, her tear-streaked face and shivering limbs. "Try me, pay nothing upfront. You lose nothing if I fail. If I succeed, pay me after!"

Instead of answering, he says, "What's that accent? Where are you from?"

"The islands, I think," she says, taken aback.

"You speak Hakka, then?" he says, and she is startled to realize that not only has he changed language, but she can understand what he's saying, mostly. His language is not quite the same as hers, but it's close.

"Yes," she says, cautiously. Trying to hide her shock. "Is that good?"

"Hmm. Maybe. There are not many Hakka speakers around, and the Japanese can't make head or tail of it. Let me think about it."

He scratches his cheek, paces a little, talks to his colleagues in a low voice.

She waits.

After a while, he comes back and says, "We will do a test. No letters, nothing written. I will give you a message in Hakka to remember, and at sundown you will go out at night and deliver it. The person you are supposed to meet will be expecting you, and will know what you are meant to say. If you get it wrong or do not turn up, no more chances."

"I am listening," she says, ears open and alert.

That night will live in her memory forever: a harrowing few hours of running, dodging, gasping. Every few steps she stops and whispers the message to herself again, because she doesn't want to survive this horseshit only to forget the actual words.

Many ghosts ignore her, while some try to talk back when she speaks to them. She is clumsy in her dealings with them, but it is a start. And for the ones who do attack, Bao deals with them savagely. It works, more or less.

Somehow, she doesn't die. Step by step, navigating across an unfamiliar neighborhood, Mei Chi staggers and stumbles her way to the designated house, repeating a nonsense message in Hakka to a baffled—and thoroughly amazed—woman at the other end.

When she returns back to Lau Yik's at dawn, trembling yet utterly triumphant, he pays up and gives her an approving nod.

She dines well that night, on a whole roasted fish. No part of it goes to waste: she eats the skin, head, tail, and the juicy little eyes. The flesh is rich and soft, the skin crisp and dripping with grease. She drinks the juices and licks her fingers afterward.

She piles the bones on a shrine for the ghost cat to eat. He can kill, but he cannot eat her food for sustenance if she does not mark it for the dead, and he needs feeding if she wants him to stick around. Ghosts linger longer if fed, and she likes having him for companionship. As well, she needs his help.

Afterward, when they are both done, she curls in the corner of the room. Resistance fighters come and go, talking among themselves.

"Fighters" is an optimistic description. They are men and women who object to the Japanese occupation, but few are military trained, and even fewer are truly fighting. Instead, led by Lau Yik—a former schoolteacher, Mei Chi gathers—they pass along crucial information, and sometimes supplies, using Kowloon like a conduit for the handful of scattered resistance forces which still hold out in isolated pockets. Most of the guerilla groups seem to be out in Sai Kung somewhere, which is not far from where she first came ashore.

As the night wears on, and the alcohol-induced moroseness kicks in, the mood drops slowly. One particularly inebriated young man with scars across his face tries to sit down on a nearby chair. He misses his seat and ends up slumped on the floor next to Mei Chi, staring unfocused at the ceiling above them.

"History will think we are ridiculous," he says to her, gulping a mouthful of raw booze. "Do you know that when the Japanese invaded, they had twenty thousand infantry coming across land, twenty thousand men coming from sea, and a battalion of fifty planes in the air? Guess what we had. Guess, guess!"

"I don't know." Mei Chi doesn't really want to hear it, but she feels it would be wrong to walk away.

"Fourteen thousand men defending Hong Kong. Scattered, disorganized, not enough support. Our sea guns did not even face the right way." Tears leak from the corners of his eyes. "One week. One week for the Japanese to capture the mainland!"

"What about the British?" she says, as much to get him to stop crying as anything else.

"What about them?" he mumbles, wiping his face on his sleeve. "There were Americans, some British, some Canadians. They fought, and we cannot complain about that. But they died or have been captured, now, and their ghosts are as angry and lost as the Chinese ones." A sobbing laugh. "No, no. Not even ghosts. The Japanese banish our dead, with their Supernatural Forces Division.

Have you see them? The soldiers kill, kill, kill. Then the division banish, exorcise, disperse the ghosts. Never in my life have I seen such a thing."

"Hey, little brother," Lau Yik says sharply. "Go to bed, you are drunk."

When the young man protests, Lau Yik walks over, leverages him up, and firmly directs him toward a room to sleep it off.

When he comes back, Lau Yik addresses the room. "We cannot become trapped in our grief for what is lost," he says. "Keep your eyes forward, my friends. Tomorrow is a new day."

Tomorrow is a new day, Mei Chi whispers to herself, over and over. *Tomorrow is a new day.*

8

OLD FRIENDS AND NEW FACES

August 20, 1975

All these years later, and a much older Mercy Chan was again looking for the man who knew everyone.

Driving wasn't a possibility in the Walled City. The roads were too dense and narrow, and some were barely strong enough for pedestrians, let alone vehicles. Once the triad cars reached the walled boundaries, they all climbed out, leaving only a couple of enforcers to park the cars elsewhere in Hong Kong.

Everyone else peeled off and moved rapidly toward Snakeskin headquarters. Mercy, though, had a different place in mind. She needed to find someone she hadn't seen in over a decade.

She picked her way through streets laden with incense and offers, past priests and hawkers offering last-minute deals on fu talismans. By tomorrow, the shops would be shutting in the early afternoon, ahead of Hungry Ghost Festival. Everyone stayed in and went to bed early on such dangerous evenings.

Rooms and addresses changed often, but Mercy still heard from Lau Yik a few times a year through his letters, and she was fairly certain he was in this part of the district. After a few wrong turns and a little bit of backtracking, she finally found the door she was looking for on the eighth floor of Kowloon Walled City's westernmost side.

At least, she *thought* it was the door; the address matched. The name on the mailbox outside, however, was someone else's: a woman Mercy did not know, and had never heard of. It could mean Lau Yik had moved, or perhaps he'd finally gotten married after all these years. One way to find out; she knocked loudly.

The letterbox flap lifted. "Who is it?" A high-pitched voice, irritable and tired-sounding.

"It's Mercy Chan." She hesitated, then amended that to, "I used to be called Chen Mei Chi, and I'm looking for a friend of mine. His name is Lau Yik—"

"Buddha's tits!"

"Excuse me?" she said, taken aback.

"Ugh." A long-suffering sigh. "Just come in, Mei Chi. Easier to explain in person."

The bolts drew back, and after some fumbling with locks from the inside, the door swung open.

Mercy squinted in the half-gloom of the alley.

A stranger looked back at her. Well, not quite a stranger. The eyes were the same—wise, dark, slightly crinkled at the corners. The dinted spectacles, so often repaired, remained unchanged. Mercy remembered them well.

But apart from that, the man she'd known as Lau Yik was gone. In his place stood a woman of nearly sixty, lean and compact as Lau Yik had been, wearing a loose black shirt and dark slacks. Long gray hair was gathered in a tidy ponytail, and fine lines etched the handsome face. Her sandaled feet were a little swollen around the ankles.

"The years have been kind to you," Mercy managed, struggling to hide her surprise. Lau Yik—was that still the right name?—had said nothing about a transformation in those sparse letters. "It's so good to see you again . . . big sister." Not so different from saying "big brother," she decided.

"Thank you. I'm glad to see you, too." A tentative smile on that serious face. "I go by the name Erika now." She gestured. "Please, come in. You too, Bao."

Bao purred, slinking inside as if he owned the place.

"Erika," Mercy echoed, stepping across the threshold. "That's nice. English names are trendy, I hear." She glanced around at the small flat: clean and minimalist, which had always been her friend's style. A TV set, some furniture, a small cooker. A bed and a shelf of books. Her friend had always preferred to live simply.

"You look like you've seen a ghost," Erika said, dryly. "And don't give me shit for an English name, not when you have one yourself."

"I don't mean offense, I just wasn't expecting it. People are allowed to change and grow. Including me, and including you." Mercy pulled out a chair and sat down at the little kitchen table. "Still. Why didn't you tell me?"

Erika settled across from her. "What was there to tell? I changed a little every day, over many years. It did not seem worth mentioning. Do you write to tell me how much you've aged, every few months?" She shrugged. "Anyway, not everyone feels about change as you do."

"Not everyone is smart," Mercy agreed. "Tomorrow is a new day, hey?"

"Tomorrow is a new day," Erika agreed, and the tension eased from her shoulders.

Mercy grinned. "How are you doing, big sister? It's been too long."

"Good, good. I run my school, and pay my rent."

Mercy nodded. With the war long over, Erika had returned to teaching unruly local children.

Erika added, "I pay my triad dues, too. You'd better not be here for money."

"Of course not!"

"But you still work for that Snakeskin woman, don't you?"

Mercy grimaced. "I don't know."

"What the hell does that mean?"

She found herself launching into an explanation of the day: the fire-breathing grandmother, to start with. Then the water fetcher, and her odd demeanor. The demolitions consultation that Cobra Lily had chosen to attend, and the trip from Kowloon into Hong Kong. The strangeness of the Executive Council member, Tsang Kit Ling. The ill-fated meeting, Kit Ling's accusations, and Cobra Lily's loss of face.

"This is serious business. Especially that dead girl you met," Erika said, when she'd finished. "Let me see those files."

Mercy slid the binder across the table. Erika flipped through it, silently shuffling through photos, eyes narrowing as she skimmed reports.

"That's a lot of dead people," she said eventually.

"Yes." Mercy drummed her fingers on the tabletop. "I can't help but think there is a connection. The girl, the demolitions, the councilwoman . . . it all feels linked. Don't you think it's a bit too convenient, this ghost arriving just in time to serve Kit Ling's agenda?"

Erika sat back, fingers interlaced thoughtfully. "Ah. You think this councilwoman has found a ghost to inflict on Kowloon, in order to make the city look dangerous, so that she can demolish it? And if so, maybe it is targeting you, specifically, because you're associated with Cobra Lily."

"Something like that."

"Where would a government official even find such a ghost, Chan?"

"That's why I'm here." Mercy scooted her chair forward a little. "I think this ghost might be something left over from the war. One of the spirits rounded up during those city-wide exorcisms. You know, something more powerful than normal."

"Ah. Down in the Murray Building, no? I suppose she would have access to those," Erika said, with a sidelong look. "Which ghost were you thinking of, particularly?"

Mercy spread her hands. "You tell me, old lady. This is your area of experience. I didn't really know much about the ghosts that ended up down there."

"Who are you calling old? Aiyah. Let's have a drink." Erika got up to fetch some bottles of beer from a nearby shelf. She popped the tops with her teeth and extended one to Mercy, who accepted it gratefully. They each took a long sip of the sour, slightly warm liquid.

Erika belched quietly, patted her belly, and said, "That's better. Beer always helps me remember things. You know . . . now that you mention it, something is coming back to me."

"Oh?"

"There were rumors, during the war years, of ghosts who fought in the resistance." Erika ran a thumb over the neck of her beer bottle. "You're right about the ghosts down in the Murray Building. They are not just any old spirits. Almost all of them were spirits of unusual strength, who helped fight against the Japanese."

"Why on earth," Mercy said, faintly astonished, "would ghosts fight the Japanese?"

"You're kidding, right? Can you truly not imagine what *a ghost* might have against invaders and occupiers who killed thousands?"

"Well . . . fair point," Mercy admitted. "Still, it seems very noble of them. Given that they are ghosts."

"Who cares about their motivation, if they're on the right side in a battle," Erika said. "There was one particular spirit who had an affinity for water. I can't remember the details, though. She was known for drowning, and strangulation. Got herself onto Japanese ships, somehow, despite all their wards."

"This is during the time I was working for you? I don't remember any stories of that!" Mercy said, eyebrows raised.

"Yep, same time. But you wouldn't have known about it, Chan. Even I know very little! The guerilla groups in Sai Kung didn't share much information about her, because they protected her existence."

Mercy nodded. "Did they catch her, this ghost? Are you sure she's one of the ones bound in the Murray Building?"

"How should I know? She disappeared after the war, so maybe she was captured and put into a gourd. Or maybe she faded naturally, as some do." Erika fished out a pack of cigarettes and offered it to Mercy, who took one. "What will you do? Curious minds wish to know!"

"The only thing I can do: investigate this Kit Ling person. And look for the ghost she has set free," Mercy said, fishing around for a lighter. "The one question I can't figure out is why she cares so much. What's it to her whether Kowloon is demolished or not?"

"Now that, I can definitely help with." Erika flicked ash. "What if I told you that our friend Kit Ling owns property in Kowloon?"

"You're joking me."

"Afraid not. She bought property here a few years ago, through a proxy. Trying to keep it quiet."

"Why the hell did she buy anything in here? Types like her don't want to live in Kowloon, do they?"

"Oh, she's not living in the district!" Erika barked a laugh. "Same reason a lot of people want property in Kowloon, no doubt. Every time the government talks of demolition, the prices shoot up."

"I don't understand."

"You just don't think like a crook, do you?" Erika jabbed the table with an index finger. "Listen. If the government demolishes Kowloon, it will have to pay compensation to its residents. And if you were, for example, some unscrupulous politician who happened to own that property, you could manipulate things. Drive the prices up, and cash in on the sale."

"Like insider trading?"

"Exactly."

Mercy sat up straight, both feet on the floor. "How do you even know all this?!"

"I used to have many contacts among the government, such as it was. Especially during the war." Erika smiled. "A few of them still write to me, every now and then. One of them is a tenant of Kit Ling's, as it happens. Though I had no idea the information would become important."

"Well. Thank you, big sister." Mercy reached across and squeezed the other woman's hand. "This has been deeply helpful. Do you know the address for this property?"

"Ever been to the Birdcage?"

"The phoenix house?" Mercy said, utterly floored. "How does a councilwoman get away with owning an opium-den brothel?"

Erika smirked. "It's registered as a residential address. And she's not the only civil servant collecting rent from Kowloon—many of them are corrupt."

"Even more reason I should visit, then," Mercy said, mind racing. "Preferably through a back window, with no one watching."

"You want to *break in*, Chan? Is that wise?"

"Are there any better leads? These shady bastards are all connected somehow, and that's as good a place to start as any," Mercy countered. "If I can show that Kit Ling or others have a corrupt interest in demolition, that will be enough to halt the process."

"Sounds dangerous and risky to me," Erika muttered.

"What choice do I have? I can't just knock and ask politely, can I?" She shrugged. "I will be cautious."

"Like *you* know the meaning of the world 'cautious,'" Erika groused, and Mercy laughed. "Listen, don't go now. Evening is here, and it is getting dark. You do not want to be roaming Kowloon in the dark by yourself, eh?"

"The streets are safe—"

"The streets guarded by triad enforcers are safe. Yes." Erika stubbed out her dying cigarette into a cluttered tray. "But if we are to visit Kit Ling's property, we should do it when the den is quiet and asleep. It will be lively and full of clients during the night."

When Mercy hesitated, Erika added, "Aiyah, what's the hurry? Are you rushing to reincarnate? Keep an old woman company for a few hours. We will have a drink, play some card games, and I can show you around my classroom. Then tomorrow morning, we can go early to this councilwoman's house. Together."

"That does make sense, and another pair of eyes would be welcome," Mercy said, giving in. "Alright, let's finish these drinks and go have a walk. I always did want to see your school."

9

A CHANCE ENCOUNTER

Thirty years ago . . .

It is the summer of 1945, in the final days of war. Mei Chi's routine is the same as always: she comes home at five thirty in the morning, drooping with tiredness from a night of running messages. All she wants to do is sleep in the small box room she rents, above Lau Yik's headquarters.

Over the past year, the Japanese occupiers have reinforced the wall around Kowloon to make it a prison for the ghosts of their enemies, but in doing so they have created a space where resistance flourishes. Mei Chi is a solid part of that resistance network, and has spent the better part of three years running errands and passing messages through a neighborhood that is increasingly drowning in spirits.

Sometimes, that work yields visible results. When she steps through the door of the street restaurant that morning, she is confronted by the spectacle of three strangers sitting on the restaurant floor.

"What's going on?" she says to Lau Yik, who is talking quietly with another man.

He turns to her. "A few prisoners, from one of the smaller Japanese camps outside the city," he says, in a low voice. "We freed them this morning, and brought them here."

Even as he speaks, one of the three people lifts their head and cries out, "My daughter! You are still alive!"

Mei Chi freezes.

The woman before her is shivering and crouched, a thin scarf wrapped around narrow shoulders. Black hair is heavily streaked with white, while hunger and worry have drawn shadows across a weary face.

"Please, I am so sorry. You must forgive me!" The gaunt woman inches forward, limping. "I did not mean to leave you, daughter. I came back to look. I could not find you, but still, I returned. You must believe me!"

For a moment, Mei Chi can almost see it. Despite the gap of years, there is something in the woman's jawline, in the slant of her shoulders and the tilt of her nose, that reminds Mei Chi strongly of her own reflection, on the few occasions she has chanced to see herself.

But then they lock eyes, and the certainty is like a stone in her belly. *No.* Mei Chi feels strongly that this woman is not, in fact, her mother at all. How she knows that, she can't explain. It just doesn't feel right.

"I'm not your daughter." Mei Chi takes a step back. "I think you must be mistaken."

"Mistaken?" Thin hands knot together, fingers entwining anxiously. "No, I would know you anywhere, I would . . ." She pauses, face growing pale. "Wait. *Wait.* Which one are you? *Which one of you lived?*"

"I don't know what you're talking about!" Mei Chi shouts, filled with a terrible panic she can't explain. She wants to run out of here, hands over her ears, but her feet seem rooted to the ground.

The woman stares with bulging eyes. "Are you . . . her?"

Mei Chi wheels toward Lau Yik. "Who is this lady?"

"Like I said, just a war refugee," he says, frowning. "She calls herself Daiyu, no family name. Do you know her, Mei Chi? She seems to know you."

"Mei Chi," Daiyu repeats, turning a sickly color. "You—you are Mei Chi. *Not my daughter!*" She begins to wail, a keening and terrible sound.

"Yes, I just said I'm not your daughter," Mei Chi retorts, both alarmed and exasperated.

"So you recall nothing?" Daiyu says, between her tears. "The island . . . the girl . . . me . . . none of it?"

"For the last damn time—"

In that moment, the world disappears briefly.

Mei Chi's senses are overwhelmed by a rush of spiritual energy and a sound that reminds her of radio static. Somewhere far to the north, reality distorts. A force so violent and destructive that it hardly bears imagining has rocked the world, sending repercussions that a spirit can feel with every wisp of their being.

Mei Chi staggers, gasping, hands clutching over her head. As if that could make any difference to the reverberant sensation she's just experienced.

"Little sister?" Lau Yik catches her elbow. "What is wrong?"

She tears out of the room, the refugee woman forgotten, stumbling outside to her knees on the concrete.

Other people glance her way, surprised by the commotion. None of them can sense it, whatever it was. They look at her blankly, exchanging glances.

But the ghosts have also noticed. And whatever knack allows a ghost talker like her to speak so easily with the dead, it has also made her sensitive to the same forces.

Every single spirit, and every single exorcist or medium, stands taut and alert, looking northeast. Staring, despite the clusters of buildings and smog. Staring in the direction of Japan.

Mei Chi does not yet know the name of the city that just died in a single breath, or its exact location. Hiroshima is over two thousand kilometers away, too far to see the nuclear blast with physical eyes.

But she feels it, oh so clearly. Every ghost and shaman from here to China to Russia to Guam and all the places in between—they *feel* the spiritual energy of a hundred thousand souls being blasted from flesh into spirit.

It is like a portal to hell has opened.

Tears are running down her face, and she can no more stop them than she can explain their presence. Her eyes are a flood, her heart a storm. Though neither scientist nor soldier, she knows in the depths of her essence what has occurred. Humankind's destructive power can impact even the spirit world.

"What is it?" Lau Yik is outside, next to her now. He hasn't missed the collective reaction of the city's nearby ghosts. "What's happening?"

"Either the war has ended," Mei Chi says, wiping her nose on her sleeve, "or the world has." Her nose is bleeding, she realizes.

It's her last thought before passing out in a dead faint.

Mei Chi does not see the strange refugee ever again. She is still unconscious when, during that post-bomb confusion, Daiyu quietly slips away, taking her secrets with her.

In less busy times, Mei Chi might have looked for the other woman. Her past is a mystery, after all, and it is possible that amidst the confusion, Daiyu might genuinely have had some tangled memory to unpick and examine.

But there are plenty of other things, horrific and immediate, to occupy her thoughts in the present. For when Mei Chi wakes a few hours later, the news is out: Hiroshima has been obliterated by American nuclear bombs, awash with a hundred thousand screaming ghosts. More and more and more civilians die after the initial blast, sickened by radiation.

By the time she even remembers the encounter with Daiyu, the other woman is long gone, and there are fresh things for Mei Chi to think about.

Three days later, the same devastation wipes out Nagasaki. Mei Chi has no love for her occupiers, but she still cannot look at the pictures. On the thirtieth of August, mere days before capitulating to Allied forces, Japan surrenders Hong Kong back to Britain. And Kowloon, by extension, also gains its freedom.

The end of the war means no more Japanese occupiers to fight, and thus, no more resistance fighters to pass messages for. Mercy is ecstatic to see the end of war—but also needs to find different work, as she realizes quickly enough.

Luckily—or unluckily, depending on your point of view—work comes looking for her.

A few weeks later, Mei Chi comes back to the cha chaan teng from one of her daily errands, only to find the entire place on high alert.

Armed men are loitering outside, wearing white shirts and dark slacks, each with a black strip of cloth tied around their upper arms. These are the early days before the triad has enough wealth to give its members uniforms and tattoos. The men do not react as she walks closer, and in fact they gesture her to go inside.

"Who are you?" she says uneasily, addressing the closest of the bunch.

"Friends," comes the curt, unconvincing reply.

She glances back the way she's come. A hard-edged young man is now standing in the alley, blocking her exit. His smile, when he offers it, is thin and unpleasant.

"Go inside," says the first man, again. "She's waiting on you."

"Who?"

He lights a cigarette and doesn't answer.

Belly roiling, Bao on her shoulder, Mei Chi steps into the eatery's dim interior.

More men lurk within, leaning against walls or sitting at tables. There must be a dozen or so in total, counting the ones waiting out on the street. It feels like more, in such crowded confines. Lau Yik is nowhere to be seen—probably out, he's forever busy—and the few people whom Mei Chi does know are keeping very quiet in the corners of the room.

Sitting at a table in the center of the cha chaan teng is a commanding young woman, dressed in a Tang-style suit. She seems only a few years older than Mei Chi, but is considerably more handsome: smooth-skinned, even-featured, good teeth, no scars. Dark hair all neatly pinned.

Mei Chi recognizes her instantly: Cobra Lily.

Bao growls softly, fur prickling along his back, and Mei Chi can't fault him.

The young triad queen is the only daughter of the man who once ran the Snakeskins. Her rise to power began when her father died during the war, which might have been considered suspicious under other circumstances. Everyone had bigger problems during the occupation, though, and she seems mostly to have gotten away with her coup.

Mei Chi offers a clumsy bow. "Good morning."

Cobra Lily leans her elbows on the table. "So you're the neighborhood exorcist. I heard a lot about you in the war. Is it true, what they say?"

"I don't know, Madam," Mei Chi says, carefully. "What do they say?"

"That you are not like other exorcists. You deal with ghosts differently, and have no fear."

Mei Chi's mouth speaks before her brain can stop it. "Of course I have fear. Ghosts are fucking terrifying."

Cobra Lily raises her eyebrows. "Yet you still deal in spirits."

"Men are afraid to die, but still become soldiers," Mei Chi says. "I like money and I want to eat, but I don't want to sweep streets, or work in brothels. My only talent is for talking with ghosts, so that's what I do. Whether it's scary or not."

"Motivated by money, then," the triad queen muses.

"Nothing wrong with that," Mei Chi says, a tad shortly. "Poor people know the true value of money better than rich people."

"Wise words, for a street scamp." Cobra Lily's smile is predatory. "I'm here because I'm looking to expand my . . . operations, now that the war is over. I have need of new employees for my plans to take off."

"I see," Mei Chi says, neutrally. "May I ask what it is you want with me?"

"The people of this city need order and protection, especially from all these ghosts, and I can give it to them. If you want to be a part of that, I think we could work together."

"Do I have a choice?" The question slips out before her common sense can rein it back.

"Do any of us? Or do we just walk the path laid out for us, by fate?" The triad queen tilts her head. "A word of advice, little girl. Don't ask questions like *what will happen if I refuse*. Instead, ask me questions like *how well can you pay*."

Mei Chi shrugs. "Okay. How well can you pay?"

"Very well. You'll have a place to live, luxury goods, and you'll never be hungry again. What do you say, little ghost talker?"

10

RED BIRD

August 21, 1975

Mercy knew at once she was dreaming.

The room was Erika's, the furniture unchanged. She herself was crammed on a small couch, having left Erika her own bed. This was normal.

But the walls of the flat were gone. In their place, beginning where the floor ended, was a long stretch of ghostly sand on all sides. Some distance away, a turgid ocean stretched.

She sat up, already knowing what she would find.

Sea Sister waited by the shore, sodden and storm blown as ever.

"Shit on everything," Mercy said. "What now? Haven't I seen enough weird things lately?" Not real, she reminded herself vehemently. This wasn't real. Somehow, that comforted her not at all.

The apparition opened its mouth, the muted screaming distorted and faint.

Sea Sister!

"Yes," Mercy said. "I know! The same thing you have said for over thirty years! What about it? Are you choosing to be extra annoying just because it is Hungry Ghost Festival soon?"

Sea Sister lifted something: Cobra Lily's jacket. The sleeves bore the same snake patterns as other triad members', but with the addition of entwined lilies on the shoulders, and a large white lily over the heart.

"That's not yours," Mercy said. "Where'd you get it from?"

Sea Sister ripped the jacket in half and flung it at her. Mercy yelped as fabric landed on her head.

Mercy woke abruptly.

She stood in the middle of Erika's flat, though she didn't remember getting up and moving. Sweat still filmed her skin, but her heart rate was slowing, and the walls were actual walls, now. Not expanses of surreal sand. No torn jacket on her face.

Did that mean she really was awake this time? The idea that she couldn't necessarily tell the difference between asleep, awake, and hallucinating was more than a little frightening.

From outside the flat, in the hallway beyond, someone coughed in a short, hacking fit. Footsteps scuffled, and another voice muttered. It sounded like the second person was complaining at the cougher. A third voice joined in, telling them all to shush.

The hairs rose on the back of her neck. Mercy got up and darted into Erika's small bedroom. She shook the older woman awake, a finger pressed to her lips.

Erika blinked, sat up, fumbled for her glasses. She was too practiced at years of resistance and spy work to cry out or exclaim in surprise. When Mercy gestured frantically at the door, the older woman nodded curtly and reached in her bedside table to fetch out a pair of chopping knives. Old habits died hard, for former spies. They took one each.

Outside, the footsteps shuffled closer. Someone tested the handle very carefully, pressing against the locks. Mercy shared a look with Erika. The other woman grinned and adjusted the grip of her weapon.

The door burst open, and the world fragmented into a series of chaotic moments. Mercy was dimly aware of herself moving, driven by a mix of instinct and adrenaline. Her first slice cut deep across the wild-eyed face of a young triad enforcer.

He screamed, startling loud against the relative quiet of the night. Mercy caught him across the throat in a backswing. He went down in a heap with blood sheeting down his chest. Erika took the next, lunging with a downward chop. Bone crunched as her heavy blade hit the joint between shoulder and neck; the second man was down, too.

In the space of a few seconds, both women stood over two dead bodies, breathing hard, blades clutched in fists and blood all over the floor, their faces, their clothes.

Two more enforcers stood frozen in the hallway beyond, still shocked and reaching belatedly for their weapons. They'd expected a couple of middle-aged ladies asleep in their beds, not a pair of knife-wielding demons lying in wait.

It only got worse for them. Bao came bounding out of the flat, transforming as he leaped into his larger size. Ghost teeth bared in a ferocious growl. Mercy couldn't help but smile fondly.

The two men turned and fled. Apparently, they'd decided the odds were no longer in their favor.

"Shouldn't we chase?" Erika had a hand pressed to her sternum, leaning against the door to catch her breath. She was nearing sixty, after all.

"I'm too old to chase people, and so are you." Mercy was already kneeling over the first body, turning it gingerly. The head lolled. "Besides, the damage is done. We've struck back at Cobra Lily's men. Look, I know this one . . . his name is Li Jun De."

A few neighbors stuck their heads out their doors, peering around at all the commotion. The sight of Bao sent them scuttling back inside soon enough, and no one came to disturb them as they searched the corpses.

There was nothing of interest on either body, beyond some ID and a set of keys. Mercy flicked through their belongings with a twinge of shame. She wondered if they'd come back as ghosts.

"I've done nothing to attract a triad raid," Erika said, then amended it grudgingly to, "Well, not in the last five years, anyway."

"They were here for me. This is Cobra Lily's doing, I'm sure of it." Mercy sat back on her heels. "But why? I'm not a traitor. I was supposed to speak to her later this evening."

"Did you make her angry?"

"A little," Mercy admitted, "but I've seen her worse. Her actions don't make sense. Also, how did she know I was here?"

"A pity we can't ask them." Erika prodded one of the corpses with a foot. "Were you followed?"

"I don't know? I didn't think so, but I must have been."

"Hmm. They know where I live, either way," Erika said. "What will you do now? Will you try to see Cobra Lily?"

"I can't go to my boss. If she tried to have me killed, we must assume she is done with talking." Mercy began cleaning her chopper with her blood-ruined shirt. "I was actually going to ask what you would suggest, big sister."

"Me? I think you should leave." Erika jerked a thumb in the vague direction of the sky. "Catch a ship or a plane out of Hong Kong. The world is big, and Cobra Lily is only one small snake. Even Kit Ling is just a councilwoman. You could be in LA tomorrow, or New York, or the middle of a desert somewhere."

"What would I do in any of those places? They're not my home. That's not my life."

Erika gave her a sidelong frown.

"What?"

"You always work so hard, for so little. Why do you care what Cobra Lily thinks? Leave that mean old woman and find a new job."

"She lifted me out of poverty, gave me purpose."

"Hnh. Are you a small child? Give *yourself* purpose, woman."

"It's not just about Cobra Lily," Mercy said, gently. "This city is my home. It is Bao's home. Good things are worth fighting for."

"Is it good, though? This life you struggle to keep."

"It's not paradise, but it's mine," Mercy said. "Besides, I'm not going anywhere without my cat, and they'd never let a maogui on a plane."

Bao lashed his tail.

Erika laughed uproariously. "You and that beast," she said. "Very well, but I'm coming with you. We will solve this problem together. I can't stay here, now that I've killed triad men."

"I'm so sorry," Mercy said, with fresh alarm. "I hadn't even thought—"

"Tch, I went for them, too! Never mind. Best if we leave together, now."

"No need to come with me," Mercy said. "Lay low somewhere, stay away from both of these women."

"I certainly will not! The sooner this is resolved, the sooner I can return. No, no, close that big mouth and don't argue! I am coming with you, and that's the end." The older woman slipped her blade back into its case, and stuck it through her belt. "But help me clean up this mess first, or we'll have ghosts of our own to deal with. All over my clean floor—look at that!"

"Yes, big sister," Mercy said humbly, and bent to haul the first body upward.

She thought briefly about mentioning her bad night's sleep, then decided against it. They had more important tasks at hand.

The bodies were surprisingly easy to dispose of. Erika had many friends in the complex, some more savory than others by legal standards. In record time, unlicensed men carrying medical equipment and ice boxes showed up to scavenge what they could of the freshly dead corpses.

An hour later, the grisly remains (which even Mercy, with all her triad-hardened years, found hard to look at) were dragged off and taken to an industrial waste site. Afterward, they mopped up a few blood smears on the already-stained linoleum floors with bleach.

"Remind me never to anger you," Mercy said afterward, washing her blood-soaked hands in the sink.

She had killed before, or assisted in killings under Cobra Lily's leadership. Triad law could not be enforced without the occasional head being removed from the occasional shoulders. But the casual butchery of corpses was a new and unpleasant experience. She hoped never to repeat it again, and wondered how often Erika had participated in such things. Her friend had many layers, and not all of them were nice.

"If you ever did make me angry, I'd give you twenty-four hours' warning, first. For old times' sake." Erika grinned around a cigarette, and Mercy could not tell whether the other woman was joking. "If you're nearly done, I think it is time we paid a visit to Miss Tsang's property."

Torrential rain plastered Mercy's clothes to her stocky frame in mere seconds. Even with a sky sheltered by buildings, the rain got in, filtered through layers of pollution and metal. Around her, the air tasted of ocean salt, undercutting the city stench of grease and pollution. Signs rattled in the sideways wind, the gutters already flooded. The first of the yearly typhoons must have landed in the night.

The weather was inauspicious, to say the least. It felt like another storm was coming.

Mercy held a folded newspaper above her head as she darted down the street, cursing the lack of umbrella. The newspaper did nothing except disintegrate steadily above her. Street lights flickered and faltered. Flooding was often a problem in Kowloon in this sort of weather, making the electricity unreliable.

It was the last day before Hungry Ghost Festival, meaning street hawkers were frantically trying to sell the last of their fu talismans, lucky amulets, incense sticks, special fruit, and paper offerings to all and sundry, before their goods became obsolete again. And before they all went in for the night, to stay safe.

The winds were strong, shaking the festival markets which clustered in streets and side alleys, rattling the hanging lanterns. The ghosts who always lurked in corners and shadows were bolder than usual, almost playful, and everyone gave them a wide berth.

From here, she could see the high-rise building which housed the Birdcage. The establishment occupied two floors, on the fourth and fifth level; beneath it was a butcher shop, which always seemed rather suspicious to Mercy.

The entrance to the Birdcage was an approximation of grandeur, though it fell short of the mark. Creaking double doors stood beneath a swinging sign, inviting entry. Red and gold paint flaked from the carved exterior, the handles patterned with the grime of many hands.

A pair of bouncers stood inside the enclosed porch; both were armed, with carved wards hanging round their necks. Even large, tough men did not wait outside at night in Kowloon, unless they absolutely had to.

"Not looking very quiet," she muttered. "Do those big nephews ever sleep?"

"Probably not, but that's okay," Erika said, and tugged her arm. "This way. There's a back entrance through the alley. I'll show you."

The "alley" had once been a gap between buildings, a few levels above the ground floor. Since then, the gap had been filled with planks, cables, and pipes, layered up with metal sheeting and a thick layer of trash compacted down by the passage of feet. It was somewhere between a garbage net and a ramshackle bridge. Mercy stepped with light feet, conscious that any of it might give way in unexpected places.

No one else was down here. This was where the Birdcage liked to empty their trash, and the rubbish heap of an opium den and brothel was not a place that most folks enjoyed walking through. On a good day, the ground was covered in discarded food and broken glass; on a bad day, one might find sacks of body parts. Today was a good day, with only a few smashed bottles and the usual sacks of garbage strewn around.

She reached a sign, staring upward. It hung dejectedly over the back door. The door had no handle on this side, and was clearly locked. A little farther along, though, Mercy spotted a small, high window. Not ideal as an entrance, but certainly better than that door.

It was also heavily warded. Iron plates etched with anti-ghost fu talismans were nailed to either side of the little window, keeping out unwelcome visitors. Mercy chewed a thumbnail, then looked down at Bao.

"Wait here, on the border," she instructed. "Don't come after me, even if you see trouble. I wouldn't want government exorcists to lock you away or banish—Hey, are you even listening?!"

He wasn't. Bao had already found a discarded box to curl up on, and gone to sleep.

"Such loyalty," Erika said, dryly. "Shall we go in?"

"*I* will go in. You, old lady, are going to stay out here."

The retired spy looked at her, eyebrows raised. "Excuse me?"

"Bao cannot go through that window, because of the wards. And if you and I both go in and get stuck, there will be big problems. Let me go in through the side entrance. If I don't come out in twenty minutes, go get help."

"You need my help!"

"*Please.* I can't have your death or injury on my conscience, and this isn't your fight." Mercy touched her shoulder. "You've already done so much for me. Besides, who will bail us out if we're both caught?"

"Fine. Fine! But I don't like this at all," Erika muttered. "Do you have a weapon, at least?"

"I always carry a blade."

"Fine, fine. Be careful and quick, Chan."

"I'll do my best," Mercy said, and hoped that would be enough.

When Erika and Bao had retreated to a safer distance away, Mercy stacked a few decrepit crates together, held her breath against the stench, and clambered up to peer through the window. She had one of Erika's knives tucked into her belt, for all the good it would do.

The sight of a public bathroom greeted her, stinking and fetid. But it was currently empty; it was early morning, and many of the occupants in the Birdcage would be going to sleep after a long night of drugs and work.

Lovely.

"Wish me luck," she said to the ghost cat, over one shoulder.

Bao tilted his head, ears twitching.

She pressed her palms against the sill and hauled herself up through the window, landing lightly on the stained, foul-smelling floor. The scent hit like a sledgehammer. She wrinkled her nose, stepped round gross puddles, and gently eased into the main area.

The main room was a moderate-sized space plastered over in dark-crimson wallpaper, cheaply patterned and erratically peeling, which seemed to absorb all the light. Guttering candles and a few electric bulbs fought the encroaching shade. Bamboo mats covered the floor, easy to replace if stained or spilled on. Lounge chairs were arranged in a semicircle around a cluster of tables, the once elegant cushions now stiff with grime. The pipes, lamps, bowls, and dishes for opium littered the tabletops, a small fortune in drug paraphernalia.

Men and women sprawled unconscious on the lounge chairs, some asleep after a late night and some still in a haze of drugs. None of them paid any attention to Mercy, who flitted past unobtrusively. She hovered at the edge of that space, listening carefully.

What she needed, categorically, was proof of Kit Ling's corruption. Something that not only demonstrated how this woman stood to gain from Kowloon's demolition, but suggested—or better yet, offered proof—that she was involved in the ghost attacks in the district.

It was a lot to hope for.

A small sign on the wall indicated that Red Bird's room was down the closest corridor, at the end. Since Red Bird was the chief tenant of this place, she might well have something Mercy could use. She began easing herself around the room, and down the corridor.

The scent of opium receded, overwhelmed by the pleasanter smell of candles, cosmetics, and fragrant tea. It was quieter down here, the bamboo mat flooring replaced with thick Shanghai rugs. There were little individual studio flats: one room, one phoenix, as the signs outside advertised.

At the far end of the hall, an intricate, solitary lamp rested atop a liquor cabinet, its doors ajar. The cabinet was large but conspicuously empty. Maybe the brothel was cutting back on costs.

Red Bird's room was right at the end, next to the cabinet. A fenghuang was painted on the door arch, in reference to the mythical creature from whom Red Bird took her working name.

Piqued by a mix of instinct and nosiness, Mercy put her ear to the door, listening.

Nothing. No sound from within. Not even breathing, or the rustle of a sleeping body stirring. Mercy was still wondering whether to wait or go in or come back, when she caught the slap of footsteps as someone approached from the other end of the curved hallway. Any second and they'd come round, see her there; it would be difficult to explain why she was here, or who she was.

Damn. She mouthed it under her breath, not daring to say it aloud.

Before she could second-guess herself, Mercy swiftly opened the empty liquor cabinet and folded her frame inside, pulling it shut with her nails just as Cobra Lily came striding down the corridor.

11

BASIN SISTER

August 21, 1975

Later on, Mercy could not say for sure why she remained hidden.

Her boss was unarmed and alone; this could have been the perfect time to confront the other woman and explain what she was doing. They had years of rapport, and were ultimately seeking the same goal—the salvation of Kowloon's community. In all likelihood, Cobra Lily was here for the same reasons as Mercy: to snoop around, and find something they could use against the councilwoman.

At the very least, it would have been far more sensible than stuffing herself into a liquor cabinet and not coming out. Only extremely suspect people hid themselves in furniture without a good explanation, and she had none. If Cobra Lily caught her, the whole conversation would get off to a very wrong start.

Even so, some primitive instinct kept Mercy frozen inside the cabinet. She peered through the wooden latticework which covered the doors, holding her breath and taking care not to move.

Cobra Lily drew closer. She was dressed in a black formfitting suit cut in the modern style, with a red collar and red trim on the sleeves. It was elegant, but in that dilapidated flat, she looked startlingly out of place.

For a split second, Mercy thought the triad queen had seen her and was going to fling open the cabinet, because her gaze appeared to be stabbing straight through the latticework. Mercy's throat grew tight, fist closing around her knife preemptively. Then Cobra Lily, with casual absent-mindedness, turned toward the mysterious room instead.

She took out a key, twisted it twice in the lock, and stepped inside. Mercy caught a brief glimpse of a lush interior, draped in finery and exotic furniture from other countries, and then the door fell shut behind her.

Moments later, a soft clunking noise echoed from within, as if a heavy drawer had been closed with too much force.

A slow flush crept into Mercy's face.

She was an idiot, three times over. Cobra Lily was likely here to visit a phoenix sister, for the same usual reasons most people visited such establishments.

The triad queen had cash, and was known to prefer women. The Birdcage was discreet and had warm beds. Who was Mercy to judge.

Except . . . that still didn't answer the question of why Cobra Lily had turned on Mercy so suddenly, sending men to attack her in the night. Also, it was a deeply strange coincidence that Cobra Lily should turn up in a property owned by her supposed nemesis.

Mercy was still conflicted on what to do about it when the door to Red Bird's room opened again. Inside the cabinet, knees burning from strain, she stiffened to statue-quiet, once more holding her breath.

And almost choked when a completely different person stepped out.

A young woman strode past in flashy clothes, high heels, and fake jewelry. Very little skin was hidden in that outfit. Mercy didn't judge any woman's occupation, but she simply hadn't expected this stranger to come sauntering out of the same room Cobra Lily had entered.

The mysterious girl clacked down the hallway in her heels and left through the front door, shutting it firmly behind her. The key turned, and silence followed.

Mercy waited, dumbfounded, until the echoing footsteps were gone.

The woman who'd left was Red Bird, presumably. Cobra Lily had gone in to see her, so she must still be in there. But what was she doing on her own, in a phoenix sister's room?

Curiosity and lingering anger made Mercy reckless. She pushed open the cabinet with the heel of her hand, crept out, and listened at Red Bird's door. Nothing; still and silent as before. She put her eye to the keyhole.

Empty. There was nobody in there, unless for some insane reason Cobra Lily had chosen to hide under the bed. Where the fuck had the triad queen gone?

Mercy sat back on her heels, frowning. One person had entered. One person had left. The only problem was they were different people.

Suddenly, getting inside felt like the most important thing in the world.

Quiet as a mouse, she took her knife and slid it through the gap to lift the latch.

Red Bird's room was much the same as when Mercy had briefly glimpsed it through the keyhole: lushly appointed, all corners and hard surfaces softened with swathes of different fabric, drapes, and little touches. The bed took up most of the space, elaborate and carved. There was no space underneath; it was solid all the way to the floor. An open wardrobe rested against one wall, expensive clothes hanging in a neat row. A dresser table was nestled on the far wall, a basin of water resting atop its surface.

The decor was extravagant, especially compared to the rest of the flat. Some of the things in here could not easily have been bought on a phoenix sister's salary.

It was also empty of people. No question. If anyone had been hiding in here . . . well, there was no place to hide. She turned in a circle, frowning at the dresser, the wardrobe, the solid bed. A small stack of books, slowly gathering dust: Chinese philosophy from various historical periods, and a well-thumbed copy of collected Song dynasty poetry.

Cobra Lily definitely, *definitely* wasn't in here. So where the hell had she gone?

"Fuck a crab," Mercy said aloud.

There had to be a secret door in here. That was the only explanation. She stood up, glancing once at the dresser table with its mess of jewelry and cosmetics.

A ghost peered up from the basin.

Mercy swore in shock, grasping her knife tight. She leaned over the wide ceramic bowl.

Her own reflection was gone, replaced by the apparition of an elegant, oval-faced woman, perhaps early thirties in age—the same one who'd just walked out in the flesh, moments before. Her skin looked damp, as did her hair, like she'd recently washed in a basin.

Or been drowned in one.

"You must be the ghost of the young lady who I just saw walking out of this room," Mercy said, low. "How is it possible that your spirit has been separated from your body?"

Another thought, more horrible: If this lady was dead, what was living in her skin? This strange business was getting worse by the minute.

The young woman opened her mouth as if to speak, but reflections could only be silent. Her lips trembled. She was a weak spirit, contained in a vase's worth of water.

"Are you dead, little sister?" Mercy knew the answer, but when talking with ghosts, it was important to find out what they knew, too. Some thought they were still alive, and needed gentle correction.

The woman nodded, her face mournful. She was well aware of her own status.

"When did this happen?"

Hesitantly, the spirit held up a finger and sketched something out. Her fingers did not break the surface, but her touch was sufficient to displace ripples.

"Eight," Mercy hazarded. It wasn't easy, trying to read backward-facing Chinese characters invisibly traced underneath water. "Eight what, days?"

Red Bird shook her head.

"Weeks? Months?"

A shake, a pause, then a nod.

"Eight *months*," Mercy said, faintly. That was a terribly long time to be trapped in a basin. "And no one noticed?"

A helpless shrug from the ghost.

"Who killed you? Who took your body?"

Red Bird put her face in her hands, shoulders quivering with silent sobs. She either did not know, or could not say. Ghosts often found their own murders hard to face.

"Don't worry about it," Mercy said, conscious of the time bleeding away. "Can we help each other? I'm looking for—for someone who was in here, very recently. I think she might know your killer, or be involved somehow. Do you know where she went?"

She would never have spoken to a ghost so boldly in normal circumstances, but Cobra Lily might come back into this room at any point, and she did not want to rely on getting lucky a second time.

Within the reflection, the dead woman pointed behind Mercy, as best she could while trapped in a basin.

Mercy spun round. Nothing to see. She glanced back at the basin; nothing in the reflection either, anymore. The mysterious woman had dispersed, for now.

She put her knife away and stepped toward the wall, next to the bed. She thought, though she wasn't sure, that this was the general direction the ghost had indicated. Nothing unusual stood out. She peered more closely.

A mosaic of small tiles adorned the wall, beautiful and intricate, arranged to form the image of a flower, possibly a lily—hard to tell, it was so stylized. Looking more closely, Mercy was struck by the realization that one of the little tiles did not line up, was out of sync with the others. It gave the flower a slightly lopsided appearance.

Mercy ran a finger over the odd tile. Slightly loose, hint of a rattle. She pressed it experimentally, feeling foolish.

The tile sank into the wall, and she swore under her breath. A gentle *clunk* followed, same as the one she'd heard when Cobra Lily had been in here alone.

Mercy stepped back as part of the wall swung open, revealing a narrow archway that was just big enough for her to squeeze through, if she turned sideways. She peered inside.

Through the secret entrance, she spied what must have once been the bathroom in this flat. Tiled flooring, moldy walls, and emptiness greeted her. The sink and toilet had been ripped out, as had the far wall. Someone had simply knocked a long hole through, and then built a chute on the other side.

"Don't think that's allowed in the rental agreement," Mercy muttered, peering over.

The chute itself descended into darkness, accessible only through a series of metal rungs fixed into the wall. Someone had done some serious conversions on this room. The chute went down at least two levels to the ground, maybe farther. Mercy wondered how that worked, with shops beneath.

She stared, wishing Bao were with her. She'd come out this morning in search of answers, but the questions were only piling up.

If she climbed down there, she would find out things she might not wish to know. Things to explain what was going on with Kit Ling and Cobra Lily and the water fetcher girl and the phoenix sister's ghost in the basin. Nothing would ever be the same again.

Didn't matter, it was too late. She had to know.

Mercy set her foot on the top rung.

She soon figured out what exactly had been built. It was rather ingenious.

Like many buildings in Kowloon, this one had a lightwell that ran down the center of it. Lightwells were narrow, vertical shafts. Some were open to the air, others were roofed. They typically ran from the roof to the lowest levels. In more expensive flat blocks, they might be illuminated and decorated, but this place was old, and cheap. It was simply a dank, narrow gap between buildings, filled with blackness and dripping water.

Someone, maybe Kit Ling or perhaps Red Bird, had knocked a hole in the bathroom wall. They'd then added rungs to the wall outside the former bathroom, to reach the bottom of that narrow shaft. That sort of building modification was illegal in most places, but Mercy had seen far worse in Kowloon.

At the bottom of the lightwell was a large storm drain. The lid had been removed, and the rungs carried on down, uninterrupted. A dank smell wafted from below, and the faintest hint of light.

Mercy took a breath, and kept descending.

Another eight feet lower, and she was well below street level. It was cooler down here, and gently damp. At the very bottom, Mercy found herself standing on concrete, with a tunnel stretching off in either direction. Several inches of water covered the bottom, but she could imagine it being much deeper when the weather turned to rain.

It seemed Kit Ling had found an entrance to Kowloon's waterways system. It was no small job, knocking through a wall and adding rungs. Surely this had taken a few months of work.

The liquid churned, and Mercy felt her stomach flip. Only shallow water, she reminded herself. Not like the oceans she'd viewed yesterday; this was no worse than a bath. Well, apart from the smell.

She took a steadying breath, forced herself to get a grip and focus. The tunnel was lit in both directions. Mercy looked toward the northward one; by her calculations, that would head farther under the Walled City, unless she was much mistaken.

Interesting, and disquieting. That meant Kit Ling had an underground path straight into various buildings. That route looked far more flooded, the water noticeably deeper as the path progressed.

She looked southward. The path curved away, and she couldn't see where it led, but it was drier and shallower, and better lit. She decided to choose that route first. Going toward Kowloon was always an option for later.

It turned out to be the smart decision. After thirty feet or so, all of which got progressively drier and cleaner, she turned a corner.

The path here widened out into a large room. It had the feel of a cavern: rock walls, damp with moisture, and a high rock ceiling, about fifteen feet above her head. Perhaps thirty feet wide, in a crude oval shape. It looked to have been some kind of reservoir or water-processing room, which Kit Ling had apparently adapted. Lanterns swung from the ceiling, casting moving shadows; the water carried a loud echo.

Mercy walked forward, fascinated. She was studying the lanterns so intently that she didn't notice when the floor ended—and abruptly stepped off its edge.

Cold, goopy water swallowed her up. She flailed in extreme panic for a full ten seconds until she found her footing, and realized with angry shame that it was only waist-deep.

She stood up, gasping from the sudden temperature change, still mad that she'd floundered in shallow depths. Too late, she spotted a series of stepping stones that would have kept her dry.

In all directions, she could see machinery, pipes, and pumps. Presumably to pump all this water in here, in the first place. Drainage grates pocked the ceiling, dripping with discolored water. No rainfall was going to waste.

She climbed out, and eyed the stepping stones. They took a winding path, branching to a series of three rocks. No, not rocks; concrete platforms, rising out of the water.

Several of the slabs had indistinct lumps lying on them, covered in heavy tarps. They looked worryingly like corpses, if the long shapes were anything to go by.

Mercy's tongue was stuck to the roof of her mouth. So many years in the city of darkness, most of that spent dealing with ghosts of one kind or another, and she had never seen anything like this. She hardly knew where to even start.

She needed to know more.

Mercy slogged to the nearest stepping stone and heaved herself onto that small rectangle of dry rock. She crouched there for a second, shivering and sodden, trying vainly to wring excess water from her trousers. Her shoes had gotten lost, down in the foul-smelling mud and sucking silt, and she didn't care to go looking for them.

Carefully, leery of her own dubious balance, Mercy reached the first concrete slab, and lifted up the tarp.

It took her a long moment to realize that she actually recognized this body, in part because the head was missing: the little water-fetcher girl, laid out to rest. The smell was bad, but this whole room stank of drainage and filthy water. So, this was where the body ended up, then.

She moved to the next one, gently peeling it back. A young businessman lay beneath, still in a smart suit and polished shoes. An expensive watch encircled one wrist, and his dead eyes were wide open.

A fu talisman of preservation was tacked to his chest; he had not rotted, unlike the young girl. Those fu talismans were common enough for funerals, or on food you didn't want to spoil, and Mercy had seen them often. This was a much darker repurposing of a very useful fu talisman, though.

A terrible suspicion crawled over Mercy.

Some ghosts could take bodies and inhabit them. But usually, ghosts took only a single victim, leaving that unfortunate person behind as a new spirit, in their place.

This ghost, though, seemed to be taking many different bodies. Instead of living in a single one, they were swapping between skins like sets of clothes. It reminded her a bit of the story about the painted skin demon, who could take different appearances and blend in as human.

But for what purpose? That was the bit Mercy found difficult. She still couldn't fathom *why* the ghost was doing all this. What need, what desire, what unfinished business drove it to such layered and complex actions? Ghosts were many things, but *complex* was rarely one of them.

Feeling sick with anxiety, Mercy turned away, stepping carefully to the final slab. With a deep feeling of trepidation, she drew back the heavy tarp.

This body belonged to Cobra Lily.

12

CATS ARE BASTARDS

August 21, 1975

Mercy bent over the cold body in that dim light, breath coming in hard and sharp.

Definitely Cobra Lily. Mercy could pick her boss out of a crowd of thousands, could—if required—home in on that triangular face. The tattoos seemed heavy and dark against the unexpected pallor of her skin. A preservation fu talisman was pinned to her chest, same as the man Mercy had just looked at.

This murder must have occurred the night before, she decided. Perhaps the ghost had come to Cobra Lily's quarters in the Walled City, through the connected waterways. From there, it would be a simple task for such a creature to drown the triad leader.

That explained the triad enforcers coming to Erika's house in the night. Cobra Lily hadn't suddenly changed her opinion of Mercy's usefulness. Rather, someone else—or some*thing* else—had taken over Cobra Lily.

And Kit Ling was definitely working with this ghost, in some capacity. Mercy wondered how the councilwoman was controlling something so powerful—if indeed she was. Maybe it was controlling her, or maybe it had gotten out of control.

Mercy lifted one of the hands, unable to stop herself. Long fingers and a narrow wrist, resting in her palm. The arm sat limply in her grasp. With her knife, she gently prodded the corpse; no response to that either. She hadn't been expecting one.

You'll have a place to live, luxury goods, and you'll never be hungry again. What do you say, little ghost talker?

Working for a triad hadn't always been easy, despite the money and prestige. The job had been a challenge, both in learning to deal with ghosts and in navigating the triad queen's wild mood swings and fragile ego. Then there'd been the whole business with the name change: Cobra Lily had insisted she take an English name, for "prestige."

But Mercy didn't hold a grudge. She'd known what she was signing up for and been fine with it. Ultimately, she had never wanted or expected an easy life, only an interesting one, and Cobra Lily had always given her that.

She would miss the violent old bat.

"I am sorry," she said to Cobra Lily's shell, wishing she knew the woman's full name. Her boss had been a complicated woman; both a benefactor and a bully, both a social reformer and a volatile criminal.

Mercy gave herself a shake, replaced the tarp gently, and stepped back. She had to get out of here. Had to tell someone.

Only, there was truly no one to tell. The ghost was working with Kit Ling in some capacity, and either was controlled by her, or was controlling her. It could appear as a swathe of different people; no one was safe.

Who, exactly, was Mercy going to inform other than Erika—someone nearly as powerless as herself?

Theoretically, she could tell the triad. But the idea of rounding up triad members and informing them that their leader was now a supernatural creature inhabiting different skins made her insides clench. No one would believe her tale, not without significant proof, and that would involve openly storming the premises and bringing people down here. Dragging a body up with her would not be enough, because you could get bodies from anywhere.

Assuming anyone in the triad did believe her, Mercy was not sure they would care. Cobra Lily was seen as powerful, regarded almost as a force of nature. The revelation that she was even more powerful than everyone had first thought would not necessarily have the effect Mercy was hoping for. A handful of skins in a secret room was unlikely to deter those loyal to her. Cobra Lily had buried her share of corpses over the years.

Maybe Mercy should just walk away. There was still time to go back up those stairs, out the side door, and flee. Meet up with Bao and Erika, get the hell out. She could catch a plane or boat or train, anything, and be on the other side of the world as Erika had suggested. Sometimes a fight was bigger than you could handle.

And yet.

Mercy stared down at the inert body, beneath its covering. Around her, the cavern echoed with lapping water. Spillage leaked from ceiling grates. Machinery clanked occasionally. The bodies, who should have been alive, were the stillest thing in the room.

She couldn't do it. If she simply left, Kowloon would certainly be slated for demolition. This ghost was working toward destroying the city she had known and loved for years. Kowloon was her world, the one constant in a life full of upheaval and change. Mercy did not know who she would even be without it.

Mercy willed her mind to focus, to hold itself sharp and taut amidst the chaos that clouded her head. Get out of this building first, then take the triad-warded streets to the city limits. Once she was out in wider Hong Kong, she could have options.

"I see you got my message."

Mercy spun round, her heart skipping beats.

Red Bird stood framed in the entryway, still wearing heels and fake jewelry. Or rather, her body stood there, inhabited by something else; the real woman's soul was still trapped in a basin upstairs.

"What message?" Mercy asked, shakily.

The tiniest of frowns crossed those pretty features. "The girl. The water fetcher. I sent her to give you a message, and she ended up destroyed. That was you, wasn't it?"

"The demon," Mercy managed. In among so many other strange things happening, she had briefly forgotten about the dead kid. "You're the demon she mentioned. The one who killed her, and made her into a ghost."

Red Bird giggled. "Guilty."

"Got a name, then?" She needed to keep this thing talking, and distracted, for as long as possible.

"Of sorts. They used to call me the Girl with a Thousand Faces." The thing that was and wasn't Red Bird offered a shrug. "You may call me that as well."

"Why not. Seems appropriate for a monster who collects bodies like a rich lady collects shoes," Mercy retorted.

The other "woman" only laughed. "Do you not like my skin room? I worked hard at building it, you know." It paused, lips curving in a cruel smile. "Kit Ling had no idea how useful this property was when she bought the place. She only wanted the land for her own corrupt, monetary gain. But I discovered the phoenix sister used to store her drug supply down here, and adapted it for my own needs."

"So happy for you," Mercy said, coldly. What did it want, a fucking trophy for being creative? "Who or what are you? What the hell is going on?"

"Both are complicated questions, with complicated answers. Would you like to guess?"

"You killed Cobra Lily." Mercy's fingers crept toward the knife on her belt.

Some ghosts liked to talk, some didn't. This one seemed like a talker, which was good. Gave her time to prepare.

"It was a busy night," said the Girl with a Thousand Faces, stretching languorously. "First, I had to walk through the storm drain tunnels as a spirit, just to get past fu talismans and guards so that I could drown your little triad leader in her own bath."

Mercy flinched.

"When Cobra Lily was dead, I brought her body here, for safekeeping." It paused to smile, thinly. "Very soon, Kit Ling will turn up as a corpse, in Cobra Lily's house. In fact, it has already happened."

"Kit Ling will . . . what?" It took Mercy a whole thirty seconds to work through that realization, accompanied by a rising sense of anxiety. "Wait, aren't you working for her?"

Thousand-Faced Girl laughed. "How funny you are! Of course not. I work for no one, little exorcist. Kit Ling is merely one of my skins, albeit very useful." Its head tilted sideways, eyes narrowing. "You didn't expect that, did you? Another thing you didn't think of."

Kit Ling was dead. *Kit Ling was dead.* All along, Mercy had been dealing with a puppet, with a demon looking out at her from dead eyes. This thing was in perfect control. It had played her like a lute from the very beginning.

"What was the point?" Inwardly, she was tense as a laundry line. All her nerves were screaming at her to *run, run, run* except there was nowhere to go. "All that murder, that complex chess playing, for what?"

"I have my own plans." Thousand-Faced Girl smiled even wider. "You don't need to know them. Not yet."

"Again, who the hell are you?" Mercy said, ragged. "What is your problem with my city?!"

"Who am I? Oh, there have been so many names, so many faces. Hundreds, maybe thousands." Thousand-Faced Girl tilted her chin up, hands on hips. "I am beautiful or plain, young or old, male or female. I am everyone, and no one, all at once."

A wave of revulsion rose up in Mercy's throat. "What you are is a disgusting body thief!"

"Disgusting," the ghost echoed, tilting its head to one side. "I am no more vile than you, Mercy Chan. Chen Mei Chi. Whatever name you choose to use."

"We are nothing alike!" She readied herself to throw her knife, angling her body ever so slightly.

"Interesting. Do you still not recognize yourself? Your lost memories . . . your lost life. Don't you remember?"

"Why don't you tell me, since you seem so keen for me to recall," Mercy retorted, silently willing the ghost to tilt her head up. Just a smidge more.

"I know some part of you still remembers." The ghost wet its lips with the tip of its tongue. "The island. The girl by the sea. *The temple.*" She gestured widely. "All of this is because of you, Mei Chi. Cobra Lily's death, my quest to destroy

Hong Kong and Kowloon . . . it is all connected to you, and what *you* can't remember. What *you* refuse to apologize for!"

"If you want my apology, then ask. You didn't have to kill people to get my attention." Mercy let her mouth do the talking, concentrating on lining up the shot. She would only have one chance.

"No! I needed you to remember first, so that you can suffer. An apology without true understanding is meaningless," the ghost hissed, tilting its chin up at last. "I need you to lose absolutely everything, by inches and degrees, including the city you call home—"

"Shut up." Mercy threw her dagger at that exposed neck.

It was a good throw: almost fifteen feet across open water. The blade buried itself in the former phoenix sister's throat. She staggered back with a gurgle. Blood jetted from the wound in uneven gouts as Mercy launched across the stepping stones in a sprint.

Fear and shock swirled like a storm inside her head. She squashed it down, forcefully holding the emotions at bay. Get away first, survive, get out. Later, when she was safe, there would be time to process the horror of Cobra Lily being dead, of all these people being dead, of the thing that inhabited her boss's skin and swapped bodies the way a child swapped shirts. And the strange things it said to her, which filled her with deep anxiety.

Red Bird's body slumped to a heap, bleeding out even as Mercy took the last shaky jump from stepping stone to concrete corridor. She botched the landing and was just scrabbling to her feet when the phoenix sister's body split open like a ripened pea pod.

Bodies were not clean, tidy things. Blood and viscera spattered the walls, the ceiling, Mercy's face and clothes. She threw her hands up, lowering them in time to see a blood-covered shape oozing out, sliding over the edge of the platform and into the water.

Thousand-Faced Girl was going for another body.

It was too dangerous to wait here. Mercy stopped to wrench the knife from Red Bird's neck, and fled up the tunnel. Back toward the rungs, the chute, the weird flat.

From somewhere in the cavern, a loud sigh echoed. Cobra Lily's voice rang out, clear as a gong, "You cannot run from me, stupid little rat! Justice is coming for you!"

Mercy ran anyway.

⁘

She burst into the tunnel like a flood, ready to fling herself up those rungs as fast as she possibly could.

Except the way was blocked. A couple of triad enforcers were crouched above the open storm drain, peering in. When she skidded into view, their eyes widened and they began shouting.

Thousand-Faced Girl had set an excellent trap.

Mercy didn't waste time trying to get past them. Instead, she kept running, and hoped Erika had been canny enough to get away. She sprinted straight past the entrance, following the tunnel northward. Farther underneath Kowloon. Behind her, the sounds of pursuit; ahead of her, the tunnel yawning into greater and greater darkness.

In her youth, Mercy had been fit enough to run or jog most of the night, all in the service of passing messages between different resistance groups. But she was fifty-three, now, and it had been at least a decade or two since she'd had to run like this.

By the time she saw a second pair of rungs leading to a closed storm drain, she was badly out of breath and her chest had knotted up. Mercy flung herself up the metal ladder, despite every groaning protest of her body.

No time to rest. From down in the tunnels below, she could still hear shouting, and sounds of pursuit.

The storm drain lid was heavy, but she was desperate. Mercy shoved it up and away, hauling herself onto the busy streets of Kowloon Walled City. Rain poured heavily; the weather had not relented since this morning.

She was in a side alley, just off the central courtyard. The only part of Kowloon where the sky was routinely visible. A pair of triad enforcers were waiting in the courtyard, in plain sight. They turned toward her, eyes narrowing. Thousand-Faced Girl had come prepared.

"Wonderful," Mercy said.

Two more enforcers joined them, making that four against one. Mercy didn't rate her odds in this fight.

She fled, shouting, "Bao, where the hell are you!"

With a roar that *did* stop pedestrians and enforcers alike, the ghost cat came barreling through the crowds, lion sized and gleaming white. He was at her side in an instant, matching her flagging pace with his supernatural energy.

"Stop her!" Cobra Lily was climbing out of the same drain, hair sodden and dripping. She had been impossibly fast. "Don't let her get away!"

Mercy flung her arms around Bao, and held tight. She didn't often ask him for a ride, but this was a serious emergency.

He ran, bearing her weight with grace.

The triad enforcers chased. Bao tore up the nearest set of stairs, seeking higher ground. Mercy clung on for life, shouting at pedestrians to get out of the way. Yelling apologies and dodging curses as they burst past. Over one balcony edge, along the eaves, jump the gap—a different street, now. Angling toward one of the gates. If Bao could just get into wider Hong Kong—

Her luck ran out. Bao halted abruptly and Mercy lost her grip. She tumbled to the ground, staggering to her feet in chagrin. They were at a dead end.

The main road leading to the southern gates was blocked off. Someone—likely the ghost, in Cobra Lily's body—had erected a barricade. Enforcers waited on the other side of it, holding menacing choppers. More triad men leaned out of windows and from walkways, and the ones behind her would catch up in a minute or less.

Shit.

Realistically, she was dead. So dead. There was too much city and too many triad assholes. She had no way of getting out.

Mercy looked at Bao.

"If you have any ideas," she said, "now would be a great time."

The ghost cat turned his gaze on the blocked alley, swiveled to look at the advancing enforcers, then back at Mercy. Still in his demon form, he licked her bruised forehead with an ephemeral tongue, gentle as a kitten.

Then he turned and fled through a crack in the barricade, oozing his spirit self away to safety.

Mercy was truly alone.

"You selfish feline bastard," she said, incredulous, and began to laugh.

She was still laughing helplessly at her disloyal cat when the swarm of enforcers caught up to her at last and tackled her to the ground.

13

THE NIGHT OF THE HUNGRY GHOST FESTIVAL

August 21, 1975

"Why did you murder the executive councilor?"

"I didn't. Cobra Lily killed her. She's even in Cobra Lily's flat."

"Stabbed with *your* knife through her throat, Chan! How do you explain that?"

"I already have, in eight different ways," Mercy said, irritably.

A knuckly fist swung at her jaw.

Mercy fell sideways, teeth rattling in their sockets from the blow. She could do nothing to avoid it; her hands and feet were bound. The sensation was there, but it did not swarm her. She had already moved to a place in her head where pain was a distant cousin banging on a locked door, and was determined not to let it in.

Even so, the blow put bursts of light across her vision. She found it harder to think and form words than she had at the start of this "talk."

"Get up," the vanguard said. "Answer the question, and don't be fucking rude. It's your fault the government are about to bear down on us!"

With agonized effort, Mercy struggled back to kneeling position, the weight of her body resting on her aching knees.

"I did answer," she said, wearily, when more or less upright again. "Cobra Lily is dead. So is Kit Ling. Their bodies have been possessed at different times by some kind of demon, probably a ghost. It moves between skins like a hand between gloves. Right now, it is wearing Cobra Lily, because that serves its purpose. Go back to Red Bird's room, climb into those tunnels. I know you know where they are, you were standing guard when I—"

"What our boss keeps in those tunnels is her business," the vanguard said, stooping to her level to meet her gaze. "I'm not going to poke around in her personal property! Do you think I'm stupid?"

"Your own mother thinks you're stupid." She grinned at him through a blood-streaked face, lips burst and cheeks bruised.

He hit her again, far too hard. Like she wanted. Mercy leaned into the blow and let it knock her into blissful oblivion for a while.

Not nearly long enough, sadly. She awoke when they emptied ice water over her head, some uncertain number of minutes later.

"Stop being a coward and kill me," she said, trying blearily to focus on the ceiling. But her vision was blurred and she couldn't open one of her eyes from the swelling. She spat blood in lieu of gagging on it.

"Dying is too easy for one like you." Fabric rasped as he rolled up a sleeve. He stood over her, the stink and sweat of him a palpable miasma. Mercy turned away, more from revulsion than fear, and kept her eyes shut. Easier if you didn't see the blows coming.

A pause. Someone spoke at a distance. Then, footsteps. He was walking away.

She cracked open the working eye.

The vanguard had left. He must have been called off by a signal she hadn't seen. When the ringing in her ears died down, she could hear muttering outside the door. Ah, talking to someone. That explained it. A small, temporary reprieve. She blew out a sigh. Blood flecked her breath.

The room she'd been put in was damp and gray, with grimy walls and a muddy floor. Maybe there was stone or concrete underneath all that grime, underneath the caked layers of blood and viscera and human feces and who knew what else. It had long been buried, though.

No windows, because obviously. And it was underground. Like the reservoir. No, don't think of the reservoir. Even so, from within this closed box of a place, she could hear the rainstorm gathering strength outside.

Mercy wasn't expecting help. Hong Kong didn't have a functioning police force in the Walled City, and had not for years. Ever since the war, Kowloon had belonged to Cobra Lily. Her affairs were her own. Besides, the police now wanted her for killing Kit Ling.

The only other person who believed Mercy, who could really help her, was hopefully long gone to safety. No one had mentioned Erika, which was promising, and she'd seen no sign of her old friend, or of Bao. Mercy prayed that meant both of them were well away, and safe.

For herself, Mercy couldn't summon up any angst about her own fate. A big part of her was beginning to believe that she deserved everything that had happened in the past few days.

Not from killing Kit Ling, because she knew she was innocent of that.

The years with Cobra Lily were fine, too. Triads had a reputation, and many of the things they did constituted a break of law. But Kowloon had been abandoned by proper countries, left to rot while China and Britain uncomfortably dodged the responsibility for its poverty and spirit infestations, refusing to deal with any of it. The schools and protections and rules kept Kowloon running, and even the triad dues were not so different from taxes.

What had led her to this sense of resignation was the conviction that she had done wrong, in the past she could not recall. After many years of being a ghost talker, Mercy had learned to believe their complaints, and the ghost had been adamant: she had caused great pain, somehow, in her forgotten youth. Even if she no longer remembered it.

After all, wasn't that what the waking visions and nightmares were about? Her own brain, trying to remind her of things her heart apparently wished to forget. Lying here, taking blows, she kept trying to pierce the veil around her mind. If she could recall what she'd done, maybe the spirit could be reasoned with.

A strange little idea popped into her head, giving her a moment's pause.

Those waking visions. Had she ever tried to interact with them properly? She talked to them a bit, answered their cries, sure. But nothing in depth, as it were. Her go-to reaction had always been to shout at Sea Sister, or attempt to wake up.

Maybe it was time for a different tactic. Mercy closed her eyes, fighting off the pain and panic. Think, she told herself.

The forlorn figure, lonely and tormented on a surreal beach.

Sea Sister. SEA, SISTER!

Dead eyes, staring out from the face of a dead water fetcher.

Do you remember the island, Chen Mei Chi?

Kit Ling, smartly dressed and smiling coldly.

Are you sure, completely sure, we have not met before?

Red Bird's nails, clacking and painted.

Do you still not recognize yourself?

A trickle of cold water ran across her cheek.

Mercy opened her eyes. Well, the one eye, anyway. The ceiling was dripping, the walls wet with moisture. The central drain was flooding, seawater welling up, the reek of brine overpowering the stench of blood and filth; a welcome change.

And Sea Sister was there. That monstrous, ocean-drenched young woman, wearing the same ragged clothes. As always.

"You," Mercy rasped, through burst lips. "You are the key to all of this. Help me understand. Why is this happening to me, and why is it happening *now*?"

Sea Sister drifted over. With every step she drew closer, the level of water rose a little in the room until it was almost knee-deep. Mercy floated on her back, unable to move, neck twisted to keep the monster in her sights.

When she was standing with her knees against Mercy's shoulders, Sea Sister stopped and peered down. Water dripped from the ends of her hair. Pearly eyes did not blink.

"I've been examined by every exorcist in the city, and they all tell me I'm not haunted," Mercy said, words slurred through her busted lips. "But even if you're not haunting me, even if you're just a dream, you carry my secrets. And on the other side of you are all the memories that I've lost. I need to know what's so bad and wrong about my past."

Sea Sister echoed mockingly, *Bad and wrong.*

"Oi!" Mercy exclaimed. *That* was different. "Endless years of ignoring me, and you choose to respond today? Why are you only talking to me now, after all this time?"

Why are you only talking to me now?

"I have always been talking, but you never answered," Mercy said, annoyed.

I have always been talking.

Disappointment swamped her. It wasn't really speaking, just parroting her words. So much for a breakthrough.

"Oh, fuck this. Are you even real?"

Are you even real?

"Eat shit," Mercy offered, experimentally.

Silence. Interesting, her hallucination was choosy.

"Answer me this, at least. Who am I, that you can't leave me alone?"

Who am I? The apparition touched its throat, thoughtfully. *Who am I?*

"You are Sea Sister, idiot," Mercy said, ragged. She was already having the worst day of her life, and this damn apparition couldn't even answer a straight question.

The green face leaned over, so close its lips were a hairsbreadth from her nose. *You are Sea Sister, idiot*, it repeated, and licked her eyeball with a sucker-studded tongue.

Mercy lurched away in revulsion, swearing loudly. In an instant, the water and vines vanished as if they had never been, the walls moldy but no longer dripping. Unsurprisingly, the green-skinned apparition had gone; she was alone again.

The door swung open noisily. Footsteps slapped the ground. And Cobra Lily sauntered over, grinning wide.

Except it wasn't Cobra Lily. Not even close. Beneath that familiar skin lurked a polluting spirit, staring out at Mercy from dead, stolen eyes.

The Girl with a Thousand Faces, in the flesh again.

Well, *some*body's flesh, at any rate.

"Sleeping, were we?" the water ghost said cheerfully. "Any interesting dreams?"

Thousand-Faced Girl had changed clothes, putting Cobra Lily's form into a smart red jacket. Hair smoothed back, collar and sleeves starched, skin lightly flushed with health and color. No indication that a few hours ago, this body had been cold, empty meat on a stone slab in a secret reservoir, with a preservation talisman slapped to it.

Mercy glared in response, saying nothing.

"Want me to make her speak?" the vanguard said, with cruel eagerness.

"What? No." Thousand-Faced Girl gestured with a languid hand. "Give us some space."

The vanguard retreated to the far corner.

The triad queen's body crouched down. "Are you enjoying the show?"

"Is this a game to you, then?" Mercy retorted.

"Not at all. My goal was simple: to spark a conflict between the police and these triad folks. That's all it was ever about, this demolition nonsense. With Kit Ling dead, apparently murdered, that will be easy to kick off. I imagine it will be quite the gunfight."

Mercy spat with perfect aim, landing a gob of blood and spit on Cobra Lily's clean jacket.

In his corner, the vanguard reached for a blade.

Thousand-Faced Girl waved him down irritably. "I said, give us space! In fact, go bring us a barrel."

"A . . . barrel, Madam Snake?"

"Yes, for interrogation. Bring it here, and bring water to fill it."

The vanguard eyed them both, then detached from the wall and left.

Thousand-Faced Girl turned back to her. "Much better. I won't have to whisper now." It made no move to clean off the bloody spit staining its jacket. "I think it's important to have the police busy in the Walled City, you see. I need to free all those other ghosts, so unfairly locked away in the Murray Building."

"I knew it," Mercy said, with a tiny flare of vindication. "You *are* one of those combat spirits who fought in the war!"

"Me, and many others. We were all betrayed." Thousand-Faced Girl sighed breathily. "Do you know what day it is, Chen Mei Chi?"

"Of course." She didn't even have to think about it. "It's the night of Hungry Ghost Festival."

"That's correct!" Thousand-Faced Girl clapped its hands in delight. "Today, the dead are strongest, and most angry, because today the gates of hell open. It is the perfect night for a prison full of angry ghosts to wreak havoc on Hong Kong." She laughed, though nothing was funny.

"What did those people out there do to you?" Mercy demanded, struggling to control her anger. "The citizens of Kowloon Walled City are innocent. So are the citizens of Hong Kong!"

"Are they? I think not." The pretense of humor fell away; Thousand-Faced Girl's features were contorted with something like hurt. "Everyone betrays me. I fought for this city, Chen Mei Chi—with sweat and tears and terrible danger. In exchange, they left me rotting in a bottle gourd, once their great stupid war was finished. Their betrayal was even worse than yours."

Mercy wanted to ask what her betrayal had been, but there was no chance. The door banged open for a third time as the vanguard returned, this time carrying an industrial barrel. He struggled with its weight, knuckles white around the brass handles, and set it down with a half groan.

That done, he unspooled a hose from the nearby wall and began filling the rusted barrel.

Mercy couldn't take her gaze off the damn thing. "What are you going to do with me?"

"Kill you, obviously," Thousand-Faced Girl said. "It would be stupid not to. But! But, the good news, Chen Mei Chi, is that dying is not the end. I have every confidence your spirit will endure. When it does, perhaps then you shall remember your crimes."

"Dying is not the 'end' for anyone in a city where we all become ghosts," Mercy retorted, but deep within her chest, a tiny spark of panic was catching alight. "But being a ghost does not count as being alive!"

"Being . . . a ghost . . . does not count . . . as being . . . alive," Thousand-Faced Girl repeated, finger tapping its lower lip. "How right you are! And how ironic that you, of all people, should say that to me."

"Done," the vanguard said shortly.

Mercy tried to speak, found her words had all withered up.

"There is no need to worry. I have everything under control." Thousand-Faced Girl smoothed down Mercy's hair, as if she were a child. "Never doubt that I will always love you," it whispered, and for a single breath, despite the incredible strangeness of that statement, Mercy found herself believing it.

The Girl with a Thousand Faces straightened up. "Goodbye, Chen Mei Chi. See you in another life."

Mercy rolled away, trying frantically to crawl toward the door. For all the good it would have done.

She didn't get far.

The ghost caught her, held her, dragged her to the water barrel, and pushed her head beneath the surface. She should have held her breath but the panic was setting in. Rationality fled, and Mercy tried—foolishly—to suck in a breath. Water burned up her nose and then down into her lungs, like a cold wet fire.

Mercy had time to think *Oh shit, not again* in confused dismay as her spirit peeled away from her body, and there was nothing left of her but empty skin.

PART TWO

14

IN ANOTHER LIFE, MAYBE

Thirty-three years ago . . .

In the distance, the city recedes like an outgoing tide.

One final glance gives sight of pale colonial-style buildings clustered like barnacles around the coastline and docks. Junk boats cut through the harbor with their red, fan-like sails and narrow prows. There are occasional cars and frequent rickshaws, schools and temples and hospitals; there are trading offices filled with people speaking multiple languages, and dusty warehouses processing a steady stream of goods.

From here, it is almost pretty. But home is never more beautiful than when you see it for the last time.

The year is 1941. You are twenty years old, and were born during the lull of relative calm between two brutal wars: a squalling and reluctant addition to an ever-growing port city. The flat in Wanchai District that your parents rented overlooked the crowded, ship-thick harbor, thronging with people and cargo and ferries. As a girl, you could see the ocean from your window, a stone's throw from the ferry docks and their ceaseless shipping traffic.

For most of your life, that simply *was* Hong Kong, sprawling on China's southeastern coast like a hungry, concrete octopus, infested with busy humans. No better or worse than a thousand such cities across the globe, except this one is—was?—your home. The only place you've ever lived.

But Hong Kong has another side.

A different face, if you will.

Here's how to find it. First, help your mother pack six suitcases on a warm December morning, with all the food and clothes you can cram in. Most of your family's possessions must be left behind. Then go to the nearest pier, and hire a small junk boat.

Pile your luggage in the hold and sail forth through Victoria Harbor and beyond it. Slip past shipping lanes and ferries, past British naval vessels and American cargo carriers, and up round the coast of Sai Kung toward shorelines softly eroded by yearly typhoons. Skirt around the archipelago islands that dot the coast, tiny yet steep, studding the ocean's face like rocky freckles. The city shrinks smaller and smaller every time you look back until, at last, it isn't visible at all.

And breathe.

Turn down the engine, embrace the quiet. No busy morning traffic, jostling with the rickshaws and bicycles and pedal-traders. No crowds surging round the ports, the buildings, the narrow streets. Pollution left behind. Open sewers too far away to smell. Shade your eyes, look outward from the small deck. On this dazzling, sunlit morning, you can see for miles; the eye travels like a bird set free.

Gaze to the left, toward the mainland. Hills are draped in clustering trees. The coastal beaches are a mix of white and soft, or else stony and raw; the ocean is a swirl of inky green. Somewhere, bauhinia flowers drift on the wind in dashes of pink, red, white. Somewhere, sharks and stingrays and dolphins are swimming.

This, this is the face of Hong Kong you will learn to fall in love with. The bit everyone else calls "city" is just a cold monstrosity.

If you wished, you could dive from the boat, let the salt water drink you up until the skin of your body is cracked and wrinkled. Beneath the surface there will be the clownfish, the urchins, the sprawls of coral. Take a moment to catch your breath while the sun runs renegade across the sky.

Welcome to heaven. It was just over the horizon, all along.

But we're getting ahead of ourselves. Those gorgeous moments aren't quite upon you yet. For now, it is enough to lean on the railings, elbows pressed against sun-stung metal. Life has been so bleak, for so many months, that you've forgotten how to be happy.

It's almost like there is no war, no distant bombs, no constant air raid sirens. No more city on the teetering edge of occupation. The Japanese will arrive soon with guns and submarines and cruel prison camps but that isn't your problem, not any longer. You're just here with Mami and both of you are doing what Baba told you to do, before he left: getting somewhere safe.

In truth, few places in the world are safe right now. But some places are less tactically advantageous than others, and a tiny abandoned island with no strategic importance is surely safer than the bustling urban jewel you've left behind. There's less chance of trouble out here.

Mami stands next to you on the deck, after stashing the luggage away. For most of the trip, she has said very little. Just stares at the horizon, as if resentful about what lies beyond its edge. If she is enjoying this, it doesn't show.

You've seen her happy in photographs, if rarely in real life. There's an old snapshot of her wedding day, black-and-white, much faded, with *Sung Ho Tung and Chen Daiyu—married Sept 1922* written on the back to mark the Western year. Unlike Western wives, Chinese women keep their names in marriage.

In it, Mami wears a traditional qun kwa, the gold dragons and vermillion cloth all bled to gray by the camera's inadequate eye. She is young and smiling, surrounded by double-happiness decorations. Baba—Ho Tung—stands next to her in a Tang suit and looks dazed, as if all his good fortune has come at once.

Unusually for most Chinese women, your Mami chose to take her husband's surname on marriage, for reasons that were never quite explained to you. Baba said once in passing that she did not wish to be reminded of the family she'd lost as a child, and you'd never questioned it.

Regardless, little trace remains of that youthful, happy Daiyu. Years of hard living have eroded her smile, and fresh worry has caricatured her into a shell, hollow and haunted. Even on this boat, with the sun a relentless shower of light above, joy can't touch her.

It's hard not to feel like this is your fault, because a lot about Baba's departure feels like your fault. Mami says it isn't, but you know in your bones that isn't true, that she blames you at least a little for not stopping him—as you blame yourself.

Your heart lives in a state of tug-o'-war between her misery and your guilt.

"Sit still," she says, abruptly. It's the first thing she's said all trip. "Always you are fidgeting, like ants are biting."

Truthfully, you hadn't noticed. Your body likes to be in motion, and becoming a statue is not easy. It's been a long couple of hours crammed on the boat.

But you want to be respectful. You fold both arms across your chest, and hug yourself to quietude. Daughters should be obedient and respectful, when possible. She seems satisfied with that, or at least isn't complaining anymore.

Since even glancing her way dampens the mood, you angle both shoulders to cut her out of view, until the searing line of horizon fills your eyes and heart. For now, it's enough. Time aplenty for unhappiness later.

The boat needs refueling. That demands a stopover at Silverstrand Beach, if only briefly. A few of the locals give you sideways looks when they hear of your destination. Everyone pointedly doesn't talk about the war, which means there is little to say.

Then the tank is full and you're moving again, on toward the island. They're almost as relieved to see you go as you are to leave.

Shek Ham Chau in Cantonese, or Shak Ham Chiu if speaking Hakka. The syllables roll off the tongue, modest and gentle. The British translation on maps says: *Stone Temple Island*, though this is not quite accurate. A closer translation would be *Stone Shrine Island*, though the nuance of that was probably lost in the English translation.

Regardless, there was a village on it once, going back hundreds of years. Your mother was born in this place, the daughter of salt farmers. That was her life and identity, until 1918 or so, when the worst typhoon in two centuries wrecked the community.

Everyone died except Mami and a few other children. Baba told you that she lost her entire family in the storm. All survivors relocated to the mainland, to live with distant relatives. Shek Ham Chau stands abandoned, now, aside from the lonely ghosts who linger in its remains.

However, fewer people means greater safety for you, because empty islands are worthless to Japanese invaders. And Mami owns the house where your grandmother once lived, with a farm attached. She's never been able to sell the land, because of the ghosts. That is where you're headed, the pair of you; a quiet refuge from the war, if there is such a thing.

A haunted island is a daunting retreat, but it's only temporary. Just until Baba can get the supplies and money he needs, and come for you in a boat of his own. And then you'll all go somewhere safe together. That's the plan, and your heart is hinged on it.

"We are almost there." Mami's voice breaks a silence that has grown thick without you noticing.

"I can't see it," you say. "There's too much mist."

She points. "Look. Look there."

The boat draws closer. It is indeed misty, the atmosphere cloying with the promise of rain. A cool breeze rolls in from the east. Squint, shade your eyes, and peer vainly into that white haze, seeking a first glimpse of your destination.

Then the sun comes out, quick as a child's smile; clouds part at her warm touch. And Shek Ham Chau seems to rise in front of you like a woman surfacing for air.

Sunlight shimmers on the water. Boxy houses, brightly painted, refract color at unexpected angles. Glossy mangroves fuzz the shoreline as the boat glides toward docking, offering glimpses of tangled forests farther inland. Scintillating peace lingers.

It's beautiful enough to send a flutter through your heart.

But it also doesn't look remotely abandoned, which is odd. After years of neglect, you were expecting collapsing roofs, rotting planks, green life creeping through everything, lots of mold and rot. Yet the village is nearly pristine, as if preserved in time.

"Mami," you say, catching her sleeve, "I thought you said the island was empty?"

She doesn't look at you. "It is."

"But the houses are so tidy. Everything looks new."

The fisherman steering the boat hisses through his teeth.

"The ghosts look after the houses."

"Oh." Another thought strikes you: "Wasn't the village destroyed in the storm?"

"I'm told the ghosts rebuilt it." Mami bites a fingernail. "They are . . . industrious."

Behind you, the fisherman spits in the water. "Ghosts shouldn't linger so long," he mutters, and Mami pretends not to have heard.

That's nice of the ghosts to do such work, you decide, and wonder why everyone finds the idea so upsetting. If you were a ghost, you'd look after your old house, too.

The boat crunches up to the nearest pier. As you finally step ashore to the perfectly empty dock, luggage in hand, Mami says, feebly, "Well. What do you think?"

Behind you, the driver is revving the engine and heading back to the mainland. He does everything in a hurry, and doesn't look back. Afraid of the bad luck that lingers, of the ghosts who still live here.

"It's amazing!" Astonishment and awe paint your features. "I love it!"

"You do?" A look of surprise flashes across Mami's face. "Well, that is very good. I hope you will not be bored."

The idea of being bored leaves you dumbfounded. This is the first time you've been anywhere more than a few miles away from home. There were a few trips out when you were younger, to Lantau Island or once to Lamma Island, nothing exciting.

Other than that, you spent most days working at a local street restaurant. Weekends involved trailing after your perpetually exhausted mother as she combed the wet markets and dry seafood stalls for cheap foodstuffs. Drifting past incense-filled temples, which your parents never visited. Listening to war news on the radio for the final hours of every day. Dreading the air raid sirens, afraid of tomorrow's dire headlines.

"I won't be bored. I'll be fine." You'd have said so anyway, because self-sufficiency is the one thing she's really needed from you these past few days. But in this case, you do mean it.

Along the shore, a small white cat sits on a rock, sunning itself lazily. It doesn't look up as you gather the luggage, but you smile to see it all the same. Cats are good luck, and this one is cute.

"I'm glad to hear that." Mami hasn't seen the cat. She's already trudging up the path, carrying her luggage: clothes, farm tools, a few kitchen things. A creased envelope containing Baba's last letter. There's more luggage on the pier; it'll require multiple trips.

Take another deep breath to compose yourself. And follow after her, burdened with additional bags.

The cat watches you go, tail lashing.

The village is sunk into the forest. Old-fashioned houses nestle sporadically in the hills, softly wrapped in mangroves and giant taro. Strangler figs engulf sweet gum trees. Banyans force their tough roots through hard rock. Creepers wind around the red-tiled roofs, framing the Chinese characters painted onto archways.

Yet despite those classic flourishes, some of the architecture is unexpectedly Western in shape and structure: squat, squarish buildings, corners shored up with stones. There is even a chapel, with a wooden crucifix nailed above the entrance. Catholic influence makes an uneasy marriage with Hakka heritage.

Every building is pristine—and completely empty. As if the owners have gone out for a walk, but will return at any moment. You are a little disappointed to see no sign of the ghosts, but perhaps they are hiding. It is still bright daylight, after all.

The house that your maternal grandmother once owned is much the same as the others. It was built on high ground, with a good view of the sea. Wooden walls are slathered in white paint. A low, peaked roof sits on it like a stony hat, the edges curling up like an old-timey pagoda.

Step up to the porch. A half-rotted fu talisman hangs on the front door, faded and unreadable from sun exposure. You wonder if it still bears any protective power. If it doesn't, you'll have to rewrite it, to keep out all the ghosts. It's not a good idea to let them into the house regularly.

The floor creaks in a friendly fashion as you step inside, like a grumpy old uncle complaining about his joints. There's a sense of familiarity to everything, and as Mami leads you through a living room full of furniture, it feels like coming home.

The bedroom that will be yours is small, and the bed is at least thirty years old. Still, the frame holds your weight; strong, well-built wood. No mattress, in the traditional style. A pile of neatly folded linens sits in one corner. They should be rotted, but the cloth is soft and clean when you touch them.

It's eerie, how fresh everything is.

The only other furniture is a carved chest of drawers. The wood is dark with age, the grain of it worn and pitted. You run fingers across it, unable to resist exploring its texture. Scratches notch the corner; scuffs layer the flat surfaces.

Your gaze skips across the window above the dresser. It is completely open, no bamboo blinds and certainly no glass; the shutters lie flat against the wall, letting in the breeze. This side of the house has a view of both island and sea. Overgrown farmland stretches out to one side, graduating into lush mangroves, roots and branches densely knotted together. Just out of sight is the cliff edge, and a dirt road leading toward the beach.

Something else: a ghost stands in the middle of the field.

It is the first spirit you've seen since arriving. The form is indistinct, and it's impossible to tell if it is man, woman, or child. It shimmers as if covered in water. The typhoon that wrecked this village also drowned a lot of people; maybe that is why the ghost looks damp.

Hard to know if the spirit sees you or not. Just in case, you give it a respectful wave. The ghost ripples, and disappears.

Now that it's gone, you realize it was obstructing your view of a rusted sign, hanging by a single nail on a rough-cut signpost. On that strip of corroded metal, someone long ago has painted 鲛人洞穴, accompanied by a rough sketch of a pointed-roof building.

Flood Dragon People Shrine.

A shiver goes through you. Jiaoren. *Flood dragon people*, or *shark people*. The Westerners have something similar in their legends—mermaids, merfolk. Fewer teeth and claws than the Chinese variety, and Western ones do not weep pearls.

Strange, to have a jiaoren shrine. You've never heard of anything like that. Ghosts are everywhere, but jiaoren are only myths, a common story in island communities.

The sign points toward the mangrove trees, and something that looks like a very overgrown path is just about visible. Maybe you'll go exploring and look for it later. That could be fun.

You begin unloading your clothes, filling the dresser with the handful of belongings which came to the island. As you open the chest's top drawer, you note that inside, someone has scratched Chinese characters. These look like a blessing, or protective wish.

There is also an old photo, water-stained and faded with age. It appears to be of a small family, standing proud in front of several salt pans. An older lady, like a grandmother, and two young children.

Of the two children, the taller one is recognizable as Mami, when she was a little girl. The same uplifted chin and delicate nose, the same set to her shoulders. It's strange to see a picture of your mother as a child; she actually looks happy.

The other little girl is a mystery. She must be Mami's sister, and the realization fills you with intense curiosity.

Obviously, you know that Mami wasn't an only child. The rest of her family all died in the island storm. But your mother has never talked about them, and claims she barely remembers them. In fairness, she was only a child herself when the typhoon struck, so maybe she's telling the truth.

Peer closer. The little girl's face is impossible to pick out, but not because of water damage. There's a burned hole, going right through the photograph. Like someone has pressed a joss stick or a cigarette end, searing off the child's face forever.

The door creaks open; you jump.

"Siu Yin?" Mami pokes her head in. "What is the bed like in this room? Mine is usable."

"Great, just fine," you say, dropping the photo back into the drawer and shutting it discreetly with your hip as you fidget uneasily. "The furniture is still sturdy, after all this time." You can't shake a lingering sense of embarrassment, as if she's walked in while you were snooping.

"Good, that's good. One less job to do." Mami almost smiles, doesn't quite make it. It's as if any emotion sucks energy from her, these days. Then her half smile collapses as she says, irritably, "Siu Yin, be *still*. There is no need to jump around."

You're not jumping, just jigging one leg restlessly, but you don't argue the point. Nothing sets her off as fast as hearing you talk back.

Instead, you opt to distract her by pointing at the sign outside. "Mami, what does this mean?"

"Ah," she says, after a moment. "That points to the Shrine of Compassion."

Understanding dawns. "The stone temple itself," you say. "The one this place is named for."

Mami nods. "On the south shore of this island, there is a cave. It is possible to swim into it during low tide, though it is treacherous to do so. In high tide, the entrance floods completely." She crosses her arms, brow bent in an emotion you can't place. "Anyway, there is a very old temple, or perhaps more of a shrine, deep inside the cavern. Carved right into the rock."

"It's *underground*?" That surprises you. Temples are almost always built on higher altitudes, with their backs against mountains. Closer to heaven. "Who made it? Was it carved by the original Hakka settlers?"

She shrugs. "It is very ancient is all I know. The shrine was there before even my ancestors came to this place. Nobody knew what it was for, but it is dedicated to Kwun Yam, sort of. Some people here called her Ma Zu."

"Huh? Aren't they very different?" To the best of your haphazard knowledge, Ma Zu was a seafaring goddess of lowly human birth. Kwun Yam, meanwhile, was the very lofty goddess of compassion.

"My people believed Ma Zu was an incarnation of Kwun Yam. Not typical, but it's what we were raised to think." She makes a vague gesture. "Anyway, it's an ocean temple to the goddess, and it has carvings of jiaoren in it. So we called that place the Jiaoren Cavern, and the building within it is simply the Shrine of Compassion."

"Oh. That sounds interesting. Maybe I could have a look? It can't take very long to swim around this island."

"I don't think you should go swimming, not yet," Mami says, drawing in her breath sharply. "The cave faces the sea, and is impossible to enter when the tides are high. Only strong swimmers should attempt it."

"That seems like a bad location to build a temple, if it's so dangerous," you say, doubtfully. "Shouldn't temples be easy to reach? And near the top of a mountain?" Everyone knows that temples should be close to heaven.

"It *is* easy to reach, if you are swimming and don't need to breathe air. And it *is* atop a mountain, if you've come from the ocean depths," Mami says, matter-of-factly. "We found the temple, daughter, but it wasn't built for us. Humans are not the only ones who wish to worship gods."

You wait for her to laugh, or turn the statement into a joke.

She simply looks at you, unsmiling.

"Oh," you say, faintly.

Carved by jiaoren—for other jiaoren, or so your mother seems to be implying. But surely not. Those are just stories, silly old myths.

Aren't they?

"We will eat supper in an hour, and tomorrow go look at the fields." She is already turning to go. "Time to see if I can remember how to farm and fish, and if that old water well still works."

"Yes, Mami," you agree, and reluctantly get back to tidying the room.

Outside, near the rusted sign in that derelict field, ghosts begin gathering in glistening silence to peer through the window.

15

FINGERS MADE OF WATER

Fifty-two years ago . . .

It is time to introduce myself. This may be your story, but you are not telling it. You can't, because you don't remember it anymore.

I am Kwan Yam, the goddess of mercy and compassion. In my heart, I still recall all of your life, and your days—before you ever left Hong Kong, and arrived to Shek Kan Chau. It is the privilege of a goddess to know such things, to be in myriad places.

I know that you are beginning to wonder why I retell you these details, but I promise that it matters. The shape of your life has informed so many other lives that it bears looking at, albeit briefly.

I recall your birth, though you do not. I remember that humid, quiet evening in 1922, your Mami laboring in the privacy of her cramped Hong Kong harbor flat. The bed was too hot, so she took to the floor, damp cloths easing her backache. Soon after, infant-you had the shock of emerging to the world, and being lifted to her chest by hands that were warm and kind.

It was one of the few times that your mother was any sort of gentle.

If that sounds like a harsh indictment of her, it isn't meant to be. Mami grew up with war and natural disaster, the way other children are raised with siblings. She has suffered much.

When you were born, she tried to put aside her disappointment, and never quite succeeded. She had hoped for a studious boy, but got a careless girl; she hoped for more children, yet no others arrived. All her expectations were therefore pinned on you, and no one child can live up to that. You fell very, very short.

As you grew, she raised you as she had been raised, with a sharp tongue and a heavy hand, her mind bent always toward worry. Your endless chatter aroused her ire, and her stern ways provoked your scorn.

Here is a short list of your "flaws," as she saw them, which drove her to frustration.

You could not sleep well, especially as a youngster. That restless nature honed her tiredness to a teetering edge of exhaustion.

You could not stop climbing on chairs, tables, cabinets, like a monkey in search of the forest canopy.

Your fingers seemed to be made of water; everything slipped through them, or out of them. You caused so much breakage. Carrying dishes was a risk and washing them only slightly safer.

And you talked too much, as if your mouth were a teapot that continually poured out its brain to the world at large. Every day, you buzzed with too much energy, a thrumming lute string of a girl, jittering into trouble. This frustrated her more than anything else.

On the worst days, Mami would chase you out of the flat in seething exasperation and point at the unlit, echoing stairwell that ran like a spine up the center of the residential building.

"Go run," she liked to say, often with an accompanying smack upside the head. "Put on your shoes and run from the bottom to the top, three times! And don't knock the offering shrines!"

It's hard to be sure whether she meant her task as punishment or some kind of bizarre therapy, but you actually enjoyed her strange command. On your own, feet pounding concrete steps, there were no dishes to break and no one to disappoint. The effort left you gasping and spent, briefly free of that frenetic energy which wore you ragged if you didn't indulge it. Sometimes you'd run an extra lap just to feel the calmness that movement brought, before breathlessly edging back into the flat.

And you were careful, didn't knock the offering shrines that lined your door and your neighbors' doors, each one displaying long joss sticks jammed into fruit. Even your clumsiness had limits. You didn't want to offend the ghosts, after all.

Ghosts were a part of daily life, in Hong Kong and elsewhere. Less in the West, where they tended to be banished, but you'd never been to that part of the world.

For example. Your local food store was kept clean at night by the ghost of a man who'd once owned it. He was efficient and hardworking but prone to roaring at anyone who disturbed him when darkness fell. The current owners often left him offerings. He was friendly if they remembered to do that.

The temples were the busiest places: a steady traffic of the dead-but-not-gone. Priests had an uncanny tendency to linger round their brethren, perhaps knew the offerings would always be good there. The sad ones, to me, were those ghosts who came to the temple in search of family who never visited, never thought of them; beggar ghosts, hungry ghosts, forgotten ghosts. The monks fed them and lit incense, but they still must have felt lonely.

Most of the ghosts in your particular building were hungry ones, with pinprick mouths and distended bellies. A few were grandmother ghosts, a couple were waiting women. Once, a fire-breather turned up, and the tenants all pooled their money to pay for an exorcist, but most were banal. They roamed the halls or begged in the stairwells, and during Ghost Month liked to hover above the food bowls, picking away at fruit and paper offerings.

Rarely were they dangerous, provided one treated them with respect. That was easy enough to do. Put out food in shrines, offer polite greetings, and give them space. The ghosts, for their part, almost never came indoors; everyone had wards, carefully placed, to dissuade them from entering private homes and causing distress.

You did not mind them at all, liked seeing them, would even try talking to them. The dead made better listeners than the living.

One of them in particular was your favorite. It was very old and almost faded away, all wispy outlines and hazy features. You could walk through it, as if it were a cloud; it wasn't solid, like some of the others.

The neighbors called it a jian, meaning a ghost of a ghost; a creature that was barely sentient, more of an echo. It must have been a child when alive, because it loved to race you to the top of the building on ethereal feet, cackling and giggling.

Though you could never win, you did enjoy the challenge. Also, the ghost never minded your chattering, or your jitters, or your fidgets. In later years, you'd swear it listened, absorbing your words happily as it raced you to the roof.

When you think of it now, you remember the jian as a friend, and hope it rests in peace.

Perhaps fittingly, it was ghosts themselves that finally began to bridge the gap between you and Mami.

Once you turned six or seven, instead of having you buzzing and fluttering around the house, Mami could finally pack you off in a stiff uniform of plain brown clothing and let you fidget your way through school.

Under the tutelage of teachers, in the company of rambunctious students, you learned to read and write, along with the basics of numbers and some rudimentary history. Instead of running up and down the stairwell with a jian, you could run outside at lunchtime with living peers. And instead of hard smacks upside the head, teachers doled out palm-whacks with rulers. You liked the changes.

Mami, though glad you were no longer underfoot, was less than impressed with their teaching.

"Who is showing you how to write fu talismans and make wards?" she said one day, exasperated by your endless chatter about numbers and reading.

"No one, Mami."

"No one?!"

"Teacher Ying says that spirit warding has no place in a modern, scientific education—"

"Aiyah! And what will Teacher Ying do the next time they are plagued by a bothersome ghost?" Mami exclaimed, squashing a stray mosquito between her palms. "You will need to know some wards before you are grown."

She sat at the kitchen table and jabbed a finger; you sat, too, not daring to contradict.

"Pass me that piece of paper. Yes, that one. Sit here, quickly please." Mami dug out a pot of ink from one of the cupboards and a small fine-tipped brush. You'd seen both of those objects many times before, but not been allowed near them.

"This is temple ink, made by monks," Mami said, matter-of-factly. "It is perfectly balanced, with blood and ash and blessings mixed in."

"Can I use regular ink for fu talismans?"

"Yes, but it will be unreliable. Maybe the glyph will work, maybe not. Temple ink will always give you a good result."

"I thought we don't go to temples," you said, forehead creasing in puzzlement. Unusually, your parents did not observe religious festivals; they were the only people you knew, other than Westerners, who refrained from doing so.

"I don't owe monks or gods anything, especially not my time or money," Mami said, with a venomous acidity. "But their ink is still useful, so we buy that." She drew an unfamiliar word with a steady hand and confident strokes. "Do you see this?"

It looked like a Chinese character, but none that you could quite recognize. From the corner of your eye, the lines seemed fluid and erratic, shining a faint glow. Like a match on the verge of snuffing out. But every time your gaze focused on them directly, it looked normal and static.

"This is a glyph," Mami said, pointing to the ink-wet words. "Put different glyphs together, and write them on paper or bottle gourds or metal with temple ink, and you have made a fu talisman." She tucked loose hair behind her ear. "Glyphs must be written very precisely. If you get them wrong, the fu talisman doesn't work. If you are trying to make a ward, for example, and your fu talisman is written wrong, then the ghosts will not be scared."

"How do you get them wrong? Or right?"

"When you write glyphs, you write the shape of a thought. Each word, each written character, tells a little story, but glyphs are more than words. They are the truth of a thing, the many layers of a thought."

"Oh." You poked one corner of one glyph; it left a dab of ink on the fingertip. "How many glyphs are there?"

"I don't know. I suppose a wise man could write many of them. But I only know a few, and that is all you will need to learn." Mami scribbled a series of symbols, showing them to you. "See these two? Put them together, and that will frighten ghosts away from an entrance."

You studied it intently; this was indeed a symbol you recognized. Many of the neighbors hung such fu talismans above their flat doors. "Is this how exorcists trap spirits, Mami?"

"No. Binding is far beyond my skill, something that takes years of practice. I can only teach you to preserve bodies for funerals, or to ward doors and windows against unwelcome spirits." Mami got up and fetched down another stack of paper sheafs. "Go on! Copy me. Copy the glyph I made. In your own hand."

You couldn't yet write your own name without getting the characters wrong, but did your best. The result was a blobby mess of wavering strokes, bearing no resemblance to her neat scripts.

"Looks like an ink spill," Mami observed.

You flushed. She wasn't wrong.

"Think more, think harder," she said. "It's not enough to just draw. Think of the ward, hanging above the door. Think of the ghosts who come to stand in front of it, then flinch at the sight, and drift away. Know what you want when you write. Know what you need. Understand?"

"No," you grumbled, but squeezed your eyes shut anyway, thinking hard about the fu talisman hanging outside the flat; you'd seen it often enough.

Opening your eyes, you put brush to paper yet again, this time trying to keep the purpose held in your brain.

A strange thing happened. Soft warmth built in your palms, trickling to the fingertips. Your clumsy grasp became firmer, more confident. For a moment, joy buoyed you.

The lines began to writhe and shimmer, struggling away from your control.

The image in your head grew hazy and your hands shook, unsure which line or stroke to draw next. The half-formed glyph devolved into a garbled, unusable thing.

You scowled at your work.

"Try again, it still is not right," Mami said, sharp as a skewer. But she sat next to you, larger hand curling around your smaller one with a firm touch. "I will help. Think of the ward, of scaring away. Whatever looks at this glyph should want to turn around. Are you thinking like that? Now go!"

A third try. You held the essence of the ward in your mind with ferocious tenacity, moving your own hand while also allowing Mami's experienced touch to guide and nudge the shaping.

Something in your head seemed to click. It was as if a weight had shifted, or a stone had been pushed into place. Suddenly, the writing flowed like rainwater down a polished gutter. The glyph crystallized, brush strokes glowing briefly, then darkening back to fast-drying ink.

And there on the page was a shaky but recognizable talisman, done in your own writing. More or less, anyway.

"I did it," you exclaimed, proud and amazed. You were tired, too, and suddenly starving, as if you'd run too many laps or skipped at least three meals.

"With my help," Mami said, then relented a little. "It's fine for a first try."

Unexpectedly, she stood and stretched, cracking the joints of her hands and shoulders. "We should go for a walk before it gets dark, have something to eat," she said, which shocked you. She often went walking on her own, but she never brought you along. "Get your shoes on, daughter."

Intrigued by her invitation-slash-command, you did as she bade and followed, feeling uncertain yet curious.

◆⁘◆

Cities, streets, and neighborhoods all have their own smell. Your street in Hong Kong was no different. Take a sniff, inhale that dizzying mix of dried seafood wares and raw fish, of salt water and ferryboat fumes, of smoked meats and soggy laundry. Summer heat wrung the sweat out of everyone even as the night rolled in.

Down by the docks, Mami bought skewers of spicy fish balls from a dai pai dong, which she shared with you. She had changed from her hospital uniform into a simple cotton qipao; that was a fashion trend she had adopted during her time in Shanghai. You had so far managed to squash the insatiable urge to talk nonstop in her presence, and your ability to accommodate her need for quietude seemed to soften her demeanor. She talked some about her day, the conversation polite and gentle.

It was a pleasant evening.

After that first venture, it became something of a ritual. Friday evenings, practice those glyphs and fu talismans until your hands hurt. Then tidy up, stretch, put on shoes, change into casual clothes, and walk down to the docks amidst the markets. Conversation was often awkward, but you both tried. It was a chance to eat snacks, if nothing else.

Looking back in later years, you were never entirely sure what Mami sought from you then, or you from her. Family piety is strong in Chinese people, an overpowering drive to make it work between members, and maybe it was simple as that. Beneath all the things that made her broken, some part of her was still trying hard, in a twisted fashion.

Sometimes, Mami would even tell stories. Some you knew from neighbors or friends, and others were unfamiliar. She liked ghost stories, and told those the most.

"Long ago, there was once a little girl, born to an island village," she said one evening, leaning against the wall to take the weight off her feet, hair tied back severely. "This girl was unique. She was a wild thing who could summon storms and talk to ghosts. They listened to her, instead of ignoring her, and they refused to harm her. Some said she was an incarnation of Ma Zu, the ocean goddess. Others said she was cursed."

You listened attentively. There were many folktales of all kinds, but Mami was telling one you'd never heard of before.

"In another life, this girl might have become a powerful medium, but there was no one to teach her how to use her abilities safely. Even as a toddler, she would anger local ghosts by crying at them, which in turn caused harm. The villagers soon learned to be cautious around her, and to take care with wards.

"One day, while the girl's father was traveling to the mainland for business, his ship was lost at sea, due to a storm. The girl's mother, on hearing this news, was filled with grief and could not be comforted. She took her own life, soon after. Only the grandmother was left, to raise the little girl by herself.

"All of this terrible luck sparked cruel rumors. The villagers came to believe that the little girl was surrounded with bad fortune. They feared her tantrums and tears, which they said summoned storms. They claimed she spoke evil words to ghosts, and could command them to curse mortals. They shunned the girl and told the grandmother to do the same, but the grandmother refused.

"Now, this girl happened to own a little cat. She was very attached to it, as she had no friends among the other children, so it was her only companion. One morning, the girl awoke to discover that her cat was nowhere to be found. She looked all over the island, and eventually discovered it dead, on the beach. Someone had crushed its head with a rock.

"The girl grew angry, and accused the other villagers of killing her cat. When no one would confess, she shouted curses at them, and threatened to raise the cat's ghost in revenge. She was not truly a necromancer, but she was upset, and the villagers were afraid anyway.

"That night, several men came to the grandmother's house and demanded that she and the girl leave the island forever. Some claimed that the girl's curse was already taking effect, that their chickens and crops were dying. Others said they had been unable to catch fish all day. The grandmother argued with them, but it did not help.

"These village men chased the girl and her grandmother out of the house, driving them toward the shore. However, while running away in the dark, the girl and her grandmother fell to their deaths from a tall cliff by the sea. The fall killed the grandmother instantly, but the girl survived—although she was terribly injured. Her back was broken and she could not move or walk.

"The girl cried for help, yet no one would help her. The men who had chased her would not let the others intervene, as they felt that implied their guilt. Eventually, the tide came in, and the girl drowned, because she could not walk. No one buried her, so her spirit could not rest. Soon, she returned as an angry, powerful ghost.

"Death only made the girl more powerful. As a raging ghost, she summoned a storm and washed away the whole island, in punishment for her death. That was the last anyone saw of the island, or the ghost girl. The end."

When it became clear Mami was done speaking, you said, "But the story can't be finished."

"Says who?" She tore a chunk off today's snack: a soft white bun filled with sweetly roasted pork. "I think it is finished."

"What happened to the ghost? Is she just a ghost forever, now? Shouldn't someone come to fight her?"

"Aiyah, what are you talking about?" Mami said, sharply. "You are thinking like a Westerner, like one of the white nuns at your school. To them, ghosts are just a pest, a villain, a monster to kill. British people—like those gweilo soldiers over there, do you see them?—they do not love their ghosts, as they do not love their ancestors. When their dead return, they are banished. When their souls cling, they are forced onward. They even ward their own graveyards! Barbarians."

"She drowned a village, in the end," you said, interrupting her rant. "Doesn't that make her evil, Mami?"

"No, it only makes her a ghost. Ghosts are driven by hurt, and cannot help themselves. Do you think a storm is evil, because it pours rain on your head?"

"No, but . . . not everyone in the village was responsible for her death. It's not fair that they *all* died."

"Isn't it? They didn't all kill her, but they all left her unburied. That was stupid."

"But why should the other villagers have to bury her, if they didn't kill her?" you say, puzzled. "Why is someone else's crime their fault?"

"Again, you think like a Westerner! If each person only corrects the crimes that they have committed themselves, then the world will be full of pain, because evil men do not care about injustice, and so never correct their own."

You mulled that over. "I guess that's true."

"The dead return when they have something to say, daughter, and we listen to them until they have said it. We help them even if we are not responsible for the crimes committed against them. Do you understand?"

"I think so, Mami."

But secretly, you wondered if that was how she saw you: a bad-luck girl, a ghost haunting her life, whom she nonetheless felt a duty toward. Whom she dared not ask to leave.

"Good." She straightened up. "We should go home. It is late."

And you followed.

When I think of your mother in the years to come, I prefer to remember her in those moments: standing by the harbor's edge in the failing light wearing her plain green qipao, eating cheap street food and rattling off stories in that flat, matter-of-fact way. Her calloused hands smelled of hospital soap, and sometimes she would even smile.

Occasionally, I look back and wonder how your lives might have unfolded, if given enough time and peace. Whether you and Mami might have built something stronger, if brutal war and long toil had ever eased their grip.

I still wonder that now.

16

BLOODY SATURDAY

Fifty-two years ago . . .

Mami was not your only parent, of course. The yang to her yin was Ho Tung, your Baba. He is a big part of the reason why you went to the island, why you stayed so long, and so his story here matters, too.

In many ways, Baba had always been a silent fixture in your life. He often came home late and tired, having talked all day as a translator—mostly arguing over import paperwork—and seemed to retreat into himself. He drank tea, smoked cigarettes, ate his meals, did the accounts, and cleaned the stove all in stoic quietude, while you bounced around the kitchen or nattered to the neighbors through the door gate. Meanwhile, Mami hung the laundry, swept the floor, and put away dishes.

What Baba lacked in words, he made up for in action. He often brought treats and small toys, purchased on his journey home, proffering them with embarrassed gentleness. Once, he brought you back a tiger charm bracelet, a nod to the year of your birth; you never took it off, treasured it always.

And when Mami scolded too hard or hit too often, he could sometimes quietly defuse her—a gifted cigarette, a manufactured errand, occasionally a kiss.

It goes without saying that you loved him.

You knew your father, and yet also didn't. You knew what kind of cigarettes he bought (American, to impress the traders), his favorite dish (mutton stewed in a fragrant broth), and the exact order in which he read a newspaper (headlines, obituaries, finance). But those things were not the man himself, just affectations he had collected.

There were a few things of importance that you learned about him, from listening to snippets of conversations across the years and nosing through his old belongings. Baba was from a small village just outside Shanghai. He left it to serve in the First World War, as a young volunteer. China sent no soldiers to that conflict, but he did work in a munitions factory, producing bullets.

Even that relatively safe exposure was enough to quell his curiosity. After the conflict ended, he became determined, from then on, to lead a peaceful life. He returned to Shanghai and met your mother, who was living with northern relatives after the destruction of her home island. They married soon after.

Together, Baba and Mami settled in Hong Kong, where the money was better and life was a little easier. Her Mandarin had never been good, and she missed the climate; Baba was drawn by the good job opportunities, and liked Southern Chinese food. Here in this city, they hoped that wealth and modernity and the heavy hand of British colonialism would protect them from strife, from war and typhoons and uncertainty.

It did not.

War came to your lives, unwanted yet predictable, like the cycle of yearly storms, like the crash of a rising tide, and drowned everything in its path.

You were fifteen years old when incendiary bombs began to fall on Beijing in the sun-soaked months of July 1937, adding man-made fire to the sun's crushing heat. People talked about nothing else at home, at school, at work.

Yet Japan was so small, China so vast—surely, despite everything that had happened to the country in the past, they would weather this, too.

"It is not so simple," Baba said, when you asked him about it over dinner. "China has been struggling for a long time, little bird."

He still called you "little bird," because of the meaning of your name. Even though you were old enough to be leaving school soon, and were already looking for work.

"Struggling with what, Baba? Do you mean the Opium War? I thought that was finished."

Even the smallest child knew about the Opium War, and how badly Britain had devastated China. At least there was a certain honesty about armed conflict, bloody though it was. But a conflict waged through drugs and extortion was just a dirty, miserable mess.

"War does not *finish*," he said, heavily. "It is not a game that stops when enough players quit. It is a wound, sinking into flesh, leaving scars and rot that cause pain for a long time."

Then he sighed, forced a smile, and told you to come sit next to him. "Look, I have a new book of poems today," he said, as he so often did; Baba was forever buying little books of this and that, bringing them home to show you. "We will forget about the news for a while. Come read with me, Siu Yin."

You were not interested in the slim volumes of Chinese poetry he found so fascinating. But you enjoyed listening to the sound of his voice, and were always willing to sit next to him, attentive while he read aloud.

◆⁘◆

The days passed, and the news grew steadily worse.

In the autumn of 1941, the Nazis reached the height of their power, and Japan's emperor turned his burning gaze upon Hong Kong. Mainland refugees streamed across the border as the Japanese broke China relentlessly, one victory at a time.

You kept your head down, and concentrated on other things. Too old for school, you had a job by then, working in the kitchen of a local restaurant. Hard and greasy hours, but it paid almost as well as Mami's cleaning role at the local hospital, and left you too exhausted to think much about what was happening elsewhere.

Then came the Battle of Nanjing—the wide-scale torture and massacre of its civilians, the weaponized mass rape of its women and children. The exact numbers sent scholars spiraling into arguments, but across the next few months, over one hundred thousand people were massacred in that region alone. The scale of that horror defied your teenage brain to comprehend; would horrify you for the rest of your life.

A few weeks later, Beijing fell to the Japanese, followed by Tianjin.

You saw the pictures in newspapers: bodies blown to pieces, limbs piled in doorways, buildings collapsing, children pin-cushioned by shrapnel. This was war as your country had never known, another level of hell bleaker and harsher than even the artillery-fueled misery of previous generations.

Tens of thousands died, mostly civilians, until the ghosts and the rubble began to outnumber the living. Worse, the ghosts created in these firestorms were neither sentient nor friendly, nor easily pacified; they were screaming, rageful, traumatized things, as much a danger to the locals as the bombings.

Sometimes you would lie awake at night, trying to imagine how it felt to live in a city being smashed to bits from a daily rain of sky-weapons, and then discover the spirits of your loved ones trying to dismember you as they'd been dismembered.

One morning, you were folding clean laundry in the bedroom when your father gave a strangled gasp in the next room.

"Baba?" You came into the living area, found him reading the paper.

An English headline dominated the front in towering black font. Pictures of a city devastated by bombing splashed the front; a small, screaming child sat among the ruins, chubby form picked out in black and white. The usual grim images of violence.

Mami, who couldn't read English, leaned over him. "What is wrong?"

"Shanghai has been captured by the Japanese empire," he said, in the quietest voice you'd ever heard from him.

"Captured?" you echoed. "What about the people in the city? What will happen to them?"

Other cities had already fallen, but Baba's brother was still living in Shanghai; children, relatives, the lot. Or had been, anyway.

Baba didn't answer. He just kept flipping through pages describing grisly deaths and mounting damage. Bloody Saturday, the papers were calling it.

"The ghosts will kill them, or the Japanese will, or their own side will in counterattacks," Mami said, when he remained silent. "Same as the other cities."

"Some will live." Baba sounded strained. "Some will run."

"If they can," Mami said, waspish. "And there will be more refugees soon, taking trains and boats and coming across borders to our city, I'm sure."

"What about us?" you said. "Will the bombs come here?"

"No," Baba said, at the same time as your mother answered, "Yes, of course."

You looked back and forth between them, unsure who to believe.

"Hong Kong is full of English refugees from Shanghai, and Westerners are everywhere." Baba gripped the paper tightly. "Our port is valuable and strategic. Most of the aid that China receives comes through Hong Kong ports."

"And Shanghai was full of gweilo people too, till they left!" Mami often called the Westerners "gweilo" behind their backs. "If this city is important to the war, then the Japanese will surely come here. They will attack us soon, and the gweilos will leave."

"They may think to do that," he said firmly, "but the British would never just give Hong Kong away—"

"Aiyah!" She flung down a dishcloth. "Who says the gweilos will *give* it? They don't have to give anything! The Japanese will take it all the same. Their empire is very strong and we are very weak, much weaker than Shanghai was, which they also took. And the foreigners care more about Malaya than us."

A shocked silence filled the small flat.

"Why do you trust the British so much?" she said, shaking with vehemence. "They bought this land, this city"—her foot stomped emphatically—"in exchange for the profits they made, off the opium they forced China to buy. A few years of repeating their English words, and suddenly you think they are saviors? Working for them has made you—" She clamped her lips together.

Baba stared at her. "Made me what?"

Mami half-turned to glare at you, as if the exchange were your fault. "Go play in the stairs," she said, in a tone that brooked no argument.

You were nearly grown, too old to be entertained by running aimlessly. The jian you'd once raced had long since dispersed. Still, you did as she ordered and escaped the kitchen.

The sounds of your parents arguing followed you down the hallway and through the stairwell, chasing you through the building until, at last, you climbed up toward the roof, and left their anger behind you for a while.

⁘

Time proved Mami right.

As summer ebbed along, Westerners began to leave the city. First the women and children, then nonmilitary men: bankers, traders, craftsmen, and the like. A trickle of flight that grew into a panicked stream as the months slipped by. That, you could not ignore. No one could.

The British began running drills, preparing the Hong Kong population for impending invasion. Soon, you learned to dread the air raid sirens.

The first time you heard one, you did not recognize the noise. It sounded like the spirit of the wind being cut open, tormented with needles, and then forced through a pipe organ. The wailing moan went right through your soul. The bombs would be worse, when they fell.

Baba continued to insist that Britain would protect Hong Kong. Mami smoked and ignored him; you listened, and tried to believe. He continued insisting that for the next few months until, on the 7th of December in 1941, Japan woke the "sleeping giant" of America by bombing Pearl Harbor.

The same morning, half a world away, they also launched an attack on Hong Kong which destroyed the city's airbase. The Americans did not talk about that as much, though.

Most of Hong Kong's northern territory was taken in barely a week. That, I remember starkly. It fell with breathtaking suddenness, leaving those who were on Hong Kong Island, like you and your parents, utterly stunned.

"We should leave, like the gweilos are," Mama said, later that day, during an argument with Baba. They argued nonstop, now. Mostly about the war. "Before it is too late!"

But Baba would only say, "Go where? There's nowhere to go!"

"We could return to my ancestral home." It was the first time Mami made the suggestion, though it would not be the last. "It's quiet there—"

"Daiyu, you were the one who told me *never again that place, not ever.* The things you said about it—"

"That was then, this is now," Mami retorted. "The worst my island has is ghosts. That's better than war. It must be. If we stay here, we will die!"

"And how would we eat, on this island of ghosts? How would we live? What happens if the Japanese land there?" Baba stormed out, and neither of you said much for the rest of the evening. By the time you went to bed, he was still gone.

But late that night, sounds of warfare woke you, the guns and shells distant yet audible. Your eyes flew open in the early hours of darkness from a particularly loud explosion, and it was then that you saw the light on in your living area.

Naturally, you got up and peeked through the door.

Your father had returned.

He sat at the kitchen table which had been the literal and metaphorical center of your life for as long as you could remember, smoking one cigarette after the next in flickering candlelight. His back was toward you, shoulders stooped with what you thought was weariness, but would later realize was defeat.

"Baba?" You kept your voice pitched low, so as not to wake Mami. "What are you doing?"

"I'm thinking and remembering," he said, without looking up. "I haven't heard from my brother or his family since Shanghai fell. Haven't seen him for almost twenty years. Did you know it had been so long?"

In fact, you did know that. Baba and his brother had never found the time for a reunion. You said nothing, though, because he wasn't really speaking to you at all.

"I'm sure he is gone, now. Obliterated when the city fell. Everything is gone." He coughed smoke. "Buddha says, *All things are transient. Every single moment we are undergoing birth and death.* That is the way things are."

You fidgeted in awkward silence, unsure how to talk to him. He'd never been like this around you, so oddly vulnerable and maudlin.

"Go back to bed, my little bird." He stubbed out the glowing end of his cigarette and lit another with hands that shook. "Don't go into work tomorrow. It isn't safe. And don't let your Mami go in, either."

With the wisdom of a goddess, I know that your Baba was afraid, and deeply ashamed. He believed he'd failed you in a fundamental way; that he should have got you all out of Hong Kong, somehow. He felt that he should have predicted or altered the course of world events, though they were far outside his control.

His state of mind was born from a toxic sense of self-flagellation, and that must have been terrible to bear alone.

At twenty, you were far too young to talk to him about the choice he was weighing. If you existed another hundred years, you would still be too young. Nobody is ever old enough to talk about war and death.

All the same, you would later wish that you'd tried. That you'd told him *No, I won't go to bed, not just yet.* That you'd sat with him, put your head on his shoulder, and said *Pain is transient too, Baba. Good things may be transient, but so are bad things*, because Buddha also teaches this.

If nothing else, you would later wish that you'd sat with him through the night. Though he wasn't a perfect human, he was the only father you had, and there would never be a shared grave for the three of you. Your family would not be lucky enough to enjoy such a fate.

But the past is written and unchanging. In my unlying memory of that evening, you merely did as he asked, curling on the bed into a tight ball. Sleep crept up on you like a mountain lion, leaping when your attention lagged.

In the early hours of December 15, 1941, you woke to Baba's absence with a haunting sense of bewilderment and trepidation. He'd left, taking almost nothing with him except shoes and clothes. There was a note on the kitchen table.

Mami had got up before you, and already read it. She thrust the slip of paper your way.

"He's written it to you," she said, and you wince; Baba hadn't left a note for her. That must have stung.

Still, you took the scrap of writing from her swollen-knuckled hands and silently read your father's blocky script, the characters so meticulously formed.

> *Siu Yin, your mother is right. We cannot stay in Hong Kong any longer. There is no time to waste—both of you must leave the city. Go to Shek Ham Chau, as your mother has suggested. She still owns property there. It is bleak and lonely on the outlying islands, and rife with ghosts, but it will be free of invaders.*
>
> *Either way, look after your Mami until I return. I will wrap up our affairs, use the money to purchase a boat of our own, and pick you both up in a few weeks.*

"I'm . . . so tired, daughter."

You looked up.

Mami had simply collapsed into a kitchen chair, the sharpness of her dulled and blunt. Her shoulders twitched but her face was a landslide of tiredness, as if all the fight and fury had eroded suddenly. The one person who could always spur her to anger had gone.

She hadn't tried to go into work, nor had you. The skin across your back tightened as you hunched in shame.

You were too old to cry, too young to know what you should do. Instead, you sat by the window, knees scrunched to chest, flinching when the air raid sirens came on again. It seemed like you should do . . . something. You felt like doing nothing. There were no words for how you felt in that moment.

Look after your Mami until I return, he'd said, but you had no idea how to do that, how you were supposed to manage this without him.

There is no time to waste—both of you must leave the city.

That directive. You thought about it, reading the words over and over, and realized the stark truth: despite his protestations these past months, Baba knew the city was not secure. He expected it to be either overrun or bombed to fragments shortly, or both. He wanted his family to flee before Hong Kong surrendered.

Go to Shek Ham Chau, as your mother has suggested.

His fears about invasion were well-founded, and you shared them. Everyone had heard what life might be like under Japanese occupation. Citizens whispered about every horror under the sun, citing the massacres and war atrocities, the wanton rape and random slaughter of innocents. That had happened in other places, and if your city fell, it would be your fate, too.

It is bleak and lonely on the outlying islands, and rife with ghosts, but it will be free of invaders.

He had underlined those words: *free of invaders*. This man, whom you adored and respected, had given you a final task. In the end, how could you refuse him? He was your Baba, after all. That brought an end to any lingering doubts.

"Mami," you said, "get up. We need to leave."

17

SAFE HARBOR

Thirty-three years ago . . .

It has been four days since you and Mami fled the city on a rented junk boat, with only a few pieces of luggage. Baba said he'd be with you in a couple of weeks, meaning he's due to appear soon. That's your hope, anyway. Every so often you touch the tiger charm bracelet he gave you, and think of him fervently.

But hope is only the ghost of a promise; it has no substance, no weight.

Somewhere to the south of your tiny refuge, Hong Kong is currently surrendering to Japan this very afternoon. The history textbooks will refer to this day as Black Christmas.

Soon, troops will move in to establish martial law and subjugate the population. Soon, thousands of men will die in prisons and POW camps, while thousands of women will face rape and sexual slavery. Thousands more will starve because there is no food coming into the ports, while many will die screaming from torture.

I cannot help most of them, and my heart bleeds for this.

The darkest hours of your city are here, and they will last for three years, eight months. The legacy of pain they leave behind will last even longer. It is everything your parents feared would happen, and more.

You do not know that, though. Not yet.

In the present, you are walking with Mami through the empty places of her ancestral island home. It is late afternoon, and you have nearly completed a circle of the island, inspecting all its various houses and buildings. Such as they are.

Her arm brushes yours and, in a rare moment of emotional anxiety, you think about reaching out to take her hand. Better not, though. She'll only pull away, which will spoil the peace. Better to enjoy the beautiful sea and the warm earth underfoot.

The little white cat you saw yesterday is here again, padding quietly along the ground. It darts into the grass, disappearing once more from sight.

"The salt fields are old, very old," Mami says, pausing to shade her eyes from the glittering sunlight. She once walked this exact path as a little girl, nearly every day; she thinks of that now, though she says nothing to you about it.

"Hakka clans first came to these islands almost four hundred years ago. They settled on Yim Tin Tsai, an island to the north, and then they came here. Yim Tin Tsai also mined salt, but our fields were always richer." She is smiling, a rare sight. "Over here"—she points to a spot some two hundred yards off—"the settlers found large strips of flat land, which shallow-flood in the high tide. They built big salt pans and water gates."

You look as directed. Remnants of panning equipment are dotted across the furrowed earth. The mangroves press in on all sides, yet none of them have grown in the salt fields. The ghosts have kept it all functional, but the fields somehow look sad anyway, when not in use.

"I can't imagine it busy with people."

"Neither can I, anymore." She scrapes back loose hair, reties it absently. "This island was wealthy, once. In my great-great-grandmother's day, the salt we sifted sold like gold."

"Really?" That *does* perk your ears up. "What changed?"

"Even when my great-grandmother was a girl, salt prices were falling. By the time I was a child, we were as poor as the other islands." She starts walking again. "No point worrying about it. We won't be farming salt with just the two of us."

There are a few other islands that you can see, on a clear day if you squint. Shek Ham Chau is halfway between Sharp Island and Shelter Island. Kau Sai Chau is quite big, and also visible from the right vantage point. The seas between are dark and choppy, though, and you wouldn't try to reach them with anything less than a very solid boat.

In some ways, any of those places might have been nicer to live, and free of ghosts. But Mami doesn't own any land or housing on those places. She cannot just settle you both in an occupied area. Besides, she prefers—and you agree with her—to stay as far under the radar of any Japanese armies as possible.

Together, you walk around the island for the next few hours. It is not big, and much of it you don't need. The farming areas are small, and filled with weeds, but you only require a smallish patch to feed two women, if it comes to staying. Since it's the wrong time of year to plant anything, you have till end of winter—a good two months—to prepare the ground for crops. Or so Mami says.

Mami has bought a lot of dried food and rations, which are already stored back at the house; that will tide you over for a while. She tells you that there's also fishing, and fruit: peaches, plums, pomelos, persimmons, lychees, dragonfruit, and cherries. Some of those are on your island already. All will grow here, if cultivated.

Most importantly, the only freshwater well on the island is still functional. It is not far from your house, though still enough of a trek to make baths awkward if you haven't planned adequately for the day.

"I thought we weren't going to plant crops, or harvest trees," you interject, looking at the overgrown earth. "Baba will be here any day now, and we have enough food to last till then."

"I suspect your Baba may decide we should stay on longer," Mami says, rubbing a blade of grass between thumb and finger. She wonders if she sounds evasive, hopes she doesn't. "If he cannot buy a good enough boat, how far can we really travel? And where is safe? Oh, I don't know. Everything is so . . ."

She sighs, leaving her sentence unfinished. She is thinking of her lost loved ones, again, and all that happened with the storm. The memories eat at her.

"What do you mean, we might stay on longer?" Your voice is an unwelcome intrusion to her reverie. "I thought we were only staying till the conflict ended."

"Till the . . ." She gives a half sob, half laugh, trying to bury her annoyance at your endless questions. "Aiyah, and what happens with the city occupied? What if it stays Japanese territory forever? Your father did not think of that one. I suppose he thought the British would win!"

"Will they not? I mean, the British are so strong, and the Americans too."

"Westerners certainly think they are strong," she says, pure scorn. "Even if they win later, the city will fall first. It will be like Nanjing, and Shanghai. Little girls and old grandmothers are not safe. The soldiers have lost all respect and honor."

"Even in Nanjing, the violence stopped eventually." You try not to think of little girls and grandmothers at the mercy of rapacious soldiers. "Maybe we can go back when things are quieter."

She shrugs, as if to condemn the insanity of that hopeful prediction. You have never met anyone then or since who could imbue so much meaning into a simple lift of the shoulders. Then she says, "Go back to what? Ruin and poverty?"

There's no solution to her question. You can only wait, and hope that Baba will turn up eventually; he must.

You don't have an easy way of leaving, if he doesn't. There are only a handful of small fishing boats on the island, and none of them big enough to take both of you plus all your luggage.

"How long do you think it will be before we hear from Baba?" Daring to voice the question that has hung over you both.

"That man? Hmph. When he shows up, I'll let you know." She stalks off ahead, arms stiff at her side.

You follow sullenly, trailing after.

To your surprise, ghosts are waiting at the house when you both arrive home. At least five of them, though it is hard to keep track. Some seem to fade in and out of existence. Two are mostly corporeal. All of them look like villagers. Their clothes are sodden and dripping, leaving puddles as they wander around.

One of them, a Western man wearing Jesuit robes, shuffles up to you and begins muttering a Latin prayer. There were Christians on these islands, usually traveling missionaries. He must have been such a person.

Just an accident, whispers a young farmer, with bulging and bloodshot eyes. Rivulets of water run from his mouth when he speaks.

"Who—who are they?" you ask, unsettled and nervous. "Are they all villagers?"

"It's the typhoon victims," Mami says, steering you roughly toward the house. "I wondered if . . . when . . . they would show."

"Oh," you say, numbly. "What are they talking about?"

"The night they died. Ghosts repeat themselves often." She dabs her eye quickly, as if embarrassed anyone should see a hint of emotion. "The typhoon killed so many, and wrecked all the farmland. A terrible tragedy."

We did nothing! An old lady steps in front of you. Her chest and head are smashed, brains dripping down the back of her skull. Snapped ribs protrude from her belly, the sight making your stomach flip.

"Get in the house, and I will speak to them." Mami says, giving you a firm push. When you hesitate, she adds, "We each find different ways to confront our dead. Please, daughter."

She should know better than to let the ghosts gather like this, and you are no child anymore to be ordered around. But beneath Mami's command you hear a plea that crackles with painful need, and out of respect, you reluctantly do as she asks.

Mami stands in the waving grass and whispers to the gathered spirits, arms outstretched in placatory tones. They flicker and flash and mill around her, seeming to listen.

It's an uncomfortable sight. You sit in the front room, peering out of the window, watching her and reflecting. Ghosts as a general hazard you are very used to. You try to tell yourself that these ghosts are really not so different from the ones you grew up with.

But try as you might, you can't extend that same sense of openness to the ghosts of Shek Ham Chau, and you're not sure why.

Maybe it's the way they operate as a group, which you find deeply unnerving. All the ghosts back home were individual people, individually locked in their own spiritual loops, trapped by personal grievances or lingering desires.

Never before have you seen a whole village, apparently caught together. All of them working, diligently, to keep their abandoned island immaculate, drifting repetitively through the houses they once lived in. Clustering around your mother like sprouting fungus.

It's a little unnerving, if you're honest.

Mami comes back after ten or fifteen minutes. Not very long. Whatever she said has stayed between her and them. She doesn't share. You decide to get cleaned up, since she isn't talking anyway.

By the time you emerge from your room, having washed down with a rag and changed clothes, she is preparing dried mushrooms and fish in the kitchen. The ghosts are nearby but no longer crowded around your doorstep. They linger at the tree line, glimpses of lost figures. Watching—benevolently, you hope—but not interfering.

"What do they want?" you ask, unable to stop staring.

"They are lonely." Mami washes the day's dust from her hands in preparation for cooking. "It has been quiet here, for a long time."

She has been lonely, too, though she does not say that to you; knows you won't understand. Knows she can't confess to you these things in her heart. She cannot even say them to herself, let alone someone else.

"I see," you say, nonplussed. "Should I write some fu talismans?" You've gotten quite good at doing warding fu talismans, over the past few years.

Her shoulders twitch. "I told you, they are friendly."

"So were most of the ghosts in Hong Kong," you say, frowning. Why is she being like this? "We still had wards to keep them out. Isn't that why we brought so much temple ink?"

"These are family, and friends, not strangers," she says, sharp and hot. "One of those ghosts is my aunt. One was a childhood friend. Another is my second uncle! You would not understand—"

"I'm sorry, I'm sorry!" you interject, awkwardly. "I didn't mean anything by it."

Mami draws a ragged breath and passes a hand across her eyes. "Please, Siu Yin, let us discuss it in the morning. I am feeling overwhelmed and exhausted. It has been a long day."

A thousand worried questions are jostling in your head, but you can tell it's futile to try and get more out of Mami right now. Besides, it is evening, and you *are* both tired.

Reluctantly, you swallow your questions and help her prepare dinner.

The days slide by. The war grinds on. Two months in, and Baba still hasn't arrived.

You and Mami have stopped talking about him. There is nothing to say; he has either abandoned you, or become trapped in Hong Kong. Both possibilities are bad and so you each dive into your own distractions.

Every morning goes the same way: scarf breakfast as fast as you can eat, blitz through chores with record speed, and help with the farming, fishing, and fruit picking. It's more efficient to split up, and increasingly you each work separately. The little garden is taking shape around you both, and at least that looks hopeful for the future.

By afternoon, you've usually run out of necessary things to do. This period of time you fill by writing fu talismans, which you hang on various places around the island. The first port of call is the doors and windows of this house, which Mami doesn't comment on but also doesn't object to. The second is the well, because you want to protect the water supply.

If there's any spare time, you spend it ambling gently around the island. It doesn't take long to learn the length and breadth of it, and the exercise does you a world of good. That jittery energy of yours, which has always annoyed Mami deeply, is greatly calmed by your body being in motion for so much of the day.

There'd been work in Hong Kong, too, which always kept you busy. Working in a restaurant had definitely sapped some of that overflowing energy. But there is something about walking around a rural island which you find particularly restful, and in daylight the ghosts are scared enough not to worry you.

That said, it is always a trifle . . . well . . . lonely.

For a girl who has lived in a city thronged with crowds, the island's quiet can feel terribly stark, at times. You find yourself wishing there were at least one other person here, since Mami is such bad company. She probably feels the same about you, which doesn't make you feel any better.

"Just one friend would do," you say to the cat, the next time you see him. "I don't suppose you feel like learning to talk?"

The cat yawns, showing a bright-pink mouth. He still comes by often, though he never enters the house.

"It was worth a try," you say, and sigh.

Still, life is pleasant enough. Despite the loneliness, and the looming shadow of your father's absence, you feel weirdly hopeful. Perhaps, you tell yourself, Baba has simply been detained, because of the war; the ports have likely shut. When the conflict ends (always think *when*, never *if*), maybe you can go look for him.

The small fishing boats on the island's far side, though not big enough for all the luggage, could at least get you somewhere safe in an emergency. You and Mami could reach a nearby island, if not the mainland.

Daydreaming about the end of the war, when you don't even know what's going on! Still, it would be a good idea to visit those other islands, sometime, even if only to get news. Mami won't be keen, so you'll have to do it quietly and perhaps not mention it, unless the news is very good.

You'll go after the planting season, you decide. That makes the most sense. That gives Baba a little more time to make an appearance.

Then the typhoon arrives, and all of those plans crumble.

18

THE NIGHT WE DROWNED

Thirty-three years ago . . .

Typhoons have always been a summer occurrence. You can't recall seeing one earlier than May, and more commonly in June, July, or August. That's the wet season, when the winds are dangerous and fickle.

This one comes on the first day of March.

It begins with a sunrise of blood-red clouds and strong winds, which seems to leave Mami unsettled. She keeps checking the sky, ignoring your questions. By midmorning, she is urging you to help her tack down loose items, and bring inside anything essential. You take down clothes off the line, though they're still very damp. Buckets, tools, other odds and ends are brought in. Mami pulls tight the shutters, binding them so they won't fling open.

Around noontime—lunch is jarred fish and raw vegetables, because Mami doesn't think it is wise to cook—the storm begins to really spin up. The house rattles from gust after gust of unrelenting wind, and the rain sounds like hail because it hits the roof with such speed and fury.

Typhoons are not unfamiliar. They come every year, albeit usually in summer, to wallow all over the South China coast and make themselves heard. But you are used to weathering them in the safety of a city, where the buildings shield each other like little concrete turtles. Out here, exposed on the high hill of an island, it is rather frightening.

Mami's reaction makes it worse. She huddles underneath the bed in her room like a child, wide-eyed.

"Mami? Are you okay?"

"I hate typhoons," comes her muffled reply. "Ever since . . ." She trails off.

Ever since one of them destroyed this island, when she was a child. She hadn't liked typhoons when you lived in the city, either, but maybe this was all just a little too personal. Perhaps the context is triggering some strong memories.

After some deliberation, you join her. At least it's relatively safe here, and maybe it will make her feel better. As much as you often grate on each other, it's hard to turn away from someone when they are clearly so terrified.

"Can I ask a question?" Reach out, touch her on the shoulder.

She recoils. "What is it?"

"Will this storm be bad?" you say. Wishing yet again that Baba had collected you both, by now. "Will the house survive?"

"It did when I was a girl." She adds, in a voice thick with emotion, "Mine was the only house still standing, at the end."

She doesn't talk after that, and you don't feel like drawing her into conversation. Together, the pair of you lie beneath the bed, uncomfortable and a little claustrophobic, while the rain pounds on the roof and the wind screams like a dying child.

Some hours later, when the tempest calms down, both of you roll out from under the bed and go to inspect the damage. The fact that the typhoon has lasted a mere handful of hours has not escaped you; that's far from normal. Not that you're complaining, exactly.

A quick inspection settles your nerves, at least initially. The house has clearly survived, though it's lost a number of roof tiles and one of the shutters has blown off. The garden is ripped up and will need replanting. The thought is a little demoralizing, after all the work it's taken.

Mami, though, has skipped looking at the house and gone straight outside. You're still sulking at the mess of the garden when you hear her choked cry. Alarmed, you dart over to the hilltop where she's standing.

"What's wrong?" you ask, reaching her side.

"The village is destroyed," Mami says, hoarsely. "Just like when I was little."

Look where she's pointing, and wince. The handful of homes you can see from this vantage point do look seriously damaged. The pristine beauty that was on display when you first arrived is now all wrecked.

"I'm sure the ghosts will rebuild it again," you say, trying not to fidget because it will annoy her. It's hard to know what to say in the face of such destruction, though. "They did last time."

"Maybe." Mami purses her lips. "I must see the village."

"Huh? Why? Wait, where are you going!"

Mami doesn't listen. She strides off through the light drizzle and you hurry to follow, unsure what is happening.

The damage soon becomes apparent. Almost every other house has been flattened. A few ghosts linger in their ruins, taking up positions that recall how they died. Some are crushed beneath collapsed roofs, others impaled improbably on sharp objects.

But overall, there are not many. Privately, you wonder where the other ghost villagers are. The death you can see is appalling, but there don't seem to be many of them around. You wonder where the rest of the ghosts have gone.

"This is just like I remember." Mami breathes raggedly, sounding close to panic. "When I was little, it was like this, too. I came out in the morning, found everyone dead. Found these houses ruined, and . . . and . . . I must get to the chapel!"

Abruptly, she starts running.

"Mami . . . Mami, slow down!" you call out, chasing after her.

She ignores you and keeps going.

Soon enough, you reach the old Catholic church. The roof has collapsed, the walls tilted in. Mami slows to a halt. "They hid in the cellar. I remember, now . . . Everyone thought it would be safe. But the church collapsed, and they couldn't get out."

You look uneasily; rubble has fallen atop the cellar door, blocking it shut. The sight of that sparks a bad feeling in your body. If the other ghosts are reenacting their death, then what waits for you in this ruined building?

Mami begins clearing the rubble in a frantic burst of energy. "Come help!"

"I'm not sure we should do that," you say, anxiously. "Everyone died years ago. Why go through this again?"

She whirls on you. *"Just do your family duty!"*

Anyone other than a parent, and you'd have considered slapping them and walking off. But since it is your mother and she's clearly caught up in some kind of distress, you reluctantly bend to help her.

When the rubble is moved, Mami yanks up the cellar doors.

Both of you recoil, screaming.

The cellar has filled with rainwater, and every single person down there has drowned. The bloated faces of family and friends cluster at the cellar entrance, buoyed up by water. Their fingers are shredded to bone from scraping at the wood, skin purpled and bruised.

The dead begin to speak.

They wail and groan, crying out to the gods, begging for forgiveness, offering anything for their lives. One by one, bloated ghosts begin to surge from the cellar in slippery, sodden lumps, dead flesh hanging from dead bones, tormented spirits raging in their bodies.

"It's not my fault!" Mami shrieks, tugging wildly at her own hair. "Forgive me!"

Never in your life have you seen her so unhinged, and the sight snaps you out of your own terror.

"We must go!" You loop an arm through hers and pull her away, as hard as you can.

Surprisingly, she comes with you, sobbing loudly as she flees.

All the way through the village, past every building, ghosts come out as the pair of you sprint past, shouting questions and garbled pleas. Mami tries to apologize in Hakka, even pausing to reach back with arms extended.

"Mami, no!" You grab her around her waist, since taking her arm is apparently not sufficient, and yank her very hard.

Once you get going, she stumbles into a run yet again. Dazed yet compliant, at least for now.

Eventually, you get back to the house. Slam the door shut and start whispering prayers to the Christian God, to your ancestral gods, anyone who will listen, frankly. Feel grateful for the fu talismans plastered over every entrance, keeping out those grasping and waterlogged hands.

"What," you say, still panting and shaking a little, "the hell was that?"

"I'm sorry," Mami mutters, forehead resting against the door. "I did not think it would be like this. The ghosts are remembering the night we drowned, acting it out in detail. The storm must have set them off. They should . . . they should calm down soon."

"Maybe we should leave Shek Ham Chau," you say, after a long, extended silence. "It doesn't seem very safe, and, well . . ."

And Mami seems extremely unhappy. But you don't say that part out loud, since she won't appreciate it, at all.

"What's the point? Where would we go?" she says, tiredly.

"Another island. Any other island. There must be space on Yim Tin Tsai, or Sharp Island. Anywhere."

She is silent, genuinely considering it. Eventually, she straightens up and smooths down her hair. The rain has made it frizzy and unkempt.

"Let me have a sleep on it," she says, at last. "It's not so easy to simply go somewhere else. We don't know where the Japanese are, or what they're doing. We don't know whether another village will take us in."

"I guess." It occurs to you that moving to a different island will make it hard for Baba to find you both, if he does arrive, but Mami doesn't seem to have thought of that.

"Let's eat something, and refresh ourselves," she says, after several more beats of silence. "We have a lot of work to do in the garden tomorrow. Can you sleep tonight?"

"I think so? I might make a few more fu talismans before bed, though."

"Yes, that's sensible," she says, already walking to the kitchen to start cooking. She pauses in the archway and says, "I'm sorry for dragging you into the village. I should not have done that."

"It's fine," you say, but she is already turning away, taking out a wok and some of the stored food.

Sighing, you go to get some paper, brushes, and blessed ink.

Mami does not sleep that night, however.

Instead, she waits patiently for dinner to end. For you to write and hang your fu talismans, and go to bed. Then, when she is sure that you are deeply asleep, she throws on a light shawl and heads out.

Darkness lies thick across Shek Ham Chau, the moon hidden by clouds. She picks a stumbling path across the night-chilled earth, toward the beach. She feels naked out here, aware of the ghosts who lurk, the taut gleam of their spirit selves grown more dangerous, and yet paradoxically unafraid. The frenetic fury of their re-enactment has passed, and they are placid once again.

Ingrained memory leads her to the right place. Carefully, she kneels in the sand, the sea crashing in front of her.

Mami cups her hands over her mouth and calls out, "Are you out there, goddess?"

From a distance, the little white cat watches her from the depths of tall, waving grass. She does not see it, and it does not reveal itself to her.

Nor do I reveal myself, for the time is not yet right.

Instead, a particularly large wave hits the shore, accompanied by a powerful gust of wind. The force is strong enough to knock her down, the accompanying spray soaks her through. Mami falls with a gasp, damp and outraged.

As a little girl, years ago, she would have found it funny to be sprayed by a wave. But she has not been a little girl in such a long, long time.

Mami stands up, fuming, and throws a rock into the ocean. What she hopes that will accomplish, I cannot imagine.

Hair dripping, breath steaming, she calls out, "Why didn't you stop any of it? Were my prayers not enough? Whenever I pray to you, disaster strikes!"

The tide advances and retreats, advances and retreats. I am silence itself.

"I hope all humans forsake you, as you deserve," Mami continues, fists clenched. "I hope you descend to the underworld and demons torment you forever! I hope—" She starts crying, the ranting choked off by her own tears.

In the tall grass, the cat looks up at me. It is the only being on this island who can perceive me, and its gaze is full of questions.

For a long moment, I'm tempted. Tempted to step forward and comfort a woman who was once a frightened child, even though I know I am the last face she wants to see right now. Tempted to kneel at her feet, seeking forgiveness. I would almost do it, just to make peace with the last living person in this place to remember me.

But Daiyu—your Mami—stopped believing in me a long time ago, and that makes it difficult to appear to her. Besides, it is not her forgiveness that matters; not any longer. A more powerful anger rules this island.

Her crying draws attention. Soon enough, the villager ghosts begin to gather at the cliffside. They stream down in their dripping clothes and bloated bodies, limbs like jelly, mouths open. Normally, they avoid coming too near the coast, but in this instance they will make an exception.

Mami is still kneeling in the sand, crying into her hands. They gather around her, whisper to her of their guilt, their longing, their suffering. She closes her eyes, and embraces them. The clouds roll back, allowing the moon to bathe the world in silvery light.

Welcome home, little one.

One of us . . .

Don't leave!

Slowly, she stands, arms spread wide. The ghosts gather, pressing around her. And alone on that dark headland, she begins to dance with her dead beneath a darkly glittering sky.

Your Mami should know better; she *does* know better. A child of three is wise enough to steer clear from the embrace of ghosts, because the past is an endless ocean on which we can sail forever without returning home. And the past is the only place the dead can take you, the only thing a spirit offers: moments long gone, days turned to dust.

But her future is a cold, narrow place. Of *course* she wants to sail on that endless ocean of the past, wants to spend her days lost in re-creations of a place where she felt happy. Tomorrow holds less and less interest for your mother.

Mami does not return home that night. She stays out beneath the star-wracked sky, hair tossed in a midnight wind and arms entwined with her ghosts. Only when the sun begins to creep shyly above the horizon line does she stagger reluctantly toward home, drawn by the one thread that still anchors her to the world of the living: you, her daughter.

I do not think that thread will keep her tethered very long.

19

AND THEN YOU LOOK DOWN

Thirty-three years ago . . .

You wake in bed with the morning light streaming across your face, unaware of what has transpired in the night.

It is New Year's Day, according to Hong Kong's British calendar, though Lunar New Year is still a way off. Not that it means much. Time hardly seems to matter, on Shek Ham Chau. The world is far away in this place.

As you get up and walk through the house, you are shocked to discover ghosts milling around as if they belong, rifling through your things and leaving watery footprints on the floorboards. At least eight are thronging around the kitchen and poking through the garden.

"Hey!" you protest, and have to snatch a bowl away from a curious but clumsy ghost child.

It warbles at you plaintively, its face too bloated in death for you to work out whether it used to be a boy or girl.

An accident!

God's will. God's will.

The drowned priest is back, standing next to an old fisherwoman with seaweed in her hair. The pair of them drip in the kitchen as they repeat lines to each other endlessly. The fu talismans must have failed.

But when you go to check on them, they haven't failed. They simply aren't there. Someone has taken them all down.

It's not exactly a mystery. There's only one other person living in the house.

You stride outside furiously, in search of Mami. She's hanging things on a washing line, basket of laundry on the ground.

Confronting a parent isn't the natural order of things, not for a young woman of good Chinese upbringing. But neither is waking up to a house full of ghosts, apparently invited in on purpose.

And breathe. "Mami, there are ghosts in the house. Lots of them."

"Yes." That's it. Her one-word reply.

"I thought we were going to talk about maybe leaving Shek Ham Chau?!"

"I changed my mind. I spoke to them last night, and we came to an understanding. It is best if you and I stay a little longer."

"What does that have to do with taking down my fu talismans!"

"I didn't want to offend them, or make them feel unwelcome." Her tone suggests she thinks that is completely reasonable.

"Offend the . . ." It takes all your effort not to swear. "Mami, ghosts shouldn't be under the same roof as us. That's what you've always told me."

"This is different. I am honoring our dead," she says, stooping to pick up another item. Spirit children chase one another in and out of the draped row of clothes while she works, and their whispers sound like water gurgling. "The island belongs to them, and we hide here in safety because of their hospitality."

"Ghosts do not own anything," you say, exasperated. "The world of the living belongs only to the living. It is they who are guests, not us."

"You understand nothing," Mami said, fingers shaking a little as she pegs a shirt to the line. "I should not have survived, daughter."

". . . What?"

"I told you. Almost everyone died in the typhoon, yet I lived." She fumbles the next peg, bends to pick it up. "Why should I have such good fortune to still be breathing?"

"Mami . . ." Your heart is heavy at her words.

Having been down to the village yesterday during its haunting, you can well imagine how terrible it must have been for a child to wake up to such destruction, death, and fear.

She shakes her head. "They said it was my sister who was bad luck, a curse to everyone."

"Sister?" you say, ears perking up. The other little girl in the photo. "What about your sister? What happened—"

"But they're wrong," she interrupts, talking over you. "It is me. *Me.* I lived while others died and ever since that day, I carry my cursed luck wherever I go. I feel I owe it to my ghosts. How can I turn them away when I should be one of them?"

That rare moment of vulnerability moves you to pity and sadness. Your mother is beginning to look like the ghosts she loves; she has stopped tying up her hair, let it grow loose and tangled around her shoulders. Her clothes, once hospital-clean, are unkempt. The sleeves are streaked, dirty, torn.

Life has been hard on her. It has been hard on both of you. In this haunted place, trapped between time and tides, your shared grief exists in limbo. As if you are both caught between the real world and the underworld, just like the drowned villagers.

"Mami, nobody is at fault for a typhoon," you say, gentle as possible. "You do not owe these ghosts any debt."

She recoils as if slapped, lips trembling. "Ignorant ugly chicken!" she shouts. "What do you know about my life, about this island?" She flings down the shirt she is holding—it is one of yours, of course—and storms back to the house, arms wrapped around her chest.

In that single moment, your brief burst of sympathy and pity evaporates like mist, burned off by the hurt and indignation of many years. How easily she kindles anger in you; how swiftly she stings and lashes out. Only family can hurt family in that way.

Slowly, you bend to pick up the discarded shirt. It is freshly muddy, and will need washing again.

Ignorant ugly chicken.

She might be your mother, but Mami can't stop acting like a hurt child. Some part of her has never healed from the past. She may be your mother, and you her daughter, and you may live together on this island, but it is through necessity of survival. Nothing more.

No point running after her, not again. You're flat-out tired of always reaching for her, something you have been doing your whole life, only to hit walls and barriers and slaps. Why should the burden of connection always be yours?

Baba asked you to look after her, and you've been trying. But everyone has a limit. This might well be yours. If Baba comes back, he can sort it out. If he doesn't . . . Well. Mami is old enough to know what she is doing, and she has chosen this.

Fuck that old cow.

Fueled by anger and fear and confusion, you kick the bucket of laundry over and storm off. Let her wash the whole lot again.

⁘

It is so easy, when looking back on our lives, to judge relationships only on how they ended or how they broke down. In the wake of estrangement and arguments, it is so difficult to remember the joy we once felt in another's presence.

There were good memories of Mami, and if pressed you could recall them. Those Friday evenings down by the dock, for example. The odd occasion she'd help with your schoolwork, or tell amusing stories from her day at the hospital.

In the present moment, however, those handful of bright spots feel very far away. They have been left behind with a war-torn city, lost along with a missing father.

Right now, you cannot remember Mami at her best: tired and trying, telling you stories, making you food. In the heat of your anger, she is only stupid, stubborn, old, and pointlessly secretive. Every unfair criticism, harsh word, scolding tongue, contemptuous click, unearned slap, stair-running punishment, bad day, or cranky argument comes tumbling into your brain and you can't bear to be around her for another *fucking* minute.

Should have let her meet those ghosts on her own. Why do you keep saving her, anyway? Why do you keep running after her? You *are* a stupid chicken, actually, but not for the reason she thinks. You're stupid for always coming back to her, for trying again.

Anger boils up and you *run*. Out of the house, down the overgrown trail toward the beach. Away from her, away from everything.

A grass-choked path unfurls at your feet. The forest sprawls on all sides, filled with birdsong and tree-rustling and wave-roaring. Empty of people, though. Behind you, the house is swift to vanish, its ghosts too slow and heavy to keep up with your flying steps.

The deep sense of isolation strikes you, sinking in all over again. The sensation is freeing, giving your spirit wings and lifting the corners of your mouth into a smile. You start singing out loud, because there are no ghosts or people around to observe an awkward young woman belting out the worst rendition of Bai Hong's "Spring Wind" on this side of the Pacific.

Skip a little, run a little, walk when tired. Following the half-rotted signage, your feet tracking through the forest and out again, along the sultry curve of coast to a particular sprawl of beach where the water is a reflective sheen and the wind a quiet companion. Sunlight skitters across surf.

Heart swells. Breath catches.

It's perfect.

Back in the city, you were never far from the shore. Beach trips were an occasional weekend thing, and Baba taught you how to swim years ago, though Mami always stayed stubbornly on shore.

Still, those trips had nothing on this place. Stanley Bay was full of litter, crowded, the sand strip narrow and speckled with crusty rocks. This is a pristine paradise, empty and clean, filling your ears with the raw smash of water.

Suddenly, the only thing you want to do is swim. Mami's warnings, like Mami's moods, feel of little consequence. What does she know about anything, anyway? It's nearly spring, now, with the days already heating up and the water looking inviting. Certainly, it will be safer than going for a dip in August, when the rains come in heavy.

Time to dive. Peel off those sweaty, grimy shirt and trousers, and leap in wearing just camisole and drawers. Why not, no one is around to see. Cool water silks over skin, washing heat and dirt away. The waves are big, crashing over and around, tumbling limbs about. Sand grits under eyelids and fingernails and you surface for air, licking salt from cracked lips. Swarms of little moon jellyfish brush your skin, gentle and quivering as they move with the tides.

Laugh, dip down again. The shore sinks deep quickly out here but it's clear water, with good visibility. Not too much kelp, either. You swim down a dozen feet, feeling like a deep-sea explorer, and touch the bottom in joyful triumph while avoiding spiny urchins and irritable crabs. Rise again to surface, pushed by natural buoyancy.

It is unholy to be this happy.

Hard to believe that a couple of months ago, your life was so completely, unutterably different: the long drudge of working in a street restaurant, the sluggish surge of city life, the war that threatened like a snarling dog in the corner. The days leading up to Hong Kong's invasion had narrowed your existence until the hours seemed to fold indistinguishably into one another.

After an hour of swimming and splashing, your limbs grow tired. Time to turn for home and swim back. The beach is a good fifty meters away, and the front crawl back to shore is filled with reluctant weariness.

But as you strike out for shallower water, the current tugs in the opposite direction, its pull noticeably stronger than an hour ago. It doesn't seem like a problem at first. You've swum on the southern side of Hong Kong Island. This is not any different.

Except . . . it is.

The current here is more of a yank than a tug. The riptide picks up force and urgency. Suddenly the water isn't a friend but an enemy—dragging you, bewildered and terrified, through churning surf.

The next time you surface, the shore is farther than it was when you started. Tired and alarmed, you strike out for home once again. There are rocks ahead, an outcropping that stretches far into the water. If you can reach it, that will be a reprieve.

Almost, you make it. At the last moment the waves push too hard, dashing your leg against the very barnacle-encrusted refuge you sought. Sharp edges cut unexpectedly into skin. Blood clouds the water and you're stunned; you didn't know such harmless shells could do so much hurt. At least from here you'll be able to climb up, reach the shore—

The next set of waves comes in, sweeping you off the outcropping and farther out to sea. Again.

The funny thing about riptides: they are most dangerous when you swim against them. Let them pull you where they will, and you're less likely to drown. Resist, and they'll pummel you into submission.

No one's ever taught you how to swim in this kind of a current, though. So you strike out for land with increasing panic and get rolled up like a cigarette by those tremendous crashers. Into shore, back out to sea. Into shore, back out to sea. No closer than where you started, fifteen minutes ago.

The next time, that current drags you under and doesn't let you go. Sand on your tongue, in your throat, up your nose. Salt searing the eyes. Forever and a day underwater and the strangest thing is that you can't seem to reach the surface, no matter how you try. The current is carrying you even farther and still you've not been up for air, the burning in your nose, throat, eyes matched only by the intense fire in your lungs.

It occurs to you with sudden, piercing clarity that you are going to die out here. In love with this place more than anything or anywhere else in your life, and it will be the death of you.

The edges of your vision are going dark and you're not sure what's up or down, where the shore is or how to reach the sky, can't imagine ever breathing again. Everything hurts and you reach both hands out, blindly, without hope or expectation.

Something grasps your wrist.

Fingers, hard and slim. Long nails that press clean edges into your flesh. The shadow of a face you can't make out with salt-stung, half-closed eyes. A flash of long, dark hair, the streaming tendrils curling like tentacles.

A figure, swimming at your side.

For the moment, there is nothing else to do except hold on tight and hope this is a savior, not a predator. Clutch at the blurred body; it is ice-cold, reed-thin. Water swirls and suddenly, you are rushing up and up and up, ears popping and a sick feeling in your belly as the pressure changes too fast.

Light. *Air.* Break the surface with a gasping wail, spluttering and sobbing. The shore is devastatingly far, and getting gradually more distant; the currents are still fast-moving. You tread and float, exhausted but too terrified to stop, too terrified to sink again.

Pain in your eyes, head, and throat, and pain in your left thigh where it was dashed against the barnacle-clad rocks. Bleeding into open water. That can't be good. Sharks come out here sometimes, and they can smell blood from a mile away.

A fresh wash of anxiety fills you. Help, you need help—

The one who rescued you. The thin form, the long nails and the dark streaming hair. Where have they gone?

And

then

you

look

down.

20

. . . JIAOREN?

Thirty-three years ago . . .

A woman lurks beneath the ocean surface.

Skin the color of palest jade, delicate as a paper lantern. Eyes that are solid white and glistening. Clouds of black hair unspool around her head. She sweeps away errant, floating strands with hands that are long as your foot, the bones strangely elongated. Each finger is tipped with claw-like nails. In her mouth is the hardness of teeth, too many for a human and jagged as a shark's. Her feet are long and flat like a pair of fins, with webbed toes.

Far from land, nearly drowned, bleeding still; inches away from a monster. You should be screaming. You should be a gibbering mess. Instead, you are only amazed.

Even . . . awestruck.

For she is beautiful, in a twisted way, and something about her sorrowful, ferocious expression moves you to a mix of pity and wonder.

"Jiaoren," you manage to croak out, dumbstruck and overwhelmed. "Jiaoren!"

What else could she be but one of the so-called flood dragon people—the magical women and men of ancient legend, who live beneath the waves in their own undersea kingdoms? Whose tears become pearls, whose love is legendary, and whose vengeance is relentless?

Everything makes sense. The decrepit signs in the fields, the ocean your mother is nervous of, the temple built for sea-dwelling people. The aura of beauty around this place. Even the strange storm, an act of supernatural influence. This woman—no, this jiaoren—is at the heart of it all.

On an island full of faded, chittering ghosts, her monstrous nature is bright and fierce and full of verve. Like a vibrant bird, flying above a field of dry bones.

It's then that you realize how cold and weak you are, strength sapped by fighting the tides, shivering in the water despite the warm sun above. The burst of adrenaline is gone and with its passing, your legs slow, ceasing to tread; you slip once more beneath the surface.

One of her hands darts through the green and grabs a fistful of camisole, her nails slicing inadvertently through fabric. She holds you tight, face-to-face with her in the waves.

Those shark teeth. Those pearlescent eyes. You're spellbound and dazed. A glimpse of her form, ravaged and unpleasantly starved beneath the rags she wears—doesn't she eat? Surely one like her is a predator—with all her bones on display, ribs protruding and hips like axe blades. Nothing about her is soft, or safe.

Time stretches as you hang in the water and she reaches out, so gently, to touch the tip of your nose with her other hand. One nail traces a cheek and, despite the lack of verbal communication, you sense her shock.

Hold on, she says, or at least, you *think* she is speaking. Her lips move and you understand what she means, which is almost the same thing.

Abruptly, she wraps both arms around you and launches into a swim. Starved or not, she's strong as a horse. No, a dolphin. You clutch at her wrists, hanging tight as she torpedoes through the waves.

It's exhilarating. Fear melts like spring frost as water parts around you both. Glimpses of fish, something that might have *actually* been a shark, sand and rocks, liquid emerald everywhere.

Dip and dive through glassy water, disrupting schools of fish, skirting typhoon-hit wrecks, dart through waving seagrass and clustered coral. Urchins roll like spiky balls, shunted by the force of your passage. She lets you surface to catch your breath before diving again, and keeps you safe as she glides through unknowable waters.

Soon enough, she reaches the shore where you first entered the sea earlier. No signal, no warning, no discussion. One moment you're tunneling through the green, as close to a fish as you'll ever get. The next she flings you from her with insane strength, strong as the ocean itself, and you're cresting through the surf to wash up like beach detritus.

Air! Warmth! Dryness! Joy expands in your chest as you lie back on the sand, foam surging round your limbs and the blessedly warm sun soaking in. After those long minutes beneath the surface, the world above feels almost too bright, too clear; unnaturally hot and dry. As if the water were a place you half-way belong, now, having nearly died in it.

"Hello?" Sit up, look up; you're alone. "Hey! Sea Sister, are you there?" *Sea Sister.* Why not. It's a polite enough honorific, since you don't know her name.

A glimpse of something pale and fast in the waves. Fleeing, or lurking? Scramble to standing, and leap back into the water, putting your head beneath it.

That moment. Where sound plunges into a muted dullness, where the raw noise of the atmosphere above is softened by the sea.

She's there, your rescuer, your personal fantasy: a little farther away where the water is deeper. Watching you as if transfixed. The jiaoren seems startled, though she's alien enough in appearance that it's hard to read her expression.

"Sea Sister!" you call out again, this time underwater. Forcing your voice to make sense in a liquid environment.

She turns uneasy circles, giving a good view of her ravaged form. The rags that barely hide her bones, the feet and hands so unusually proportioned. She looks hungry, lonely, haunted; an isolated legend, living among ghosts. Yet she is inexplicably beautiful despite the monstrous traits and the painful starvation.

The jiaoren stops circling and swims toward you, cautious and hesitant. She seems to be waiting for something. An invitation, maybe?

"Swim with me again," you yell underwater, expelling all the air from your lungs to enunciate-shout the words. Needing breath, you stand up in the chest-deep waves, gulp oxygen, and duck back down again. "We can be friends," you plead.

She watches, unblinking and statue-still despite the fast-moving tide.

"Are you hungry?" you bellow, feeling stupid and rude for shouting, but it's not possible to speak underwater otherwise. Assuming she can understand you at all. "Can I get you food?"

At your question, her face changes, lips drawing back and teeth clacking. A long, black tongue flickers, the surface of it covered in tiny suckers like an octopus's tentacle. Her dark eyes squeeze shut, then reopen, and she drifts close, so close the tip of her nose brushes against yours.

Unwittingly, you gulp. Not afraid, exactly, but definitely intimidated.

She pulls backward, shakes her head, and smiles—or bares her teeth, you're not sure which—as she takes your small, suntanned hand in hers, bony fingers rigid against your palm.

Come back tomorrow, Shore Sister.

Tomorrow, you mouth back, exaggerating the lip movements. Showing her you understand.

The jiaoren bares her teeth again, and flashes away. Faster than a motorboat, melting into the depths.

Despite her instruction, you climb out and wait around on the beach for a little bit anyhow, telling yourself it's better to dry off. Trying to understand what's happened to you, why it doesn't faze you like it should. Ghosts are one thing; this experience was something else entirely.

Other people would be afraid, but the things you fear and the things you love have never quite lined up with the fears and loves of other people. The island, the beach—it's like all of this was fate, like everything that has happened till now was just a series of steps allowing you to move onto this path, and meet Sea Sister.

Destiny is unfolding. You still don't know what the future will bring, and hate to guess. But for the first time in years, that isn't a worry.

The sun is setting, you are famished, and it's a long trudge back. Time to go home, for now. It has been one wild day.

As you set off for the house, the small white cat watches you from the shadows, its whiskers quivering.

I watch, too, but you do not see me at all.

The walk back just about dries your cami and drawers, enough to throw on the shirt and loose slacks that you left on the sand. Conveniently, the longer clothes hide your scraped thigh (barnacles), scuffed shins (rocks), and scratched arms (monster claws).

Inside, your heart is broken open from too many new experiences, brain thrumming with awe and overwhelm. Lost in your own thoughts, you don't pay attention to your surroundings for most of the walk.

The whitewashed walls of your house emerge quietly from the greenery as you draw closer to home, and it's only when you're a dozen yards away that you finally notice the low but audible murmur of talking. Something else, too: music playing.

What the hell.

Then you see her, through the front window. You see your mother.

Some of the ghosts are dancing and some are playing spirit instruments (where did they get those from?) in the background while Mami watches, hands clapping to the rhythm and a smile on her face. She bounces from foot to foot, not quite dancing. This is no traditional performance, but a modern dance, of the kind one might have found in a Shanghai jazz bar before the bombs wiped it away. You recognize the tune as one she used to hum sometimes, while doing her chores.

Has she taught these ghosts to play modern music? Surely not.

The sight is unnerving. You stand there for a good ten minutes, roiling with uneasy emotions, until she notices you with a jolt through the window and straightens guiltily.

By the time you come through the front door, Mami is in the kitchen, make-work tidying as if nothing unusual happened. The only tell is a guilty flush to her cheeks. The ghosts are present, doing chores and milling around, but the instruments and music are gone.

You could swear the ghosts speak louder than they did before. Some of them are definitely more active than they used to be. You wonder uneasily if Mami has been feeding them, and if so, on what; there is nothing on the shrine, no bowls of food with joss sticks.

"Back so soon?" she says, lifting the lid of a clay pot. Regardless of whatever she was doing with the ghosts, she hasn't forgotten to cook.

"It is almost evening," you point out, watching her, wondering whether it's okay to ask about what you've just seen. "If I got back any later it'd be nighttime."

"Yes, supper is almost ready." Her response doesn't really make sense.

"Thanks for cooking." Fumbling for words, trying to sound normal even though your day was the literal definition of otherworldly.

"No need for thanks. Just wash up for me, afterward." She plonks chopsticks on the table. "Where did you go?" No mention of the argument earlier today. Maybe she's forgotten about it.

"Um . . ." You're a natural chatterbox, a chronic oversharer, and that tendency to spill your life on other people has long been a source of conflict with her. Meeting the jiaoren is the most important thing to ever happen to you.

Which is exactly why you can't seem to summon up the words.

It's too much. You're not ready. Your brain has only just begun to process the things that your eyes and hands experienced. Speaking about it to someone else is out of reach, a distant mountain surrounded by churning rivers. Especially when the "someone else" in question was the target of your boiling anger only a few hours ago.

Mami is looking at you, waiting for an answer.

"Just walked around the island," you manage, and she nods distractedly. Neither of you mention the argument from before, which only makes it loom taller.

Together, you sit and eat. She's made clay pot rice with chunks of preserved sausage, dried mushrooms, rehydrated bok choi, scallions aplenty, and a blend of salty-sweet sauces. These are the very last of the good ingredients brought on the boat; there won't be food this nice for a while. You try to enjoy every bite, making it last.

It doesn't escape you that she seems as averse to discussing her afternoon as you are to discussing yours. Better to leave it. To not question her, as she is not questioning you.

With hindsight, you should have talked to Mami about what was happening. About Sea Sister reaching for you beneath the waves, even as the village ghosts reached for her. The warning signs were there, all along.

But Mami isn't easy to approach. She dislikes difficult conversations, seems to dislike conversations full stop. You have long suspected this was a consequence of her days working in a hospital, where she made endless polite chatter with endless patients, even as a cleaner.

Doesn't help that Mami has never seemed to like *you*, specifically. She goes through phases of being almost affectionate, like those Friday evening walks. But it always feels like a slipup, like some kind of weak moment.

Again, lack of life experience is working against you. You are too young to understand how afraid she is of losing people she loves, yet again, and what that does to her: how she labors to keep everyone at a distance. That's a lesson you've yet to imbibe, much less have sympathy for.

In the end, you're both comfortable with things as they are, each willing to sue for peace, mutual secrets skinned in a thin varnish of mundane life. So you say nothing, and eat your damn food without complaint.

It's a nice meal, at any rate. Mami always was a good cook.

When the bowls are empty and you're both licking fingers clean, she says quite suddenly, "Are you worried, living here?"

The jiaoren's ethereal face fills your mind, unbidden.

"No, I'm not worried." The truth, mostly. You like the bits that don't involve the village ghosts milling through your private spaces. "It's beautiful. Quiet. No one has told me lately how annoying I am."

More bitter than you mean to sound, and she actually winces.

"Good," Mami says, not meeting your gaze. "Good." For once, her sharpness seems abashed, even subdued, which is unlike her.

Despite feeling irritated, you ask, "Are *you* worried?"

Unspoken between the lines: *Are you safe here, talking to these stupid ghosts?*

"I miss your father," she says, once again catching you off guard.

She is thinking, with rare wistfulness, of the ring he bought as part of the dowry for their wedding. The gold was pure and soft as chilled wax, its square top carved with lotus blossoms. Not much, but all he could afford, and she'd loved it. Regretfully, she sold it to pay for the fare to this island.

"Me too." You don't say that for her sake, but for your father's; you owe him that admission. "Every day he doesn't come, I worry more."

"It takes time," she says. "Selling our things and buying a boat is not a quick business, not with the war going on."

"I know." But you can't help wondering if something has gone wrong that Mami isn't telling you about. After all, Baba was so worried about the invasion that he didn't think it safe for either of you to stay behind with him.

"I wish more of my family had survived the storms here." Mami looks out the window, and you don't miss how she's changed the subject. "I wish that we had come back to a thriving village and not to . . ." She trails off.

Not to a walking graveyard, you finish silently.

The spirits in the house turn toward you both, one at a time, suddenly alert and attentive. They're difficult to ignore.

Aloud, you remind her, "If living people were here, it would not be so safe. We came because the Japanese will ignore Shek Ham Chau."

"Yes. There was nowhere else to go. And we are home, now." She smiles, but not at you—her gaze slides over your shoulder to fixate on the ghosts.

The rest of the evening passes in wary silence. While you tidy up the bowls and chopsticks, and rinse the dishes, Mami studies the evening sky; she is trying to ascertain tomorrow's weather. Wet season will start soon, and that affects the planting of crops.

Afterward, she reclines against her kitchen chair with a bottle of beer and a cigarette. She only brought three packs to smoke, and one crate of beer; despite her efforts to stretch them out, both will soon be totally gone.

In this light, the gray strands in her hair seem more prominent. The lines of her face rest deeper, sink a little sadder. She is not an unhappy person by nature, despite her sharp tongue and abrasive edge. Instead, life has gnawed her joy away, loaded her with care and worries and guilt and exhaustion.

With a brain that won't stop churning, you curl up and read one of Baba's few poetry books that came in the luggage. The pages smell of his cigarette smoke. You wish you'd brought one of his jackets, but there wasn't space to bring his clothes. He was supposed to bring those himself.

After a little while, though, the nosey ghosts are starting to put you off, hovering too close as you flip slowly through the pages. Besides, your thoughts keep drifting toward a certain green-skinned woman in the ocean.

Tomorrow. Tomorrow.

Tired to the bone, you wish Mami good night and get up to go sleep.

"Daughter," she says, as you rise.

Hand resting on the doorway, you pause and look back. "Yes?"

"When you were out walking around, did you go by the shore at all?"

Stillness pools in the room.

"Why do you ask?"

"Well. I was wondering if you saw . . ." She hesitates, pulling at her lip.

"What?" you ask her, almost daring her to say it. "Saw what?"

"Nothing," she says, retreating immediately. "It doesn't matter. Foolish question."

"If there's something I should know," you say, carefully, "maybe you should tell me before letting me wander by myself. Are these ghosts dangerous?"

"The island is fine. We're among friends." She tugs at the hem of her shirt in short, repetitive gestures. "Just—just be careful. There are sharks in the water."

"Sharks," you echo, flatly.

She says nothing.

"Well, I haven't seen any . . . sharks. I'll let you know if I do."

Mami seems to wrestle with that answer, and you get the sense she regrets being so evasive, which only solidifies your sense of satisfaction at shutting her out. For once, you're the one closing the door in her face, instead of the other way around.

There's not a lot she can do about it.

She says, finally, "See you in the morning, daughter."

"Good night." And you turn on your heel, feeling pettily victorious.

21

ISLAND DREAMS

Thirty-three years ago . . .

You wake abruptly in the middle of the night.

The walls and roof and ceiling are the same; the bed you lie in is unchanged from when you fell asleep. Yet something feels different, feels off. A flicking tail catches your eye; you are startled to see the little white cat, which you've occasionally spotted around the island. He (for it seems to you like a "he") is sitting at the end of your bed, gazing with an unnerving intensity.

How did he get in here? Very strange. You reach a tentative hand forward, curious to see if he'll let you stroke.

A voice beside you says, "Little sister? Are you up?"

You jerk abruptly and turn over.

Someone else is lying in the bed behind you; a young girl. She looks frightened. Her face is familiar; like your mother's face, but younger, softened by childhood. She is the spitting image of the photograph that you found in the dresser, many days ago.

"Who—" You gasp, then stop, caught off guard by another shock.

The voice coming out of your throat is not your own. It is reedy and high-pitched, the voice of a child. Lift your hands; look at them. They are not yours, either. Small hands, short and stubby. Look down at your clothes: fisher-girl trousers and loose top. A braid swings from your scalp, neat and tightly pulled.

This is a dream. Of someone else's life, someone else's time, from years distant.

But whose dream? And why are you seeing it?

"Daiyu?" you say, cautiously, because the girl next to you looks so much like your mother, and you are sure she's the girl in the old photo.

"I'm here," she says, and you realize she's trying to soothe you, though she is just a child herself. "It will be okay."

"What will?"

The door bursts open and a frightened-looking old woman comes into the room, her gray hair drawn into a tight bun.

"Ahpo!" Daiyu exclaims. "What's happening?"

"We must go, we must go," your grandmother says, and takes each of you by the hand. "Hurry, they are very angry!"

There are voices, you realize suddenly; men shouting outside the house. The words are indistinct but the threat of them carries, clear and stark.

"Why are they angry?" you say, unnerved by the strangeness.

"The men think you have cursed them." Ahpo half-drags, half-pulls the pair of you toward the back of the house. "They want us to leave. We must go, or the men may be violent!"

How strange, you think dizzily. This is just like the folktale your mother recited once, about the girl who was chased away by superstitious villagers. But how did it end again—

The front door caves, forced open by red-faced fishermen waving sticks and other implements.

Cursed child! Bad-luck demon girl! Storm bringer, ghost talker, ugly bad-luck sorceress!

You know their faces, and feel a wash of anger. These are the men who killed your cat, because they blame you for typhoons and revile you for speaking with ghosts. You *know* they did it, because the cat told you so. When he came back from the dead.

Where is he now? His ghost should still be around.

"Run!" Ahpo says, breaking your chain of thoughts, and the three of you do. Out the back of the house, into the mangroves. Away from the furious, violent, unreasonable villagers.

And still, still, you cannot wake, though you want desperately to do so.

Distance skips and scatters, as it often does in dreams. One moment, you are in the village, holding hands with Daiyu and Ahpo.

The next, you are on the coast: running across the headland cliff, under a lumbering silver moon. With no light pollution, the sky is a bright swathe of celestial bodies, reflecting their shimmer across the sea.

"What are we doing?" you say, to no one in particular.

"Praying at the stone temple. It is beneath our feet," Ahpo says, sounding anxious. "The goddess will keep us safe. Tomorrow, we must leave Shek Ham Chau."

Words come out of your mouth, words that you don't intend to speak: "But the tide is high. We can't cross from the beach to the cave."

"No need to go that far. We can pray from here." She points at the ground.

You look down.

The headland has a crevice, a crack that runs across the top. It is wide enough for two adults to fit comfortably, were it a vertical passageway. Directly beneath it is the Jiaoren Cavern, and within it a stone temple, carved directly into the rock. The roof is visible through that crevice, about thirty feet below you.

"Will she hear us from this place?"

"I believe so," Ahpo says.

"I've brought an offering!" Young Daiyu reaches into her pocket and pulls out a fistful of flower petals, partly wilted and slightly crushed. "Will that work, Ahpo?"

"It will have to do. Hurry, kneel here!"

The three of you kneel. Daiyu and Ahpo begin to whisper a prayer, in soft sync.

> *Goddess of Mercy, Bodhisattva of Compassion*
> *She who hears the cries of the world.*
> *Hear my cries, see the heaviness of my heart.*
> *The waves of sadness that threaten to drown the spark of my spirit.*
> *Help me find the light of hope in this darkness*
> *And follow it back to wholeness—*

If there is anyone who will listen to the sadness of a grandmother and two lonely children on a remote island, it is surely the goddess of mercy.

When the prayer is finished, Ahpo says warily, "I can't hear a ruckus anymore. We can go to my cousin's house, and spend the night there. In the morning, I will find us a way to the mainland."

She stands, giving you a hand up. You take it, and stand with her.

But the ground near the crevice is weaker than any of you realize. It gives way abruptly as Ahpo walks, earth crumbling like the crust of a sweet tart. The ground collapses beneath the three of you, earth and grass shattering like a dropped vase.

Young Daiyu is the farthest away. She leaps to safe ground, panting.

But Ahpo falls through the widening hole in the cavern roof with a frail cry. And you, still holding her hand, fall with her.

"Siu Yin?"

The drop takes seconds. The drop takes thousands of years. Ahpo's bony arms snake around your body as you both plummet, holding you close. There is earth and dirt raining on all sides, hard dark rock rushing up to meet you both—

"Siu Yin!"

⁘

—and you wake.

Nighttime, Shek Ham Chau.

You are in your own bed, soaked in so much sweat that the sheets are damp. Immediately, your skin itches with irritation.

Mami is standing over you, and for one awful, confused moment, she is both old Daiyu the middle-aged mother, and young Daiyu, who is an elder sister.

"Siu Yin!" she says again, looking worried but sounding angry. "Wake up! It's only a dream."

"I'm awake," you protest. "My eyes are open!"

"They were open when you were shouting, too," she says, which shocks you.

"How . . . how long was I . . ."

"A little while. I heard you making noise, and came in when you couldn't seem to wake." Mami looks up and down, adding, "Best if you change out of those clothes."

Nod slowly. It won't do to sleep in clammy, sweat-soaked fabric. Carefully, feeling weirdly embarrassed, you climb out of bed.

"What were you dreaming of?" She hands you a fresh shirt as you peel off the soiled one.

"A nightmare."

"That's obvious," she says, sounding annoyed. "What kind of nightmare?" She's so cold and stiff, not like the younger version you saw moments before.

"I dreamed about your sister."

Mami is still for a long moment. "What do you mean?"

"It was like that folktale you used to tell me, years ago. About the little girl who was driven to her death by superstitious men, because they thought she was a necromancer? Only in this dream, the unlucky girl was your sister." For some reason, it feels weird to admit that *you* were her sister, in the dream—so, you don't. Some inner sense warns you that this will upset her deeply.

Mami grimaces, and says nothing.

"Mami?"

"A ghost dream." She pulls the damp sheets off your bed, piling them on the floor. "It happens, on places which are haunted. Sometimes they can bring on a fever, but you seem to be healthy enough."

"A ghost dream?" You've heard of such things, but never experienced one before. "Was it real, then? What I dreamed about?"

“I’m not a mind reader, I don’t know exactly what you saw,” she snaps, spreading a clean sheet atop the hard, wooden bed. “But the folk story I told you is mostly true. My sister was that girl.”

You stare at her, aghast. “That’s awful. I didn’t know they treated your sister so badly.”

“Most people didn’t. A few of the men didn’t like her, that’s true, but many of the villagers were kind and good,” she says. “Can you get back to sleep?”

“I think so, but I want to write some more wards for my room, first.”

“If you must,” she says, already walking to the door. “Don’t stay up too late.”

“Alright,” you say, but she is already out in the hallway, retreating back to her own room.

Sigh, reach for some paper and ink, and start drawing your fu talisman.

Swiftly, the shape of your days begins to change.

The dream doesn’t return, probably because of your fu talisman, and its details fade with time. It helps that you’re relatively busy in the day. The garden still needs weeding and watering. There are still everyday chores like drawing water, or cleaning the house. Apparently, the ghosts no longer feel the need to do it, now that you’ve moved in.

Between you and Mami, those tasks get done, more or less. If there’s the odd day that someone forgets to tend the garden, or a few extra plates are left lying around, neither of you comments. Truthfully, you’re rushing through those activities, mind elsewhere, and she is doing the same.

After lunch, you both drift apart to separate worlds. You don’t even make excuses to Mami anymore, nor does she in reverse. Simply disappear to swim, and she hardly notices. Mami spends her free time talking or dancing with the dead, locked in a fantasy where you are not welcome or needed.

It would bother you more, if you didn’t have Sea Sister.

Always, you seek out the isolated places, the bits of coastline that require a scramble in low tide across slippery rocks—and you’re mindful of those barnacles now, having learned your lesson there—to reach little strips of shore where the riptide is a fiendish trickster and where your friend, your Sea Sister, is likely to lurk.

You arrive at the beach to find, always and every time, that Sea Sister is waiting as usual. She circles in the depths like an ocean serpent.

“I’m here,” you call out, feet planted in the sand.

Beneath the water, she smiles wide in answer.

Step free of your shirt and trousers. Throw your hair into a tucked bun, tie it tight, and leap into the cool green sea with hands splayed and knees bent. As the currents swirl round, you reach out, taking her extended hand; she pulls you close and the pair of you cut through the water at her knifing, lurching speed.

You play tag games in the water most afternoons, which of course you cannot ever win, even when she closes her eyes and twists a hand behind her back. Still, it's fun. She catches fish, caging them in her long-fingered hands so that you can see them up close. Sometimes urchins, too, and once an octopus. The octopus isn't afraid, and wraps a tentacle thoughtfully around your wrist before jetting off.

Sea Sister is as dangerous as the ocean itself. Logically, you know this. She has those teeth for a reason, and once or twice—when meeting a shark in the open waters—she has snapped her jaws in their direction. None of them stick around; animals have enough sense to recognize death when they see it.

But also like the ocean, Sea Sister is magical and beautiful, and you can't get enough of her. Of the two options—spending time with a monster, or spending time with ghosts—you know which you'd rather choose.

Sometimes, she peers through the tendrils of her dark, water-logged hair, and you glimpse how others might see her: lurking, cruel, dangerous. A twisted and hungry creature. Sometimes, she will dance by spinning through the water in a whirl of gaunt limbs, a sight as terrifying as it is fascinating.

Then she smiles, dives, cavorts, and there is only Sea Sister again. Fierce and fiercely lonely, savage and savagely beautiful. She belongs only to you; the light that dazzles your eyes alone.

And you know with every filament of your being that these are the good days, the bright hours and best moments of your life, and that their like will never come again.

There is only one thing amiss: communication is difficult.

You can hear her just fine, but she cannot hear *you* so well. Human speech is not meant for watery atmospheres, and sound carries with difficulty. Whatever anatomy that allows her voice to carry is something you don't possess.

You develop a system, of sorts. When you have something complex to say, you make a sign, indicating she should come close. Sea Sister swims right beneath the surface, ear cocked toward you, while you murmur words just above the water line.

Increasingly, you find yourself talking to her a lot. Sometimes you'll spend a whole afternoon just floating in the water, or clinging to rocks, whispering to her about yourself, almost skin-to-skin. She is the sister you never had, the mother you always wanted; that alone is addictive.

You tell her about growing up in the city, how your first memory is of the small, cramped flat, exhausted parents and pollution and streetlights. Later, a memory of playing on a sticky floor with the neighbors' children. They are quiet and well-behaved; you are rambunctious and restless, earning frustrated scolds from Mami.

Even then, you were slowly realizing that the world didn't want your noise and movement; it wanted your silence, your easy presence. Society desired that you never make yourself heard, never be inconvenient.

You talk to Sea Sister about school, and the stern nuns who followed a faith that bored and confused you, of their Western deity who eschewed wealth and animal sacrifices, yet demanded tithing and killed his own son.

About your mother, difficult and sad and struggling, who forgot how to be happy and never remembered. Her anger, her unfairness, her wild reactions and unnatural attachment to the ghost villagers.

About the war that overshadows everything, about the jewel of China—Shanghai, that is—falling and taking all its culture, its Eastern jazz and modern poetry, its trade and glitz and glamour, into fire and ruin forever.

About the agonized ghosts who multiply across the country, millions upon millions of traumatized dead inflicting fresh woe on those left behind. About the air raid sirens that scream like demons, about the torture and starvation of Chinese people in other cities.

You talk about Baba's abandonment. He would have joined you here by now if he were still alive. Something must have happened to the city, after you left. Mami thinks so, certainly; it is driving her mad.

You talk about the disconnection and surreality of it all.

And Sea Sister puts her hand on your cheek, nodding with sorrowful understanding. She murmurs in liquid tones: *Lonely girl. Sad girl. Ghost girl, living on a ghost island.*

A lump forms in your throat. You feel like a ghost girl, certainly.

Partly deflecting, mostly curious, you whisper, "Are you lonely, too?" The first real question you've dared to ask her.

Sea Sister flashes away from the rocks, swims a long slow loop, then returns to say softly, *In the ocean, no one can cry without drowning. Sorrow is silent beneath the waves.*

Her answer makes your heart hurt.

Unsure what to say, you tell her that in the city, all the noise drowns out the sorrow. A girl can cry there, but no one will hear it over the noise of people, traffic, vehicles. And that's before the air raid sirens, the bombs exploding.

Talking about the city interests her a lot, and soon you're describing Hong Kong in-depth. Streets, cars, buses, thronging crowds, docks full of ships are alien concepts to Sea Sister. You wonder why she never ventures past the coast of Sai Kung, why she doesn't just swim down to the harbor, but you decide not to mention it. Selfishly, you're afraid that putting such an idea in her head will encourage her to abandon you for other adventures.

Whatever the reason, she eats up your chatter about the city eagerly enough, and you get the sense that it appeals to her. She isn't sharing your indifference to that cancerous urban sprawl.

When you get tired of describing it, you bring her clippings from old newspapers—Mami used them to pack fragile things in your luggage—and show them to her.

The first time you give her a photograph clipping, passing it to her underneath the water, she stares and stares, those sea lion eyes grown huge and round in her face. Her fingers tremble as they trace the outlines of a burgeoning cityscape that she has never seen.

It doesn't take long before the thin paper crumbles from the ocean's wet erosion, taking her delighted smile with it.

The sea washes everything away, she says, and looks so mournful and listless that you can't help but want to fix it for her. Anything to see your closest ever friend smile.

It's then that you have your best idea yet: glass bottles.

"Wait here," you tell her. "I'll be right back!"

22

THE TEMPLE

Thirty-three years ago . . .

The house is cold as ice as you set foot across the threshold. It is almost a relief from the boiling heat outside except that the unnaturalness of it makes you feel uneasy. Maybe you should be moving out? It's not the first time the thought has occurred to you lately.

Mami is standing in the kitchen, smiling vacantly. To your shock, she is wearing her one fancy dress that somehow made it to the island: a blue and pink qipao, beautifully embroidered and brought with her all the way from Shanghai. In all the years of your childhood, she has only ever worn it once.

She wears it now, singing a modern Chinese jazz song you've never heard before. The ghosts gather around her to listen and are bolder, less concerned with what you think. Her voice trails away as you come in, though.

"Why are you here?" Mami says, distractedly. "What are you doing?"

"I need a bottle to store water, while I am out." The lie springs to your lips with ease. "It is so hot these days." The sight of her makes you uncomfortable, so you busy yourself digging through the cupboards, because it's an excuse to keep your back turned.

"That's fine." Her finger is tapping the wooden table. Keeping time for the music. Several of the ghosts start playing on bamboo flutes, filling the silence her singing left. "Try not to get sunstroke out there," she adds, kind of randomly. Like she's grasping quickly for something motherly sounding to say.

"Try not to freeze in here," you shoot back, unable to resist a barb.

"It is my turn to sing again, soon," she says, and it's unclear whether she is talking to you or to them. Either way, you get the sense she's just waiting for you to leave.

You manage to find one old beer bottle, long empty and dry, and put it into a canvas bag. There will definitely be others around, but this will do for now. Some stacks of old newspaper go in next, along with a fishing knife for cutting, some oilcloth rags, twine, one of Baba's old notebooks, a few other things.

As you head for the door, Mami says suddenly, "Wait."

You pause in annoyance, fingers on the handle. "Yes?"

"You will stay out of the water." She isn't phrasing it as a question. There's a curious flatness creeping into her voice. "Please, daughter."

"Isn't it your turn to sing?" you retort.

A few months ago, she'd have berated you for such a rude reply, and yelled till your ears glowed red. Strange to think how you used to cringe from someone whom you can just ignore these days.

No scolding this time. She just blinks, very slowly. "Yes, I should . . . get singing." And she wanders back into the living room, attention focused on the deathly music.

You can't get out of the house fast enough.

Back at the beach, out again in the hot, soothing sunshine, you put your worries into a mental box. One thing at a time: the mission for Sea Sister is occupying the moment. Worrying about Mami's madness can come later, when you have to deal with her in the evening.

Squatting on the sand, open the bag and set to work. The knife is used to shred the old newspapers, clipping out pictures of Hong Kong with its boats and ferries and trading houses, all bustling around a choppy harbor.

Next comes the bottle. Pick up a photograph, partly roll it, and drop it in. The picture curves convex against the bottle's interior. Next, though it feels almost disrespectful to do so, you rip out a sheet of the paper from one of Baba's old notebooks, scribble a quick message, and slot it lengthwise into the last glass bottle. You don't know if Sea Sister can read, but it doesn't matter. You can read it to her, if she needs.

And because there is extra space (the paper is only narrow) you also slip in a single photograph of you and Mami on the other side: taken two years ago, at great expense. In it, you and she stand side by side, stiff and pale in the black-and-white grain, hands clasped at the front. Mami wears a severe frown to match her dark clothes; you have a slight smile, undermined by an ill-fitting cheongsam. Not much of a photo, but all you have to give.

When all of that is done, the bottles get returned to the carry bag and you stand, striding toward the beach. Splash back to the ocean with these newly made prizes.

This is the sort of kindness you are capable of, and as a goddess of mercy, I have always loved that trait in you.

Sea Sister appreciates it, certainly. She trembles like a reed when you hand her the bottle with its preserved pictures inside. A picture frame for ocean dwellers.

"Yours forever," you say. "Bottles will last a long time."

She turns it over and over in disbelief, handling it with amazed reverence. Finally, she traces a finger over the scrap of paper, with its small message.

"A message from me, in case you forget," you say, and can't quite meet her gaze.

Sea Sister whispers the words you have written:

From Shore Sister to Sea Sister: may we always be friends forever.

Sea Sister looks at you for a long moment from beneath the water. Then something extraordinary happens: she lurches out of the ocean, crouching on the rocks under the sun's bright gleam.

You yelp and fall backward, more startled than afraid. The entire time you've known her, she hasn't surfaced, and the natural assumption has been that she can't.

Quickly, you realize why she doesn't. That beautiful, pale-green skin begins to dry out, tiny cracks forming at the creases of her joints. Just like a stranded jellyfish. Her pearly eyes turn red and veiny, as if exposed to a hot oven. This creature belongs in the ocean, and being out of it surely causes her pain.

She presses a clammy palm to your sunburned cheek. *Thank you, Shore Sister.* Her touch drops away, but the coolness of it lingers.

"Do you like it? Is that okay?"

I love it, she says, in a voice like foam on rocks. *No one else gives me gifts. No one else remembers me. Everyone left me.*

"Who left you, Sea Sister?" Strange chills are going through you, despite the warmth of the day, despite the soupy water. There is something here, a moment happening and you do not want to miss it. "Who forgot you?"

A question for a question. There's a challenge to her voice. *Who do you think I am? When you know that, you will know who left me and forgot me.*

"I think," you say, carefully, "that you are the reason my mother warned me against swimming. I think when she speaks of sharks in the water, she is thinking of you."

Sea Sister makes a strange noise, low in her throat; after a moment, you realize she is laughing. *What do* you *think, Shore Sister?*

"I think you are like nothing else on this island. Everything here is so dead, but you are so alive, so fierce." You pause, searching for the words. "I wish I was like you. I wish I could be free and strong, swimming the waves as a jiaoren."

Is that . . . what you want? Sea Sister peers from beneath the sweep of her kelp-tangled hair. *I can make that happen, Shore Sister. I can make you like me.*

"Really?" Astonishment blooms in your heart. "Do you have that power?"

I do. If you trust me, if you want it, then come with me. And she extends sleek green fingers, skin frazzling in the sun.

You don't even hesitate. Her hand fits neatly against yours, and you squeeze it tight.

Sea Sister smiles and murmurs, *Hold your breath!* as she tucks the gifted glass bottle under her other skeletal arm, and pulls you into the water.

Sea Sister swims a long way.

Amidst the whirl of water and fish and sunlight and coral, you become disoriented, losing all sense of direction. The shore is visible to one side but she's swimming so fast there's no time to gauge how far it is, or which bit of the island.

One last surface breach for a gulp of air, and then she dives a second time.

This is deeper than you've ever gone, ears popping. Fifty feet? More? Hard to say. Strangely, it's easy to hold your breath, easier to see than it was before you met her. You're getting used to doing that, after all these months. Still, the suddenness of the descent is a little unpleasant.

Your lungs are beginning to ache again by the time she starts angling up and it is hard, hard, hard not to panic because she's drawn you somewhere with a strong current and no light. Rock walls scrape your arms, and the space is extraordinarily narrow.

She has pulled you into some kind of undersea tunnel. The realization is alarming. Press tight against her, not wanting to be smashed against the sides, trying not to flail in that deep-set darkness, the cold salt, the long slow crawl. As if you are passing through death itself.

Up she rises, much too fast. But the pressure on your body eases as you ascend to shallower depths, and it gets a little easier to keep that breath in, air expanding in your lungs. That much is a relief.

Light grows around you, softening the dark. The tunnel widens rapidly. Deep ink giving way to paler and paler shades of verdant water until, finally, whole body hurting, you break the surface.

Ten extended seconds while you pant and gasp. Chill air floods your throat and chest. A pulse hammers in your head; it's too much, too soon. You have the vague idea that diving and surfacing the way you have been is not really a good idea, though you don't have the technical expertise to be more specific. All you know for the moment is that a headache is festering in your skull, and your joints feel a little odd.

Sea Sister is beside and beneath you, keeping your fatigued, dizzy head above water. You turn on your back and float, inhaling until the starbursts disappear from your vision and the rush of adrenaline dies down. Only then do you look around.

The underwater passage has brought you to a cave.

Wet walls drip and shimmer in the faint light. The rock is layered in striations of red and brown, the color of blood at different stages of freshness. Not all of it is enclosed; the wall behind you is partly open, with a large hole facing out toward the sea. Like an enormous window set into stone. Technically accessible by land, but you understand why Sea Sister did not take you that way.

Although it has a good view of the horizon, the cave's "dry" entrance is treacherous: there would be a sheer climb to get in or out, and on the other side a maze of whirlpools and sharp rocks, which one would have to edge around to reach safer terrain.

The ceiling is high and rent with gaps. Sunbeams pierce the darkness, creating odd refractions and shadows. In heavy rain, this place becomes a forest of waterfalls, all dribbling and rivuleting away.

It is the Jiaoren Cavern, you realize with shock. Whose sea-facing entrance is difficult to access. The one containing a shrine to Kwun Yam, or possibly Ma Zu.

Slowly get to your feet in that chest-deep pool. Slowly turn around, half knowing already what you will see.

A stone temple rises at the far end of the cavern where the water is shallowest, carved straight into the rock itself, and illuminated by faint light, which trickles through gaps in the stalactite-riddled ceiling.

A thousand details catch the eye, all of them coalescing into a strange and surreal picture. Rough-hewn walls rise from the water. A pyramid roof protrudes outward, edges curled up like ancient pagodas, with a spike at the top. The entrance is open, no door in it, and within you can see something that looks like a statue, with a low-lying table—altar? shrine?—in front.

"Amazing," you whisper aloud, and the sound reverberates in a multitude of soft echoes.

There is no one else here, yet the cave is noisy as a crowd. Every drop—and they are legion—seems to echo and reverberate; every lapping wave is a ringing slap. As you stumble forward, relieved to be in water shallow enough to stand, your sloshing is cacophonous. Sound cannot escape this place, bouncing and snagging on every surface.

Sea Sister stands up, comes to walk beside you. Water sluices off the bony angles and flat planes of her form. She doesn't instantly burn or dry when out of the water, and that's either from lack of direct sunlight, or something about the cave is special. Perhaps both.

She drifts to the side of the cavern, where there is a sort of crevice in the rocks, and wedges your glass bottle gift into it, very carefully. Preserving it where she can see. It's rather sweet.

"It's beautiful, this cavern." The words boom and echo. "But why did you bring me here?"

This place is special to me. Her voice is the same as always, yet for the first time it strikes you that it doesn't sound . . . quite right. *Go, Siu Yin. Step within the temple.* She lifts one hand, and points.

Cloudy water stirs with each step. At no point are your feet dry. Even in low tide, the ocean flows into the temple itself; the entire floor stands in several inches of salt water.

You hover just beyond the archway, unwilling to venture farther. The cavern isn't well lit, and the interior of the shrine has no light at all, beyond what seeps through the archway.

A commanding statue waits within, and you recognize the figure at once. The peaceful face, the modest half smile. The multitude of arms and eyes, to reach all living creatures on earth. Long robes flow from head to toe. One hand holds some kind of relic, though time and tides have crumbled it to dust. The hat and clothes and relic remind you of Ma Zu, and you remember what your mother said about the villagers: that they viewed Ma Zu as simply an incarnation of Kwun Yam. An interesting belief, if unorthodox.

Step closer, peering into the temple. You have always known Kwun Yam as a lady goddess, but older texts sometimes portray them as a man. This statue is somewhere in between, the gender indeterminate and the features neutral. Kwun Yam transcends gender, and can be either. The statue is stunning regardless.

Curiously, you feel starkly different in here, in a way that is hard to explain. Cleaner, almost; as if your mind has been sinking into sand from the moment you arrived at this island, and something has rinsed it all away. You're more awake.

Yes. Definitely more awake. The days on Shek Ham Chau have been congealing together like soup left overnight. Standing in this temple is a cold slap of clarity.

"Why are we here?" you say, out loud. "Is this where I can become a jiaoren?"

You turn around, or try to, but Sea Sister grips your arms, keeping you facing forward.

Keep moving.

Is she even speaking? You'd think that would be an easy thing to determine and yet, for the first time, you're unsure whether she is actually, physically talking, or you're just . . . hearing her. Inside your head.

Keep moving, she says again, insistent, and points. *Go into the temple. Go see.*

You do as she suggests, stepping beneath the archway with extreme reluctance.

Carvings are etched into the stone walls, beautifully done but—like the statue—suffering from the erosion of centuries. Most are barely discernible, now, which is why you did not see them straightaway in the half-darkness. The closest one looks more like someone has attacked the stone with an axe.

Hesitant, reverent, uncertain, you edge a little farther into the temple, trying in vain to get a glimpse of the stories depicted within.

Against the far wall is a shrine, on which a collection of pearls and shiny ocean rocks have been piled by unknown hands in ages past. A curious and unconventional offering, but you suppose incense wouldn't work well in so damp a place.

The carvings are easier to see from here. Most are ruinous beyond deciphering, but three of them stand out. The biggest mural shows a scene you don't recognize: of Kwun Yam descending to an underwater world, while strange beings surround her with offerings. They have fins and scales and fish-like faces with lidded eyes, their appearance closer to aquatic than human. Tails instead of legs, too.

Jiaoren. *Flood dragon people.* You touch the carvings thoughtfully, entranced by the depictions. Again, this is a story you'd associate more with Ma Zu, and the bleed-over with Kwun Yam is as weird as it is confusing. You take another step forward, and something crunches beneath one foot.

Glance down.

And almost retch, despite yourself. For here on the temple floor are the long-rotted remains of a girl's corpse.

Mami's story flashes through your head, mixing with the strange ghost dream you had some weeks ago. A little girl, thought to be unlucky. Chased to the headland where she fell into this cave, and then left to die.

It should be impossible. A body in this damp, ocean-washed place would have disintegrated long ago. Yet somehow, you sense innately that this is indeed the sister that Mami spoke of, and whom you dreamed of. Preserved by some supernatural influence.

A hideous suspicion is beginning to creep over you.

Hesitant and slow, you walk back out into the echoing cavern. For the first time in months, your brain is alert and sharp as the rocks underfoot, your senses unfogged by the island's strange, dreamy atmosphere. The temple has that effect, its divinity cutting through like a knife.

There in the dim light of Kwun Yam's sacred temple, Sea Sister stands revealed.

Gone is the heady aura that made her seem alluring. You perceive her as she truly is: the starved ruination of her body, bones sketched beneath graying skin. The ragged claws and serrated teeth. Her eyes are not divinely white, but dead and filmed over. Like that of a corpse.

"You . . . are not a jiaoren," you say, swallowing. "This temple to Kwun Yam depicts her as Ma Zu going beneath the sea. She extends her compassion to all creatures, above and below the waves. But you are not like the jiaoren she met."

No fins, no gills, no scales. No fish tail.

No magic, only horror.

Please, Sea Sister says, except she really isn't speaking in the physical sense. Her words are a whisper inside your head, watery and echoing. *Please, Siu Yin. Don't run.*

"Sea Sister," you say, shakily, "tell me who you are."

You need her to say it. The truth matters.

She inches closer, holding your face with her long, clammy hands. *Let me show you,* she says, and presses her forehead to yours. *See for yourself.*

23

WATER GHOST

? years ago . . .

Water laps you to wakefulness, cold and fishy-smelling. Cough and splutter; you are lying on an uneven, rocky surface, covered in several inches of seawater that swirls gently back and forth. If you had landed face-down, you might have drowned, but you have landed on your back.

Above, the cavern roof gapes larger than it did before. The edges of it have crumbled in, widening the crevice. The temple itself—a mere handful of steps away, you have landed within clear sight of its arched doorway—is the same as always: quiet, peaceful, beautiful, ancient. Nothing changed there.

Head spinning, you try to sit up. It is hard work. Your legs do not move, nor do your hips. You cannot feel any pain, only heaviness, and that worries you. Dazed and anxious, you look around.

And start screaming.

You've landed atop your grandmother, whose body has cushioned the fall. Ahpo's head and belly are smashed open, entrails and brain matter and bones everywhere. She is very dead. Like the victims in Shanghai and other bombed cities, you think, then feel confused because that thought makes no sense.

A shadow drifts across the patch of light. Look up; it is Daiyu, face full of terror and horror. She cries at you with confused, warbling words that are choked through her tears.

"Are you okay, little sister? Where is . . . oh, no! Ahpo!"

"Help me," you plead, because everything feels real and not any longer like it is a dream. A real and visceral terror is spreading through your veins. "Please, big sister!"

"I will!" she promises, sobbing. "I will go get help!"

"Don't leave me alone!"

"I can't get you out on my own, there's no path down anymore," Daiyu says. "I'll be back." She disappears from sight, her promise lingering as an echo that bounces off the cavern walls.

The time passes.

The tide rises.

Tears are all that remain. You cry for a while, because you are still just a girl, not even six, and the shock of it is awful. You regret everything you have ever done, your whole life and existence, and all that you have brought to this world; none of it is good.

But soon enough, the self-recrimination fades, replaced by resentment. The islanders who came knocking share this blame. They feared you, used you as a convenient excuse for everything that went wrong on Shek Ham Chau. Including the death of your parents. It is their fault you are here.

And above it all, your grandmother did not deserve to die like this. She did nothing wrong.

You are angry. So terribly, terribly angry about all of it.

Waves wash higher, slapping your belly. The tide is coming in, and when it does, the cavern will flood. You must not lie here crying, and need to get out first. Anger can come later.

Surge upright, away from the soggy, stinking mess that used to be Ahpo. Already, the ocean is dispersing the flesh and blood into a miasma. Leaning forward, you try to pull yourself along the ground.

Agony fires nerves in your back and sides from the heave of movement. That, you do feel, but only in your ribs, which are extremely tender. Something in there is broken, or at least bruised very badly. Your legs still feel nothing.

The panic becomes cloying. If you can't walk, you can't get out of here, and that will be a death sentence. At the moment, the cavern is covered in half a foot of water, and that's in low tide. In a few hours' time, it will rise enough that you will be in over your head.

No one can swim or climb with paralyzed legs. If someone doesn't help soon, you will drown down here.

Just when you are about to despair, more shadows populate the shrinking patch of sunlight. Again, you look up, and again, you find the view obscured. Not by one head, but by several. The villagers are here, leaning over the edge. You can't quite pick out their faces.

A fragment of joy lifts your spirits. Daiyu has kept her promise, and told someone.

"Help me," you plead, anguished that your weak voice doesn't carry very well.

No one answers you, but snippets of conversation trickle down in drips and fragments.

". . . girl . . . too weak now . . ."

"—is that the little girl? Horrible—"

". . . high tide! High tide in a few hours!"

". . . treacherous . . . stairs damaged . . ."

". . . Heaven's will . . . God's plan . . . is what she deserves."

You stare up in horrified disbelief. They really are going to do it: they will leave you here to die.

As the villagers leave, one figure leans out farther: your big sister, Daiyu.

"I'm sorry!" She is crying, begging for your forgiveness. "I'm so sorry, little sister!"

"Stay," you beg her, because you know she can't help anymore. "Just stay with me!"

"I can't," she wails, sounding desperate. "I don't want to watch!"

She disappears from sight for the last time. Your wordless screaming follows her. It is a sound that will pursue her for the rest of her life.

The time passes.

The tide rises.

No one comes.

Every so often you try moving your legs, pinching them even, but it's as if the legs are no longer there, just a strange and inanimate curiosity attached to the body.

Even sitting up, the water is at your chest now. Your head is clear and you can breathe, though not for much longer. However, your body is floating, you realize. Eventually, you'll sink again. But for now, it's a help; you can move, slightly. Enough for one last effort, one last burst of energy.

You twist round, crawling on your hands, dead legs buoyed by the ocean. Crawl inch by agonizing inch into the temple and hold on to the carved statue of Kwun Yam. Things are not working in your body. Dark patches of bruising are spreading all along your skin; you feel cold, a sickly chill in your very marrow that simply will not abate. Small cuts abound, trickling with blood. Still, you persevere.

Ocean water rushes into the cavern, and you begin to flounder. There is very little light here, just darkness and water and echoes braided with shadows. Grab the statue, struggling to pull yourself a little higher out of the tide.

A soft meow; you look up.

Your cat is there, or rather his spirit is. Still small and white, the way he died when the men of the village crushed his head with a rock out of spite. He deserved better, and you were relieved when his ghost returned.

"Bao," you say, softly, and it fills you with wavering joy to see him.

The cat curls in the crook of Lady Kwun Yam's arm. He peers down at you with red, red eyes.

"Goddess," you rasp, and the stone temple catches your soft words, flinging them around the crags and crevices of the walls and ceiling. "Please do not forget about me, the way my village has. Please remember my death!"

Almost, you could swear that the statue turns its head, ever so slightly, to look down.

The tides flood as you dip a finger into your own blood, and write your name on the statue's cold surface. And because you want to be sure, you don't just write it once. You write everywhere you can reach on Kwun Yam's statue. Even if the water washes some of it away, you keep doing it. There's plenty of blood, at least.

Over and over, you beg the silent goddess to remember you, pleading with the heavens and the underworld and any other being you think will listen, to let you return as a ghost.

"Let me catch them," you whisper into the dark, "and hold them, and drag them to the water, and keep them down until their blood is salt and their eyes are food for fishes, and there is nothing left of them but empty skin!"

It is the curse of a little child: simple, repetitive, mean-spirited as only children can be when angered.

The villagers were right in one respect: you do have a kind of power. When you are angry, bad things can happen. And now you are angrier and sadder than you have ever been. Though you cannot prevent your own death, you can certainly twist your own spirit in the process.

You don't know that, not yet. All you know at this point is exhaustion, and agony. Pain conquers every part of your body that you can still feel; numbness has claimed the rest.

Alone and defeated, you open your mouth to the waiting sea and draw it in like breath—

⁂

The ghost dream fades.

You are yourself once more: cold, damp, shivering in a dark cave. Nose to nose with Sea Sister, her forehead pressed against yours, her horrifying gaze locked with your own.

Fear rockets through your body. You've been close to her before, swum side-by-side and face-to-face, but it's different now, in this sacred place, with the glamour stripped from your eyes.

For beneath that cold skin, she is made of stillness: no heartbeat, no rush of blood, no intake of breath. She is not thin from hunger or malnutrition, but from decay. Internal organs she no longer needs have atrophied into almost nothing.

She is no mermaid, nor even a monster. Sea Sister is a corporeal spirit.

Shuigui. Water ghost.

I don't think you should go swimming.

A memory rises in your mind: Mami's anxious face, the first day you arrived.

You will stay out of the water.

Sea Sister, beautiful and dangerous, sharp-toothed and luminous.

In the ocean, no one can cry without drowning.

Clawed, green fingers, snaking around your wrist.

No one else remembers me.

The sharks who feared to approach, watching you from the depths.

It was an accident.

Words crowd in your head, only to fade in your throat. Hot and cold, hot and cold. Your body moves from flushed to a slight shiver, and back again; your hand, still clutched in her emaciated grasp.

"Ghost!" you cry, ripping free of her. "You are a dead person, like the other islanders, up in the village!"

She nods her head slightly, a single dip and lift of the chin.

"It was you." The words croak from your throat. "The little girl I dreamed of. The one who summons storms, and speaks to spirits."

Sea Sister hides her face. She looks like she wants to cry and you remember what she told you days or perhaps weeks ago, that sorrow is silent beneath the sea.

Idiot. *Idiot.*

You should have figured it out sooner.

Except, a small part of you has always known. If you're truly, unflinchingly honest. This is a ghost island, after all, according to the people on the mainland—a place inhabited and overrun by its former storm-wracked villagers.

What else could Sea Sister have ever been, but another one of Shek Ham Chau's lost spirits? No different from the creeping, selfish dead who hound your mother day and night.

Worse, in fact, because this girl and her rage are what summoned a storm and killed the village. She's not just a dead child. She's an angry, twisted, *vengeful* dead child, and she has brought you to the place she died so that you can die where she died, your corpse keeping her remains company.

A terrible revulsion is growing in you, where there was only certainty and excitement before.

"Please let me go home," you whisper. "I want to see my mother!"

Home? She lifts her head from her hands. *But you said you wanted to be like me. To become as I am, free and strong and forever swimming. We will be together in the ocean, forever and ever and ever.*

Her words fill you with ice. You thought she was your friend, but she was only doing what a ghost always does: trying to charm its victims, for its own dark reasons. How many stories have you read or heard about ghosts who trick men into marrying them? About demons who weasel their way into homes, only to kill at their leisure?

How stupid you've been.

"Sea Sister, you are dead, and I am alive!" The shout tears from your throat. "The dead have no claim on the living. I want to go home!"

No. NO. This isn't how it was supposed to go! Sea Sister bares her teeth, head thrown back. The temperature in the cavern drops from cool to a crisp chill. You shiver violently, teeth clacking. *Everyone leaves me. It isn't fair! You were supposed to be my friend! MY FRIEND. That is why I brought you here, to where I died. I trusted you to* love *me, when you saw how they treated me!*

She reaches for you, claws extended, and fear snaps your paralysis like a shard of ice. You leap away from her, back into the temple.

Come here! Come here, right now! Sea Sister surges out of the water to follow, but stops at the temple's doorway. She does not cross the threshold; can't set foot on it. Her pitiless dead gaze bores into you. How did you ever find such a creature beautiful, or loving?

Sea Sister senses her mistake. She tries to soften, baring her teeth in a smile. *Come out, Siu Yin. It is time to swim.*

"Where are we swimming to?" you call back, shakily.

You said you wanted to be like me. Don't you still want that?

"I thought you were a jiaoren, not a ghost! You *tricked* me!"

Sea Sister shrieks like an oncoming train and you clap both hands over your ears, because the sound is unbearably loud in this echoing cavern. She is in a rage, and it is the rage of a child being thwarted.

Surrounded by a swell of water, she flings herself against the temple doorway.

Water floods through, leaving you soaked and gasping. But that's all it is: ocean water. She cannot pass temple doors as a ghost. Not now, not ever. Even in this forgotten place, my presence has a power she can't defy.

One final scream, and the ghost of Shek Ham Chau flings herself violently into the cavern's waters. A sucking whirlpool forms from the speed of her departure as she plunges down and out, away from the cavern.

"Go, young one. Now, while the tide is low, and the rocks can be crossed."

You whip your head around. There is no one else here.

But within the shadows of the temple, light is glimmering across the statue's stern face. My eyes, looking out at you, through one of my many avatars.

"Lady Kwun Yam?" you whisper. "Do you speak, goddess?"

The lights flash stronger. "GO! There is no time to explain. Get your mother and leave, before it is too late!"

Shakily rise to your feet, and look upward through the crevice. The sky is darkening, thickening. A storm is brewing. Sea Sister's childlike rage is building to a storm.

Exhaustion fills you. It is years in the making, this tiredness. Grief, fear, stress, loneliness are all things which wring the body and tax the heart, and you have carried so many of those for so long, despite your youth.

But the murdering spirit of your aunt is coming to drown Shek Ham Chau yet again, until you are as dead as the rest of the village. Until you are a lonely raging spirit, like she is.

So you get to your damn feet and you run, out of the cave mouth over jagged, slick rocks, on hands and knees. Fast as you can, like your life depends on it.

Because it does.

24

IF SHE'D LOVED YOU MORE

Thirty-three years ago . . .

One upside to Shek Ham Chau being small is that it does not take you long to get home. Perhaps fifteen minutes of running hard, and you finally arrive, still caked in muck. Feet sliced and battered by sharp rocks.

A vision of the underworld greets you. Ghosts drift, lumber, and throng near the house. Some sit on the ground outside, their dripping and storm-lashed forms looking almost relaxed. Others pick away at the garden or the roof, as if working. Some are lost in re-enactments of their own deaths. Most of the village is present, not just Mami's family.

Guilt creeps over you, for ignoring your mother so much these past few months. It hasn't been healthy, the way she's been drawn into the ghost life of her childhood. And sure, it isn't fair how Mami prefers the company of the dead to spending time with you. She chose to reject you first. But she is your mother, and you gave up on her. You found it easier to escape with the shuigui and let Mami speak to those who could never answer her with joy, light, or life.

That decision is on you.

"Mami?" Calling out in advance, in case she is spooked by your unexpected return. "Mami, where are you?" Up the two creaking steps, press your palm to the left-ajar door and ease in.

Mami kneels in the living room, eyes closed, surrounded by a swirling tangle of spirits. Some caress her hair, her skin. Others speak or sing in her ear. Some play their bamboo flutes, as if soothing her. Mami's skin is tinted with a strange, sickly pallor, and her body sways to a disjointed rhythm. It is far worse than simply speaking to the ghosts; this is intimate and intrusive, grotesquely so.

You are reminded of yourself, not an hour ago, in the cavern. Standing outside the temple, charmed by a dead girl. Maybe you and your mother are not so different after all. It strikes you with a sudden cold fright that, just perhaps, both of you are equally lost in this place.

"Sung Daiyu, wake the hell up!" Yelling her proper name, because you no longer care about disturbing her, and she isn't responding to "Mami." Time to rouse from the nightmare. To the ghosts, you yell, "Stop dancing, you demented pieces of shit!"

The dead villagers halt their chaotic whirling, turning to look with eyes bulging from bloated faces. Being rude to ghosts is extremely shocking.

"You . . . are back early," Mami answers at last, sounding drunk. But there's no alcohol on the island, hasn't been for months since she finished those measly few bottles of beer. "Early . . . why are you . . . early?"

"Aiyah, will you listen to me!" Can't help it; you grasp her shoulders, giving her a hard shake. Her teeth clack from the force. "Little Sister is summoning a storm. Just like the one that drowned your village! If we don't leave the island, we'll be caught in it!"

"You . . . swam with my sister," she says, in a flat, confused tone. "I said . . . I told you to stay away from the temple. The ocean."

A hot flush is creeping through your face. "Why? So I wouldn't find out how everyone abandoned a child to her death? Is that what you don't want me to know? Because it's too late for secrets!"

"We didn't kill her," Mami snaps, anger pulling her together. "She fell, *she fell*! It was an accident, Siu Yin! It could easily have been me."

"Ghosts come back when they aren't laid to rest!" You're shouting and can't stop. "Her bones are in that cavern, Mami! Why didn't anyone bury her?"

She cringes. "Some of the men, the elders . . . they said it was fate. Said she was cursed, and touching her would bring us back luck. The Catholic priest spoke a prayer over her bones, and everyone thought it would be enough."

"Well that clearly wasn't true, was it?"

Mami buried her face in her hands.

"I deserved to know all this," you say, wound tight with raging anger. "You've lied to me, from the moment we landed here."

"I was trying to protect you!"

"By bringing me to an island of ghosts?" Fury swarms you. "By dancing with your dead, submerging in your memories, insulting me, and chasing me away when you find me annoying?" Somehow, your voice has risen to a near scream. "I hate being here with you! I wish Baba had come and you had stayed behind!"

"*Baba is already dead!*" she shrieks back.

Your mouth is hanging open. Surely it can't be true. You want to speak but your voice seems tangled in your throat.

"He took his own life!" Mami wails, fingers knotted through her hair. "That man is a coward who walked off into the night and threw himself into the harbor. Your precious father left us alone to our fate!"

"No." Head shaking, whole body rejecting this revelation. "His note said—"

"I wrote that, not him. His real note, you never saw. I read it before you woke. It was cruel, and sad. I couldn't let you have that truth. But now . . ." Her strength is gone; she slumps in your grasp.

"I don't believe you—"

"I kept the note," she says. "It's in my room. Inside the blue vase."

Wordlessly, you stalk away from her, down the short hallway, and into her space. Usually it would be tidy, but dishes and dirty clothes are lying on the floor, poorly attended to.

Almost, you don't want to find it, but there it is: a crackling slip of paper, tucked into the vase's narrow mouth.

You read it in absolute silence. Then you read it three more times, until a veil of tears obscures the written characters. The paper slips from your fingers and you don't bother picking it up.

I won't repeat the last words your father ever penned. Better that they stay lost.

Though it feels like an age, it can't be more than a few moments till you walk back into the living room, greeted by a room of ghosts, your mother almost indistinguishable among them. All eyes on you.

Poor Baba. Desperate, trapped, hurting. The thought of him dying alone, so close to your Wanchai flat and feeling like a failure, is almost enough to break you. If only you had spoken to him that night. If only you'd sat with him, how things might be different. It isn't fair to think that, but your brain can't help seeking the blame.

And Mami, carrying that burden by herself, holding it tight in her heart. She was wrong to lie, but some truths are too difficult to share. No wonder she retreated from you, from all of reality. Sympathy and fury war against each other in your heart.

You hear yourself saying, "Obviously, you knew all along that he was never coming for us."

". . . Yes." She slumps miserably.

"So why did you bring us here?"

"I thought it would be safer. I thought we could hide. I thought, even if my family were ghosts, perhaps they could help, or . . ." She dashes the heel of her hand against her eyes. "I'm so sorry, daughter. I have failed you. I let grief destroy me. I took comfort from my ghosts, and lost myself. I have not been a good parent."

"Finally, we agree." But you are crying, too. Haven't stopped since reading Baba's note.

Her hands flutter, useless and anxious. "I was wrong to return."

"It doesn't matter." It does, actually, but there's no more time to argue. "Mami, we need to get off the island. Can you row one of those little fishing boats?"

"I think so. There isn't one nearby, though. We will have to cross the island."

Thunder rolls like cannonballs, and lightning flashes in the distance. Outside, the wind is already picking up with rain smattering lightly; the storm is not far.

You look at the sky, and swallow. "I don't think we have enough time to get there. We want to be on the eastern shore, if we are to get to the other islands quickly."

"Then perhaps the village will help us." Mami looks at the ghosts, eddying around her. She kneels on the hard floor, palms held up. "Aunties and uncles, cousins and friends, will you help us? Will you take care of your own? We need a boat, to leave the island before my little sister brings her storm. Can you bring it to the closest shore, to the east of here?"

The ghosts murmur and whisper and converge on your mother, as spirit hands stroke her graying hair and promises of aid mist into echoing words.

"They will help," Mami says, dabbing her eyes. "Heaven bless them, they will help us." She gets up, knees gone crimson from being pressed to wood. "The ghosts will meet us there with a boat, after they have steered it round the coast. Hurry!"

There is no time to grab more than basics. You throw a few spare clothes into rucksacks, along with some skins of water. None of the food you have is suitable for travel; best to leave it. Grab a rain cape and straw hat, and you're set to go.

The rain is solid, the sky ink-dark by the time you both step outside again. Time for one last glance at the little house that has been a home for the past four months, and then you're off. For the first time in what feels like forever, you and your mother have a single shared goal.

It's another quarter hour of winding paths, mostly overgrown with so little foot traffic on Shek Ham Chau.

Many of the remaining ghosts come with you. They tumble and skip, flutter and creep as appropriate, through the steadily increasing rain. Some on both legs, some on no legs, some on all fours. None are as uniquely adapted and striking as Sea Sister, but then none are as powerful as she.

"Hurry, daughter, hurry!" Mami hisses, picking up the pace.

Soggy and sweating in the growing downpour, the pair of you arrive at the rocky beach, where the water grows deep quickly. Bad for swimming, good for boarding a boat.

"Where are they?" Shade your eyes in the gloomy half-light; only this morning, it was bright sun on crystalline waters.

Mami points. "There!"

Incredibly, they have done it. The ghosts have liberated the little fishing boat from the docks where you left it tied. The fishermen spirits prove surprisingly adept at fading in and out of corporeality as they take it in turn to steer its course.

It's a bit of difficulty getting to the boat, but you manage. It can come into shallow water, being small, but not all the way into shore. The ghost fishermen pull it up close to an outcropping of rock and you both clamber in.

By now, the ghosts behind you are starting to mill in agitation. They seem distressed, with signs you have learned to recognize: teeth baring, heads swiveling, seeking danger. Those who can speak are whispering or muttering.

"What's wrong with them, Mami?"

Then you hear it, echoing through the rising winds: the high-pitched scream of a little girl.

"Sea Sister," you whisper.

"Let's go!" Mami picks up the oars to begin rowing, and so do you.

Ten feet from shore, lightning strikes.

God-bright beams come arcing from above. The first bolt lashes the assembled ghosts, branching into multiple forks which each hit a different spirit.

The second bolt hits you.

A booming clap drowns out all other noise. White heat strikes every nerve in your body, pain like a million acupuncture needles, and then blankness. For a split second you exist in a place without sound, sight, or feeling. Then your eyes open, your lungs gasp, skin tingling as a body-wide ache sets in.

The blast has flung you clean out of the boat, slammed you into the water. Everything hurts and you smell like a bonfire.

Ears ringing, vision blurred, you struggle to the surface of the ocean, miraculously still conscious, fighting the choppy water. At least all those months with Sea Sister have made you a good swimmer. There is blood coming from your ears, your nostrils, your mouth. A livid burn sears down one shoulder, as if lightning has patterned itself on you; it hurts like hell.

On the shore, the milling ghosts are gone, either frightened away or temporarily dispersed. The fisherman ghost who steered the boat is also gone.

Again, that eerie cry on the wind. Only now it is more of a howl, a scream heard through the rising storm. The typhoon is landing, and somewhere at its heart is the anguished water ghost of Shek Ham Chau.

"She's here." Mami sits frozen on the boat, eyes so wide that the veins show around the edges. "My sister is here!"

"Wait!" You are trying to swim toward her even as the current carries the boat away, but feel so dizzy, sick, and weak. "Bring . . . the boat . . . closer! Please!"

Mami doesn't appear to hear you, or else no longer cares. "No, no, no," she cries. "I refuse to face her again!"

You cannot believe what you are hearing. "Mami, don't go!"

She begins rowing, then, energetically throwing her weight into the oars, crying and gibbering incomprehensibly. Complete terror has driven her over the edge.

"Mami?" A wave rolls you under and you struggle yet again to the surface, pummeled by rain and battered by wind. Still bleeding and burned from the lightning strike. "Mami, wait for me!"

The boat grows smaller. The waves grow bigger. Down you sink, hollering in the green. By the time you breach the air for a third time, her little vessel has caught a current and is picking up speed. There is a heaviness in your body; you won't stay afloat for long.

One last try. "*Mami!*"

Sung Daiyu doesn't look back. The last sight you have of her is the curve of those rigid shoulders, forever bowing away, head fixed in another direction.

If she'd loved you more, perhaps she might not have abandoned you.

But her fear was stronger.

You sink for a final time.

That moment. When sound plunges into a muted dullness, when the raw noise of the atmosphere above is softened by the sea.

Reach both hands out, grasping at nothing. A foolish instinct. Mami can't save you now, even if she wanted to. Terror and trauma have driven her into madness, and away from you. The way despair drove Baba from you, months ago.

Someone else, though, reaches back.

The ghost you call Sea Sister rises from those shadowed ocean depths to catch your wrists in hers. Just like she did the first time you met.

There is no joy or surprise in her face today, only a stark and filthy darkness. She is not here to show kindness. Not anymore. You have joined the ranks of those who abandoned her, and she will not forgive that.

For what it's worth, I truly believe Sea Sister did love you, in her twisted and warped way. In another life, perhaps she might have even loved you enough to let you live. But in the end, Sea Sister has been too hurt by existence. She cannot bear to slink back to the ocean and watch you depart. She knows that if she saves your life, you will go forever, and she will be alone.

The heart can live with loneliness if it has never known anything better. What it cannot live with is finding companionship, and then losing it again.

I told you, Sea Sister says, but she only sounds sad, not accusing. *I told you she would leave. Everyone always abandons us. Everyone always will.*

You can't argue with that. First your father, now your mother. The world at large recedes from you like a tide, impossible to hold. Your fingers are made of water, and life slips through it.

Stay with me, forever, she murmurs, and brushes a kiss across your cheek. Shark teeth leaving a scrape across your skin. *You can be just like me, free and strong and swimming endlessly. Isn't that what you wanted, ghost girl?*

It isn't, not anymore, but it's too late. One of her claw-like nails stabs into your ribs. The lung deflates, crushing what little air was left out of you. You open your mouth to scream underwater and your throat seizes up, closing reflexively.

She gathers you close amidst the churning currents. *Never doubt that I will always love you*, she whispers, and she dives.

This time, there is no going up. No return to the surface. There's a certain strange peace in that knowledge.

At least you won't be alone, you tell yourself. Even if the only person who stays with you is your murderer, it is still better than dying by yourself.

You do not resist as she bears you down, nor do you cry (no tears beneath the ocean, after all). Instead, you think of Baba, crouched over the kitchen table as he whispers, *All things are transient*, because now you understand him, so perfectly well.

Darkness encroaches, still and quiet; the storm cannot touch these depths. Pressure compresses your lungs and bursts in your ears and it doesn't matter. It doesn't matter at all. Your silence matches Sea Sister's in this salt-tinged world she inhabits.

Then death arrives like a sudden breeze, and blows your spirit clean away.

25

AFTER LIFE

Thirty-three years ago . . .

Time changes when you die, though not in the way you expect.

It doesn't slow, so much as expand. You find, in death, that there is more space between each second as transience stretches itself thin. It takes an eternity to finally drown.

Followed by a darkness that lasts forever, and only an instant.

The next thing you recall is opening your eyes in the depths of the ocean, crying out reflexively.

A rush of water floods your throat, but otherwise silence. No speaking, no noises. You feel a great and terrible need for air yet you cannot breathe, the way a rabid dog thirsts for water yet cannot drink. In that moment, you would have torn apart babies for a chestful of oxygen.

Up you lunge from the ocean floor in a cloud of sand, dust, and murky water. Seagrass and old fishing lines clutter the water. All is darkness but somehow you can see as you shoot straight upward, picking out the swirls of movement from fish and fragmentary lights above.

Burst through the surface of the ocean. A nightly breeze stings your face, the sky a riot of stars above. Each of them is ringed by a nimbus of light, weird and unwaveringly bright.

All this you see in a kaleidoscope moment of perception, absorbing without truly processing. You are too busy trying to breathe to take in anything else. A cold, heavy wetness sits in your lungs that will not go away. Struggling to breathe does nothing but send a twisting sensation through your chest, worsening the pain.

Memory returns to you in drips.

The lightning strike.

She's here . . . She's here!

Electricity flinging you from the boat.

I refuse to face her again.

Your mother, shattered by fear, rowing for her worthless life.

Mami, don't go—

Waves carrying you back into the ocean. Sea Sister's face, looming in your vision.

I will always love you.

Fearful and anguished, you lift both hands out of the water. Bone-white fingers, tinged green in the creases and tips. The digits elongated and skeletally thin. The nails have grown into something approaching claws, cruel-looking ones.

These aren't your hands.

Except . . . they are.

When you look closely, there is a hint of transparency to your skin. A lightness to your form that belies its size; you weigh almost nothing, can feel that lack in yourself. Your physical body is gone, and all that is left of you is a semicorporeal spirit.

Shuigui. Dead girl. *Water ghost.*

Sea Sister has made you like her.

Shiver and wrap both arms round your shoulders. There are no words for the transcendent hurt you're experiencing. It's not just the lungs, burning you inside out with a desire for air that cannot be met. It's everything: Baba's death, Mami's abandonment, Sea Sister's murder.

Every fucking person in your entire fucking life, who has ever mattered in any capacity, has done badly by you. And you *hate* them all for it with a power that cascades like a celestial flood.

Where is that disgusting monster, that vile Sea Sister? She was right next to you when you died, promising she'd stay with you forever. Surely she couldn't have gone far. Didn't she want to drown you to keep you close to her, after all? Wasn't that the point?

It occurs to you that your skin isn't burning, as Sea Sister's did when she was out of water. Dry, yes, but not withering up. Look up; it is nighttime, judging by the stars and moon. The night sky looks as bright to you as the day. Ghost vision must work differently.

More importantly, it wasn't night when you first died. Closer to midafternoon. Maybe the "returning" of your spirit took a while. Has it been hours? Days? Weeks or months?

Some ghosts come back straightaway. Some don't return until Hungry Ghost Festival, or at other times of year when the veil is thin between living and dead. Supposedly they spend time flying around to the underworld, but that hasn't happened to you. Well, not that you remember, anyway. If there are rules about these things, they feel flimsy.

The beach is empty and quiet, the waters bereft of any boats. Your gaze furiously scans the shoreline—and stops, catching on the mouth of the cavern as it yawns beneath the rise of headland cliff.

The cavern, and the temple. Surely, if she has gone anywhere, it is there, where her body lies rotted. At least it's a place to start. Anger hasn't gone away but it is, for now, a cold, hard thing, rather than lava in your undead veins.

You dive.

Waves part for you as easily as air, and darkness does not blind your eyes any longer. Dip, dash, slink through the tunnel with unnatural grace, and return again to the cool bliss of the cave.

It looks different to ghostly eyes than it did when you were alive. The temple glows with unpleasant light, raising a faint rash on your skin. No wonder Sea Sister was not able to enter it. Everywhere else in this underground pit heaves and seethes with dark energy, though; the collected misery of an abandoned little girl, and her desperate rage.

The shadows shift, interplaying with the light of the temple. Someone is moving there, near the temple doors where the water is shallowest. Definitely a person.

Rise to your full height, and stride dripping out of the sea.

A woman is waiting.

No, "woman" is the wrong term. If you tilt your head, from one angle she is an elegant lady of ageless features, draped in flowing robes. Tilt the other way and he is a young man with high cheekbones and a sculpted body. Viewed straight on and unblinking, they are an androgynous figure, handsome features and a beautiful head of hair, an infinity of arms curving from an impossible number of shoulders.

It is me, of course.

It always has been.

"Hello, Sung Siu Yin." I meet your dead gaze with my divine one. "Do you know who I am?"

You stalk through the shallow water, approaching slowly. Even at night, in a covered cave, the dryness begins to tighten your skin and make it itch. The ocean does not relinquish a water ghost easily. But what is a little more pain when you are already suffering without end?

Lady Kwun Yam. Lips move but no sound comes out. You're communicating as Sea Sister once did, and your words don't need air. Only thought. *Or is it Lady Ma Zu? I never did get to the bottom of that.*

"I am they. Kwun Yam, or Guanyin, or Avalokiteśvara. All those names and more. Some believe that I incarnated on this earth as Ma Zu, among others."

I saw your statue, in the temple. And in the dream.

"That's right." I incline my head.

My aunt, Mami's sister, asked you to remember her.

"I did as she asked. She was one of my worshippers, blessed with a touch of my power, and she deserved to be remembered."

Is that why she became a ghost?

"The memory of a goddess is a dangerous thing," I say, a little sadly. "There is a hint of the divine in that girl. She had a great connection to the sea, and to the spirit world. A soul of her power would always have returned as a ghost, but because of me, she is *even* stronger. Her body lingers here, never fully deteriorating, the bones trapped in perpetual rot."

So you've been here the whole time, just "remembering" her? you say, caught somewhere between incredulity and anger. *Don't you have better things to do?*

"I am, and can be, in many different places at once. In all places where I exist, I am busy."

Why speak to me now? Why did you not help me sooner?!

"It is easier for gods and ghosts to speak than it is for gods and mortals," I say, gently, "and you are now numbered among the dead, Sung Siu Yin. But I did try to help you, when you were in my cavern. I let you see the truth of her, and I told you to flee."

What good did that do? you demand, fists curling tight in fury. *She still killed me!*

"I am sorry. I cannot puppeteer mortals or ghosts, however much easier that would make my work."

Just tell me where she is! You cannot howl, so the wind does it for you, screeching over the headland and whistling down into this cave. *Where is my cowardly murderer?*

"She is gone. Days ago, now."

Gone?! Gone where?

"She came to the surface, and a passing patrol picked her up." I pause. "For whatever it is worth, Sung Siu Yin, I am very sorry."

None of that sentence makes a jot of sense.

How in the hells did a boat pick up a spirit?

"It didn't. The boat picked up a living woman." When you continue to stare, I say, in a low voice, "Did your mother never tell you stories about water ghosts?"

She did, of course, but you've forgotten in the moment. The facts were lost amidst the shuffle of fresh wounds and bewildering betrayals.

So I explain it to you again.

⁘

The legends about water ghosts vary from place to place, sometimes story to story, but some basics are the same.

First, a person—usually a woman, for most ghosts are women—must die by drowning, and return as a spirit with unfinished business. In stories, she spends many years feeling lonely and lost, consumed with the perpetual agony of suffocation, yet afraid or unable to leave the one place she haunts. Trauma is familiar, and always calls us back.

When a victim finally approaches the body of water where she lurks, the woman's spirit lures them into the water. Sometimes she does this through seduction and sometimes through a hypnotic spell; the details on this vary. Others will simply grab anyone foolish enough to go swimming during Ghost Month, when the undead are strongest.

Once she and they are both in the water, she will pull them down into the depths and hold them there until they drown.

It is here the stories begin to differ. Some say that once a victim is dead, the water ghost can rest, its spirit journeying on toward the underworld and eventual rebirth. Both souls simply pass on.

Other stories have a darker claim. They say that when the soul has detached from the body, the water ghost can inhabit the skin that remains, her corrupted spirit possessing the empty shell her victim has left behind.

In that version, she climbs out to dry land, encased in the body of the person she's just drowned. And their spirit—if it is not dispersed before it can form—becomes a new water ghost. Taking her vacated place. Thus the cycle of pain continues, passed from one person to another like a torch of misery.

That is how it went, for you and Sea Sister.

You, as her niece, were the first foot across the threshold of her heart in many years. Yours were the first acts of kindness, the first gifts. Your compassion obliterated her loneliness and she loved you like a daughter, like a sister, like a friend. For a time, her anger had been quelled.

But ghosts are not rational. Ghosts are what is left of a soul who has been so hurt that their pain lingers, imprinting on the corporeal world. When you rejected her, she lost control.

Sea Sister was lonely, so she tried to keep you. Sea Sister was a water ghost, so she tried to drown you. It is not an excuse, and she is still guilty.

But I am telling you this so that you will understand: even if you had stayed with her, as she demanded, she would still have drowned you. There was nothing you could have done. It is difficult for ghosts to think clearly, doubly so for those who die as children. As you yourself will soon find out.

Her anger-fueled storm hit Shek Ham Chau like a kick to the throat, just as it did all those years ago when she first died. The lightning that struck you was born of a spirit's anguished heart. The wave that swept you back was the force of her desperation. Her arms, as she bore you down into the darkness, had the strength of grief.

Then you died, and she was left holding an empty shape.

The sense that your body was a husk, a hollow, an empty thing, began to grow in her mind. It looked to her like a dress waiting to be draped across her spirit, a coat longing to engulf her form.

And she leaped into your dead, lifeless body. A thing she had never done before.

The feeling was exquisite and horrifying all at once. Decades of pain fell away in an instant. One moment she was pressing her cheek to yours and the next your cheek was hers: heavy and real, flesh and blood. Suddenly a person again, after a lifetime as a ghost.

Sea Sister floated, deep underwater.

Then the weight of drowning crushed back down, all the worse for having been briefly alleviated; she had nearly forgotten what it was like not to have sodden lungs. Except now that dim memory was a bright and recent experience. She struggled to the surface, broke the water. Gasped air for the first time in decades, stunned and aghast.

The unexpected happened.

Hands grabbed her as she surfaced, hauling her up. Hands wearing military sleeves, attached by arms to men dressed in Japanese uniforms.

Was it luck that a stray ocean patrol should be diverted by Sea Sister's storm, and find her/you floating in the ocean? Or a curse of the heavens? Either way, it was not my doing, and that is the course of events as they occurred.

"She's alive!" one of the men shouted, while someone else yelled, "It's only a local girl! Throw her back!"

An argument broke out. The invaders were enemies to the region, but still human. Some of them were men with daughters or sisters, and felt they should help. Others disagreed.

She tried to stand, and collapsed against the soldier who had pulled her out. Something was wrong. Your body had been injured badly, bleeding, and though she was now in it, it was still barely functioning. The right lung couldn't breathe at all. No air. Suffocating all over again.

Everything is wrong, she thought, dizzily and vaguely.

The last thing she felt before passing out was a thin, hard blade sliding between her ribs, and she could not tell if it was meant to kill her off, or save her life.

⁘

As I relate this story, fury builds in you.

Are you telling me that this filthy cow turd has killed me, stolen my body, and left me to take her place?

"I'm so sorry, child."

Sorry? You're SORRY?

In life you were never an angry person, but cruelty and an unfair death have changed that. The parts of your soul which were soft and gentle are damaged, left behind in the body that was stolen from you and gifted, instead, to your murderer.

All that remains to you is rage unending, a consuming need for justice, and a terrible desire to breathe air. Such is the existence of a ghost.

Throw your head back and scream like an oncoming train. Even that does nothing to vent your cascading anger.

Why did she wait? you say, gnashing your teeth. *Four months she swam with me. Why keep me alive so long?*

"Every day, a ghost fights their nature. She likely did not intend you harm, not in the beginning. But in the end, her own darkness won."

Then tell me her name, you snarl, standing almost toe-to-toe with me. *I must find her.*

"It will do no good, Siu Yin. There is a strong chance she won't remember you."

What do you mean?

"When a water ghost takes the skin of another, they begin to lose themselves. The process is not unlike reincarnation," I say, quietly. "If Sea Sister does not return your body soon, she will be trapped in it—forgetting who and what she used to be. She will only know herself as a young woman without memories."

No, that can't be! The realization of that horrifies you beyond measure. The idea that Sea Sister won't even recall her betrayal and theft is somehow worse than the act itself. *I need her to know! I need to find her, at once!*

When I still hesitate, you fall to your knees on the dark, rocky beach before me. *Please, Lady Kwun Yam—I am begging! Who else can help me, but you? Who else knows my fate, except yourself? I can have no peace till I have spoken to my killer. I deserve an answer!*

"What you seek is folly, but I cannot ignore such a plea," I say, full of sadness. "If it will help you on the path to peace, then the truth is yours."

I'm listening.

"Against tradition, and out of shame, your mother abandoned her family name when she met your father, and became Sung Daiyu. But as a child, her family name was Chen—and her sibling, who you know as Sea Sister, was called Chen Mei Chi."

Chen Mei Chi, you murmur, repeating the syllables over and over until they are seared into memory. *Chen Mei Chi. Chen Mei Chi. Chen Mei Chi.*

"What will you do with this knowledge?"

Instead of answering, you bow low, palms pressed together in a show of gratitude. *Thank you for your answer, Lady Kwun Yam.* Straightening, you turn away from me and wade back into the deeper waters of the cavern.

"Where are you going?" I say, with rising unease. "Ghosts are not supposed to go wandering."

Says who? There is steel in your voice. *I will not be a weak prisoner spirit, lurking sadly in an ocean puddle, waiting for my next victim. This ghost goes to seek her truth, and her vengeance. I will have it if I must travel every continent, and live in every human skin.*

"Do that, and you will lose yourself," I warn. "You *can* do that, but only through committing murder each time. And if you do take another's form, you may well become trapped in it—as she has in yours. The strength of a water ghost is also her weakness."

I am already lost, goddess, you say scornfully. *Don't worry on my account.*

In legends and stories, water ghosts are lurking spirits who haunt the places where they died. Even Mei Chi was like that: tied to her sad little island, doomed to beg for validation and love from the very people who rejected her, and then tormenting their spirits when they withheld it.

But you, Siu Yin, are determined to be different. Because you have realized that you are not tied to a location, only to a person. Whether it takes five years or fifty, even if you have to slaughter dozens or hundreds, you will go forth into the world.

For the first time in your life, you are powerful. And you will never let the world make you weak, ever again. In that at least, Mei Chi has inadvertently kept her word: she has made you strong, and free.

Violent and unstoppable in death as you never were in life, you fling yourself back into the ocean.

"Wait," I call, voice supernaturally loud despite my humble form.

But, much like Mei Chi in her ghost years, you do not care to hear me anymore.

26

WOMAN OVERBOARD

Thirty-three years ago . . .

Mei Chi awakes to a world of confusion.

She is lying on a pallet in a cramped, poorly lit room, with bandages around her chest. Nothing is familiar. She tries to gasp, and winces. Her left lung feels soggy and bruised.

Still, the lung moves and breathes. She hasn't breathed properly in such a long time. Another inhale, and this time she holds it before releasing slowly. Such an easy thing to take for granted. Until one can't do it anymore.

Scrubbing grit from her eyes, she sits up.

This is a medical room of some kind: poorly stocked, rife with maggots. Two men and a few other women lie stretched on rickety pallets. One of the men has flies crawling across his open eyes, and smells like a corpse. The floor is stained with repeated drippings of blood and viscera.

Badly made cabinets hold a smattering of unsterilized equipment, bandages that appear to have been used and washed again, and various pill bottles without labels. Shek Ham Chau had no hospital, but this is still grim to her eyes.

Shek Ham Chau. Yes. That is the island she was born and raised on. The island she died on. Because she is decades dead, long since become a ghost, and all of this is impossible.

Mei Chi looks down at her hands, daring to examine herself. Gone are the clawed fingers, the algae-stained flesh, the emaciated form with its atrophied innards. Living human skin covers living human meat and bones, prickled everywhere with small, soft hairs, unevenly tanned from months beneath a bright winter sun.

She touches her lips; chapped, salt-stung, damp with saliva and perspiration. Blinks her eyes, stretches her hands. Her toes wiggle expertly. She rolls her neck, hearing it crick.

The truth is here, obvious as daylight. What she remembers is no nightmare, no flight of imagination. She is—

Can't say it. Not yet. Needs to see it, first.

There's a small shaving mirror on the nearest cabinet. She picks it up.

Sung Siu Yin's face gazes out at her, head and shoulders reflected hazily. Mei

Chi touches her cheek; in the silvery, flat surface, Siu Yin raises a hand to touch Siu Yin's face.

A blood-red mark winds from neck to wrist on the left side, where lightning from her own storm struck Siu Yin's boat. Still red and angry, and it will scar terribly, but it is healing. A gold tiger charm bracelet encircles one wrist; a gift, from Siu Yin's father.

Mei Chi drops the mirror as if it were a poisonous snake and crawls back to the pallet, curling up like a frightened pangolin.

As a water ghost, the need to take a skin had warred with the soul's desire to have companionship, which had collided horribly with Siu Yin's rejection. She had fought the urge to drown Siu Yin, even as she'd found her niece's company irresistible. A balm against the unending loneliness.

But Mei Chi is not a ghost anymore, not with a body to complete the parts of her soul that were missing, and she can feel the horror and regret for everything she has done. She may have died as a child, but she has years of accrued memories. Plenty of awareness to understand the devastation her spirit has wreaked.

What now? Sit and wait for Siu Yin to return, as one of the dead? What will Siu Yin think, finding Mei Chi alive and breathing in Siu Yin's body? Can she leave, vacate this form, give it back? Can a spirit ripped from its flesh live again, find itself again?

The idea of giving back the body fills her with fresh fear. The memory of that eternal drowning pain is not pleasant.

Yet she *should* get back to Siu Yin, if she can, or at least to the place where Siu Yin died. It is her duty. Maybe she can exit this body, crawl back to the ocean. But for that to work, she'll need a clear run to the sea, with no soldiers. This boat will be difficult to escape.

No, doesn't matter how difficult it is. There must be a way to fix it.

Mei Chi puts a hand to her chest, inspecting under the bandages. The stab wound is healing well. Whichever Japanese doctor treated her has done a good job. They've drawn the excess oxygen out of the lung, allowing it to reinflate. Though bruised and a little weak, this body will live.

She can hear men outside the door, speaking in Japanese; someone is standing guard outside. She is a prisoner of war, then? Something like that. From one prison beneath the waves, to another above them.

"Are you the girl they pulled from the ocean?"

Mei Chi turns her head.

On the next pallet over, a young woman about her age is leaning close to whisper. She's been injured in some kind of explosion, and her thickly crusted bandages are in need of changing.

"I don't know." Siu Yin's voice coming out of her mouth. No, out of Siu Yin's mouth. From Siu Yin's throat. She cringes, feeling like the world's filthiest thief.

"You must be," the bandaged woman says, insistent. "I saw the soldiers bring you in here."

Mei Chi swallows a *Then why did you ask, if you already know* response. Best not to alienate her one source of information. Instead, she says, "Why would the Japanese soldiers save my life?"

"Not soldiers. The military exorcists," the bandaged woman says. "They keep an eye on the ghost islands in these parts, and they're kinder than soldiers. Former priests, most of them."

Military exorcists, Mei Chi echoes silently. She would have assumed they'd take one look at her and realize she was possessing this shell, but they clearly haven't.

That itself is interesting. Perhaps she does not look like a possession case because possession happens to the living; two spirits crammed uncomfortably into a single body. What she has done is . . . corpse animating, possibly, or something akin to reincarnation. Indistinguishable from simply being alive, unless they examine much more closely.

As a ghost, her mind was clouded with anger and grief and loneliness. In a human skin, her thoughts are clear and cold—for the moment. She wracks her tattered memory. Everyone knows what a water ghost does to its victims, but she can't recall any tales about what happens to them once they've found a living person to switch with.

Do they just . . . disappear into society? Live normally, like a human? Strange that the stories always stop with the murder, and never discuss the aftermath. Maybe they just carry on living, having found a second life to exist in.

The idea makes her chest constrict in horror and shame, even as her cheeks flush with excitement. Being in Siu Yin's body means no more drowning. Freedom to live, breathe, be real. But it comes at someone else's expense, someone she has killed and betrayed. She does not know if Siu Yin has become a water ghost, or moved on to the next life, and can't tell which outcome is worse.

"—and they said we were insurgents, all of us. I am only a farmer!" The bandaged woman is still talking. "Now I am here, going to heaven knows where." She grimaces, reliving some private memory.

Mei Chi tries to refocus and pay attention. "Where is here, exactly?"

"Some military ship. We're being transported."

"Oh. Where are we going?"

The bandaged woman gives her a look, like she is a child who insists on poking an anthill with bare fingers. "To where all the prisoners go, idiot," she said. "If we are very lucky, we will live in Stanley prison camp. If we are unlucky, a soldiers' brothel."

Mei Chi crosses her legs reflexively. "How long have I been unconscious?"

"Two days, I think. A long time."

"And we're still not in Stanley?" It should only have been a few hours' travel.

"None of us were well enough to travel till today," the bandaged woman says, irritably. "Don't you remember the military hospital?"

"If I did, would I be asking questions?" Mei Chi retorts, sitting up carefully. This body is weak, worn to death and dragged back again by an unfamiliar spirit; it is barely holding together. Slowly, through sheer willpower, she stands once more.

The bandaged woman eyes her uneasily. "What are you doing?"

"Getting out of here. I can smell the sea. I must swim to shore." And find her way back to the island.

"Idiot," the bandaged woman says again. "How will you get past the man outside our door? Let alone all the others."

"I'm not staying here, and I'm not getting shipped away to become—" She can't even say it. "I have to get back to someone. She . . . the one who needs me . . . she is on the island, still."

"Aiyah, we all have people depending on us. Dying won't get you there any faster, unless you hope to meet them in hell."

Her patience is used up. "Do you have a better idea, or are you just pissing on mine?"

"I was only trying to help you," the bandaged woman says, reprovingly. "Who is she, anyway?"

"Huh?"

"This woman, whose life depends on you returning."

"Oh, she is . . . Erm." Mei Chi pauses, flummoxed when she draws a blank on the name. Her best friend, her only friend in years. The woman whose body she has stolen. They've done so much together, like . . .

Like what?

Bottles with pictures, one bottle with a poem. Yes, those are good. Also diving and swimming, hand-in-hand, around the waters of . . .

. . . of . . .

A swell of frustration rises within her.

The island. Her home. The place where she has lived for so long. What is it called.

What is it fucking called!

This is ridiculous; it is on the tip of her tongue, just out of reach. Yet the name has fallen out of her head, disappeared like a wild rabbit through an unlocked gate, and she cannot seem to summon it back.

Bandaged Woman is still waiting, expression unreadable beneath the gauze.

"A friend," Mei Chi concludes lamely, and hopes the flatness of her tone sounds evasive rather than distressed. "She is a friend."

"So you said."

The fading of her memories is not a good sign. The flesh that encloses her seems heavy, like she's stepped into a pit of wet clay. She has a terrible sense that if she does not get out of this skin very soon, it will be too late to ever leave it.

Especially since she has, apparently, already been wearing it for over two days.

Guilt clamps down. Her life is a disaster. All she has ever done is make trouble, anger other people, get her cat killed. (Wait, where is her cat? Doesn't his ghost usually follow hers?) And now she has killed her only friend. (Who? What was her name?)

She needs to go back. Somehow. She can't recall exactly where that is, only that she feels sure she'd remember it if she saw it again. First, though, she needs to make sure she does not forget the things that are important. Before her disintegrating memory takes even basic details from her.

A tiny fragment of glass glitters on the ground next to her pallet, where someone has dropped a vial or a syringe. Mei Chi picks it up and presses the jagged edge to her skin. She chooses the arm that doesn't have a lightning scar, since that one is still sore and healing.

"What are you doing?" Bandaged Woman says, uneasily.

"Mind your own business." Mei Chi scratches her name into the skin, deep as she dares. The characters of *Chen Mei Chi* are shaky but readable, already welling up with blood. Got to have your own name.

The vessel rocks suddenly, caught by a high swell. Everything in the room rattles. The other patients groan with pain or fear. From somewhere outside, thunder booms.

"That doesn't sound good." Mei Chi clutches the edges of her bed, blood dripping along her arm.

"Typhoon season," Bandaged Woman agrees, and she looks troubled, too. "The storms have been bad this year."

More thunder as the ship lists again, and men shouting orders from other levels. Mei Chi does not speak Japanese, but she can detect a hint of rising panic in their voices. She is in the midst of wondering whether this could be used to her advantage, when the silhouette of boots from under the door moves away abruptly; whoever was stationed outside has left.

"Are you coming?" She looks at the bandaged woman.

"Are you crazy? It's dangerous out there! Soldiers, storms, oceans—"

"Fine, stay here. Thanks for answering my questions." She doesn't have time to stay and argue. Besides, the other woman is right: it's dangerous out there. Only a fool would try to leave.

Or someone with nothing to lose.

"Wait for me. Forgive me," Mei Chi whispers. "I'm coming back!"

But she can no longer recall quite whom she is talking to. Her memories are like a pool of water, drying fast under a midday sun.

The door is locked. Mei Chi finds a metal ruler and jams it into the crack, leveraging it open; the lock is cheap and gives quickly. An empty hallway greets her, the floor wet with sodden bootprints. She can hear shouting, though she can't see anyone yet. Ahead of her are stairs, leading up to another landing.

Her body is weak, injuries still aching. Every step is a trial, especially as the ship begins pitching steeply from side to side. On the next level, men in uniform are scurrying down corridors in all directions, shouting and wild-eyed. Few seem to notice her, and none care enough to stop. Their vessel is in trouble, and so are they.

The ocean. She needs the ocean.

She keeps going. Another set of metal stairs, and now she is out in the open air.

Chaos dominates up here. Wind and rain lash the deck, making it slippery as dolphin skin. Men scream orders and counter-orders while thunder is one continuous roll above them, the sky illumined by sheets of lightning. As if the gods are flicking a light switch repeatedly.

Mei Chi clings to the railing, unable to stand on that rolling deck without assistance, unsure what she should do. For a moment, she is convinced that this is a terrible mistake. If the storm doesn't kill her, these soldiers will, once it calms down. There is no hope of swimming in these seas, let alone getting back to the island whose name now eludes her.

And then a wave as tall as a cliff knocks their vessel up and over, and it's too late to worry about anything else.

Picture a girl, floating in a storm-churned ocean.

Her arms hang limp, eyes lidded and unresponsive. She has a worker's build, strong all over, hands blooming with calluses. Dark hair fans out in the water, forming a cloud around her face. A gold bracelet with a tiger charm encircles one wrist.

The current stirs and swirls. She does not.

Dead things surround her. A few drowned men drift in the water, limbs rigid and possessions scattered. The broken remnants of freshly sunken boats lie half buried on the ocean floor. History is eroding down here, rusting in the mud.

Beneath the water, her eyes open . . .

We know the rest of Mercy's tale from here, I think.

Your story, though, is just getting started.

PART THREE

27

LIKE A SUIT OF CLOTHES

Thirty-three years ago . . .

Swimming as a ghost is a revelatory experience. Cut through emerald water, following the coastline up and westward. A tilt of the head changes direction; a flick of the feet alters speed. You don't fully realize how fast you're going until you overtake a pod of pink dolphins, who scatter at your approach with chittering cries.

Oddly, you have never felt more grounded and aware than in that moment. The living walk through life half asleep; the dead are wide-awake. They are connected deeply to the spirit world, and they cannot shut their eyes or rest.

The burn of suffocation in your chest grinds on, a relentless ache. Oddly, knowing there is no way to ease it makes it possible to bear. When pain becomes a way of existence, we stop hoping for an end to the suffering. The death of hope is its own resilience.

In the darkest hours of the night, you wash up through the cresting waves along a barren stretch of shore. You're still far to the north, in the rural Sai Kung districts; the city is not visible from here. To reach the rest of Hong Kong would be several hours' walk through mountainous paths.

But you aren't thinking of going to the city just yet. For now, all you want is to stand on dry land, if only for a moment. As if in a dream, you rise slowly, night air drying your skin. Surf rolls across your feet, caking them in sand.

Glancing down, you catch sight of your reflection in a still pool of water, trapped between rocks.

A pallid face, tinted ever-so-slightly green. Hollow cheeks, gaunt features; the blood is all washed out. Some cultures prize slender delicacy, but this is not beauty. Your body is shriveled rather than slender; you are sinewy and twisted, rather than delicate. Despite the corporeality of your form, translucency hazes every line and edge, giving a shimmery appearance. The filmy white of your eyes is clouded and dull.

The tide roars, the stars burning in the heavens as you huddle in a sullen knot of withered limbs over a rock pool, haunted by the reflection within. Even knowing what you would see, it is still a momentary shock.

An ache tightens across your body, catching you off guard. The skin on your arms is flaking as the dryness accelerates, cracks deepening and spreading with rapidity.

Alarmed, you scuttle back to the cool relief of the ocean, ducking your head beneath the waves. The symptoms stop. Though still drawn and papery, your spirit-skin is recovering.

Trying to leave the water is dangerous. Same as it was for Mei Chi, whose limitations you now possess. You regard your limbs with grim discontent. Are you bound to the ocean, then? Not a very useful kind of ghost.

If Mei Chi were here, the hell and fury you'd wreak—

But she isn't here. She's gone, took your skin and ran. Probably she'll end up in a prisoner of war camp, somewhere. Heaven knows what will happen to your body then. Perhaps she'll even die again, and take your body with her this time.

Helplessness wells up, swamping you. In stories, ghosts always seem to know what to do. They come back overwhelmed with compulsions and rote behaviors, perhaps even enslaved to them.

Not you, though. You're lost, aimless. Grateful to have autonomy, as if you've won a kind of hellish lottery, but also at a complete loss for how to use it. Where are the stories about ghosts who are just confused and unsure?

Frustration drives you to move, even though you scarcely know where you want to go. Swim farther out to get a better view and begin following the coast. Every so often, you lift your head above the surface to scan the area.

A mile down the shoreline, closer to the city, and you finally see something. A group of men have made camp on the beach, clustered around a fire in the wilderness. Five of them together, and all heavily armed as they laugh and chatter and cook their food.

They are wearing Japanese uniforms.

Fate has brought you here this night, to an encounter that will alter the course of your un-life.

Edge closer, careful to keep behind an outcropping of rocks, and watch from the water. There is, you realize with interest, a sixth man among them, whom you hadn't seen before, because he's lying down. He doesn't wear a uniform, and appears to be a citizen. His face is bruised and his limbs are tied; a prisoner, of some kind.

Interesting. Despite all that is going on, you feel sorry for him. The need for air still batters at your senses but you find, while watching the soldiers, that it dies down a little. In its place is an urgent and moaning urge for violence that grows the longer you lurk.

The soldiers laugh at jokes, passing food and drink around. The bound man tries to sit up at one point, and a soldier knocks him over. Your shoulders tense. The hate in you that exists for Mei Chi is bleeding into your senses, attaching itself to these men.

The invading soldiers, after all, are the ones who bear responsibility for upending your world, throwing your parents into despair, and ruining your home city. Without them, you'd never have gone to Shek Ham Chau. Without them, Mei Chi would not have escaped your grasp. And without them, it'd be so much easier to find her again.

Besides, you need a way of testing your powers. Of finding out, exactly, what you can do as a ghost. Isn't this just the perfect opportunity?

In the shadowed darkness, your lips draw back in a silent grin.

The hour grows late. Darkness falls. Eventually, the soldiers finish eating and put out their ill-advised fire. Most of them bunk down and sleep. Only one remains awake to keep watch, leaning against a tree by himself as he stares out over the darkened world, and the hunger inside you is a terrible, dark thing.

The prisoner is awake, too. His eyes are shining in the dark as he glances around. Like you, he is a fighter. Even outnumbered and bound, he hopes for escape. It's hard not to respect that.

You will spare him, you decide. There is no hate in that ghost heart for a fellow oppressed.

Whisperings and fevered fantasies crowd your brain, blending with the rage you carry for these men, and all they represent. Rise quietly from the water, slow and sinuous.

Your spirit-clothes are a mimicry of what you died in: battered shirt and trousers. Hardly a fancy dress, but it will suffice. You walk along the shoreline, in sight of the soldiers' camp but not too near it, arms wrapped around yourself and head bowed. As if you are lost, exhausted, grieving. You faux-stumble and kneel on the ground, just within reach of the water, with your back toward the tree line.

Boots crunch down the shore. The soldier has seen you and is approaching, and he hasn't yet woken his comrades. Rationally, that is a foolish thing for him to do, but he does not recognize you as a ghost.

It is nighttime, and your influence is strongly seductive. To his gaze, you look the way Mei Chi did to you, once: inexplicably beautiful despite the ragged clothing, alluring despite your obvious monstrousness. Vulnerability is a powerful charm.

Shrink back at his approach, feigning a fear you do not feel.

"I didn't know there were any civilians left in Sai Kung," he says, in heavily accented Cantonese, and his voice contains a cruelty that sets your teeth on edge. "Where are you from, pretty girl?"

Huddle small, saying nothing.

"Did you hear me?" He puts a hand on your shoulder.

Twist round, serpent-quick, baring sharp teeth in the moonlight.

The soldier blanches. "Oh shit—"

You lunge. He is a grown man and trained soldier but you are a vicious water ghost full of power and fury and you *drag* him into the fucking sea like he deserves.

He gets out one garbled scream before you both go under and then you are swirling down the steep slope of ocean floor, clutching him to you like a dear and treasured lover.

It does not take much depth to drown. A human can die in four inches of water. You only have to haul him a dozen feet out, where the ocean is chest deep—this is a steep shoreline, not a shallow beach for children—and it is plenty for your needs.

Bubbles burst from his mouth, panic driving him to exhale precious oxygen. He writhes like a snake in a bag, twisting in your arms. Face contorting in an expression of utter terror.

Lock eyes with his, and smile.

You know so precisely what he will be feeling: the building burn of no air, the desperate claustrophobia of waves pressing down, the coldness that seeps into everything and the specks that tinge one's vision. Time slowing to a single point of finality.

Then he dies in your arms, and his death is the most beautiful thing you've ever seen.

Ghosts perceive much that the living do not. Energy flows through the world in currents, and souls are like little knots of energy; his knot unwinds, the soul phasing through his body before dispersing in a scintilla of colors. For one extended, glorious moment, you feel no pain, the perpetual sensation of drowning briefly lifted from your chest; his death eases yours.

It would take your breath away, if you still breathed.

He isn't a woman and so likely won't return as a ghost, not that it matters to you just then. That problem is not yours to manage. All you know is that his body floats limp, eyes bulging open. His hair billows with the currents.

And then the oddest thing happens. There is a hollow in him, forming. You wouldn't know how else to describe it. Not a physical gap or wound; outwardly, his body looks the same. But you are struck by the overwhelming sense that you are holding a husk.

It calls to you, fills you with an unbearable urge to put him on like a sack, like a . . . a suit of clothes. Yes, a suit of clothes. A thing to be worn.

So, you do it.

You put him on.

⁂

Moments after entering the sea, the same soldier climbs out onto the sand. He moves woodenly, like a puppet. Feet stumble and he jerks to a stop, swaying and dripping.

By the fire, the prisoner—who has been wide-awake and watching this whole time—goes perfectly still. He saw you lure the soldier in, and has figured out what is happening.

The other men are awake, now. They heard the yelling and shot to awareness. As the soldier stumbles out of the water, his brothers in arms exclaim in Japanese.

He blinks at them, looking uncertain and embarrassed.

First their faces are incredulous; then, one by one, they each begin to crease in laughter. *Toma, you drunk idiot*, they chide. *Did you fall in while taking a piss?*

Toma doesn't laugh. He points behind him. "Something . . . in the water," he says, thickly, in Cantonese.

The other men pause and exchange glances, their laughter dying off. They've been stationed in South China long enough to pick up a smattering of the local dialect, but none of them choose to speak it among themselves, unless there is good reason to do so.

"S-s-something . . . water." Toma gazes blank-eyed at the lapping ocean, then backs slowly away toward the land. Seeming to ignore them entirely.

The sergeant, who is most senior, hoists his gun and steps forward, scanning the waves warily. The other three men do the same, muttering in low voices that their companion is surely drunk or sick, yet still doing their due diligence in checking. Better safe than sorry.

While their backs are turned, Toma lifts his dripping Mauser and fires repeatedly.

He lacks experience with guns, but it doesn't matter at this range. They're not expecting it and two die immediately. A third falls into the surging waves, already bleeding out. The sergeant is the only one left standing; Toma's shots missed him.

The sergeant returns fire with his own weapon.

Bullets strike Toma's body. The sound is like flour bags being whacked. One of them pierces the left chest, straight into the heart. Blood jets out erratically. The soldier remains standing, gaze fixed flatly on the sergeant.

"Toma?" the sergeant stutters, rendered inane by fear.

"Sorry," you say in Cantonese, looking out through Toma's eyes. Your spirit moving Toma's lips. "He's dead."

You leap at the sergeant, taking him into the water with you. His gun goes off again but the bullets are just annoyances, destroying flesh you don't care about, and soon enough, you've caught a second victim for the night.

"Where is she?" you ask, hands around his throat, reveling in the air that fills and departs your lungs in a blessed cycle. "Where is the girl you pulled from the ocean?"

He yelps in bug-eyed terror, attempting to speak with broken Cantonese. "What girl? Who? Please—"

You dunk him repeatedly and reiterate the question. He only grows more confused and desperate, thrashing in your arms.

Eventually, tired of playing and bored of his ignorance, you drag him under one final time.

It's only after you finally climb back to dry land for the second time . . . and wearing the sergeant's skin . . . only then, do the realizations dawn.

First, you didn't die from being shot. Even after you took a skin, the body being harmed meant nothing. Yes, it hurt, but so what. When weapons make the body unusable, you can simply slip free.

And second, possessing someone means you can breathe without pain, and walk on dry land like a human. This gross act is like being alive again. You don't have to exist as a ghost, not if you don't want to. You're conscious of my warning in the cave, about what happens to water ghosts who stay in a body too long, but that just means you'll have to be careful.

Careful is good. You can do careful. With a little foresight and common sense, you can functionally be immortal, now. Because whatever it is that puts water ghosts to rest, it's not having their stolen bodies destroyed.

And what *does* put a water ghost to rest? An interesting question. Perhaps if you take enough damage in the sun, or your spirit body is destroyed with weapons. Not that you want to test this theory anytime soon. There is a more pressing matter, at the moment.

Still dripping from the ocean, walk to the dying fire and look down at the captured prisoner. He tilts his head and meets your gaze boldly. He is alarmed, sure, and alert to what is happening, but not afraid.

How interesting.

Bend down, remove the gag.

"Hello," you say calmly. "Who are you?"

"Chiu Wing Yun." He looks to be in his late twenties, suntanned and square-shouldered. A shock of dark hair falls across his face. As a living girl, you'd have found him strikingly handsome. "I'm part of the East River Column."

"The *what*?"

"Haven't you heard of us, Lady Ghost?" He gives you a shrewd, thoughtful look. "The Sai Kung resistance network. We are Hakka people who fight against Japanese occupation. Those men you killed had captured me."

"I see." A pause. "My mother was Hakka. I speak a little, if that helps."

"If you wish, but my Cantonese is good," he says needlessly, because that is obvious. "Forgive me, but who the hell are you? Why did you help me?"

"I am what you called me: a lady ghost." You begin slicing his bonds with the sergeant's knife. "One who can wear skins. And who has no love for the Japanese invaders. It is partly their fault that I am this way."

The questions are clearly hovering in his mouth, so you decide to preempt them.

"I fled with my mother to the outlying islands, just off this coast, to avoid the invasion," you tell him. "The occupiers have caused so much pain and strife, and we feared them."

Even as you speak, it occurs to you that you're so much more lucid and chatty than Mei Chi was. Is this the influence of being in a physical body, or a result of dying as an adult? Hard to say.

"It is right to fear them," Wing Yun says, interrupting your thoughts. "Occupation has been cruel in our city."

"Fleeing didn't help, did it? I've died a bitter death anyway." Your teeth are grinding, you realize; look away from him and try to gather yourself.

"What were those questions you asked the soldiers?" he says.

"I'm looking for two people. A young woman, and an older one, traveling separately. They fled south and may have been picked up by boats."

Wing Yun's eyebrows climb up his forehead. "Forgive me, Lady Ghost, but there are tens of thousands of displaced people in Hong Kong right now. Millions across China. Refugees are everywhere. If your friend—"

"Not my friend," you snap. And then, to avoid the questions in his eyes, you add reluctantly, "My mother and my aunt."

"I'm sorry you've lost them," he says, and bows his head briefly. "But I don't think you'll find them easily. Not with this war going on. Citizens cannot move freely. Resistance fighters struggle to evade notice. Until the invasion is done and the Japanese are gone, you might as well be looking for a leaf in a typhoon."

For a moment, searing rage grips you. Who is this mortal man, thwarting what you want? Doesn't he know who you are? Your hands twitch, mouth twisting in a snarl.

No. *No.* You struggle for control, forcing down the unhelpful urge to lash out. Wing Yun is right, and it is not his fault that he is right. Take a steadying breath, and look at this cocky, handsome young soldier. Your tormented reaction hasn't escaped his notice, and he watches you with narrowed eyes.

"If I cannot find those I seek until after the invaders are gone, then I must do my part to remove the invaders," you say, with a cool reserve you don't feel. "Tell me, Mr. Chiu. How would your East River Column feel about welcoming a ghost into its ranks?"

Wing Yun sits back on his heels, and begins to laugh. "A ghost as a resistance fighter? Whoever heard of such a thing!" But he sounds amazed rather than contemptuous.

"Why not?" Move to crouch in front of him. "I can kill. You've seen that. I can wear skins, and infiltrate places with ease. I can lure unwary men, and survive terrible wounds. Your people need me, and I need this war finished. What do you say?"

"I think," he says, after a long, thoughtful moment, "that it will be a tough sell, to convince my superiors." He gives you a conspiratorial wink. "But you know what? I'm willing to argue the case. I believe we can talk them round." His grin is dazzling. "Do you have a name, Lady Ghost?"

A moment's hesitation. Then, "Sung Siu Yin. But please keep that to yourself, I don't wish my name to be widely known."

"No problem. I understand." He sticks out a hand. "Welcome to the resistance, Miss Sung."

28

A HUNDRED THOUSAND SOULS

Thirty years ago . . .

The date is August 6, 1945. The time is 04:30 hours.

A Japanese boat rocks on choppy water. No moon, the sky wreathed in clouds. Men make their rounds on the decks.

Gorō makes his last loop of the night and pauses to lean against the railing. He fans himself, sweats, takes his cap off, and puts it on again. Sometimes it feels like August is the only month Hong Kong ever exists in: rainy, on the cusp between summer and fall, perpetually warm and sticky.

He misses his home in Kotohira. It has actual seasons which vary and cycle. He misses the winter snow and the spring blossoms. He misses not being at war, too, though he's wise enough to never voice that sentiment aloud.

Still, the long night shift is nearly over, and he can snatch a few hours' sleep soon. Perhaps he will dream of home. That always improves his mood. He checks his uniform, his gun, with a quick once-over. The lieutenant is strict about appearance, and tidiness.

He straightens and is about to go inside when he hears a distinctive splashing sound, as if something heavy has fallen in the water.

Odd.

After a hesitant moment, Gorō shoulders the gun and walks round the corner of the deck's curve. He surveys to the left and right, scanning for any sign of disturbance. No one is there, nothing is wrong. Still, the skin on the back of his neck prickles. Uneasy, he turns around.

Private First-Class Tōshirō is standing right behind him, dripping with water.

"Hhhah!" he gasps. "Where did you come from? Why are you soaked?"

"Splashed by a wave." Tōshirō speaks with a flat tone, not quite an accent, but unusual-sounding. His dark eyes stare slightly past Gorō. "I need to change."

"Splashed by a wave?" Gorō echoes, incredulous. The sea is choppy enough to unsettle his stomach at mealtimes, but not so bad that water is rolling over the ship. "What wave?"

He glances down. A trail of watery footsteps leads from Tōshirō to the railing. As if his friend has crawled out of the sea.

"You fell in, didn't you," he says, accusingly. "Clumsy idiot! Were you drinking again?"

"No! No, I . . ." Tōshirō hesitates.

"What? Spit it out!"

"I saw something in the water," he says, not meeting Gorō's gaze. "A girl, drowning. But when I reached for her, a wave splashed me. Then she was gone."

Gorō stares. "Where was this? When?" The ship is ghost-warded, or should be, but he never feels entirely safe with that. There are simply so many ghosts, these days. Some very powerful.

"Over here." Tōshirō gestures, leading him to a particular spot along the railing. "She was in the water, just there." He adds, glumly, "It was a spirit, wasn't it? I've been a fool."

"It certainly wasn't a living woman, floating out in the harbor," Gorō says sharply, then leans over the railing, gun gripped tight. The water is dark and gloomy, with no sign of ghosts. Not that he expects there to be. Whatever apparition his friend saw is likely long gone. "Nothing there now, but we will report it. Did you touch her, or just reach for her?"

"Oh, he reached for me alright," Tōshirō murmurs, and slides his arms around Gorō's chest.

Gorō has one confused moment to panic before they both go over the railing, and down into the dark sea below.

A brief silence settles over the ship.

Two minutes later, a dripping wet Gorō climbs back up the emergency ladder, and over the railing of the military vessel. He blows water out of his nose, rolls his shoulders as if trying to get comfortable.

"Idiot," he says aloud, in perfect Cantonese. Then he goes to raise the alarm.

Men come running. Steps, guns, restless hands and anxious eyes.

Something in the water . . .

. . . she grabbed Tōshirō . . .

. . . tried to save him.

Tōshirō's floating corpse is plain enough to see. The other sailors begin reeling in the body, shouting and swearing, bringing out wards, hanging extra ones on railings. It's a good distraction, exactly the kind of thing to get many hands on deck.

Gorō watches impassively. He even helps hang a ward or two. Why not, it doesn't hurt him. Talismans only work on ghosts without a body.

"Get belowdecks, and get dry," says one of the officers.

Gorō throws a salute, and does as he's told.

⁂

Two hours later, and the ship is in chaos.

It has mysteriously run aground in Victoria Harbor, crashing into another docked military vessel. The resulting damage has pierced both hulls, causing the lower levels to flood with water. If that weren't enough, a fire has broken out on board. Men are dead, the survivors fighting among themselves.

You take full advantage of the confusion you've caused.

Wrecking the ship was your main goal. That enemy soldiers will also die is a nice bonus. The irony of the Japanese being so meticulous in warding against spirits is that the men who die aboard won't come back as undead. That means you are the only spirit anyone has to worry about, and you are not on their side.

You limp through flooded corridors, still wearing Gorō's body. His flesh has accrued a few stab wounds and a couple of bullets, and it stings like hell. You can mostly shut it off, though. There is something quite freeing in knowing that a body doesn't belong to you.

The plotting room is occupied by only two men, both junior engineers. There would normally be more but things are a little hectic at the moment. One runs off in fright when you wave a gun; the other starts yelling. You shoot him dead, and lock yourself in.

Switches flip beneath your hands. Lights beep and blink. Somewhere up above, whatever remains of the warship's artillery will be firing at surrounding vessels, blindly. If it goes on long enough, other ships will eventually return fire, just to sink this one.

Fine by you.

Someone begins yelling and banging on the door. A part of you wants to let them in, kill them with your own hands, feel them clinging to you as they seek comfort in death. Even from a murderer.

But everything in you that is sensible, and reasonable—a hard balance to maintain, as a ghost—reminds you that victory is the goal. If you open this door, someone might be able to reverse your sabotage.

So you sit, and wait. Put your borrowed feet up on the desk, hands behind your head.

Shots rock the warship. Return fire, at last. Maybe they evacuated the men on board, maybe not. Enough have died, either way. You no longer hear anyone banging on the door of this room, and that's promising.

Creaking noises; is this ship about to sink? Also hopeful. You open the door, finally. Water pours into your room, and you welcome it. Water is pain, but a familiar one. Everyone still aboard will drown as you have drowned.

And really, that's the heart of it all, isn't it? You want everyone to know your pain as you do. Especially those who are responsible for it.

The man who was banging on the door is still there, to your surprise. It's the first junior engineer, the one who initially ran off; his courage must have sent him crawling back, keeping him firm even as everything is going to hell.

His gun is empty so he attacks you futilely with his fists. You ignore him, mildly intrigued by the way his knuckles leave marks on your ribs, and the meaty places of your body. When that has no effect other than to make you bruised and bleeding, he tries to strangle you with his bare hands.

You let him, out of morbid curiosity, because strangulation isn't something you've experienced yet. It's not very nice, and you decide not to experience it again.

Afterward, he sits there sobbing and shaking while the water rises around him, your freshly throttled corpse floating nearby. The water is almost waist-deep, and still pouring in.

Feeling bored, you slip free from Gorō's ruined shell.

The junior engineer sees you ooze out, a green-hued spirit girl, and screams horribly loud in that small, enclosed space. Your form reasserts itself to the alluring, ethereal water ghost that death has shaped your soul into. His screaming stops as the glamour takes hold; you recognize the familiar look of awestruck entrancement in his gaze.

"Beautiful," he whispers, in Japanese. You've learned a lot of that language, these past three years.

My turn, you think, and close your fingers around his soft, soft throat as you push his head beneath the swirling water.

In wars, the presence of ghosts is factored into calculations: for roughly every thousand men killed in battle, generals assume that at least one of them will return as a spiritual force, angry about their death and in need of dispersing by exorcists or appeasing through offerings. Hence the Japanese and their careful warding of the Walled City, their efforts to corral angry spirits.

Sometimes, ghosts will even fight for one side or another. They may or may not appear right away; they may be stronger or weaker when they do appear, depending on the time of year, and how much of their spirit has endured. Some can throw punches and fire weapons, while others drift past in a hazy cloud.

This sort of thing is not new, though textbooks prefer not to discuss it. The American Civil War was a short-lived affair, thanks to the legions of furious ghosts who had suffered so abominably as abused, enslaved people while alive, and fought against the South.

George Washington frequently sought counsel from his two dead sisters, lost to childhood illness; their foresight gave him an edge.

The witch hunts of the 1600s ended abruptly when the ghosts of murdered women began slaughtering witch-finders.

King Henry VIII was eventually found dead under mysterious circumstances, the artifacts of his many queens lying scattered across his body.

And poor Puyi, China's unlucky last emperor, was frequently plagued by bad luck—arising, many said, from the haunting of the previous empress's displeased spirit. She always considered him inadequate to fill her shoes.

It is notable, too, that most of these ghosts were women or members of the underclasses. That should surprise no one. Those who lack power in life carry an unequal share of injustice into death. Returning from the grave is their only recourse to right those wrongs.

And you, as a ghost, definitely have a lot of injustice to be angry about.

The first of these was Baba's death, and the lies your mother told to cover it up. Mami's abandonment was the next such event; it severed any lingering belief you had that familial love could ever be enough.

Being betrayed by Mei Chi was the next one. You will never forget that night, the shocked realization filtering through: this unfair death is what happened to Mei Chi. Followed by, *This unfair death is what Mei Chi did to me.*

If she'd done it by accident, that would have been forgivable. But she stalked you, lured you, tried to charm you into drowning, all to sate her egotistical loneliness. And when that didn't work, she drowned you by force, taking everything.

In the wake of her disappearance, you have nothing left except your anger: at her, at your mother, at the world, at the invaders who have derailed planetary peace. Mei Chi was out of reach while the war was going on, the city too dangerous to search. So you have chosen to go to war, and see if you can't do your bit to end it that much faster.

War, after all, is nothing more than a collective societal excuse to kill each other with skill and style, and celebrate it proudly. In peacetime you'd be a monster of legendary violence, but in the heart of the Second World War, you are well on the way to being a hero.

Three years of fighting, three years of drowning soldiers, taking their skins, infiltrating their camps and boats and once a submarine—admittedly, that venture was unsuccessful—to disrupt their plans.

All in all, the days have been running by in a blur, so fast you can hardly count them. And suddenly you are here, August 6, 1945.

Another landmark moment in your life.

The resistance fighters almost shoot you when you return, but you're used to that, and so are they. It's hard for them; you leave as one skin, come back as another. Almost always you are wearing a Japanese soldier of some description, and they can't keep track. If they don't stay vigilant, then one of these days an actual soldier will walk up and they'll not kill him in time.

You shout out the password, which changes every three days.

"Stand down," says one of the veterans to a trigger-happy youngster; he's new to this group. "It's only Thousand-Faced Girl."

The Girl with a Thousand Faces, or sometimes just Thousand-Faced Girl. That's what they call you in this camp. It's not strictly accurate—your count is barely above two hundred, if that—but you rather like it. A nice myth, as it were.

There are other ghosts among the resistance fighters. You joining up opened the door wide for other supernatural helpers. Few as versatile or powerful, but plenty can help in other ways. Little grandmother ghosts who sew uniforms, for example. The waiting women who wander the woods and catch Japanese patrols unawares with their ribbon necks and savage teeth. Fire-breathers who cause havoc in guerilla raids. And others, many others. The main criteria is being able to listen to orders.

Offer up a cheerful smile to the men on guard, and saunter along past. They fall back at your approach, saluting respectfully. Only Wing Yun has ever seen your true form, or known your real name, and even then he couldn't see through the glamour.

It's Wing Yun's tent you head to first. The whole of this resistance cell is based in the forests and hills of Sai Kung, makeshift tents pitched among the trees and rain and boggy ground. It is always humid, rarely comfortable, but still better than a POW camp. Which is the only alternative for these men and women.

"I hear it was a rousing success." Wing Yun doesn't even look up as you enter. He's bent over a folding desk, rickety from age and rust. "But I'm keen to hear a direct report."

He's benefited from your success. Together, you have taken on a slew of impossible operations, the pair of you rising through resistance ranks in record time. You've tried working with other soldiers, and didn't like them nearly as much. None of the others were as charming, or as intelligent. The fact that he is extraordinarily good-looking doesn't hurt, either.

"What you heard was correct." Grab a seat, slump into it lazily. "The boat sank like a stone. Lives were lost and it did a lot of damage in port. The information you gave me was gold. As usual."

"That's a relief," he says, grinning, and you grin back.

Sometimes his information isn't, and the infiltration jobs go wrong, but you rarely mind. Unless the men have an exorcist aboard—and those are in short supply these days—there isn't a fucking thing they can do to you.

The best part: there are never any witnesses. If it goes wrong you simply leave, and the Japanese think they had a traitor in their midst. If it goes right, they all die, with no one left alive to spread awkward rumors. They have no idea that a single "lady ghost" is causing them so much havoc.

"What's our next action?"

"Already moving on?" He sounds amused. "How nice it must be, to never sleep, hey?"

"I would tell you that I'll sleep when I'm dead, but I'm already dead and that hasn't happened," you say dryly. "So, I'll sleep when my spirit moves to the underworld. How's that?"

"Fair enough! Well, we dealt an incredible blow tonight. But this location"—he stabs a finger at the map on his table—"will be of vital importance if we—"

The world disappears briefly. Your senses are overwhelmed by a wash of white lights and a sound that reminds you of radio static. Somewhere far to the north, reality distorts. A force so violent and destructive that it hardly bears imagining has rocked the world, sending repercussions that a spirit can feel with every wisp of their being.

You stagger, gasping, hands clutching over your head. As if that could make any difference to the reverberant sensation you've just experienced.

"Siu Yin?" Wing Yun approaches, hovering near you with worry on his face. "What is wrong?"

You tear out of the tent, stumbling to your knees in the dirt.

Hiroshima is over two thousand kilometers away, too far to see the nuclear blast with physical eyes. You do not yet know the name of the city that just died in a single breath, or its exact location.

But you feel it, oh so clearly. You and every other ghost or medium from here to China to Russia to Guam and all the places in between—you all feel the spiritual energy of a hundred thousand souls, plus other living animals and plants, as they are converted from flesh to spirit.

"What is it?" Wing Yun is outside, next to you now. He hasn't missed the collective reaction of the camp's gathered spirits. "What's happening?"

"Something terrible," you say, surprised to find yourself weeping. "A horrible act of destruction. I don't have words—"

Wing Yun takes your hand, giving it a squeeze. Hesitantly, you squeeze back, both of you kneeling in the damp earth beneath a quiet sky. He doesn't understand, can't know yet what you've sensed. But he knows you are distressed, and that's enough.

Against all the cruel and dark things you've experienced in this world, that one act of kindness is precious, and you hold it close in your fractured heart.

29

THE LONG NIGHT

Thirty years ago . . .

Nuclear devastation ends the war, eventually. The Japanese resist for a while, although that collapses shortly after the second bomb.

But even as the opposition folds, even as hope grows in the hearts of the resistance fighters, your own hopes are fading. While it's a venerable occupation to possess the bodies of enemy soldiers during times of war, that kind of ability makes people uneasy in times of peace.

When the Japanese capitulate, the British will take over. And they are none too keen on the "ghost regiments" of Sai Kung, however useful they found you during these past three years. Even Wing Yun's recommendation isn't going to help. The messages coming from the remnants of Hong Kong's government have made that clear as day.

The developments frustrate you. All this work you did was driven by the desire to find Mei Chi and your mother, but the return of peace doesn't seem to be making that any easier.

Still, you can't do anything if you're caught by exorcists. Angry and bitter, you take off in the night, the day after the second atomic bomb falls. And you go to hide in the forest, intending to lay low until you can see which way the political winds are blowing.

You are therefore rather surprised when Wing Yun comes to find you one morning, in early September.

The resistance fighters have mostly disbanded by now, and all gone home. But you have remained, lingering in your military tent and stolen body like a bad smell, continuing to squat in the tree-riddled hills of the New Territories. Away from the rest of humanity.

The resistance camp held a few Japanese POWs, before the war ended, but it doesn't anymore. You brought them along when you left, and have been "going through" them like disposable gowns. They were up for execution anyway, not that this makes it any more ethical. But ethics have stopped mattering to you as much as they once did.

"Siu Yin? Is that you?" Wing Yun kneels outside the battered tent, peering in. His nose wrinkles at the stench of your stolen, unwashed flesh. "So, it's true. You are still out here, lurking around."

"Where else would I go?" You sit cross-legged beneath the grimy tent, shirt worn to rags, flesh emaciated from days of not eating. The only bathing you've done is whatever the rain chooses to bestow.

It isn't comfortable squatting in the woods, and there are few facilities. Even less food. Fortunately, you don't care about comfort, or taking care of your body. It's only a dead enemy, and their corpse doesn't require your respect. Let it starve, let it be dirty.

"Fair answer." He crouches outside the tent, fingers interlaced. "How long have you been in that body?"

"Why do you ask?"

"I thought you told me once that staying in the same vessel for too many days is bad."

"My memories start to fade, if I inhabit a skin too long, and I forget myself." You don't admit that some memories are already slipping from you, like soup through a sieve. "But I wouldn't call that bad."

He raises an eyebrow.

"Everyone likes to forget, sometimes. Living people drink beer; I stay in my skins an extra day."

"Beer doesn't erase an entire person," he counters.

"Doesn't it? I think it does for some. Besides, the memories come back when I shed the skin." You've done it twice before, by accident: stayed too long, started to lose yourself, then fortunately gotten "killed" in action. The death brought it all back. Since then, you've been more careful.

Well, usually.

You add, "I won't stay much longer. Since you seem worried. This body is on the verge of fatal dehydration, and that will clear my head."

"Shouldn't you be near water, if you're about to leave this body behind?"

"I can look after myself," you tell him. "Why are you here? Isn't there a victory to celebrate, or something?"

"I am more of a fighter than a partier." Wing Yun scratches his chin thoughtfully. "I miss our chats. Ghost or not, you've been a good friend and fought well, and earned us many victories. I respected you. Still do."

"Futile, what we did," you tell him, shortly. "We could have just sat in the trees and waited for that bomb to drop."

"Not futile," he says, with quiet conviction. "It is never futile to fight for freedom. What we did mattered."

No idea what to say to that. Wing Yun is an idealist, which you both admire and dislike in him simultaneously. It's not a worldview you can even begin to parse.

When he gets no response, Wing Yun sighs and says, "I came to warn you, one friend to another. The British are in control again. We all know how the Westerners feel about stray ghosts roaming the place."

"No surprise! Why do you think I left? I could see how that was going to go."

"Smart choice." He grimaces. "They've already rounded up the other ghosts who were in my division."

"And you just let them, did you?"

"They came in the night and gave us no choice."

"How I hate them," you say, with real bitterness. "Years of my existence given to service of this country, and for what? They want to exorcise me—put me in a bottle gourd!"

"It is unfair," he agrees, quietly. "I will fight for our warrior spirits' rights however I can. But in the meantime, you must stay safe."

His concern brings a lump to your human throat, and you are forced to look away. If only you weren't a ghost and had your own skin. If only you weren't dead and could pursue this man, have a courtship, have a life. Grow up, as you were meant to do.

Desperate to change the subject, you say quickly, "How do the European exorcists compare to the Japanese and their Supernatural Forces Division?"

"Far worse." If he's noticed your moment of emotion, he doesn't comment. "The Japanese respect their own ghosts, at least. It was only enemy spirits they feared. The Westerners, though, would rather see no ghosts at all, and they mostly revile spirits, unless they get classed as Catholic saints. For some reason, their saints get a pass."

"I see. Are you advising me to . . . what, hide? Return to the ocean, lurk there drowning forever?"

He spreads his hands. "Have you ever listened to my advice? I am giving you warning, that's all. They're already doing sweeps through the city, cleaning out spirits. Good, bad, friendly, unhelpful. I just thought you should know."

You want to ask him what he thinks you're supposed to do. Sit in the sea, rotting away and murdering random victims? Or perhaps take a body, forget yourself, go among the living? Likely enough, that's what happened to Mei Chi.

Fucking Mei Chi. She's probably a thousand miles away by now, if not dead herself. The anguish of that injustice, that unsolved rage, eats at you daily. But regardless, Wing Yun has no answers for the questions in your head. He's already standing, shaking mud and grass off his trousers, getting ready to leave.

"Will you help me?" you say, on impulse. Needing to know, before he disappears. "The women I'm looking for, who we've talked about. I can't search them out easily or safely. But now that the war is ended . . ." A hesitant pause.

"I can move around freely?" He finishes your statement, not missing a beat. "Siu Yin, I thought you'd never ask! Of course, I will look for them. I have my own relatives to search for, too."

You could hug him just then, if you weren't so exhausted and dirty. "Thank you, my kind friend. I appreciate that."

"It's the least I can do," he says. "What can you tell me about them? Names, descriptions—"

"No need." You stand up and press your forehead to his, as Mei Chi did to you once, three years ago.

Memories and experiences flood from your mind to his. Not the full thing, because you don't want to share every moment of hurt with him, but enough: glimpses of your face, Mami's face, the island, snippets of Hong Kong.

It's intuitive, this action. You know how to do it in the same way that you know how to swim. Ghosts long to share their stories, after all. When it's done, he rocks back on his heels, blinking hard and a little stunned.

"Was that . . . your life?" he says, amazed.

"Part of it."

"And the two women—"

"The older one is my mother, Daiyu. The younger one is my aunt, Chen Mei Chi. You know their faces, now, and their names."

"I can work with this," he says, recovering his composure with admirable speed. "Are there any relatives you can think of who they might seek out in Hong Kong?"

You're about to reply when the snapping of twigs catches your mutual attention.

"Friends of yours?" you ask, with sudden wariness.

"Shit. I think I've been followed here!" Wing Yun catches your arm, pulling you to standing. "Siu Yin, you need to run. Now!"

"What?" You let him pull you up; this body is very weak, after all. "Who is it?"

"Government exorcists. I thought I lost them in the woods, but clearly not." He gives you a shove. "Go! If they catch you, I'll do my best to free you."

"Promise," you say, struck by a sudden pang of fear. "Promise you won't forget me."

He looks at you, unblinking, and nods. "I promise. Now get out of here!"

With a hiss, you whirl away and begin to run through the woods.

Any other day, and you'd have destroyed them. Any other body, and you could have outrun them.

Just your bad luck—and bad planning, if you're honest—that today this form is tired and weak, distracted from having worn this skin too long. Severe dehydration and lack of food means there is only so far you can push shaking legs.

The noise of footfalls is growing louder in the surrounding forest, and you can hear men calling to each other in a mix of English and Cantonese.

What will they even do to you, these exorcists? No, doesn't matter. Don't think of it. There will be time later to process their betrayal (again! More betrayal!) and your own need for revenge.

The body you're in stumbles, knees briefly giving way. It won't last in this chase much longer. Realistically, you need water to escape these men. If you can get to the nearby stream, they'll not be able to catch you. Eject from this skin and slide off to freedom. Maybe kill a few as you go.

Looking back, it's tragic how close you came to escape. A little more luck, and it would have all worked in your favor. But it is not, and has never been, your destiny to be lucky. The heavens were not so kind when plotting the course of your life.

In short, you reach the stream only to find that some of the exorcists have anticipated your thoughts. Two of them are already waiting.

Skid to a halt, bare feet dug into the damp forest earth. Breathing hard, parched and tired.

"Good afternoon, Thousand-Faced Girl," says one of the men, in clipped English.

He is Western: fair-haired and too tall; pale-eyed, like a dead fish. His robes are long and black despite the heat, clothes designed for a chillier European clime. Delicate spectacles rest on a nose that could break rocks. In one hand he carries wooden rosaries; in the other, a fat old Bible.

The other man does not greet you, only stares coldly. He is dressed similarly but instead of rosaries, he carries old scrolls and what look like cannisters. Some of that famous holy water the Catholics are known for, and blessed salt. You don't know how supernatural banishment works in other cultures, other than that Europeans are especially good at doing it.

"Get out of my way. I only want to exist, not cause harm," you snap, pointedly answering in Cantonese. It's been ages since your schoolgirl days, and your English is rusty. Besides, why accommodate a man who has come to hurt you? You don't owe this gweilo any kind of courtesy. "Didn't I fight well in the war? Don't I deserve as much respect as someone living?"

"We mean no disrespect, Thousand-Faced Girl," says the first Jesuit, even as he lifts his rosary beads high. His Cantonese is very good, which makes it even more annoying that he tried English first. "Your sacrifices and hard work will be engraved on a memorial—"

"A memorial! How wonderful and kind!"

"—but your time to rest is here," he finishes, and then begins chanting in a language you've never heard before. Latin, Greek, Hebrew, something unknown to you. The other Jesuit joins him.

You try to dart around them, conscious of the other priests who are catching up. Needing desperately to reach the open stream not twenty yards behind him.

The second Jesuit opens a cannister and flings holy water in your face. It stings and hisses on your skin, as if he's thrown boiling-hot acid. The pain is great enough that your spirit self is in agony, and your already weakened shell of a body staggers to one knee.

Immediately, both men begin throwing a ring of salt around you, still chanting in unison. You try to run over it and cannot, to your horrified shock. Strange, that; salt has never bothered you before. Whatever they've done to it, however they're using it, is oddly powerful.

Things only get worse from there.

More priests arrive, some of them Taoist rather than Catholic. Between their disparate groups, they trap you in salt and keep you cringing with their holy water. Blessed smoke and fu talismans written in temple ink seal the ring into an impenetrable, painful prison. It is almost as bad as being back in the ocean, perpetually drowning.

For the first time in years, you are again a scared young woman, far out of her depth.

The exorcism is excruciating, all the more because you are strong. It takes two attempts before they can force you from the corpse you've hidden in. When you finally crawl forth, trembling and wishing that water ghosts could cry, the sun is beginning to sink behind the hills.

Small mercies: between the cooling off of late afternoon and the shade offered by this valley, you do not die right away.

Thankfully, the Catholic priests do not seem to recognize how deadly the sunlight is. You are a different kind of ghost than anything they've seen in the West, and when their third exorcism fails to disperse your withering spirit, they decide to bind you, instead.

You'll wonder, later, if the Taoist priests knew and said nothing. Perhaps they were young and ignorant of water ghosts, or perhaps they felt disinclined to assist their Catholic cousins in dispersal and exorcism. You are not a normal ghost, after all, and have made a name for yourself during these war years. Anyone with a conscience would feel the weight of guilt.

Right now, you do not have space to consider this, and know only searing anger, wrenching betrayal. Even at Wing Yun, who unwittingly led them straight to you. His promises feel hollow in that moment, like everything else.

As the ritual reaches its climax, one of the Taoist priests steps forward with a large bottle gourd, elegantly painted and etched all over with glyphs. A fine, thin net stretches around it, shimmering slightly.

You know what's coming. Bottle gourds have a long history of uses, from medicines to spirit-trapping. They're not easy to make for one as powerful as you, but these men have come prepared, and are clearly willing to spend the resources.

Their chants rise louder, Latin and Chinese entwining in awful disharmony. Weakened, sun-frazzled, exhausted, and in pain, you begin to turn into mist. And that mist flows into the bottle gourd, like a genie in reverse.

Your last thought before darkness clamps down is that, if you ever get out of here, you will *never* forgive this city.

30
A MUTUAL PROPOSITION

One year ago . . .

Death is final, so we fear it. Even if a spirit reincarnates to a new life, that is no comfort to the self that is lost, or the possibilities that went with it. A fresh start is no guarantee, either, of a better experience.

But there are worse things than death. Your torment was one such thing.

Time doesn't freeze for the being caught in a bottle gourd. The experience is not like falling asleep or slipping into a coma, where unconsciousness is a gift to protect the mind. Humans either don't realize that, or don't care, when they trap spirits within.

You are aware and awake in that gourd, for every excruciating moment. Pinioned in pitch blackness with nothing to see or hear, no one to speak to but your own thoughts. In Chinese and Christian hells, there are at least other people to share the misery. Demons to bargain with, gods to plead with.

This is simply nothingness. Pure isolation and loneliness, distilled.

No wonder ghosts and demons who are bound always come out so angry.

You're not immune to the strain, and periodically lose your mind. Minutes and hours and days and weeks and months and *years* of screaming, singing, crying, pleading in the empty dark. Insanity descends on you like a flood, and then recedes in time as your spirit mind cycles through suffering and healing and yet more suffering.

It is an unimaginable experience, and I am sorry for any sentient being—living or dead, human or demon—who must endure that.

A lesser ghost would have fragmented. Many of the other captured ghosts do just that: quietly expiring within those gourds, which themselves are locked away in a secure storage room in a well-guarded basement facility. Their souls cannot even reincarnate, and they are nothing more than bottles of discombobulated energy.

But you, who have always been fierce and focused, overflowing with energy and now newly warped by multiple betrayals all feeding your hate . . . You, you persevere. The little girl who couldn't stop moving, who jittered restlessly, is now the not-so-little ghost who still can't let go, relax, disperse. What's left of your soul is too restless.

Even knowing it is futile and that you might easily spend a hundred years, or indeed forever, in this stupid fucking fruit husk, you refuse to collapse into nothing. Because the alternative is that there can never be justice for the things done to you; no resolution, no vengeance. That is more unbearable than any death or torment.

No one else will ever know this struggle you faced, this great unheralded battle in your life. But for what it's worth, Siu Yin, this goddess saw you, and was impressed.

You had almost made peace with such inconceivable torment, when fate again intervened.

Dates and hours are hard to quantify in a dark place with no functioning senses, no companionship or presence. All you know is that the suffering and madness has gone on interminably, until it suddenly stops.

There comes a ring of brightness, forming around. It is the first light you have seen in what feels like eons, easing the unending and unresponsive darkness. That frightens you, makes you worry that death is at hand. Nothing you can do about it except brace.

Then a spiraling sensation, as if you are being drawn upward through a drain, in reverse. Corporeal reality slams down with the force of a truck smashing into a concrete cliff. The world reasserts itself.

Floor. You are lying on the floor, cheek pressed to chilly concrete. There is pain, all over; it is too dry in here. For a moment, the sheer overwhelm of existing in any capacity is too much, and your mind can't take it. After so long existing in nothingness, this small enclosed space is a vast, sensory-laden expanse.

Try to scream, find you can't breathe. As usual. The familiar drenched feeling in your dead lungs. Look down; clawed, green-tinged hands. A bony and monstrous form. Yourself as you are, in ghost form.

That's bad. It is too dry in here, no water anywhere. Already, your spirit skin is cracking. The room itself is a small stone cell, eight feet by eight feet. No furniture, only a single pedestal on which to rest the gourd. Fu talismans hang from the walls, and a ring of salt surrounds the pedestal. The talismans are rent, but the salt circle is intact.

Someone has set you free.

Well. Partially, anyway. You can't leave this stupid ring of salt, not in your weakened condition.

"So *you* are the famous Girl with a Thousand Faces. The memorial plaque they made doesn't do justice."

Tilt your head up painfully, straining against the rapid dehydration and sensory overload.

A youngish woman peers down from her vantage point in the doorway. You did not notice her before, because there was too much for you to look at. She is in her late twenties, older than you when you first died, with a hard edge to her cynical smile. Smartly dressed in a gray tweed suit. Lean arms fold against a slim body, and her front teeth are charmingly crooked. The opened gourd sits on the floor next to her, along with a jug of water.

Water . . . I need water! Point at the jug. She must have brought it for you.

"You can have water later," she says, impatiently. Her Cantonese is crisp and clean, with no trace of accent; a native Hong Konger. "I brought you out of binding to talk."

No, you don't understand. I need water, now, or I will die*!*

She hesitates, caught off guard by your insistence.

Please. The fight with the exorcists has left me weak. Look at me! Extend your hands, the skin already like withered parchment, cracked all over. *I will talk about anything you wish. But first, water!*

"Fine," she says, exasperated, and picks up a jug next to her feet. It is full to the brim, and she throws it over you. "Better now?"

Water pools around you on the floor, but does not breach the circle of salt. Interesting. Normal salt would wash away, but this stuff is presumably blessed or sanctified in some way.

Thank you. It's an effort to keep your voice sounding humble. The water is good, but it's only a temporary relief, and you resent this arrogant young woman who acts so dismissively. *How long was I in there?*

Her lip curls. "Today is the tenth of June, and the year is 1974."

You clutch the pedestal, reeling in shock. Exorcists trapped you in 1945, which means it's been twenty-nine years, locked in that tiny pocket of torment. *Twenty-nine years.*

"I tried three ghosts, before yours," the young woman says, watching you avidly. "The others had dispersed into nothing. Yet you have endured, after nearly three decades. Very impressive."

I will not succumb to darkness. The water that pools around you on the floor has nowhere to go; the concrete is sealed. You sit in that shallow puddle, taking what comfort you can from the barest of liquid. *I will not yield to time. Not after all I have endured.*

"Wing Yun said as much," she says, then grins as you sit bolt upright. "Ah, you recognize that name!"

He was my brother in arms. We fought in the war together. Is he still alive?

"He is, and he's petitioned for many years for your release. In fact, it was his petition that first drew my attention to the ghosts down here, and gave me the idea."

An uncomfortable itch settles between your shoulder blades. *What idea? Who are you, and why have you freed me?*

"At last, you ask sensible questions! My name is Tsang Kit Ling, and I am a councilwoman on Hong Kong's Executive Council." She unhooks a folding stool from a nail on the wall, and sits on it cross-legged. "You are the Girl with a Thousand Faces, and you fought for the Hong Kong resistance during the war. Very brave."

Hong Kong betrayed me.

"The British government did, when it took over again," she corrects. "But I suppose my government did yield to that order. Not like there was a lot of choice."

Same difference!

She ignores that. "I have come to offer a deal, Thousand-Faced Girl. If you are willing to negotiate."

That gives you a moment's pause. You will never trust living humans, ever again, but you do need out of here, and this smug young lady seems to have the proverbial keys. Whatever she's offering must be better than a return to the bottle.

I am listening. What kind of deal?

"It's very simple. Either you go back into banishment until your spirit collapses and you die a true death, without even reincarnation"—she gestures languidly at the gourd, and you shudder—"or, you agree to do me a favor. For whatever it is worth, I think you will like the task I have in mind."

That doesn't sound like much of a "choice" to you. But though your anger is a towering mountain, you rein it in. The memory of twenty-nine years' worth of lonely torment is more than enough motivation to keep your ghost urges under control. For now.

Because honestly, as much as Mei Chi dominated your thoughts for years, you only have one overriding desire at the moment: to stay out of this hellish bottle they've kept you in. Going back is a horror that frightens even you to think about. Worry about the rest once you've persuaded this arrogant young woman to set you free.

Of course. Smile as best you can, with your monster teeth. *I would be honored to know what favor the wise councilor requests.*

Kit Ling actually claps her hands in delight. "I'm so pleased! Very well. Have you heard of Kowloon Walled City? I'm sure it was around even in your day."

Surprise flits through you, though you don't allow it to show.

I have, yes. It is a small neighborhood where the undead were driven by Japanese forces, who feared their retribution. Refugees also gathered there. We coordinated many resistance operations with the people in that place, though I never met any of them in person.

All of that is true. You were always out in the field, busy wearing stolen skins. You add, *What of it? Does it still exist?*

"Oh, it exists. As a rotten little slum." Her lip curls again, with fresh disdain. "I have made it my career mission to have Kowloon Walled City demolished and built over."

You keep your silence, and say nothing lest your own contempt leak through. The sheer pettiness of human ambitions never ceases to amaze you, even after all this time. "Career mission" indeed.

"I suppose financial gain means little to a ghost," Kit Ling says thoughtfully, with a flicker of self-awareness. "But you see, I own some of the property in that place. Demolishing the city means I will benefit from the government compensation payouts, and as a Council executive, I can influence the amount we compensate the residents and landlords." Her smile is wolfish and unpleasant. "There are also certain building contracts which will fall into place, and again benefit me, if all comes to fruition. However, the clock is ticking, and these businesses will not wait forever."

I respect your clever financial ambitions, Miss Tsang. A good thing that ghosts can lie, and very easily. You respect nothing about her, not an inch. *Yet I remain confused as to what you require of me, willing though I am to serve and be of use.*

The obsequious language seems to please Kit Ling. She practically wiggles, like a child who has been praised for good school marks.

"It's very simple. There is great resistance to demolishing Kowloon, from within and without the neighborhood. Therefore, I hope to unleash you on the Walled City. It is the perfect place for you: dark, with many underground waterways, and lots of ghosts. The triads who control it insist that only they can keep the ghosts in check, but if you are running wild and causing chaos, it will give me the perfect excuse to seize control and have it all knocked down. We both benefit, and some nice buildings can replace that ugly slum."

You're far from stupid, but she clearly thinks you're an idiot, and that rankles.

It's obvious that once she's used you to wreak the havoc she needs, she'll either step back when the exorcists and ghost hunters come calling, or send them in herself. No way would she let you simply wander free at will, especially if she thinks you're dangerous. Doubly so if your existence implicates her actions.

Not that you can call her out on this, unfortunately. Anything suspicious and she'll likely force you back into the bottle gourd with fu talismans and chants. Best to assume she's able to do that, even though she gives the air of someone with more confidence than competence.

Your main priority needs to be getting out of prison. The next words you say to her matter greatly.

Forgive me, Miss Tsang, but what happens to me when Kowloon is demolished?

A little risky, but your gut instinct whispers that not mentioning it at all will be suspicious. She might be inclined to think you are insincere if you leap to accept her offer without question, and you don't want that. She must believe your capitulation is real.

Kit Ling's eyes narrow in response, and she examines you the way a housewife might examine a cockroach who has dared crawl into her house.

"What do you want to happen?" she says, acidly.

The ocean, you say, immediately. *I long only to return to the sea, to the island from which I came.*

"Huh. And how do I know you won't do that straightaway, if I release you?"

Because my soul cries out for justice. That is certainly true. *The people of Kowloon betrayed me, and caused me to be locked away here, even though I once worked with them. I seek retribution, and you kindly offer me this chance, Miss Tsang.* Not quite accurate, but close enough that the truth rings through it. *When that is done, I yearn only to retreat to the waves. Will you let me?*

"Well. I think that can be arranged." Her self-satisfied smile fills you with loathing. "I won't ask you to sign a contract, Thousand-Faced Girl. Paper agreements cannot restrain a ghost. But here is what will happen. First, I am going to bind you back into that vessel."

She pulls out a second bottle gourd, similar looking to the one you inhabited before. "I'll swap gourds, leaving this empty one behind. Then I will walk out, with you tucked safely in my bag. Your old prison will be put away, and no one will know you have been released. Later, when I am out in the city, I shall set you free. Are we agreed?"

You agree, after pretending to think about it. There's no other choice, except to trust her. If you don't agree, she'll only force you back inside, anyway.

Still, stepping willingly back into that tiny prison is one of the hardest things you've ever done. The trauma of that bondage is fresh, the relief of being "out" immense in so many ways. It takes all of your resolve, your years of forged inner strength, to let her bind you anew.

She begins to read a chant from a piece of paper, and you close your eyes, willing yourself to yield. Darkness closes in again, and your final horrified thought as she seals up the new gourd is that you can, in fact, tell there is less room in here.

A while later.

You're not sure how much time has passed, only that it was a much shorter span than before. When you come to, you're lying in a bath of water, groggy and exhausted. Still not fully recovered from the exorcism which first trapped you, never mind the second one that Kit Ling has put you through. There is very little light in here; the windows are boarded up, and the taps leak badly.

At least the bathwater is helpful, and very soothing. It's good to be submerged again. The darkness is nice, too.

"There you are. Feeling yourself, yet?"

Sit up slowly. Water sluices off languidly.

Kit Ling is perched on the edge of the bath, a smug grin plastered on her pretty face. That expression offsets any beauty she would otherwise have.

Where are we now, Miss Tsang?

"In a property I own and lease, within the Walled City. People come here to gamble, hire girls, and take drugs." The casualness with which she says this, as if immune to the stench of her own corruption. It is staggering that this woman is a city official.

I am . . . free? To kill, to hunt, to roam?

"Yes. Cause all the damage you like." She stands up. "I must go, now that you are awake. It won't do for me to be seen in this place. Have fun, Thousand-Faced Girl."

You sidle out of the bath, standing between her and the door.

The councilwoman frowns. "What are you doing?"

You call yourself a city leader? Disgusting, "Miss" Tsang. Your first blow slams her head against the bathroom door. She squeals pitifully, tries to start chanting an exorcism ritual; you snatch the bottle gourd from her hand and smash it.

"No! We had an agreement," she gasps, and then immediately wets herself when you pick her up by the throat.

I know that you plan to betray me, as humans always will. Our agreement was therefore void, the moment you made it.

She begins wailing, scratching feebly at your wrists. Her face is a mess of bruised cheeks and busted lips.

This idiot, you think dismally, would not have lasted an hour under Japanese occupation. She is all cocky privilege and corrupt self-satisfaction, with no character or strength. The world will not miss her a jot.

"Please, please, please!" she sobs, shameless and pathetic in her begging. "I'm so sorry, so sorry, please forgive me, I didn't mean it!"

Be sorry in your next life. This one is over.

Drag her into the bath and force her head beneath the tepid water until she stops fucking struggling. It's done in less than two minutes. With so much blood on your hands, another pointless death is not remarkable.

Afterward, it seems only fitting to take her body as your own. She is a well-connected, financially secure woman, and that is really quite perfect for your needs. Should have thought of that before hitting her so hard, but never mind.

You step into her skin, and stretch languorously. Next, you reach down and scoop out some of the water, splashing it on the floor before mopping it up with a towel. The rest you allow to drain away.

Water ghosts make water ghosts, especially if the victim is a woman. You got lucky with those Japanese soldiers the first time; they were men, which greatly reduced the likelihood. It's trickier with women victims.

But her spirit can't return to dryness, and thus her death is final if you displace or clean up all the water she died in. That's a trick you worked out during the war, and it is as handy now as it was against soldiers. The water-ghost curse didn't account for intelligent manipulation.

It's a trick you'll use later, to keep Red Bird's ghost under control: a small spirit trapped in a small basin, virtually powerless. There is a certain creativity to your malice.

Later, as you stand in front of that mirror dabbing blood from your (her) split lips, applying ice to your (her) black eyes, a smile steals across your face.

"Thank you, Miss Tsang," you say, into the mirror. "You don't know what you've done for me."

Not only has this idiot politician freed you, she's given you the keys to the city. Her money and her life are yours, to use as you see fit. Everyone thinks you're dead and captured, and no one will know to look for you.

The quest for vengeance—against Mei Chi, against Mami, against Hong Kong which betrayed you—can finally, *finally* resume.

This fucking city will never know what hit it.

31

BRAVE NEW WORLD

One year ago . . .

Hong Kong of 1974 is unrecognizable to your eyes.

Back in the '40s, it was a bustling, ex-colonial settlement, where locals often wore traditional clothes and the buildings were a mix of European and South Chinese. Very busy, yes, and jostling for sure, but few structures were taller than five or six stories, and the streets were mostly cluttered with rickshaws and trams and bikes. Even the war hadn't changed that.

What confronts you now is an alien landscape. Concrete towers knife upward along the skyline. Cars stream in a murmuring flood through asphalt arteries. The government is, you hear, beginning to dig tunnels beneath, to create a rapid high-speed rail of some sort. Even the harbor shape has changed; developers keep filling in bits of the coastline to expand the landmass. Everywhere you look, new buildings and roads and shops are going up.

Such a complex structure will require a lot of work and planning to exact revenge against. This place is an enormous mountain to topple.

First, you have some personal business to wrap up.

You take two weeks of holiday from Kit Ling's job, to adjust to her body and her life. It takes a day to even find her flat, much less get into it.

The sense you get, walking around those polluted and surging streets, is akin to walking around a large, endless shopping arcade. It is both overwhelmingly vast and terribly claustrophobic at the same time. It never ends and yet everything is repetitive and the same. When you first go out, it is only for a few minutes, and then a few hours at a time. Getting used to space again is not a quick transition. At night, you huddle in small, confined spaces that remind you of the bottle gourd. Barrels are a particular favorite.

Another few days to learn the ins and outs of Kit Ling's life, studying her diary and journals and trying to figure out how to pass in a job you aren't trained for. This will be an ongoing process, but at least you have some basics, now.

You also establish a routine, for your own safety: every two days, you fill a bathtub or barrel and slip out of her skin. Then you spend at least ten to twelve hours soaking, reclaiming and reasserting yourself so that Kit Ling's body doesn't submerge your consciousness. This is important, if you are going to live as her without being swallowed by her.

On the seventh day of escaping confinement, once you've figured your way around the city and gotten accustomed to Kit Ling's strange life, you manage to find Wing Yun's contact details and reach out to him. It's not difficult, because he's been petitioning the Council for years, as Kit Ling already told you. The hard part is simply working up the nerve, and that does take you a few hours.

The message you send him is simple:

Let's meet, old friend. It's been too long.

Twenty-nine years was a solid amount of time to reflect.

Initially, you endlessly replayed the memories of your life, the moments of city and island and sea and wind. Of your parents, your childhood, your school, the war. Every grain of existence was examined, over and over. There was nothing else to do, after all.

By the time you emerged, there were three truths engraved on the tattered remnants of your soul, and they became the mantras that you would exist by.

The first truth: humans did not have true sympathy for another person's pain, unless they experienced it themselves. The wealthy dismissed the poor, the healthy dismissed the sick, citizens dismissed refugees, men dismissed women, and so on. It was not until the wealthy became poor, the healthy became sick, citizens became refugees, or men suffered as women suffer, that people could truly understand another's experiences. Even you hadn't really grasped Mei Chi's pain, until you became a ghost, too.

From this, you concluded that suffering was not a thing to be transcended, as Buddha had taught, but a thing to be universally shared as widely as possible. Only through suffering could compassion flourish. Pain was the greatest of all teachers, and humanity was chronically ignorant.

The second truth: those who lacked sympathy were also those who caused the most suffering. This was ironclad and immutably true. If the wealthy knew poverty, they would be kinder to the poor. If men understood women's lives, they would behave with more gentleness. If politicians suffered in trenches, they would think twice about sending young men to war. And so on. Therefore, it was imperative to inflict on them what they had done to others, or society could not improve.

Third: the most unbearable thing about pain was knowing that those who hurt you did not even comprehend your hurt. Often they neither saw nor cared about it, and carried on with their lives, wrapped up in their own concerns. This forgetting, this ignorance, torments victims more than the actual crime in many cases.

Therefore, when you thought about revenge during those long dark years, it was not the redressing of karma that you sought or imagined. The betrayal of your mother, of Mei Chi, of the city you'd fought for, could not be undone or rebalanced.

No. Vengeance, as such, was about *understanding.* You needed those who had hurt you to understand what they had done, in a visceral and deep way. And the only way to do that was to disseminate as much pain to as many of your enemies as possible.

Now that you are free, teaching that pain is your new goal. Not just to the city which betrayed you, but to the one person who truly failed to grasp the hurt they had caused—none other than Chen Mei Chi herself.

You would make her understand, no matter the cost.

Thoughts whirling in your skull, you stride into the Peninsula Hotel on a sticky June afternoon and head straight for their far-too-expensive cafe.

The decor is an arrogant array of white and gold, every chandelier and marble tile immaculate. The outside fountain is a pleasing rush of water, and a part of you longs to take off your shoes and put your feet into that cool spray. That would get you thrown out, though, so you don't.

As a girl, you walked past the iconic Peninsula Hotel on the way to and from work. Those gilt staircases and glass-fronted exteriors meant it was far too upmarket for you to ever get work there, let alone visit as a customer. The cost of an afternoon tea in their high-end cafe would have been months of your wages.

But you're a councilwoman now, from a well-off family. Though it's still an expense to drop in, it is an affordable one. Especially for such a special occasion.

Take a breath, compose yourself, walk in grandly.

Wing Yun is already there, seated calmly by the window, an untouched cup of coffee gone cold in front of him. Twenty-nine years have changed his face greatly. A map of lines runs deep across his skin. The brawny young soldier, so cockily defiant to his Japanese captors, is now a tired and skinny man in his late fifties.

But he is still the smart, thoughtful person you knew during the war. The same shrewd intelligence behind those kind eyes. There was no room for love or even affection in the relationship you had with him; even if you weren't dead, the war took up all the oxygen.

Still, looking at him now, you can admit quietly that he will always occupy a space in your heart. Even after all these years, and all the bodies you've lived in, and all the things you've each endured, his face is comforting to look on.

He glances over as you enter, clearly recognizing the figure of Kit Ling and looking puzzled.

You throw him a military salute.

His solemnity breaks into a familiar grin. "It's been a long time, Siu Yin." He rises to standing, clasping your hands in his.

"Thank you." You surprise yourself—and him—by squeezing back tightly. "Thank you so much!"

"I haven't done anything," he protests.

"Yes, you have. You remembered me, when everyone else forgot. You tried to help me, these past three decades, and kept a promise few others would have cared about." An unexpected lump forms in your throat. "In a world of betrayers, I am truly honored by your friendship."

"It was the least I could do." Wing Yun extracts his hands and claps you awkwardly on the shoulder. "After all you and those other spirits did for us, in the war . . . shameful, the way those exorcists locked you up. Especially when it was my fault they found you."

You nod your head, saying nothing. Internally, though, Chinese politeness is warring with a spike of ghostly fury. He's the closest thing you have to a friend, the only person who has always shown up for you, but it *was* his fault, intentional or not. Across the past twenty-nine years of captivity, you've had plenty of time to curse his name, even if you've mostly made peace with it now.

That realization briefly surprises you. Making peace with things isn't something ghosts usually do, but searching your heart, you find only lingering resignation for the unwitting role he played in your capture, rather than burning anger. How curious. Maybe forgiveness is occasionally possible, for ghosts.

"Well," he says, into the dragging silence, "the point is, I'm glad you survived." He takes his seat again, leaning back slowly. "I must admit, when I first began petitioning the government for your release, this result"—he gestures vaguely at your stolen body—"was not quite what I had in mind."

"Does it upset you, what I've done?" There is no malice in your question, only curiosity. Always, you have been frank with each other, and even after nearly thirty years, speaking to him is like slipping on a familiar jacket. "One could argue she was innocent. I would understand if you disapproved."

“That depends. Why did you do it?” He sips from his cold coffee, and makes a face. “Can’t believe the Americans drink this stuff.”

“It’s better with milk and sugar, I’m told.” You perch in the chair across from him, and signal politely to a waiter. “As for Kit Ling, she heard about me because of your petition, but she didn’t agree to free me, as you asked. She wanted to use me.”

He raises an eyebrow. “Use in what way?”

“She wanted me to terrorize Kowloon Walled City to demonstrate that it was unsafe, and get the government to finally demolish that place. My understanding is that she owns some property there, and she’d stand to gain from the compensation payouts should it be demolished.”

He blinks. “I see. And what would happen to you, once that job was complete?”

“Nothing good. That’s why I took her skin. She was never going to truly set me free.”

“In that case,” Wing Yun says gravely, “I am not upset about what you did to her. I’ve done too many dark things in my wartime days to judge you, Siu Yin.”

The waiter comes over, interrupting the chat. You give him an order of shared afternoon tea. It’s more for the experience of the fancy three-tiered trays than because you have any liking for bland, overpriced cakes. Some working-class part of you is still tickled to be eating where wealthy expats like to take lunch, and that is its own kind of satiation.

When the waiter is gone, Wing Yun says, “What will you do now? And what about the other ghosts, who fought in the resistance?”

“I would love to set them free, if I could. It is complicated, though. While I can visit most of the ghosts that are bound in the cells beneath the building, there are wards, guards, all sorts of things. I will need time to plan.” Offer him a wan smile. “I have not forgotten them. Nor the debt this city owes me.”

He nods. “I won’t ask what you mean by that. Think I’m happier not knowing about your plans for revenge.”

“Not going to talk me out of it?”

Wing Yun looks at you hard, his gaze steady and shrewd. “I don’t have the right to do that, Siu Yin. No one does. Only you can decide what is justice.”

“That’s . . . very philosophical,” you say dryly.

“I’m not finished.” He leans forward. “I won’t judge, but I will say this. I am an old man, after many years of living in Hong Kong. You are forever young, the spirit of a girl shunted between skins, collecting pain and yet never growing up. So, we look at life differently. What I see, Siu Yin, is that my life is running out, and I number my days carefully now. What time I have, I spend on good things. What energy I have, I spend on carrying my own bones. There is not enough of my time left for hate, or enough energy to carry anger."

Irritation makes your shoulders twitch. "What's your point? Like you said, I'm not you. Death already came for me and now I am eternal, something beyond mortality. I have plenty of time and energy for my hate, my anger, my unfinished business."

"What you have," he says, a little sadly, "is a chance to live life anew. You do not have to take more skins, you do not have to exact revenge. *There does not need to be more death.*"

"There is always more death," you say, stiffly. "The world owes me a debt."

He shakes his head. "I am sorry for all you have lost, but life is not an abacus where we get to balance the accounts. Humans simply carry on, looking for good when we can find it, and enduring our difficulties when we cannot."

"For you, maybe, but I don't accept that anymore."

The waiter returns, putting down the elegant little tray with its tiny sandwiches and cakes. He flutters around annoyingly, making a fuss of it all while the two of you sit in awkward silence, before eventually leaving.

When he is gone, you say in a low voice, "You were right about one thing. You don't understand. I am not doing this to 'balance' any universal books. Those can never be balanced. One death doesn't cancel out another. Mei Chi's pain doesn't pay for mine. Karma is not an exchange system, and I know that keenly."

He spreads his hands. "Then why? Why not rest, move on, forget yourself, have a new life?"

"Because I need my pain to mean something." You take a cake and bite into it, but his words have soured your appetite; the cream and sponge tastes of ashes. "I can't bear that my death was meaningless, or that those who made me suffer have never had to face what they've done. I don't want or need them to make amends, because that is impossible. I only want them to understand the pain they've caused. Is that so much to ask?"

"It is and it isn't." He sighs. "I can see your mind is made up, Siu Yin."

"Correct." You chew through the remainder of the cake slice with wooden efficiency.

He studies his hands, seems to be thinking, then nods slowly. "In that case . . . in that case, I have news you may wish to hear."

A flutter in your stolen stomach. "What news?"

"I found her," Wing Yun says, simply. "You asked me to look for your mother and your aunt, so I did. Can't help with Mei Chi, but I did locate your mother, a few years ago."

Shoot to your feet, tense as wire. "Where?"

"She's in a government-run old folks' home. It can wait till after you've eaten—"

"I don't care about cake." You fish out some bills and toss them on the table. "Take me there right now. Please?"

32

ALL THAT REMAINS

One year ago . . .

The Joyous Residential Home, as its sign proclaims itself, is full of loud echoes, but very little joy. In the crowded games room, chairs scrape continually on a cheap linoleum floor, accompanied by the endless clacking of mahjong tiles. Most people are smoking, including the staff, and the furniture reeks of tobacco. Underneath that stench, the sharp scent of bleach cuts through. Those who aren't gambling slump tiredly on folding chairs, staring in the middle distance.

"I'd rather be dead than end up here," you say to Wing Yun, without thinking.

"Then you've already got your wish, Lady Ghost," he says, and rings the little bell on the reception desk. One of the nurses skulks over. "Excuse me, miss, but we are looking for Sung Daiyu. I've visited before, if you recall."

The utterance of that name sends a quiver through your body.

"Ah! We are so glad you are here. We have been trying to reach her relatives, but not had any success. Have you found one of her family members?"

Wing Yun looks at you.

"I think I'm the only one," you say, a little numbly. "Most died in the war."

"I understand," she says, with courteous sympathy. "This is very auspicious timing, in that case. I am glad you could make it."

"What do you mean?"

"Mrs. Sung has been ill for a long time. She had two strokes earlier this year, and has been very frail for weeks. She has recently stopped eating. I'm sorry, but we do not expect her to live much longer."

You have no idea how to respond to that. Too many things are colliding in your head.

Eventually you settle on, "I see. In that case, I would love to see her as soon as possible."

There are a few forms to sign, some explanations to go through. A few lies about being second cousins or a grandniece, something along those lines. In truth, no one probes very deeply. They're probably hoping you'll agree to take Daiyu away and lighten their workload.

Eventually, they bring you to a small bedroom down one of the corridors.

"She doesn't speak much," the nurse warns you. "I can't promise anything."

When neither of you say anything, the nurse makes an excuse and returns to other duties.

You peer into the dim little room. Wing Yun peers in, too. There's not much to see. The room is clean but very small, and not well furnished. A small table, a folding stool, and a wardrobe occupy this end. A narrow, iron-framed bed rests against the far wall. There is one window, looking out onto the busy streets below.

An elderly woman reclines on the bed. She bears so little resemblance to your mother that, at first, you do not recognize her face. Daiyu's hair is cut short, her feet are bare, and her clothes are strange: plain, discolored shirt and trousers, almost like pajamas. The obsidian black of her hair has grayed out, and the skin of her hands is rice-paper thin. Rice-paper pale, too, from lack of sunlight.

From a short distance away, you stare and stare, feeling overwhelmed. It has been thirty-two whole years in total since you've seen Mami—three years of war, twenty-nine years of entrapment—but she looks older than seventy-five. A far cry from the stern, handsome woman who raised you.

Wing Yun touches your arm. "Are you alright, Miss . . . ah . . . Tsang?"

"How?" you manage. "How did you find her? Where has she been?"

"Diligence, and time," Wing Yun says, keeping his voice low. "Like I told you years ago, I had my own family to look for, as well as yours. After the war ended and the government locked you away, I spent time in former Japanese internment camps. Then the refugee camps, then homeless shelters and psychiatric hospitals. Just searching."

He shakes his head and grimaces. "After the first twenty years, I started looking in homes for the elderly. There are a lot of them, and not all the patients know themselves anymore, or have good records. I didn't have any luck with my parents, but I did see *her* name on a list. Plus, with those memories you gave me, her face looked familiar in the photographs. I came here and tried to speak to her myself, just to be sure."

"What did she say?" You can't tear your eyes away from the old woman in front of you.

"She started crying and begging forgiveness, though she wouldn't say what for. The old lady wouldn't talk to me much." He shoots you a curious look. "What happened between you both? You never showed me the details. Is she the one who killed you?"

"No. She's the one who left me to die."

You walk through the doorway before he can respond, and raise your voice. "Hello? Is that you, Sung Daiyu?"

She looks up from the bed, making a sound halfway between a sob and a laugh. "Who wants to know?"

Almost, you tell her. But you are not wearing your own skin; you are too young, too different looking, to pass as yourself. Besides, she might panic. Better to go slow.

"A friend of your daughter's," you say, after a pained pause.

She wrings her hands anxiously. "Friend? What friend? How did you know her?"

"At school, long ago." Too late, it occurs to you that this wouldn't be possible. Kit Ling is twenty-four years younger than Siu Yin, and they would never have been at school together.

Thankfully, Daiyu doesn't seem to realize this. "If you are looking for her . . . you are . . . too late. She is dead. Drowned." Her gaze skitters around the small room, from one thing to the next. "I left her behind . . . like I left everything behind. The island, my husband, her . . . then her again—"

"Her, then her again?" you cut in. "What does that mean?"

She flinches, as if startled by a strange noise. "I saw her," she whispers. "I saw my daughter drown . . . and then I saw her alive."

Mei Chi. Your mother must have found Mei Chi, out in the world, wearing your body.

You kneel down next to the bed, and catch her wrists. "Where?"

"In the city of ghosts. Where else?" Mami sags against her pillows. She is so sick, so exhausted. "I went to the land of ghosts, thinking . . . thinking she'd died. Thinking . . . if her ghost was anywhere, it would be . . . with the others. But she did not remember. Not me, not the ghosts . . . not the island . . . not even . . . her father." She shudders. "But I was wrong. It was not my daughter. My daughter . . . my daughter is dead. I left her to drown."

Disappointment floods you as her words sink in. This is no reveal, no sudden clue. The old woman is rambling and confused.

"If you grieve her death, then why did you abandon her?" Disgust drives your tongue to bluntness.

"It's not . . . like that," Daiyu says, weakly. "I went back for her later. Truly, I . . . I . . . I did. But . . . she was gone. The ocean had swallowed everything." Her voice sinks low, barely audible. "If I could just see her again . . . Just one more time, oh heavens . . . I would ask her . . . No, I . . . I would tell her . . ."

She pauses, seeming to struggle with the words even more than usual. Her head bows forward and she shudders.

Unexpected tears well up in your eyes. A combination of grief, anger, and yearning. The brittle anger inside your heart trembles, almost undone by her half admission.

"What?" you manage, thickly. "What would you tell your daughter, if you had the chance?"

Daiyu remains where she is, slumped against the pillows, head tilted forward and resting on her chest. Her wrists limp in your grasp.

"Sung Daiyu?" Give her a slight shake. "Mami? Mami, *what would you have told me*?"

Her head tips back, eyes sightless and mouth slack. There is no pulse at the wrist, no rise and fall of the chest.

Mami is gone.

All the things you wanted to say, shout, or thrash out with her, die in that instant, dissipating alongside her spirit. Always, your mother has denied you—first her love and affection, then her help. Finally, she has denied you any closure or meaningful answers. Even in the last, her heart is a door fixed shut, which you may never enter or even attempt to knock at.

There will never be a chance to tell her who you were and what happened after she left you to drown, let alone demand an apology. No reunion, no resolution. No good ending, not even a bittersweet one.

The realization is agony.

You are nothing more than a lonely ghost girl in a stolen body, holding a frail and faded corpse.

Later that day, when it's all over, you and Wing Yun are both seated in a cha chaan teng around the corner, drinking tea and smoking while the city tramples past in all directions.

"I'm sorry about your mother," he says, eventually.

"*All things are transient*," you quote, tiredly. "*Everything single moment we are undergoing birth and death*."

You find yourself wondering, for the first time in years, where your father's body ended up. It's not a question you ask yourself often, because there are no happy answers to it. Even so, you wish you knew.

Wing Yun lights another cigarette and says, "What will you do now?"

"Arrange for a burial." The last thing you want is Mami returning as a ghost, with unfinished business. A good funeral and an honest priest will help with that. "There is nothing else I *can* do."

"Did she have a lead for your, uh . . ."

"My auntie?" That's how you're referring to Mei Chi, since it's factually true. "No. She said her daughter is dead. And Mei Chi had been in that body."

"Do you believe her?"

"I don't know? She seemed convinced, though it was hard to work out what she meant. Her words were very confused." A helpless shrug. "I will say that I have never found any trace of my aunt, whenever I looked. Even you, searching all these years for me, have only found my mother. I must admit, the odds are not in Mei Chi's favor. It is more likely that she died during the war, especially if she stayed in Hong Kong."

"There's one other possibility which is worth considering," he says. "I believe your mother mentioned something about . . . the city of ghosts?"

"Did she?" You frown, sifting your memory. She said so much jumbled nonsense. "I suppose so. What about it?"

"I've heard some of the old folks use that term. They're not referring to the underworld, but a place in Hong Kong. A city within a city."

The penny drops. "Wait. Do you mean that district in Kowloon? The Walled City, with all the crazy triad people?" The place Kit Ling wanted to knock down and pave over.

"Before you get too excited, I've looked there before," he says. "They did take a census in Kowloon Walled City, sometime after the war. Of sorts. There were a few Mei Chis, and many Chens, but no one with that exact name who was anywhere near the right age."

"Oh," you say, a little crestfallen. Then you straighten again. "Perhaps she changed her name? Lied about her age?" Or changed her body. All of those might be possible. All options add complication, too.

"Could be," he agrees. "How would you find her, though, if she had? What if she *was* there, like your mother claimed, and she's moved on or died since then?"

"I don't know, but it is still a place to start, and that's more than I had before today." Reach across the table and squeeze his hand briefly. "Thank you, again."

"What for?" he says, surprised. As if he can't see the many favors he's performed on your behalf.

"For your loyalty and friendship. For keeping your promise and always advocating for me, even when I was locked up. For never treating me as a monster. And now you casually give me the only lead I have for the woman I seek."

"Well, I am glad to have been of some use," Wing Yun says, quietly. "Makes me feel like I've paid some of my debt."

"There is no debt," you insist. "Not with you. If anything, the debt goes the other way."

"Siu Yin, you saved my life the night we met," he says, very seriously. "As you saved the lives of so many resistance soldiers in the years that followed. Did I ever tell you how close my hope came to fading?"

You say nothing, too startled; he hasn't confessed such things before.

"When we met, a fire started again in my heart, one I thought had gone out forever. I saw in you the victory that could be won for our city. I believed again, after I had thought my faith in the cause turned to dust. In the darkest moments of that war, you burned through my despair." He pauses, and you get the sense he's fighting back tears. "Whatever else you may have done or be guilty of, I will never forget how you fought, or the gift of hope you brought to me and my soldiers."

"I feel like all I did was destroy." The words tumble out of you, unbidden. "I'm not a builder of anything, hope or otherwise."

"I think you do yourself an injustice, Siu Yin." Wing Yun dabs his eyes, and smiles. "The price of peace is always death. Every year of good fortune is paid for in war, and the cost of those lives means you and I can sit here, now, and breathe air quietly. You paid for us to live."

"And when will it be my turn to live?" Heaviness squeezes your chest, a feeling not unlike the ache of drowning.

"That, I don't know. But I believe the future holds more for you than vengeance. If you want it to."

No idea what to say to that. As much as you adore this one human, his way of thinking is so alien. He sees by a light invisible to your eyes, and you cannot know the sunlit world that he looks at. Ghosts only understand darkness and shadows.

A little while passes in companionable silence. Tea is drunk, cigarettes are smoked. Sometimes, the best company is passed in silence, when no words need be spoken because each person understands the other.

Eventually, though, Wing Yun stirs again.

"Well. It was truly wonderful to see you once more," he says, draining the last of his cup, "but unfortunately, I can't stay much longer. I have a long journey coming up, and I've not finished packing."

"Journey?" Sit up in alarm. "Where are you going?"

"It has been years in this city, Siu Yin," he says, a little sadly. "What's left of my family have already emigrated to other countries. Now that I have paid this debt to you, I will be leaving to join them. There is a ship, going to Liverpool in a few days' time. I plan to be on it."

"Liver-*where*?"

"It's a city in England. I have a cousin there, and a job waiting. The British make it easy for Hong Kong people to immigrate these days." He stubs out the end of his cigarette. "Anyway, it's a fresh start. Sights to see. Nieces and cousins to meet. I'm told they have big European castles."

"Oh," you say, nonplussed. Then, "Isn't it cold, in Britain?"

He smiles. "I'll buy a coat."

"It's on the other side of the world! Why there?"

"Siu Yin, I am not from Hong Kong, not originally. I actually don't really like it here. But I can't go back across to Shen Zen, either. There's nothing for me in China, and the country is so changed now. Not for the better under Communist leadership," he adds, muttering.

"I see." You rotate the cup slowly with your fingers. "I think I can understand that."

"You could come with me," he offers. But kind as he is, you suspect he hopes you'll refuse, despite how much he likes you. It would be awkward for him to have a body-snatching spirit hanging around.

Luckily for him, you have no intention of accepting. "Thank you, but my place is here. England is a hostile land for ghosts, and I have unfinished business in Hong Kong."

"No problem. I understand, too." Wing Yun rises stiffly, with an old man's gait. "Still, it was good to see you a final time. My heart is calmer, knowing you are freed from that cursed binding."

"Wait," you say, standing, too. Unsure what to say, but fully aware that you may never see him again. He is pushing sixty and going to a far country; that hurts. Your one good friend, the soft spot in your ghost heart, and he is leaving you as everyone leaves.

Even though you can't blame him, it stings a little. Maybe a lot.

He pauses dutifully. "Yes?"

"I will miss you deeply, Chiu Wing Yun," you say simply. "You'll never know what you've done for me." Or what he's meant to you.

"Ha!" He throws a salute. "Goodbye, Sung Siu Yin. I'll tell my nieces many stories about our adventures. The Girl with a Thousand Faces, who sank Japanese ships! The little lady ghost who revived a resistance! They'll never believe me."

He disappears through the surging crowds, swiftly lost from sight and gone forever.

You are alone once more.

33

YOUR FACE

One year ago . . .

Early the next morning, you get dressed and take a taxi to the edge of Kowloon Walled City. If Mei Chi is in there, you'll find her. Even if you don't, there is still the matter of your wider vengeance to organize.

The first three times you visit are a nonevent, and you leave empty-handed. Maybe not a surprise; there are so many people, most of them suspicious of an outsider like yourself. If anyone does know this Chen Mei Chi, they're not saying, and you don't want to make too much noise in case you scare off the person you seek.

After the second time, you tell yourself that returning is futile, and yet you go twice more anyway. Because on every occasion, the district is increasingly fascinating; it's almost enjoyable to walk around. To most outsider eyes, it's a nothing place, full of squalor and crime and broken people, shattered on the hard edge of war. You, though, look at it and see . . . an ecosystem.

The city has layers which remind you of the archipelagos and lagoons around which you spent so much time swimming, both as a girl and later as a ghost. The strata of buildings are tiered, and so are the residents; bottom feeders and mud dwellers, normal swimmers trying to get by, and little pipsqueaks who hide in others' shadows. There are prey, parasites, lone sharks, huddled groups. The buildings sprawl and creep like coral, and wetness sticks to everything.

It is an ecosystem, alright. One of ruthless survival and errant growth; it teems and heaves and thrives and surges, a snarled tangle of darkness and human vivacity. All of that is like an ocean, too.

The only thing it is missing, really, is the water.

Now *there* is an interesting notion. Your imagination wanders into strange places, prompting you to smile. In your head, you conjure up a wall running round this whole area, building on existing foundations to reach several stories high. It could be like a reservoir, a vast aquarium filled with water: briny or clear, it wouldn't matter.

Keep walking. Though crowded, Kowloon is not very big in area. There is one semi-open space at its center, where the old fort's courtyard used to be. The sky can be glimpsed here, along with the planes which pass overhead frequently.

It's also the part of Kowloon that most looks like a lagoon reef.

Tilt your head up, gazing around. Imagine: water flowing through those windows, these dank and ramshackle alleys, making every crevice or gap between the city a swimmable passageway. Imagine: water washing everything clean, and a legion of drowned ghosts appearing in its wake.

"Young lady, are you sick?"

An elderly gentleman is at your elbow, peering up into your face.

You straighten, startled to realize you are bent over, fingers snaked through your hair, gripping it tight. On the street around you, people are shuffling past on all sides, a few casting vaguely interested glances your way.

"Thank you, grandfather, but it is only a bad headache," you say, lamely, still caught off guard by the sudden wave of dark thoughts.

"Drink less beer, then. Or else drink more beer, and improve your tolerance," the elderly man says, with a grin, then pats your arm and goes on his way.

"Thanks," you call after him, feeling wryly amused.

You're still considering how best to begin today's search when you realize, quite abruptly, that the crowd in Kowloon's single courtyard has come to a standstill. No one is moving, everyone is watching—something, you can't see what.

Unexpectedly, the skin of your arms begins to prickle with goose bumps. A sudden curiosity to see what they're looking at overcomes you. Push your way to the front, ducking beneath elbows and stepping around hips. And stop in your tracks.

A ghost sways and weeps, hands pressed to her face. She is corporeal and glimmering, hair falling like a veil of ink across her shoulders. Burial robes drift around her in a haze of white, stirred by a cold and unnatural wind.

Another woman stands in front of the anguished spirit. Short, stocky, approaching middle age; tattoos all over her body, cheap sandals on her feet. Hands in pockets. You can't quite see her face; she's angled away from you, toward the ghost. She must be some kind of medium, or exorcist.

The woman speaks to the ghost in a low tone, the words too indistinct for you to pick out above the bubbling, chattering crowd around. Definitely a medium, if she's talking and not exorcising. The ghost is listening, its eyes narrowed in guarded interest.

Strange shivers run through you. There is something familiar about her voice, even at this distance.

When the medium is finished, the ghost whirls away and cries out, "Where is my husband?"

You raise an eyebrow as the ghost's head detaches from her body, neck extending like a stretchy noodle. Been a while since you've seen a ghost of that type.

The crowd is far less calm. People scream, and someone faints. The ghost screams back and then the head dives down, its neck a taut ribbon, flailing body following after. It is going after one particular person in the crowd: a young man whose nervous expression ripens into horror when he realizes death is coming his way. He tries to flee.

A small white ghost cat comes bounding out of nowhere. You have enough time to think *That looks like the cat on the island* before it transforms into a large, lion-sized feline, with ferocious teeth and claws. The man yells as the maogui knocks him over and pins him down, and then his wife's ghost is upon him.

The ribbon neck winds and twists as the ghost unhinges her jaws to snip his head off in vengeful glee. Blood explodes in a shower, jetting from the neck stump. People cheer nastily.

"Good for you, big sister! Get your justice!" shouts the medium, half turning to keep the spectacle in view. And you finally get a full, clear view of her features.

Sound fades. Awareness dims. The world narrows to a single point of vision. You stare, and stare.

The woman is wearing *your face.*

For a moment you are unsure, recognizing but also not recognizing the features in front of you. It's been a damn long time, and you didn't own a mirror for most of your life. Maybe it is another woman with similar features. She is well into middle age, too, which makes it trickier.

Then she raises her hands to cup them around her mouth, shouting something above the fray, and you see her bare skin exposed.

All the way down her left arm is the blazing, blood-red scar of a lightning strike. The tattoos obscure the scar, but can't fully hide it. The mark runs from her shoulder down to her wrist, which is encircled by a slim bracelet strung with a tiger charm.

The face. The scar. The tiger charm.

All of them, yours.

Definitely your body. Scarred and lined from years of hard living, sure, but familiar down to the tilt of the eyes and the mole on one cheek. With every step you take toward her (yourself?), more and more details reveal themselves, and the certainty cements.

Compared to the body you now inhabit, your original vessel is shorter and heavier, dark hair straight and slick in a short bob. The years have worn lines of wisdom and humor around the mouth, cheeks, and forehead.

Can it be? Can it really be, after all this time, all these years? The records you searched, the camps Wing Yun looked in, the years of digging . . . How the hell has she just been here, this whole damn time?

Daiyu's words from many days ago rise to your mind: *I saw her alive. In the city of ghosts.* Those aged shoulders spasming in a shudder. *It was not my daughter.* Mami must have seen your body, and mistaken it for you. Only to be repulsed on finding Mei Chi inside it.

"Rest now, beautiful lady," Your Face cries out to the raging, blood-soaked ghost. "Justice is done. Find your peace in the next life."

The ribbon-necked ghost sighs breathily, head slowly winding back into her body even as her form frays at the edges. She begins to shrink, robes growing loose around her diminishing form until the remnants of her spirit disperse into shimmering mist. The empty burial robes fold in on themselves into a pile of fabric, which in turn seem to melt into the ground. In moments, the ribbon-necked ghost is gone as if she never existed in the first place. Nothing remains.

The crowd claps and cheers. Ghosts don't normally listen to advice or suggestions, but this one did—once its fury was spent, anyway.

Your Face bows respectfully to all and sundry, and makes a sharp gesture. The maogui lumbers over, size compacting with every step until he is once again a small, harmless-looking kitten, albeit fuzzed at the edges with a wisp of transparency.

Definitely the same kitten that Mei Chi owned as a child, and whose ghost used to wander the island. Insane that he's come all the way out here. He must have real affection for his mistress. The thought of its misplaced loyalty fills you with irritation. If you can kill that cat spirit, you will.

Meanwhile, Your Face gathers the cat up and puts him on her shoulder with genuine affection, then turns and walks through the crowd in the other direction. Her sandals slap the concrete in irregular rhythm.

Still reeling, you grab the sleeve of the nearest person and tug hard to get their attention. The man you grab looks down. "What is it?"

"Who was that? The woman we just saw?"

He laughs around his cigarette. "Don't you know? That's Mei Chi Chan. She works under the Cobra Lily triad. One of those exorcists, or mediums. Something like that." A note of admiration enters his voice. "She's a strong and canny little auntie. Never met a ghost she was afraid of!"

For a moment you are confused, unsure why he would say the name back to front. He's also slurred "Mei Chi" quite badly, and transposed "Chen" with "Chan."

Then you realize, with a jolt, that he hasn't said Mei Chi: he has said *Mercy*. An English name, or perhaps just an Anglicized version of the Chinese original. Similar, ish, in sound. Very different in meaning.

"Thanks," you say, distractedly, brain already churning.

Chen Mei Chi . . . to Mercy Chan.

Your guess was right. She's changed her name. She's *changed* her *fucking* name, dropping the Hakka for a mix of Cantonese and English. Because of course she has. And before that, there were probably no records of her anywhere, thanks to the war. She's been safely hidden away until you casually found her, today.

Fate, you decide, has a spiteful sense of humor.

The crowd disperses, everyone going back to their daily routines. Mercy, or whatever the hell she calls herself now, is already gone. Time for you to go, too. At least for now. A heat is building up behind your stolen eyes, though you try to ignore it.

You make it two blocks before ducking into a nearby doorway and bursting into tears.

People mind their own business in Kowloon. No one comes over to bother the grown woman who is crouched in a dark, filthy corner, bawling her heart out uncontrollably. Just as well; you'd have probably wrung the neck of anyone who tried, in that particular moment.

Seeing Mami again rocked you, but not like this. You never felt a connection with Mami, the way you once had with Sea Sister—with your aunt.

So many emotions collide that you can barely think or breathe, choking on your own sobs. The whiplash of adoring her, fearing her, hating her, then seeking her all these years, to thinking she was gone, then finally stumbling on her—as a person of local importance, it seems—in this small neighborhood . . . the staggering breadth of that emotional journey, culminating in this moment, has your head and heart spinning in different directions.

When the storm inside you calms and your skin has run out of human tears, you drag a dirty sleeve across a snotty nose and allow your lungs to take deep, steadying breaths.

Crying is good. Crying is sweet. You've learned to value it when in human form, since water ghosts can't weep. In the wake of that turbulence, your mind is serene and calm again, like the surface of the ocean on a clear summer day.

You know exactly what you want to do, and precisely how you're going to do it.

Several hours later and you're back in Kit Ling's flat, showered and changed and sitting at her desk as you look through all her resources. All her notes and files, her plans and collated knowledge. If you want to make this city suffer, and make Mei Chi understand the pain she's put you through, then you'll need every scrap of it.

As Kit Ling, you have access to government records on wartime ghosts. These records indicate that there are 446 "significant spirits" who were captured by teams of Taoist priests and Catholic exorcists, working in tandem, for a few years after World War II ended.

Every single captured ghost was either involved in the resistance, or somehow survived the Japanese occupation. All but a handful had never been a threat to Hong Kong, but their existence had offended the returning government. There was no official term for this operation; it was simply referred to as a *city-wide spiritual cleansing.*

It's likely that a majority have expired into nothingness and bad energy, but you are determined to free as many as possible.

The difficulty is in the details. It's possible to get a few bottle gourds out, as Kit Ling smuggled you out. But start stealing hundreds of ghosts, and you'll likely get caught. Attempting to set them free is also dicey: there is still a lot of security in the building, and many of them would be recaptured swiftly.

What you need is a way of tying up the city's resources, even if it is just for a single night, while you launch a multipronged plan from different angles. It is not unlike the sort of military strategies that Wing Yun used to work on, with your help.

You pick up a pen, and start making notes. Hours go by unnoticed. Day darkens into evening, then full night. Still, you work.

Only in the early hours of the morning do you sit back in the chair and stretch. Your stolen body aches, its vision blurry from overuse and its back creaking from being bent over a desk for so long.

The plan, though, is done.

It goes something like this.

First, you'll keep pursuing Kit Ling's schemes with regard to Kowloon, because it suits your agenda of punishing Hong Kong, but most importantly, because

Kowloon is her home, and she does not deserve to keep it. Cause havoc in the district, as a ghost—you can do this yourself, though it means getting your hands dirty. Log those deaths, and keep tabs on everything. Use this rocketing rate of murder to push for demolition of Kowloon, and create tensions between the district and the wider Hong Kong government.

Second, arrange for a high-profile murder to happen in Kowloon. Who exactly, you're not sure yet, but you'll figure that out when the time comes. This will necessitate a police raid, if handled correctly. They will likely be accompanied by regiments of exorcists and priests, to handle the sheer number of spirits inside.

Third, set a trap within the district. Once the police go in, make sure they're locked within Kowloon's walls, busy fighting the triad. Busy fighting ghosts, too, hopefully. This part, you have some ideas for handling; a few options to explore.

Fourth, free the ghosts locked away in civic building basements. With the police busy and chaos rampant, you're confident of overpowering those who remain.

Fifth, step back and allow the havoc to unfold. Even if only half of those four hundred ghosts have endured, they will be angry and strong, and happy enough to unleash their fury on the city in one explosive wave.

That, combined with much of Hong Kong's police and supernatural forces being tied up in Kowloon, will batter the city badly.

While all that is happening, you'll also be dealing with Mei Chi. You have ideas for that, and they cause your lips to twist into a dark grin every time you play out those little scenarios.

This is going to be fun.

34

THE PAST CATCHES UP

August 20, 1975
(Two days ago)

It is more than a year before you see "Mercy" again, under very different circumstances.

Across the past months, you've relentlessly pursued the demolition paperwork for Kowloon Walled City in your day job as Kit Ling. You also do extensive research on "Mercy" Chan, in your spare time. There is little enough to find: she came to the city as a war refugee, displayed a knack for talking to ghosts, and now works for a known triad leader.

By night, you hunt through Kowloon's waterways, taking lives and racking up murders, sowing quiet discord. Not that it truly justifies your actions, or makes you feel better, but you try to stick to the cruelest and worst of humanity: the human traffickers, the little drug lords, the abusers and known killers. They are, to your mind, less innocent by far than the soldiers you slaughtered during the war. The only difference is the context in which society views your actions. Killing during wartime is heroism; killing during peacetime is murder.

Some of the bodies you keep, though it takes a while to work out how to store them. That's new for you; storing bodies wasn't something you had the luxury of doing, during the war. It requires space, and fu talismans of preservation, and proper access.

Kit Ling's property in Kowloon proves extremely useful, in that regard. It's a simple matter to drown her tenant—a drug-addled young woman called Red Bird—and make certain adaptations to its rooms. Chiefly, connecting them to the waterways that run beneath Hong Kong and Kowloon alike, and fitting out a sealed-off underground pumping room as a place to hide spare skins.

You still have a need for some of those identities, even if trying to keep them all straight gets a little tricky at times. Luckily, you don't need to sleep, and that helps. Some skins you only wear in the day; others only in the night, or at certain times of the week. It all balances out.

In short, though, it's a lot of work. All of it building carefully, relentlessly, toward that perfect single moment. And you're not fully you, after everything you've endured; you still flinch at loud bangs, still huddle in barrels when not in a skin.

The world perpetually feels too big, too shocking, after such long years of war and confinement. Still, you manage.

As the date draws near and your plans reach completion, you at last offer up the demolition consultation to Cobra Lily, the self-declared triad queen of her little rotten empire. She takes the bait, as you expected.

Also as expected, she brings along her vaunted second-in-command, Mercy Chan.

An entourage of assistants and security guards flank behind and around you as you approach Cobra Lily. An altogether unimpressive woman of middle age, whose real name is Wong Jing Yi. You've seen her birth records, are privy to facts about her history.

Still, you keep your gaze fixed on Cobra Lily's severe features, unwilling and unready to look at Mercy Chan just yet. Already, the triad queen is balking at your rebukes, your subtle humiliations.

"We are not thugs." Mercy steps forward mid-conversation, defiant and saucy. You can no longer ignore her. "The Snakeskins manage crime when your police force does not dare enter Kowloon. We run schools. We look after the elderly. We protect women. Even the girls who work in opium dens. Yes, there are drugs, but you have that, too, out here! As for the ghosts, we have long managed their infestation, without government support. The Walled City is our home, and you do not have the right to destroy it, when you have done nothing to help it!"

"Well-spoken." You turn toward her, composure tightly gathered. "And who are . . ."

The words die away as your eyes lock with hers. A torrent of emotions freezes you to the spot and you're aware of your mouth open, eyes widened despite your best efforts. How desperately you planned for this moment, intending to stare at her coolly—and yet you can't help being thunderstruck.

Your face. *Your own face*, looking back at you with eyes that should be yours. Time has knocked your body around the edges, added a little weight to the middle, flicked gray streaks through the hair. But it is you.

The experience is far more intense than the first time, when you merely saw Mei Chi from a distance.

"This is Mercy Chan," Cobra Lily says. "A trusted aide, and best of my exorcists. It is with her work that we successfully contain the ghost problem in Kowloon."

"I see." Your nostrils flare. "Who gave you that scar?"

Stupid to ask. Stupid, stupid, stupid. But you can't help it; you want to hear what she has to say, even knowing that she can't possibly remember her past anymore, because she was in your skin far, *far* too long.

"Huh? Nobody gave it to me."

"Nonsense," you retort. Her coy pedantry is grating. "That's not a birthmark, it's a scar. How did you get it?"

"Not that it is any of your business, Miss Tsang," Mercy says, "but I have had this scar for as long as I can remember. A doctor told me it is probably from a lightning strike."

It is *my business*, you want to scream. *It is literally and entirely my business, you murderous thief!*

"What is this rude questioning?" Cobra Lily says. "We are here to—"

"I know why you are here, and I want to be sure your exorcist is a reliable person," you snap. To Mercy, you say, "What do you mean, *as long as I can remember*?"

Hasn't she wondered, all these years? What kind of self-centered, unaware person doesn't question the huge gap in their memory? The body she inhabits was fully grown when she took it, she must *know* her childhood is missing.

But your murderer merely says, "I don't remember my life before 1942. I arrived in Kowloon in the middle of the war, without family or memories." She adds, "That's a little before your time, Miss Tsang, unless you are much older than you look."

You need to get control of yourself, before this conversation spirals off. Remember the plan. Stick to it.

Aloud, you say reluctantly, "A little, yes. I was born in 1945."

"Then why does it matter? Am I offensive to look at?"

"No. But your face, and that scar, are extremely familiar to me. I could have sworn . . ." One more time. Give her one more chance to consider. "Are you sure, completely sure, we have not met before?"

"Never that I remember," Mercy says. "In another life, maybe."

"In . . . another life." A raw pain squeezes your heart.

She truly, really doesn't remember you in any capacity. Though you knew that intellectually, having it laid out so categorically still burns.

Oddly, the feeling works like an antidote against the raging chaos inside your head. Smile, rally yourself, and straighten up.

"My mistake. You are quite right, I am too young to remember the war years." Turn your gray-suited form back toward Cobra Lily. "Please accept my apologies for my confusion, Ms. Wong. As I was saying . . . your whole entourage cannot come into the building. Perhaps I can suggest a compromise? You are welcome to come to my office, where we can speak in private."

Eventually, Cobra Lily and Mercy Chan both leave, looking suitably anxious. As they should be, if they knew even half of what you hope to do.

You start the ball rolling.

It's going to be a busy day, *and* night.

Under cover of darkness, you infiltrate Cobra Lily's flat. That involves breaking in, but this is easy to do. You have infiltrated Japanese ships, and this is far easier. One of her enforcers is in the opium den, a not uncommon occurrence. It's easy enough to drown him on the premises, in one of the bathing rooms, and take his skin.

Afterward, you walk into triad headquarters, go up to visit Cobra Lily, and give her the same treatment. She puts up a fight, with that sword of hers, but not for long. Her sword does nothing other than prize you out of the man's skin, and you cheerfully drown her in her own toilet.

Things are easy after that. Put out a few feelers, ask a few questions. Discover that Mercy has gone to visit an old friend or contact. You send some enforcers to frighten her, keep her off-balance. If they capture her, then fine. If not, it doesn't matter, not yet.

As it happens, they don't come back, but you don't really care. All paths lead back to you, whether that's through the opium den or to the triad directly. Set spies on them, keep tabs.

Those spies alert you when Mercy and her strange friend finally decide to head for the opium den, and you—at last—make your move.

Mercy is captured, of course. You're prepared in every sense. Her friend escapes, but you don't care about that. The person who matters is here.

You go to confront your killer.

She is defiant, this one. So bold for someone who is so wrong. Her bemused suffering is pleasing to witness, and when she realizes her time has come, it's hard not to laugh at the expression of fear on her face.

The woman who used to be Chen Mei Chi lunges away, trying frantically to crawl toward the door. You don't let her get far.

Catch her.

Hold her.

Drag her to the water barrel, and keep her head beneath the surface. Water burns up her nose, then down into her lungs, like a cold wet fire, and then there is nothing left of her but empty skin.

For a long moment, you contemplate the body left behind. Once, you dreamed of reclaiming your skin, but that prospect holds little allure for you now. Not when you can choose to be an endless succession of young, fresh-faced bodies instead.

No. She wanted your body so damn much, she can have it, for all you care.

Disdainfully, you slam your old body fully into the barrel, still part-filled with water, and tamp down the lid. *That* brings you satisfaction. A gourd would be safer, but this is a far more poetic justice. Besides, you don't want her to stay in there forever, not really.

Let her see what it feels like, to be trapped in confined environments. Let her escape in a few months' or years' time, and see what destruction you've wrought. Let her know and remember, and be too fucking late to do anything about it.

"She dead, then?" the vanguard says, glancing over his shoulder.

You smile. "For now." Point at the barrel. "Help me carry that, please. We're going to the basement."

When her ghost is locked away, you climb to the roof of Cobra Lily's headquarters building and lie atop the concrete, staring at the tempestuous sky.

It's very strange, but you're so calm, and so flat. You thought you'd feel . . . something? Anything, really. Seeing Mercy had an effect on you. Why hasn't vengeance done the same?

A tiny voice whispers that maybe what you sought from Mercy was never vengeance in the first place. You push it away, flushed with sudden anger, and sit up. Of course you wanted vengeance. Of course you wanted her suffering. That was the point of it all.

Wasn't it?

Yet the anguish in your soul has not dissipated. Not a drop of it. You feel the same now as you did a year ago, or thirty years ago, or even at the moment of death: betrayed, adrift, furious, unfulfilled. It doesn't make sense; this is everything you've worked for.

Why can't you *feel* something? Aren't ghosts supposed to disperse, or calm down, once their objectives have been achieved?

Ah, but maybe that's the problem. You haven't done everything you set out to do, yet. There is the city to wreak chaos and havoc on, after all.

Get to your feet, and contemplate the situation.

At present, Kit Ling's body has been found, and reported. That's good. A police raid will likely take place, very soon. With Cobra Lily's skin, you have prepared a trap for that raid; the gates of Kowloon will be barred shut once enough of them are inside, and your triad enforcers will tear into them.

Once that conflict is well underway, it will be time for you to get to the civic buildings and start freeing ghosts.

Focus on that next step, you decide, and then see how you feel.

Perhaps if you can expend enough rage and hurt on others, that pain which haunts you will finally ease.

PART FOUR

35

THE TRANSMIGRATION OF MERCY CHAN

August 21, 1975
(Yesterday)

For the second time in her long existence, Mercy Chan awoke underwater.

Her first sensation was one of confinement. The space she occupied was small, barely enough for her body to cram into, limbs folded tight to her chest. The sides of it were metallic, rusty, and curved; some kind of storage barrel.

The same one that Thousand-Faced Girl had shoved her into.

Panic set in. Mercy twisted in frantic flurries of motion. There was a horrible wet sogginess to her lungs that she didn't like. She needed to get out of here, to breathe. Her hands shot up, seeking a rim to pull up against, and instead, her palms slammed against a well-fixed lid.

There was no exit. She was sealed in.

Fury and fear blended with her panic. Mercy pounded against the sides of the barrel with closed fists. *The lid*, she thought. Surely the lid will be the weakest point.

She braced her feet on the floor of the barrel, as much as she could in such a tight space, tucked her chin to her chest, and slammed her shoulders upward. And again, and again.

It should have hurt. The force she was applying was enough to bruise anyone's shoulders. Yet she felt nothing except a deep panic to get out, get up to air, get to where she could breathe. How was she even still alive? It had been minutes without breathing. A distant part of Mercy was aware of this, but refused to think about it because the alternative was hideous. Instead, she kept trying.

On the seventh slam, the lid gave way, barrel falling over from the force of her motion. Mercy slopped out of the drum on hands and knees amidst a splurge of water.

From darkness, into darkness. The room was small, barely the size of a large closet, and half full of water. The only light came from a small grate in the ceiling.

No, not a "room"; that was the wrong description. The walls were slick with mold and slime, the "water" dank and fetid, with an overpowering scent of rot. There were no doors or windows or any exit except that grate.

Mercy tried to breathe. Instead of easing, her pain intensified. Dry air scraped her skin raw, drowned lungs straining futilely to inhale. A transcendent horror kicked in, feral and spiraling. Mercy attempted to scream, couldn't manage it. Thrashed like a fish out of water.

Dying is not the end for you.

Shivering, Mercy looked down at herself for the first time.

Her hands were unnaturally elongated, the fingers ending in nails that curved long like claws. Her body, if it could be called that, was a starved and emaciated scrap, skin tinged the color of bile, the edges of herself indistinct and blurred. Gaunt, withered, deadly.

Corporeal . . . almost. But not quite.

Slowly, anxiously, she turned around.

Her body, or what she had long thought of as her body, lay crammed at the bottom of the barrel, waterlogged and unmoving. It had drowned in there, and she hadn't even noticed in her panic to get out, or else had mistaken its limbs for her own.

There was no hiding from the truth anymore. She died in that barrel, and her spirit was peeled away.

The fear and panic faded, replaced by a curious calm. Even the crushing pressure in her lungs seemed bearable, all of sudden, like an old auntie whom you found exasperating but had nonetheless gotten used to over the years.

A glimmering reflection caught her eye; something was written on the walls. Mercy took a step forward. Red paint formed sloppy characters; the strokes dripped with moisture. But it was readable, if only just.

From Shore Sister to Sea Sister: may we always be friends forever.

She had seen these words before, written on a scrap of paper. The heart of a lonely girl, offered up freely and stuffed into fragile glass. Once belonging to—

Sung Siu Yin, she whispered.

Lost memories returned in a torrent and cratered through her consciousness with such force that Mercy slumped sideways, held up only by the slime-drenched walls.

Fuck everything, she groaned. *I* am *Sea Sister!*

It made sense, now. All of it. She was guilty of so much. First for killing

Siu Yin and taking the other woman's body, then staying too long in a skin that wasn't hers, until her memories had faded and she had become someone new.

Of course the water ghost hunted her; it sought justice, like the many other spirits Mercy had talked to over the years. When the Girl with a Thousand Faces had killed her for the second time, Mercy's spirit must have slipped from its stolen skin into that barrel, hiding in the water.

Then the lid had been sealed on top, and the barrel placed . . . here, wherever this was. The intent was for her to rot in stinking darkness, forgotten and trapped, as she deserved. Mercy could not even complain that it was unfair.

So many were dead, because of her. Along with a slew of other unnamed, countless dozens—hundreds? More?—whose existences had been snuffed out in Siu Yin's endless quest for justice and vengeance. All paying a price that Mercy had evaded for years, against the balance of a debt she could never fulfill.

Nor did she have any hope that things would improve now that she'd been shoved in this hole. The Thousand-Faced Girl was a water ghost unbound, free to wear skins and wreak havoc. All this was surely only the beginning.

A clear voice cut through her despairing thoughts, like a hot knife through pig fat:

"Finally, you got there. Took you long enough."

Mercy spun. *Who said that?*

"Some call me the goddess of mercy. I have been your friend for years, though you never pray to me anymore."

Lady Kwun Yam? she said, stunned. *Where . . . where are you?*

"Everywhere. Nowhere. All around. It is easier for us to speak, now that you are dead again. Flesh dulls spiritual senses." I manifested myself, coalescing from the darkness to hover in front of her, my robes dry and pristine despite the rotting damp of this pit. "Is that better? Mortals like to look on faces when they speak, I'm told."

Her mouth opened and closed, fingers twitching. Trying to process it all.

"You were born special, like Ma Zu was, long ago. As a child, you came to my temple often. You asked me to remember you when you died. I took pity on you, Mei Chi, and I kept your name in my heart," I said, sadly. "But the memory of a goddess is a dangerous thing."

Why are you talking to me, here and now?! Mercy exclaimed. *Haven't you had years to speak to me?*

"I've always been talking, but you don't listen," I tell her. "I sent you dreams, for decades. Dreams so strong they broke into the waking world. I pushed you to remember, to think, to reflect. At every turn you chose to bury yourself and hide from the past. There is a limit, Mercy. Even for a deity."

. . . Oh. That was you?

"Who else?"

A clear dream with a clear message would have been far more helpful!

"Would it? Would it, really? And how do you think you would have reacted to a dream that claimed you were a long-dead water ghost accidentally stuck in the body of the niece she murdered? Would you have believed that?"

She glowered.

"Precisely." I adjusted my golden headdress primly.

Why are you here now? she said. *Is it to stop Siu Yin?*

"No, that's your job. I am just here to confront you with the truth."

What . . . what truth?

"What is happening today in Hong Kong is your fault, Mercy. Your actions created a monster, and you bear responsibility for every soul she drowns, every life she wrecks."

Mercy's shock was visceral. *I never intended any such thing! How are you pinning that on me?*

"Pinning? You took her life, little one. *You* made her into a ghost, like yourself. Gave her your curse and your pain, selfishly. Then you took her skin and lived the life she should have had."

I tried to get back to her, she protested. *I would never have chosen—*

"Except ultimately, you lived in her body, for years and years. Whatever you meant or didn't mean, the choices you made still had consequences. Intent does not excuse harm. The pain we carry does not negate the hurt caused. In the end, the path you chose to walk has led us here today."

She stared at me, stricken. *But I haven't lived a bad life! I became a good person, didn't I? The kind of good person I never had a chance to be as a child!*

"You have been wonderful," I told her, which was not *precisely* true, but I wanted to be compassionate. "However, that goodness and that redemption came at the cost of another's pain. The price of your peace was her death, and that is too high a cost."

What about her *choices? Doesn't Siu Yin bear any responsibility?*

"Yes, she does. But right now, we are talking about you and your mistakes, and how *you* must move forward to set them right."

I don't know how, she said, flinging bony hands into the air. *Where do I even start?*

"With what's in front of you," I said. "Even as we speak, Siu Yin is working her way toward the Murray Building. She will scare off or kill those she encounters, and begin breaking free the surviving ghosts who are trapped, as she was once trapped."

I mean. Is that part such a bad thing? Mercy asked, doubtfully. *It's not really a fate they deserve, is it?*

"Freeing them would be kind. Freeing them as a rabid mob, without precautions or warnings, is dangerous and unhelpful."

Fair enough, she said. *I still don't know what you want me to do, though. I have nothing. She has a city, months of planning, power, skins—*

"You are the water ghost of Shek Ham Chau, who destroyed a village and summoned storms, and kept an entire island haunted!" My exasperation brimmed over. "Isn't that power? You knew it, once, and wielded it ferociously. Won't you use that strength for good?"

Are you joking me, goddess? she said, hands on hips. *I can't even get out of this pit!*

"Oh, you will get out. Help is coming. That much I can promise. But that is why we must talk, now, while there is time." I lifted my head, gazing through the grate at the world beyond. "Tell me, child. How do you feel?"

Her mouth opened and closed. *What . . . what do you mean?*

"Are you calm? Sane? Thinking straight?"

Of course, she said, then frowned. *Ah, I see. You mean I don't feel ghostly rage. Wait,* why *don't I feel ghostly rage?*

"Because I am here. I am your goddess, and still have some hold on you, though my restraint cannot save you forever. When I go, your anger will return. Like the cycle of seasons, like the typhoons in summer, deathly fury will descend again. If you are not careful, you will lose yourself."

I don't want to lose myself, she said, anguished. *I want to be . . . to stay . . . as a human. Emotionally, anyway.*

"Then fight it," I told her, simply. "You are capable of doing so."

You don't know that, she said. *I could not control my rage as a child. You saw what I became!*

"That was then, this is now. Thirty-three years you've had in this body; thirty-three years of memories, love, sadness, joy, long days and hard nights. As a child, you weren't able to conquer your ghostly rage. As a woman, though, you *must*. No excuses, Mercy Chan."

She jerked like I'd slapped her. *You don't mince words much, for a goddess of compassion.*

I chose not to comment on that. It would have been counterproductive to remind her of all the years I'd been patient and enduring. Besides, I *was* mincing words, and she just didn't realize that.

Still, you're not wrong, she added grudgingly, and I repressed a smile.

She always got there in the end, this one. Perhaps it was why I remained so fond of her, despite everything.

This is my to-do list, then. Mercy held up a finger. *Get out of here, with help you say is coming.*

"It *is* coming."

Right. She held up a second finger. *Next, conquer my impossible rage through sheer willpower.* Third finger. *Then save Kowloon from being demolished, and Hong Kong from being overrun. Somehow.* Fourth finger. *And finally, save my niece from herself, even though she hates me for murdering her.*

"A concise yet accurate list."

All in a day's work, she muttered. *What happens after I succeed?*

"In what sense?"

I'm still dead, I'm still a ghost. I have no body to return to; I can't claim my niece's body again.

"Walk this path one step at a time." My voice grew soft, my form fading to mist in front of her eyes; the manifestation was dissipating. "You will know what is right, when you see it in front of you."

Are you sure about that? she said, alarmed. *I think you might have too much faith in me for that one, goddess.*

No answer. She would have to do without me, for a little while.

Shit, she said.

Grimly, Mercy looked upward at the grate. She rose from the water, reaching up with cautious fingers. It burned with heat, and she winced, withdrawing her hand to a safe distance.

Corporeality was a double-edged sword for ghosts; Mercy had a form that could touch, hold, push, interact. That also meant she had a form which could be trapped or held, as she had been in the barrel. Or in this room.

Her only exit was the grate, on which a talisman of warding had been thickly painted. The fu talisman was on the inside of the cover, so there was no getting around it. If it were on the top, she could perhaps simply have lifted it away.

Mercy ground her teeth in frustration.

In her human skin, fu talismans did nothing against her. As a ghost without a shell, it burned if she came too close. The glyphs were well-formed, large, and painted with a mixture made from blood and sacred ash. Priest-made, and glazed in protective paint, to keep it safe from the damp and humidity. No amateur job.

Even if she could somehow force this grate open through sheer effort, time, and will, the fu talisman would keep her prisoner.

THUNK.

Mercy jerked back. *What in heaven . . .*

THUNK.

Another strike. Someone or something was whacking the manhole cover. Another loud clang and then, impossibly, a pair of red maogui eyes peered at her through the small patch of grating in its center.

Bao! she cried out, and he growled in recognition. His claws found their grip in the grating, and with roaring effort, the ghost cat began to lift the cover.

Mercy burst out laughing. The fu talisman had been painted on the underside of the grate, but nobody had painted it on the topside. The fu talisman could keep her in, but it could not keep Bao out.

Siu Yin, or possibly her minions, hadn't prepared for another ghost coming to help.

Mercy scooped up the wretched shell of her old body with one arm and held it close. Then she jumped, catching the edge with clawed fingers, and hoisted herself like a greased serpent out of the cesspit.

36

THE PRICE OF PEACE

August 21, 1975
(Yesterday)

Up. Out. Through. Dragging the battered corpse with her.

Clawing forth onto solid concrete, and out of the pit at last. If she were still human, she'd have been gasping from relief. The best she could manage was a damp wheeze, soggy lungs compressing painfully.

Almost straightaway, she recognized her surroundings: she was in the basement underneath the main triad building. Exposed electrical wires snaked across the low ceiling. Boxes, crates, and other discarded junk cluttered the concrete floor, which was riddled with stagnant puddles. Darkness sat like a heavy cloud, and what wasn't damp was dusty. Hardly anyone came down here, unless they had to.

But the important thing was that she could see exits. There was a door, albeit locked, and a basement window, the glass smashed in from where Bao entered. Outside, it was raining heavily, water already trickling into the basement window and staining down the walls.

Bao himself was drifting, light and ephemeral, above the filthy floor. He licked her forehead with a chilly tongue, and seemed pleased at having found and rescued her. Again.

Look at you. Mercy reached over and gave the spectral ears a gentle scratch. *Following me through hell and back, from one life to the next, one mistake after another. Saving me after I called you a bastard. What did I do to deserve such a friend?*

The ghost cat regarded her loftily, as if to suggest there was no answer he could give that she would ever understand. And he was probably right.

Muffled shouts filtered through the broken window, capturing Mercy's attention. She eased over with the corpse still in her arms, acutely aware of her rapidly drying skin despite the cool dampness of the basement, and peered out.

The ground-level street outside was typical of Kowloon: dark, a little dank, strung with wires and strewn with rubbish. The handful of moldering decorations for the Hungry Ghost Festival did little to lighten the view.

There was more space than in most of the district, though, because this side of the triad building faced into Kowloon's one courtyard area. In decades past, it had been the center of the fort; these days, it was a narrow rectangle of concrete, open to the sky, with buildings clustering tight on all sides.

And in the center of that courtyard was none other than Erika, surrounded by a group of four triad men. Her hands were held high, her face pale as she spoke rapidly. They held choppers, circling her like sharks. There were people peering out of windows, or looking through cracked doors, but no one came out or interfered. Not for triad business, and not during such a spiritually dangerous evening.

She came with you, to find me, Mercy said to Bao, the realization unfolding. *Despite the danger, and the risks.*

Bao lashed his tail.

I won't let them hurt a friend. Mercy launched herself up and out through the basement window with all the grace of a vengeful spirit. Her cat followed, growling low in his throat.

The nighttime air was sticky with humidity and the darkness was heavy with spiritual energy. The full force of the Hungry Ghost Festival filled the space around her, writhing with yin energy that only spirits could sense. Wards were hung above every window and doorframe, which normally would have been painful for spirits, yet she was barely aware of them at this distance.

The triad men turned abruptly as Mercy clambered unglamorously from the broken basement window. Their eyes widened and one of them said, hoarsely, "Is that Chan's spirit? What the hell!"

Erika stiffened, eyes going wide behind her glasses.

Mercy threw her head back and shrieked. It was an intuitive cry, one embedded in her memory. The haunting, anguished wail of a child left to die before her time.

The typhoon answered, as she knew it would.

Heavy clouds stirred to a sudden boil. The wind accelerated, rattling shutters and signs and buildings alike. Thunder rolled like a stampeding horde and the heavens opened abruptly, pouring forth torrential rain. The deluge was a welcome relief to Mercy's skin. She'd been starting to blister, even under cover of night.

That's better, she said, then set down her old shell of a body and walked toward Erika. Rain lashed in sideways, and it was almost like being in water again.

The triad enforcers shouted, brandishing weapons at her approach. Two of them Mercy recognized as her tormentors, from earlier in the day, and a wash of searing anger suffused her. She must punish them, catch them, drown them all—

No. Mercy couldn't breathe deeply to calm herself, so she ground sharkish teeth and shook her head to disperse the surge of ghostly fury. Be calm, be rational. She needed only to help her friend; that didn't have to mean killing these men. They could not harm her anyway, not anymore.

To their credit, they at least tried. The first one swung his watermelon chopper with full-body force. The blade cut through her atrophied flesh, but there was nothing to damage, no blood to flow. Her arm healed almost immediately. The second pulled a peachwood dagger, while the third brandished a pair of fu talismans.

Mercy caught the chopper blade with one hand, the sharp edge pressed hard into her dead palm, and flung it away. The other two were slightly more dangerous, and *could* hurt her, in theory.

But she wouldn't allow that. A stomp of her foot sent hurricane winds spiraling across the courtyard, knocking over the man with the peachwood dagger and the man brandishing fu talismans. They tumbled and rolled like leaves, losing their precious anti-ghost items in the process.

The fourth man stood frozen and alone, too cowed to move.

Go home, little boy, she said, and bared her teeth.

He turned and fled, yelling swear words.

Bao, who had not yet changed from his kitten form, watched with impassive curiosity. He seemed to recognize that Mercy did not need him, and so had not expended the energy. For once, she was strong enough to stand on her own.

In moments, all of them were gone.

Mercy allowed it. She did not pursue, or wreak death. The rage was still within and around her, but it was merely the storm for which she was the eye, and she could be calm at its center. She *would* be calm.

The sense of control was freeing.

Are you alright? Mercy walked over to Erika, quieting the storm around them into mere rain. For now. *Did they hurt you?*

"Holy shit!" Erika's eyes were wide as saucers. She fell to her knees on the concrete, drenched and shivering. "Oh my gods. Are you—"

Your old friend Chan, Mercy answered, gently. *This is my true form, as I really am. That body over there contained me for many years, but it is not me. Do you understand?*

Erika stared at her, mouth working but no words coming out.

I'm so sorry . . . This is so complicated. There is a lot going on.

"But *what* the hell are you?" Erika sputtered, speaking at last. "A spirit?

A goddess? Something worse? No, you can't be evil, you're . . . so lovely." She blinked, as if shocked and embarrassed to have said that aloud.

Mercy understood. Her friend was not seeing a monster, starved and vicious and dangerous. In this driving rain, on the night of the Hungry Ghost Festival no less, the water ghost glamour was in full effect. To human eyes, she would be a vision of transcendent beauty.

The glamour wasn't something she could turn off or on, like a switch. Still, it was useful. Erika might have been trying to kill her or running away, if not for that power. Mercy was oddly grateful that the curse had given her space to explain.

Let me show you, she said, kneeling down to Erika's level, and pressed her forehead to Erika's. As she had with Siu Yin, long ago, and as Siu Yin once had—partly—with Wing Yun.

A cascade of memories and emotions swamped the other woman. Only a few moments passed, but Mercy knew it would feel like much longer to Erika. She gave freely the story of all she had been and done as a child, and the betrayal committed against her niece. When it was done, she stepped back, giving her old friend space.

Erika gave a gasp and a cry, patting her face and body as if to check it was all still there. "Let me get this right . . . You've been a ghost in a stolen body *this whole time*? Ever since I've known you?!"

I'm so sorry, Erika. I never meant to deceive you. I did not know myself, until Thousand-Faced Girl "killed" me. Only when I died for a second time did my memories return.

Mercy paused, trying to gather her thoughts. There were too many to gather, though. It was like chasing down a yard full of baby pigs.

"Don't speak to me like you know me!" Erika leaned away, palms pressed to her eyes. "You're just some dead woman. Not the person I thought I knew!"

For a moment, Mercy was once again Sea Sister, standing in a dark cavern and hearing Siu Yin shriek *You are a ghost!* The rage rose in her heart—

And she quashed it, hard. Patience. Peace. Self-assuredness. The things she had fought to cultivate in herself were the pillars she must lean on, and through sheer effort of will, her heart kept an even keel.

I am not *just some dead woman*, Mercy said quietly. *I lived thirty-three years in that body. I had friends, have been a friend, survived war and death, saw poverty and brutality. I made a life, I made a difference. Haven't you known me through all of that?*

Even as she said it, the full weight of that truth settled on her like a blessing, a strength to draw upon. Her choices in the past had been monstrous, but she was capable of being human, and had been for years. Perhaps one day, she would be again.

The rage within calmed further. Even the ache in her lungs seemed to dull.

Bodies matter, but they are not the only thing that matters, Mercy continued. *My life is the sum of the choices I have made. I am shaped by my skin, but not defined by it. I am a human, I am a woman, I am Mercy Chan. No matter how divorced my body is from my spirit, no matter what face I wear, this remains true.*

A long moment of silence stretched while Mercy kneeled, waiting. Around them, the curious watchers seemed to have shut their curtains and gone in. If there was anyone to see a water ghost speaking to a woman in the street, they did not show themselves.

Erika took a ragged breath. "You don't have to lecture me about souls and bodies feeling disconnected. I know all about that," she said, gesturing to herself. "If anything, Chan, I could give you tips on coming to terms with it."

Mercy laughed, or something approximating a laugh. It sounded like a child choking on seawater.

Erika reached across and squeezed her hand. "The Mercy Chan I knew was always smart, loyal, and a good friend. She was also bad at keeping in touch and perpetually short of money. That hasn't changed, I guess. Even if you're a ghost."

Who are you calling short of money, Mercy huffed. *My job made me wealthy, you sarcastic old bat! More than you ever made as a teacher.*

It was Erika's turn to burst out laughing, and a surge of joy ran through Mercy. It would be okay; her friend would not leave her, or reject her. The memory of Siu Yin fleeing tearfully seemed to ebb, and a tension she hadn't been aware of eased from her shoulders.

The anger in her hadn't been this soft since she first swam with her niece, all those years ago. Oddly, she felt that this might be a permanent change, as if the brittle sourness in her had sweetened.

"What will you do now?" Erika said, when her laughter subsided.

I don't know. Mercy bowed her head. *Everything that is happening is about me and her. It's all my fault, all the bad shit in Kowloon and in Hong Kong—*

"Oh, hell. Take a minute and sit down, will you?" Erika shifted from kneeling to a cross-legged position on the hard, puddle-laden concrete.

There's no time—

"Sit, kid. Before I catch my death of chill out here."

Mercy sighed, and joined her. They huddled shoulder-to-shoulder in the pounding storm, tarps and shutters and signs clattering in the ever-present wind, warm typhoon rain drenching both of them. Mercy's old body—or rather, Siu Yin's old body—slumped on the ground nearby, lifeless and cold.

"In all your years as a ghost talker, you always told me that the first step was for someone to just listen to a spirit. Most people are too busy being scared or hanging fu talismans to talk. That's the difference between you and exorcists, and always has been." Erika fished out a packet of soggy cigarettes from one pocket, grimaced in disappointment, and chucked it away. "I'm not trained, I don't have your knack. But I have been your friend a long time, and now that you're dead—again—I think you need me more than ever. Talk to me, Mercy. What do you want?"

The answer came naturally.

To fix things. To put things right.

"What went wrong? I don't mean the details. You've shown me those, and you're getting lost in them. What's the heart of the matter, Mercy?"

She had to think about that. *Someone loved me. I was too damaged to love them back. When I tried, I hurt them beyond measure. Now they're spilling that hurt everywhere into the world, and the only way I can think to stop them is to hurt them again. Which I don't want to do.*

"Why do you have to stop them?" Erika said, puzzled. "Since when were you in the business of stopping ghosts, Chan? I thought your thing was giving them the justice they craved."

That's the thing, I can't give her justice, Mercy said, trying not to groan. *She wants me dead, but I've already died, twice. Yet she's still raging, her hatred undimmed.*

"Then maybe your assumption is wrong." Erika took off her rain-spattered glasses and gave them a shake. "If your second death didn't bring her peace, could it be that she doesn't want you dead?"

Mercy stared at her with a hollowed, ghostly gaze. *How are you so smart?*

"Dunno, but that's why I'm a teacher, and you're a triad goon." The other woman gave a gap-toothed grin. "I think you're looking for solutions in the wrong places. Try thinking about it objectively, like a ghost talker. Think how you'd approach this case if it were someone else. Draw on all the experience you have, and don't be afraid to question the past. The answer to what Miss Thousand-Faced Girl wants, lies in you."

In me, Mercy echoed. Already, an unsettling idea was forming in her mind, one she was half afraid to consider. *I see. Thank you, that* is *helpful.*

"No problem." Erika sighed. "You mentioned all the 'bad shit' that might happen soon. What does 'bad' mean?"

It means every ghost in the Murray Building being freed on the night of Hungry Ghost Festival to wreak havoc on the city. Then the damage being blamed on Kowloon. This district being razed. That kind of bad.

"It's always something with you, isn't it?"

Sorry, Mercy said, cringing. *I do have an idea for how to fix things, I think, but I need your help. I know I have asked a lot of you today—*

"No shit, Chan!"

—but I promise, this is nearly over. Will you help me, big sister? One final time?

"Do I look like I would dare refuse a ghost?" Erika grumbled. "What do you need?"

If you can, go back to Red Bird's establishment, and fetch some of the documents from her room. They prove Kit Ling's corruption. That will at least halt the demolition process, and give the district time to build a new case.

"Isn't it guarded?!"

It won't be now. The triad have no need of it. They're too busy trying to find their leader, who is dead.

"You'd better be sure about that," Erika said, doubtfully.

Bao padded over, yowling inquisitively.

I haven't forgotten you, don't worry. Mercy kissed her ghost cat on the nose. *I have one more request for you, too, most loyal of creatures. If you ever loved me, go with Erika, and keep her safe. Do this for me, and I will never ask anything of you, ever again.*

He hissed, as if she had trod on his tail.

Please, Bao, she said. *Erika needs someone to keep her safe. And you'll be destroyed if Siu Yin sees you. I can't bear that. This isn't your justice to face, either of you.*

His teeth bared in a snarl.

She stroked his ear, understanding the question intuitively. *If I don't see you again, then know that I always loved you most of all, above any other living thing. I hope you are able to find peace one day, and I hope that it is not me who is keeping you from rest.*

The great furry head bobbed in reluctant acquiescence. Loyal to the last, he turned and padded closer to Erika, nudging the older woman.

"I'm going, I'm going!" Erika was shivering badly from the rain, and hunched down into her sodden clothing. "Will I see you again, little sister?"

I don't know. Mercy scooped up the forlorn body, its limbs slack in her grasp.

If you don't hear from me, come look on the island of Shek Ham Chau. I might be there. Or you might get some answers, at least.

"The island of where?!"

Shek Ham Chau. It's off the Sai Kung coast. Mercy added, *Good luck, big sister. Stay safe.*

"You too, Chan." Erika gave a slight bow, then turned and began hobbling away through the rattling winds and driving rain. Bao padded along at her side, casting uncertain glances over one ghostly shoulder.

Mercy did not watch them walk away, because it would only have distracted her. Instead, she looked toward the main gates, which were just visible at the far end of the courtyard. Beyond their perimeter lay the rest of the city. Hong Kong was a big place, but I had already told her where to go.

She murmured, *I'm coming, Siu Yin*, and did not know if it was a promise or a threat.

The water ghost of Shek Ham Chau ran toward the barricaded gates of Kowloon Walled city, Siu Yin's body in her arms.

37

THIS WILL HURT

August 22, 1975
(Today)

Several miles from Kowloon Walled City, you are walking through the empty Murray Building, alone and unseen. And unaware of what is transpiring in Kowloon, which you've left behind.

It is nighttime, and a public holiday, so none of the staff are here. You have Kit Ling's keys, and her security passes, but not her face, since you left it to be "discovered" by the police in Kowloon. That means you can get through doors, but guards need bribing or killing. You have Cobra Lily's sword, though, and are not afraid to use it. The consequences don't matter anymore.

It takes a little time, but you finally arrive in the depths of the Murray Building's secure supernatural lockup. Where you were once held, for nearly three decades. Fingers trembling, you input the last of the codes into the electronic systems and step inside.

Lights come on automatically. In front, shelf after shelf of bottle gourds await you. To the left is a small room, the very same one where Kit Ling brought you out the first time. It exists to interrogate ghosts safely, though that is almost never done. You won't be doing it, either.

Instead, you pull out a luopan, of the kind used by fengshui masters, among others, and begin scanning the gourds in each aisle. Ghost-finding is not what the luopan is meant for, but it can work that way in a pinch. The needle spins frantically in the presence of spirit energy.

A crushing number of bottle gourds turn up empty. Those you smash, feeling a twinge of pity for the spirits who withered away in agony within. At least this way there's a chance their spiritual energy will recycle in some fashion, eventually, though you wouldn't put money on it happening.

The "filled" bottle gourds go into a large sack. There are too many for a single trip, so you take several dozen at a time and lug them to the roof. Annoying, but you don't mind the exercise.

"Your time has come," you tell the bottle gourds, even though they can't yet hear you. "I'll set us all free. This city will be sorry!"

On the final trip, you also pick up a jar of temple ink from the nearby storage.

You will be writing lots fu talismans tonight, but not of binding or banishing or warding, or even preserving. It is time for a fu talisman of breaking.

Encumbered by the burden, slowed by the limits of human flesh, you leave the basement and begin the long, tedious climb to the roof. The elevators are switched off, and you aren't quite sure how to turn them on again, nor do you want to risk creating light and noise. Best if there's no risk of anyone disturbing these proceedings.

Besides, what's the rush? You have all night.

Outside, rain begins to beat against the window. A storm is coming, you think, but only fleetingly. You're too busy planning what to say to your soon-to-be-freed horde to pay the weather much mind.

When you reach the roof again, the storm is in full tilt. Rain sheets down hard, soaking every surface. The rooftop is flooded with water, and excess flow tips over the edge in a miniature waterfall.

If you were less focused on the task, that might have alarmed you, or prompted you to wonder why it feels like a typhoon is drawing ever closer to you specifically. But it has been a long time since you worried about the kind of supernatural beings who could summon storms.

Instead, you focus on the ritual. Set about carving a wide circle of symbols around the gourds, using Cobra Lily's sword to score the concrete.

When that circle is in place, it's time to fill it with monk-blessed ink. It flows gradually into the grooves, the process hampered severely by the wind and rain. But it's far faster and easier than doing each of them individually, and worth the cost in time. Despite the weather, the monk-blessed ink takes hold as you apply it, in defiance of the elements.

When it is complete, all of these gourds will shatter at once. That's the moment you've been working toward. Three hundred–odd ghosts of exceptional strength and anger will pour out across Hong Kong, killing and wreaking hell as they go. As well they should.

The end of your fu talisman is in sight when the unexpected happens.

Mercy Chan vaults over the railing, feet landing with a sharp splash on the overrun balcony, deliberate in making noise. The noise is a disturbance, and you twist round with alarm in one smooth, continuous motion.

The sight of her takes your breath away.

Skin the color of palest jade, delicate like a paper lantern. Eyes that glow white and pearlescent. A wealth of black hair streams over her shoulders. In her mouth is the hardness of teeth, too many for a human woman, and jagged as a shark's.

Your enemy should be locked in a barrel beneath a triad building, safely out of the way. The sight of her should send chills of anxiety through every nerve ending.

Instead, you are only amazed.

Even . . . awestruck, if only briefly.

For she is beautiful, in a twisted way, and something about her sorrowful, ferocious expression restores a hint of the wonder you once felt, long ago. You're not fully immune to her ghost glamour, not when clothed in human skin.

Tilt your head up, hold her gaze. Neither of you speaks, because neither of you can. It doesn't matter. Some moments don't need words. She is holding your body, you realize with shock; somehow, that detail escaped you till now.

Your mind is awhirl. A part of you is angry that Mercy broke out so quickly. The rest of you rather admires her for it. The prison that was supposed to last years has done about three hours, if that.

Perhaps this is just divine destiny. If so, who are you to argue with heaven?

Hello, niece, Mercy says.

"You remember, at last. Took you long enough." Incredibly, a torrent of emotions stirs in your chest. As it did not do when you killed her again and locked her away.

I do remember, she says. *It has come back to me . . . all of it, everything. I'm afraid I have not behaved very well.*

"That's a hell of an understatement!" you hiss. "You *dare* show your face to me, even still?"

Because I have to stop this madness! Her gesture takes in the half-finished fu talisman, the city at large. *Kit Ling and Cobra Lily, all the other people in this city, these ghosts you want to free . . . none of that is necessary. You can have your body back. You've already killed me. What else is there to do?*

"Why would I even want that, Chen Mei Chi? My old, tired body, that you have used, abused, riddled with scars, and worn out? No, thank you! I would never settle for my own skin when I can have a closet full of them."

She blinks slowly. *You want . . . immortality?*

"I don't want immortality, I simply *have* it, and so do you. This is a powerful curse, Mei Chi. We can live for all eternity with a thousand different faces. Which you wasted by sulking on an island for years, then traipsing around in *my* body for even longer."

Do you know, she says, thoughtfully, *I think you might be the first ghost in history to outsmart her own curse. Niece, I must applaud your creativity in learning how to exist forever, even if I disapprove of what you're doing.*

Her attitude is grating. "It's not about living forever," you snap. "It is deeper than that. You wouldn't understand."

Try me, little girl. You have destroyed a city and killed people I care about to get my attention. Don't you want to talk? I am here, I am listening.

Almost, you shout that *No, I don't want to talk, I want to punish you forever* but you realize with faint chagrin that isn't true.

Maybe it's the influence she has, that strange unspoken knack which drives ghosts to speak with her, when they should not. Or maybe it's simply the full force of the history between you both, bearing down on your tongue with the weight of a thousand angry words.

Whatever the reason, words come pouring out.

"How little you know," you say, voice crackling. "To be killed, betrayed, and abandoned is one thing entirely. To have your tormentor forget about you, as if all the pain you have ever known meant nothing and could not touch them, is something else entirely. Can you even begin to understand that?"

Of course I can, Mercy says, sincerely. *I am the one person in your life who understands that pain so perfectly.*

"Then why did you inflict it on me? Do you drown and abandon all the nieces you like, or only the special ones?" Your volume ratchets louder with every word. "It's as if all that I am, or ever could be, means nothing. *I* mean nothing to the one person who defines my whole existence. It's not fair!"

Then what would make it fair? she says.

"Your destruction!" Point at the gourds beside you with a snarl. "That is also what they will want, when I free them. To hurt those who betrayed them. The price of peace is always death, and we need death for our peace!"

Did you feel better when I was stuffed in a barrel, or did you feel the same? she retorts, and you hiss at her in fury, because she's not wrong. *I may be a silly old woman, but I do know this much, Siu Yin. When I drowned the village of Shek Ham Chau, my heart was not calmer at all. Not a jot, not for a second. I am sure that yours isn't, either, despite trying to punish me. You might think that unleashing hell on Hong Kong is going to heal your heart, but it won't.*

She's thinking of Cobra Lily, telling her a few days ago that this is justice and wishing she'd questioned it. Justice can involve death, and certainly has, but Cobra Lily's outlook was far too narrow. Just like yours is now.

"Then what *will* heal me?" you snarl, unable to stop yourself from asking the question. "Since you're so wise and have so much wisdom!"

Nothing, she says, simply and sadly. *Pain and grief are holes that never fill. We just learn to step around them as we walk.*

"Not good enough," you say, ragged and shaken. It's eerily similar to the sort of thing your father might have said, back when he was alive. "Not fucking good enough!"

One lightning-fast lunge and you swing the flat of Cobra Lily's sword. All those years of living and training during the war have not gone to waste.

Mercy surprises you. Even as the blade swings down, she is already moving, diving and darting past your left side. You twist to block a blow, but are shocked a second time to find she isn't attacking. Only moving to a safe distance.

She should be trying to kill you; it's her only chance to survive. Why else would she come back? She has no options, no possible other plan. You are her monster legacy, existing only to be defeated. Surely, that is how she sees you.

Oh, well. Her weakness is your advantage. You leap forward, sword singing and hair flying in the roiling tempest.

It shouldn't be close. Mercy never took any kind of formal fighting training, in all her years and lives. She fiddles around with knives and has a good aim, but that's not the same. You have fought in literal wars and spent time learning weapon techniques.

Except she is fast, an unencumbered spirit compared to your heavy, sluggish body. Every swing is met with empty air. You are burdened by the weight of flesh, moving only as fast as joints allow. And she is less interested in hurting you than avoiding you, which you don't understand.

Maybe you should be slipping out of this body, too. But that's risky. If she decides to dissipate her storm, normal sky will return and you'll die quickly up here without the constant pour of water. It would end her life, along with yours, but you can't be sure she wouldn't take that trade.

It has always annoyed you that summoning storms is not in your repertoire. That is all Mercy, and nothing particularly to do with being a water ghost.

She darts to the side, swinging again with furious intent. No point overthinking it. You will stay in this body for now and cut her down, because you are a far better and more experienced fighter than this bumbling middle-aged woman, even if she is a ghost.

And once you've trapped her a second time, you'll make sure she doesn't get out. Mercy will know what it is like to be forgotten and alone, forever and ever and ever. Then, maybe then, the rage you feel will start to cool. It must.

Leap, and swing. Down comes the blade.

She catches it in her claws, wrests it from your grasp. But instead of striking, Mercy flings the sword out and over the balcony.

"I have more," you snarl. "More weapons, more bodies, more hate for you!"

So do I, Siu Yin. We can go on like this forever, both of us—immortal in our anger, endlessly cruel and destructive. Is that what you want?

"I've told you what I want! I will be the storm that washes away your whole world! I will punish everyone for forgetting, for betraying, for hurting!"

I see. You want to do this the hard way, huh? Mercy draws herself upright, teeth gleaming and claws hanging, the tattered rags of a water ghost plastered to her skeletal form.

You take a step back, wary and tense.

Sung Siu Yin, she says, in a voice as deep and cold as the ocean, *before you were even born, I was already dead. Before you drew breath, I bathed in rage. Before you killed a man, I had already drowned a village.*

You want to fight? Then we fight! This is my storm, little girl, little niece, and I remember how to sing to it. You wanted me to remember everything? Well, I do. And I had forgotten more than you ever *learned.*

"Oh shit," you manage, and then all of that tempestuous power bears down on a single building.

It is like heaven itself has reached down to punch you, with a whirlwind of air so strong that every window shatters in the Murray Building. Debris smashes against nearby buildings, and the air is full of glass. The noise is enough to burst eardrums and you careen wildly, hopelessly off-balance.

Mercy grabs your wrist.

She stands impossibly still amidst that chaos, spirit feet braced on the slick linoleum, ghostly skin sheened with rain. She is light as a feather and should blow away, yet she stands solid as a marble pillar. Her claws hold you fast, keeping you from fleeing.

You stare at her with eyes wide, clutching back at her wrist. Temporarily forgetting that you, too, are an undying ghost.

I'm very sorry, niece, she says. *This will hurt.*

Lightning strikes directly. It's just like on Mami's boat, all those years ago. Only this time, there is no ocean to displace the energy.

Your body explodes.

38

GHOST TALKER

August 22, 1975
(Today)

Smell returns first. The air smells like seared bacon; the realization is almost funny. Gasping, you crawl at last from the smoldering remains of Cobra Lily's skin, like a demented butterfly emerging from a tainted chrysalis.

Rain greets you like an old friend, like a blessing long denied. With Mercy no longer calling upon the skies to deliver a storm, it is already beginning to slacken from typhoon into mere downpour.

The top of this building is a war zone of cracked concrete and wrenched struts. Debris has scattered everywhere. Mercy releases you, stooping to gather up your discarded physical body before it can tumble off the roof like so much clutter.

"I'm not gone," you snarl, shaking off the viscera. "It was only a body, and I can get more!"

"I'm fully aware." Her lips don't move, and neither do yours, yet now that you are both in ghost form, you hear her voice more clearly than any human speech. "I wasn't trying to end you. If I wanted to do that, if I wanted to just kill us both, I'd hold you close and banish the storm until the dry air turned us to dust. That's the only way I think we could 'die' a true death, at this point. Ghosts like us are more akin to demons."

"So do it," you snap, unnerved at her casual depiction. "Unless you're too afraid to die?"

"Niece, I must insist you stop being dramatic." She jams claw-tipped fists on her hips. "I know this is very difficult, because ghosts are driven to be angry and full of drama, but please *try*. We are better than our ghostly urges. And if I can learn to control my fury, you sure as shit can do it, too."

Your jaw drops. In all your years of preparing for revenge, nothing has quite readied you for the infuriating sass of her.

"Dying would be so, so easy," Mercy continues. "But what would be the point of that? We'd both carry so much grief and trauma into the next life that our existence would be misery from birth. Nothing would be healed. I'd hate to see the kind of asshole I become with *that* level of spiritual baggage hanging over me."

"Then what did you want, bitch? My forgiveness?" The last bit, you inject with heavy sarcasm.

"Yes," she says, and you are so dumbfounded by the audacity that you are, once again, momentarily without words. "I want your forgiveness, and I want to give you mine."

"You *destroyed* me!" Slam your fists down on the wrecked rooftop floor; everything shakes. The people you could have loved. The life you could have built. All gone, because of this woman. "Everything I thought worthy in myself, you have stripped away, and shown to be false. I used to be good, Mei Chi. Truly good. Now, because of you, I know how awful I can be. Because of you, I have killed and killed and killed, hated and loathed and lied and stolen. *I can't go back to being better.* How the hell could anyone forgive that?"

"No one can go back, that's true." She inches closer; you scoot away suspiciously. "But we can go forward. Become something stronger, newer, wiser, kinder."

"Do you think I'm stupid? There is no way you want that. I am trying to kill your city, just like I killed your boss, and just like you killed me!"

"I know," she says, with terrible sadness. "I know. I know exactly what you've done to me, and what I've done to you. Isn't that the point, that you wanted me to remember? Well, I do, now. I remember it with horror, and I remember it with shame. I remember it with the eyes of a grown woman, who can look back on her life as a little girl, her death as an angry spirit, and understand what she allowed herself to become. What hurt she perpetuated."

"Then you, as a grown woman with her two lives' experience, should know better than to even suggest it! You can no more forgive me than I can forgive you. We might as well ask China to forgive Japan, or Japan to forgive America. Look at the world around us, Mei Chi. Look at the war, the ruination. If humanity could forgive, we would already live in heaven with the immortals!"

"I don't know if it is possible," she says, with a helpless shrug. "All I know is that we must try, or the feud will go on and on. You call this immortality, Siu Yin, but I call it eternal hell. Hate is like a burn that sits in the chest, choking the life away, keeping a body from breathing. It is suffocation. And I *know* you understand that feeling."

She looks down at your skin, its limp form curled around her feet. "Pain doesn't end with death. Karma doesn't die with the body. Hate and anger continue, one generation to the next, as souls return damaged and we build an ever more twisted society. I think humanity must have always been like this. I think this is why we all hurt, all the time."

From a long time ago, your traitorous memory summons up the mental image of Baba seated at the kitchen table, and the words he'd said once so long ago: *War does not finish. It is a wound, sinking into flesh, leaving scars and rot that cause pain for a long time.*

"I . . ." Your hands clench. "We don't deserve forgiveness."

"If we deserved it, then it wouldn't be forgiveness, would it? Besides, Siu Yin, life isn't about what we deserve. It's about how we change, and who we love." She looks up, holds out a hand. "Please, niece. Fight the ghostly anger and sit with me. Let's talk about this, like the humans we once were. While we still can."

The rain softens into a drizzle, light enough that your ocean-adapted skin is beginning to tighten uncomfortably. It will be the same for Mercy, you're sure, and only a matter of time before one or both of you start to suffer the effects. Yet neither of you move.

You should kill her, strike her down, trap her, any of that, all of that, summon greater and greater storms, inflict worse and worse agony and . . . and . . .

And then what?

And then, like Mercy says, you will each be reborn into some other life, carrying pain you can't explain or remember, and so never address. Like your mother, haunted by feelings she could never speak of, driven from joy to cruelty; well meaning, yet ultimately lost and harsh. Trauma perpetuating pain.

The despair of that fate stretches out before you, a long and unrewarding path.

"It won't work," you insist, voice sounding cracked even to yourself. "It . . . we will *fail*."

Above you both, the rain is slackening, the clouds beginning to thin. The effect is immediate; your skin and hers are starting to dry out, already.

"How do you know, when we haven't even attempted it?" She tilts her head up, eyeless gaze on the grayed sky above. "Let me put it this way, niece. What's the worst that happens if we fail? We go back to destroying each other, and everything around us. Just like you say we must. But Siu Yin, *what happens if we succeed*?"

"It's already too late," you snap. "I've already killed so many, brought these ghosts up here—"

"Nothing can be done for those you've killed, but that doesn't mean you have to keep doing it. You can choose to stop. And as for the ghosts—they deserve to be freed," she says, which shocks you. "Just, not like this. Not all at once, without safeguards or warded rooms. You know?"

". . . Are you being serious?"

"There's a middle ground between avoiding the past and having it shoved forcefully up one's nose. Most people have forgotten those ghosts are there, which is why they keep languishing. We can help them without risking hundreds or thousands of lives."

Your mouth opens and shuts. "But . . . Kowloon! You have fought for your district, Mei Chi. Don't tell me you are going to walk away from it!"

"I am already dead," she says, gently. "Of course I care for Kowloon, and I haven't walked away from it. A good friend is going to make sure the demolitions come to a halt, and that real talks begin. However . . . this is not my life or my world. So, I must leave that task to others and focus on my truest duty: to put right the island, and to offer healing in your life. If I can."

You fall silent, thinking harder than you ever have before. Trying to process everything she has said, fighting against the ghost fervor in your brain and heart. Attempting to imagine a future not soaked in hate and hurt, as Wing Yun once urged you to do.

"It occurs to me that I haven't actually said the words. Let me fix that now." She lets go of your body and kneels in front of you, her forehead and palms pressed to the floor. "Siu Yin, I am so sorry. There is no excuse for my actions, no justification for your murder, or the hurt you've endured. Please, return with me to Shek Ham Chau, the place where it all began for you, and let me try to save what future you have left."

Sentiments you never thought you'd hear, and they strike to your core more deeply than even the lightning did. Ghosts can't cry, yet your eyes ache and burn with the desire to do so anyway.

"I'm . . . so tired," you confess, dropping to your knees next to her. "Everything hurts, all the time. I wish I could breathe."

"Me too." She looks up. "I'm beyond tired, at this point. That's why I think we must go to Shek Ham Chau and speak to a certain goddess."

It takes you a moment to remember who and what she means. You have not thought of me for a very long time, or our brief encounter after your death.

"I don't know about that . . ."

"But I do. I'm the ghost talker, remember?" She grins with a mouthful of jagged teeth. "The island is where it all began, and the island is where it must end. Everything else follows from that. If it doesn't work, you can always destroy me after. Come with me, Siu Yin, and let's try. Please."

She reaches out, jade-hued skin frazzling with dryness in the slacking rain. Dawn will be coming soon; if neither of you move, you'll both die a final death. Still you hesitate, thinking and agonizing.

Mercy gives you time, and waits.

As the sun begins to set the world alight, you finally take her hand.

39
DEATH AND REBIRTH

August 22, 1975
(Today)

In the distance, the city recedes like an outgoing tide.

One final glance reveals modern skyscrapers wreathed in rainclouds. All the ferries, boats, and ships are huddled in their docks, cast into shadow by the arriving dawn.

The bottle gourds with their trapped ghosts have been gathered up and returned to the canvas sack. You have left them at a seaside temple, with a note explaining what needs doing. The priests will be able to help with the duty that government officials have neglected for so long.

Individually, the people of Hong Kong are not responsible for decisions that led to the "spiritual cleansing" when the occupation ended. Only a handful of individuals chose to lock away spirits, rather than placate or honor them. Nonetheless, ghosts are a legacy of pain that belong to a whole society. Everyone in the city must bear the cost of that trauma. Pain cannot be left buried, or it will grow and put down roots, like a cursed tree.

That is not to say you are innocent, either. Mercy is guilty of her sins; you of yours. This is irrefutable, as are the deaths which lie at your feet. In your ghost heart, you sense there will be a reckoning someday, when you must go and confront the aftermath of the lives you took, examine all the harm you caused.

For now, though . . .

"Faster," Mercy murmurs. And she dives.

You, carrying your own body like a precious possession, dive after her.

It has been a long time since you've swum like this. Ironic, really, that you have spent more time in the water as a living woman than you ever did as a ghost. Even in your days of infiltrating ships, you preferred to be on dry land, in a variety of skins. Water was something that bound you, rather than something that freed you.

Today, in ghost form, you feel anything but bound as you propel rapidly through deep green waves, with Mercy at your side. Ocean rushes past, as do wrecks and fish and litter and coral. Clouds of moon jellyfish brush your limbs as you wind through them.

Time passes along with the miles. Both of you are fast and untiring, single-minded in purpose. The burn of suffocation still crunches the lungs in this form, but you are very used to that, and almost consider it a fair exchange for the exhilarating speed that death has granted.

Gradually, the seascape begins to look familiar. You recognize the shapes of certain rocks or islands, certain wrecks and reefs. The water in Sai Kung is a little clearer, a little brighter in its green, especially this time of year.

A strange nostalgia seeps over you. As if you are, once again, a girl on the cusp of adventure, leaving behind the strife of a conflict-riddled city.

In a way, you are.

"Up," Mercy says, softly, and guides you both to the surface.

At first, you can't see anything. The typhoon's presence has cast clouds and mist over the region, even this far out. A cool breeze rolls in from the east, cloying with the promise of rain. It eases the dry tightening of your ghost skin. Squint, shade your eyes, and try to peer vainly into that white haze, seeking a first glimpse of your destination.

Then the sun comes out, quick as child's smile; clouds part at her warm touch. And Shek Ham Chau seems to rise in front of you like a woman surfacing for air.

Sunlight shimmers on the water. Boxy houses, brightly painted, refract color at unexpected angles. Glossy mangroves fuzz the shoreline. Scintillating peace lingers.

Your breath catches. Not from the beauty, though it is beautiful—but because the entire village is gathered on the shore in all their drowned, horrifying misery. They stand together on the docks in a cluster of whispering dead, watching and waiting.

Strange how they fill you with anxiety, even after all this time.

"Not yet," Mercy says, skin blistering from sunlight. "We have someone else to see first."

You both dive again, this time angling around to the island's south side. Toward the cave and the stone temple within.

Down, amidst the whirl of water and fish and sunlit coral. Along the rock tunnel, which you notice—for the first time, despite having been through it twice—is carved, rather than natural. You think briefly of the jiaoren depicted in the temple, and wonder what happened to them, and why they never visit this place anymore. But that mystery is not yours to solve, and is a story for another time.

Then up, out. Light grows around you, softening the dark. The tunnel widens rapidly. Deep ink giving way to paler and paler shades of verdant water until, finally, impatiently, you break the surface.

Wet walls drip and shimmer in the faint light. The rock is layered in striations of red and brown, the color of blood at different stages of freshness. The ceiling is high and rent with gaps. Sunbeams pierce the darkness, creating odd refractions and shadows.

Touched only by tides, the cavern is much as you remember. There is even an old bottle, the glass fogged by waves and time, wedged into the crevice of a wall; it looks to be clustered with barnacles. The sight of it jogs a memory of better days.

Slowly, get to your feet in that chest-deep pool, your body cradled close. Slowly, half knowing already what you will see, you turn around.

A stone temple rises at the far end of the cavern where the water is shallowest, carved straight into the rock itself, and illuminated faintly by light which cascades from gaps in the stalactite-riddled ceiling.

All is quiet; the walls are merely stone, the statue within just a statue.

"Where is she?" you ask, nervously. "Where is the goddess?"

Mercy does not reply. Instead, she is riffling around in the water. After a moment she straightens, holding a handful of oysters. You watch with astonishment as she prizes them open, digging out the pearls within.

"There's a wealth of riches down here," you say, amazed. "I never knew!"

"I think maybe the jiaoren grew them, once. Just for this." She discards the shells and carries the pearls and lays them at the doorway, since she cannot enter.

You are not overly familiar with religious rituals, but you know enough to follow her lead as she bows three times, murmuring words of thanks and gratitude. It is shaky, as offerings go, but sometimes the intention matters more than the material reality.

On the third bow, something changes.

Within the temple, the statue begins to stir. Color spreads across the flat stone, taking on life and texture. Fabric softens, limbs twitch. In moments, carved rock becomes divine flesh, and a divine being stands before you on a plinth.

Tilt your head from one angle and she is an elegant lady of ageless features, draped in flowing robes. Tilt the other way and he is a young man with high cheekbones and a sculpted body. Viewed straight on and unblinking, they are an androgynous figure, handsome features and a beautiful head of hair, an infinity of arms curving from an impossible number of shoulders.

It is me, of course. I have been waiting for you both.

"Sung Siu Yin." I incline my head. "And Chen Mei Chi. Together, here, at last." So saying, I stoop and gather the remains of Mercy's bones. Fragile, bitter things. After more than half a century, any normal body would have eroded to nothing, lost in a matter of years to time and tides. But she asked me to remember her, and thus—impossibly—something of her still remains.

"You knew we were coming?" Mercy says.

"I am a goddess, little one." Bones held close, I drift quietly out of the temple, to stand on that dark and tiny beach.

"Then why not get involved sooner?" you protest, wading farther ashore. "Always, you watch us from the sides, like a spectator at a game."

"My power is not without limits, and the weave of human life is complex," I say, gently. From a human, your comment would be intolerably rude, but I am willing to give a ghost more grace. "I am in many places at once, and also in none of them. I hear prayers, but erratically. I have powers, but only in certain places—like my shrines—or at certain times of year, like my birthday. I am wiser than most, but not omnipotent. My existence is infinite, yet also very narrow. I am not what mortals think; I am both less and more than what any of you imagine. Touching one life touches others, and even deities must be careful how they tread across the tapestry of destiny."

"We recognize that, and acknowledge with gratitude what you can give," Mercy says, bowing low. "I know we have asked much already over the years, but can you help us one last time, Lady Kwun Yam?"

"That depends. What are you seeking?"

"I wish to set free the ghosts of this island." Mercy is still bent forward with hands clasped. "To make amends to my niece, as much as I can. And to find my peace."

"I see." I come to stand in front of her, looming inhumanly tall in the semidarkness. "Do you understand, Chen Mei Chi, that this will mean the end of your existence in this life?"

There is a heartbeat of silence in the cavern, but Mercy is unfazed.

"I understand, yes," she says, straightening up.

"And you're still willing?"

Her shoulders rise and fall in a helpless shrug. "I've had a damn good life.

Never easy, but always interesting, which is the best anyone can ask for. Though my death was cruel and unmourned, my existence can't come at the expense of another's pain. I want to give Siu Yin what I can."

If you were human, there'd be a lump in your throat.

"Very good," I say, pleased. "This act cannot give back the years lost, but her life can at least move forward, if you are both willing." I turn to you. "How do you feel in all this, Sung Siu Yin? On the surface, what we do will be an easy task. But the truth is, forgiveness is never easy. The heart is afraid to let go. When hurt is all we've known, we are reluctant to relinquish it, and we fear to venture into unfamiliar lands."

Your hands curl and uncurl, thoughts whirling in your head. It is, you find, easier to think clearly in this place, without the oppressive ghostly anger saturating every action or intent.

"I have done so much wrong," you say, finally. "I can't imagine an existence other than what I have."

"Don't be silly, niece," Mercy says, reprovingly. "If you can fight in wars like a legend, *and* run government offices, *and* wreak epic vengeance on your old auntie, then there is nothing you can't do as a living woman. If that's what you want."

In the moment you are grateful water ghosts cannot cry.

"Let's do it," you whisper.

"Step into yourself, Siu Yin," I say. "We will go from there."

Look down at your body with a fresh and critical eye. See the lines on that face, the gray in that hair. The lightning scar up one arm. This form is a stranger to you, a different woman from the one you remember being.

Then your gaze falls on the tiny tiger charm bracelet. Though the cord of it has been replaced, the charm endures; a tiny yet physical link between past and present, death and life, you and Baba and Mei Chi.

It's enough.

You step into your own skin, for the first time in thirty-three years.

Raw sensation floods you. The heart judders into rhythm, jolted by the invasion of a spirit. This body has a belly full of water, thanks to being dragged around through oceans. You roll over and throw that up at my feet. Gasp for air, taking in ragged breaths. The sensation of relief that comes with breathing has never gotten old, no matter how many times you've escaped into a skin.

Sit up. Examine your hands, touch your wrists and ears and nose. Is this home? Maybe. It was once, could be again. This does feel different, you realize, from other skins you've inhabited. There's an underlying familiarity that resonates.

"I feel old." Your own voice, coming out of your own throat. For the first time in so long. "This body has seen many years, and multiple injuries." The left eye is still swollen shut from the beating your enforcers gave it; very uncomfortable.

Fifty-three isn't old! There's plenty of life left in it yet, Mercy says, a little defensively. Once again, her voice is but a watery echo in your mind. *I never considered myself to be old, and you shouldn't either. As for those injuries—they will heal. Probably.*

"It's fine, I was just commenting. I understand already that the life I could have had in my youth is gone forever, and I've accepted it." Even as you say so, you really do accept it with quiet resignation. "I can only make the most of what comes."

You stand shakily, feeling hollow and exhausted. This body has seen two deaths and a recent beating, in addition to its share of life, and is worn to the breaking point.

What now, goddess? Mercy asks.

"Now, the true work begins," I say. "Mei Chi, step forward."

She does, if a little anxiously.

"Little one, you once asked me to remember you, in the same breath that you cursed your own village and railed against all who lived on this island. Will you now revoke those words to forgive the friends and neighbors who played their part in your death, and let the village of Shek Ham Chau be at rest?"

I'm not sure I'd ever describe any of them as friends, and they definitely killed my cat, Mercy mutters. *But you know, it was a long time ago. A woman's got to move on. After everything I have done, I still hope someone forgives my mistakes, too. Therefore . . . yes, I can forgive them.*

"Then let the haunting of Shek Ham Chau end." I stomp my foot.

As my heel hits the ground, green vines surge from beneath, pushing up through rock. Foliage, leaves, and moss rocket in all directions, spreading across the cavern walls like a spill of green ink. You flinch, and come stand next to me for safety; I allow it.

Mercy, meanwhile, swears vehemently and retreats to the safety of the water. This must look like her nightmare made flesh, but my dreams were never meant to terrorize her, only awaken memories of the spirit that her flesh had long buried. And my power, used now, is likewise not intended to harm. I am only here to help.

Living tendrils force cracks and crevices to widen in the unfeeling stone, crumbling away years of lime and sediment and crusted earth. Rubble begins to rain down in the cavern.

Then the headland bursts open from the force of new growth and the cavern roof collapses, smashing all the way through the ancient temple. When the dust stops, you lift your head and look around.

The cavern is gone completely, the weak headland having collapsed under its weight and my power. Open sky pours from above, bright blue and heavy with hot sunlight. Rock has fallen along the former cave entrance, blocking it off from the sea and forming a crude wall that will keep out the tide. The tunnel has collapsed, too, though you cannot see that from here.

At our feet, the ocean still pools, but it cannot be replenished any longer. In time, the sun will dry it out. When it does, this will just be a grassy hollow near the sea, ringed by rocks and filled only with earth.

As for the temple—that is destroyed beyond recognition. What wasn't smashed by the cavern roof has been destroyed by vines and bamboo, those stark green shoots engulfing the ruins. Lotus blossoms—a symbol of my power—explode into bloom, the pink-tipped petals opening wide and white to the sun. Giant taro spreads huge leaves, covering many sins.

Soon, in a matter of weeks or months, this place will be swallowed by nature, with no trace of its past remaining on the surface.

The growth doesn't stop there. All around the island, vines and trees and bamboo groves and mangrove shrubs are surging, engulfing buildings and smoothing over their presence. The land remembers what was done to it, but it will find ways to grow around the damage. Much as the human heart can also do.

"You . . . destroyed your own shrine," you say, stunned.

"All things come to an end. No one has prayed at my temple in almost half a century." I pause. "Once it was a place of light and joy, but now it has become a nexus of darkness, sorrow, and pain, to which these unfortunate souls were bound."

A wind picks up and on it, you can hear the cry of a multitude of ghosts. Their voices are a chorus, loud and searing. The noise rises to its peak and then, one by one, they begin to gradually fade. I feel each one like a plucked lute string as they dissipate, and an invisible weight seems to lift from the island.

"Is that it, then?" you say, awed. "Are they finally at peace?"

"Until the next life, yes."

I'm glad, Mercy says softly, from the shrinking pool where she lurks. *I never meant them to suffer so long.*

"Nor did they mean that for you, I am certain." I turn slightly, her bones still cradled in my arms. "Siu Yin, if you are both ready, the time has come to bury Mei Chi's remains."

"What will happen, when I do?" you say, suddenly apprehensive.

It's a natural reaction, that fear. After all, Mercy has been the center of your thoughts for decades. It's terrifying, the thought of letting go.

Who even are you, without your hate?

"Truthfully, I am not quite sure what will happen," I admit, and smile at your startlement. It is not every day that a deity confesses to ignorance. "I know that in a few days, you will settle into your body, as you would into any other skin. Likely, you will forget your memories of being a ghost, experiencing a kind of rebirth. But after that—well, it is anyone's guess."

"A death and a rebirth, all at once," you muse.

"Yes. And I will be there to guide you through this rebirth," I say, holding your mortal gaze with my divine one. "Only when you are fully human can your forgiveness have enough power to lay Mei Chi to rest. It is no longer her own anger that keeps her here, but yours."

You stare back and forth, between me and the mostly submerged Mercy. "Am I not human now?"

"No. You are still a ghost in a transient shell. It is not quite the same."

"What happens if I settle into my skin, you tell me the truth about myself, and I can't then forgive?"

"Then what will be, will be," I say, simply.

"I see." You glance up at the island, rapidly greening in the distance, all soft and quiet and empty; you look back at Mercy, hovering and silent in her tepid pool—all that remains of the cavern.

Slowly, you walk over to her and crouch down.

She gazes out at you, just beneath the water's surface: surreal and green-hued. The glamour has no effect on you because of my presence, or your experiences, but neither do you find her grotesque. She is simply a sad, lost spirit, acting on urges that you have also felt, and are now free of.

"Auntie? Whatever happens next, I want you to know that you were right to bring me back here. I can see that, now that I'm becoming human again." You pause, gathering your words. "I won't pretend I'm not angry or hurt, and I won't pretend this makes everything right between us. But I can be all of those things, and still try to forgive."

Thank you, Siu Yin, she says, rising out of the water. Despite the sun's heat searing her skin. *You have the strength of a thousand lives, and I believe you will find the way to peace.*

Tears well up, and you're relieved to let them fall. Crying cannot embarrass you after all you've been through in life, and death, and life again.

Grasp her hand and give those stone-cold fingers a squeeze.

She squeezes back.

Rise slowly, still weary from the long journey which brought you back, at last, to Shek Ham Chau's cursed shores. Turn and face me, tired and frightened and determined.

"I'm ready," you say. "Let's bury those old bones, and free some ghosts."

40

THE PEACE OF HEAVEN

August 26, 1975
(Four days later)

Picture yourself, a woman of fifty-odd years, lying flat on a quiet beach.

Beneath the shade of a giant taro tree, your form lies still and quiet. Dark hair fans out on the sand, forming a splash of ink around your face. Gray streaks add touches of lightness. Bruises bloom across your skin, though they will fade in a few days.

Trees sway, mangroves twist, birds call in low voices to one another. Waves unfurl like rolls of silk and still, you do not stir.

In the distance, someone calls your name.

Your eyes open.

Halos of refracted sunlight send you blinking, turning your head. Heave a breath, feeling strangely relieved that you can, and unsure why that would be. It seems like a long time since you've breathed so easily.

It's beautiful, here.

You just have no idea where "here" is, how you got to this place . . . or even who you are.

If one were to look closely at some of the distant foliage, they might catch a glimpse of what look like buildings, long overgrown by lush green life. Lotus blossoms grow in clusters, out of season but still beautiful. Nature has reclaimed humanity's brief habitat, yet the shape of old things remains.

To the left, there is a small, makeshift shrine; it was built for me by you, almost a day ago, though you don't remember that right now. Crude joss sticks sit cold, alongside a pile of freshly harvested pearls. You're about to examine it when, out on the wind, a lonely sound echoes and reverberates.

A shiver runs through you, every hair on your body standing up. It sounds like singing, but the voice—voices?—blends two melodies at once. Rise slowly, brush yourself clean. Unfamiliar clothes, but everything is unfamiliar. Things niggle at the edge of your memory. Whispers and thoughts, just below the surface.

Here is the truth: it is the morning of the fourth day since you retook your body, and that means your memory of being a ghost has faded fully. You've moved into a life that is new and old, at the same time, and you are not yet done adjusting.

It's going to be a hell of a transition.

Later, I will come to you as a friend, as a deity committed to mercy and compassion. Later, I will sit with you as your memories struggle to return, because it is not straightforward when a water ghost is bound back into her own body, after so many years apart from it.

There are very few rules for that. We are all in uncharted waters.

When that is done, I will tell you the story of your own life, explaining about yourself and about Mei Chi. About the long history that tangles between you. I will tell you the things that she has told me. I will tell you thoughts I have kept in my heart, all these years.

And we will all hope you can forgive, becoming a disciple of compassion.

If you can, then the next time you die, you will no longer be a water ghost. Just another quiet spirit, going to her quiet rebirth. That is the outcome we all hope for.

If you can't . . . Well. There is no path forward if you can't; no rest for a spirit who remains angry. And you are so, so tired, in the depths of your being. So in need of spiritual sleep.

For now, though, I keep my distance from you and keep my stories to myself. I watch as you walk along the beach as if in a bewildered dream. Sand cushions every footfall, and the tide smooths over your tracks.

Something has washed up on the beach, and it catches your eye. Drift closer, bend and pick it up. To your surprise, it's an old glass bottle. You can tell it is old, because it is worn very smooth by the tides, though it is still—miraculously—intact and whole.

I have kept it safe, all these years. Some barnacles have clustered on the side; they fall off as you pick it up.

Lift it to the sun. Inside the fuzzed glass, you can make out a very old photograph in black and white, of a young girl standing next to her mother. Turn it over. Curved outward against the opposite side is a snippet of writing on a scrap of paper. Something about staying friends forever. Reading the words sparks something in you, though you're not sure what, exactly. Only that it seems familiar, and comforting.

An eerie cry sings out again, tugging strangely at your heart.

Cup your hands, hold them to your mouth. "Hello? Is someone there?"

Out on the horizon, water swirls. Someone is swimming amidst the swaying kelp, and they are waiting for you, and this feels right.

It is a second chance. For you, for her, for life to prove you both wrong: that not everyone leaves, betrays, or abandons forever. That forgiveness is real, and that sometimes—just sometimes—there can be peace, even after long war.

Step into an ocean that glitters like crystal, foam brushing your knees and surf rolling over your thighs. Swim without fear, letting the currents of fate and time draw you to waters where the ground falls away, leaving you suspended in the green. Draw a slow, singular breath.

And

then

you

look

down.

Author's Note

Spelling conventions for Chinese names

Chinese given names are commonly two-syllable combinations, prefaced by a family name, or surname. There are different ways to represent that two-syllable construction in English; sometimes those first names have a space between syllables, or a hyphen. Sometimes they are written together as a single two-syllable construction.

I've been inconsistent across the book in how I represent those names; this is a deliberate choice. When possible, I combine syllables because I don't want readers to interpret Daiyu as two separate names, for example. This is also how my own name is written; my mother chose to write "Sunyi" rather than "Sun Yi," because she knew that in English the "yi" might be misconstrued as a middle name, when it is not. She also chose to spell it "Sunyi" instead of the correct jyutping representation of "Sanyi," because she knew that Westerners would mispronounce the vowel otherwise.

However, for other names—for example, Kit Ling—I opted to add a space between syllables, in order to guide the pronunciation a little more. If it were written like "Kitling," I think most Western readers would understandably rhyme that with "Kipling." This is due to how different languages handle stressed and unstressed syllables.

In other cases, I sometimes made an aesthetic decision. I felt intuitively, for example, that "Lau Yik" looks straightforward when written with a space, whereas "Lauyik" might give English readers pause.

The topic of how to best present non-Anglo names can be really sticky, and I hope that I have not been insensitive in my methods. My goal is only to make the names as accessible and accurate-sounding as possible, while still respecting both the pinyin/jyutping systems and the original language.

On the subject of English names in a Chinese setting

Hong Kong has a long and complex history with English-sounding first names. For many young people, choosing an English name—especially before going abroad—is something they spend time and effort on. Not all Chinese names translate easily to English, and also some folks just enjoy the fun of it.

When my mother moved from Hong Kong to Texas in the late 1980s, she picked the name Lisa for herself. To this day, even though she has now reverted to her original given name, there are still a few people who know her as Lisa. When I was much younger, I often used my middle name, Robin, while in America. Some of my Texan relatives continue to use "Robin" even now. In this book, Mei Chi opts to acquire the English name of Mercy, partly to reinvent herself and partly to reflect the changing world she lives in.

I will also freely admit that giving a slightly different name is a useful tool for helping the reader to keep track of the varying timelines, which do get quite complicated in places. However, having known many people who move seamlessly between their English and Chinese names, I think she would fit right in.

On the subject of translated names

For the most part, character names are untranslated in the book, but not always. This inconsistency is something I wrestled with enormously; there's a weirdness to having certain terms or names translated in a book which is set in a non-English environment, while others remain the same.

Ultimately, I decided that leaving names in their original form was truer to how Chinese people think about names. For example, my own name means God's Child, but nobody who says my name is thinking of me as God's Child. They think of me simply as Sunyi, even among Cantonese speakers. Despite the fact that most Chinese names have a directly translated meaning, the context shapes how people perceive/hear those names.

In a similar way, we might meet someone called Pierce Brosnan, and think of him only as the person called Pierce—and not as the action verb, "pierce." Therefore, I felt that writing "Mei Chi" gave a better sense of how her name would be "heard" by Chinese speakers, rather than writing "Beautiful Energy," fun though that would have been.

In Mei Chi/Mercy's case specifically, I thought it was also useful to show the phonetic similarities between her English and Chinese names, which is a part of why she picks Mercy in the first place.

The two characters who buck this trend are Cobra Lily and Red Bird. This is because their situations are unique. Cobra Lily's "real" legal name is a secret, known only to herself and the government officials she briefly speaks to; her "triad name" is a chosen identity, meant to represent her status as its leader, and to convey her power. The same is true for Red Bird. Her name is taken to represent her identity as a sex worker, and to protect her privacy from the men she encounters.

In both cases, the meanings of their names are more important than the sound of them. When other people speak of Cobra Lily or Red Bird, they are hearing the words individually, because their names are more like titles. A similar example in English might be the famous 1980s wrestler Shirley Crabtree, who was known as "Big Daddy" in the ring.

On the subject of other translated words

I mostly use English terms throughout because that's the language this book is written in. However, some words actually convey better through context than they do through crude translated terms, e.g., dai pai dong or cha chaan teng. I could say "café" instead of cha chaan teng, but that has an association for me which is European in origin. Besides, modern Hong Kong has cafes, too, and they are often quite different from a cha chaan teng.

In short, I've tried to use common sense or artistic license for what feels appropriate, and to convey a sense of cultural flavor in things that I particularly love about Hong Kong, without drowning English readers in unfamiliar vocabulary. There's a fine line between authenticity and exotification, which I am always trying to balance.

A note on Cobra Lily, and the historical figure of "Mother Snake"

The character of Cobra Lily is entirely fictional, but she does draw from a real-life lady gangster named She Aizhen. Originally born into a wealthy Shanghainese family, Aizhen was fascinated by the criminal underworld at an early age, despite her privileged upbringing and expensive education. At fourteen, she fell pregnant with a gangster's child. When he refused to support her, she threatened him with a knife until he agreed to marriage. When her second husband cheated on her, she stormed the house of his mistress, threatened the other woman with guns, and clawed the skin from her face.

She Aizhen's life was marked by extraordinary violence and unusual contrasts. She was beautiful and intelligent, but also brutal and viciously cruel. She defied a thousand different gender barriers and social strictures, but also tortured and murdered wantonly, and even sided with the Japanese during World War II. Much like Cobra Lily, She Aizhen was a difficult person to categorize: a compelling force of nature, both monstrous and revolutionary.

A further note on Guanyin/Kwun Yam, and Ma Zu

Historically, Guanyin/Kwun Yam is a wholly separate entity from Ma Zu, and better known as a powerful and important goddess of mercy, rather than as a sea goddess. Guanyin originated from Hinduism, specifically the male bodhisattva known as Avalokiteśvara. Buddhism shares much of its lore with Hinduism, including some of the deities.

As Buddhism/Hinduism spread and diverged across distances, Guanyin was sometimes portrayed as a gender-fluid deity, or more commonly as a woman in East Asia. As my mother put it, "Guanyin was born a man, but we know her now as a woman."

The reasons for this are complex and fascinating, and draw in part from Guanyin's ability to incarnate in different bodies and take different forms, as well as their emphasis on compassion and mercy. I have attempted to capture some of that gender fluid history here, in how Guanyin/Kwun Yam is represented.

Meanwhile, Ma Zu's origins differ enormously. Unlike Guanyin, who has always been divine, Ma Zu was born a human child with selective mutism (hence her human name, Lin Moniang, which means "Silent Girl"). She had the ability to control storms and astrally project her spirit, and eventually ascended to godhood; the exact story for this ascension varies across different myths and regions.

Over time, and in certain locations, Ma Zu cults and Guanyin cults became enmeshed. Though Ma Zu is widely accepted as an elevated human, some believed that she was actually an incarnation of Guanyin in human form, which would go some way to explaining her devotion to Guanyin (Ma Zu's goddess of choice), and her amazing supernatural gifts.

The historical literature leans heavily on them being separate figures with separate histories. But in this novel, I've adopted the interpretation that Ma Zu was an incarnation of Guanyin, hence the strange sea-cavern temple and the carvings that depict interactions with jiaoren. (For context, Ma Zu famously threw herself into the ocean after the death of her father, and in some legends she encountered strange creatures beneath the waves.)

As always, there's a balance to be struck between respect for beliefs, and the desire to weave those rich traditions into story form. I hope that what I have done will be of interest, rather than of offense, to those who worship both or either of these deities.

Acknowledgments

I struggled with this novel more than I've ever struggled with any other piece of writing. From first idea to final copyedits, it's taken me five frantic years (August 2020 to August 2025) to get *GWATF* across the finish line. In an industry where a book a year is the norm, this was a terrifying amount of time to spend on a manuscript.

My research was extensive, and the rewrites were numerous; I don't know how many new drafts it took. I lost track after number eight. Everything from setting, to plot, to main character, to all basic aspects of the story kept changing. For one particularly bad rewrite, I got to eighty thousand words and threw all of it in the bin, starting over completely from scratch.

The only things I knew for certain: This novel was a story about lonely women who were lost and adrift. And it would be set in Hong Kong, with ghosts. It is therefore the height of irony that I was a bit lost and adrift myself while writing it.

The end result is a novel that I and my editors are finally happy with: a tribute to the city and the islands of my youth, a love story to Hong Kong's ghost legends, and a heartfelt nod to my grandmother's personal history. If there is one thing that I hope readers take away from this story, it is a sense of how devastating the world wars were to China, and how the echoes of that unacknowledged mass trauma still linger today.

And on that note, I want to thank a lot of different people for helping me bring this story to completion—because there were definitely times when I worried that day would never come!

Firstly, I want to give a shout-out to my acquiring editor, Lindsey Hall, who pushed me to be ambitious and try something "completely different" from *The Book Eaters*, and who took the time to check in with numerous video calls. I'm glad of the challenge and I'm proud of the book that emerged from the rubble and ruin of these many drafts. I would never have attempted something so structurally complex without her encouragement.

I must also follow this up with many sincere thanks to my next editor, Aislyn Fredsall, who stepped in to take over the project and pick up where Lindsey left off. Her vision and her edits never wavered, until she finally brought us all the way home. She has been a guiding light that helped pull this novel back from the brink.

I would also like to thank my previous literary agent, Naomi Davis. Though we are no longer business partners, I remain eternally grateful that she picked me up when no one else did, and that she always believed in my work long before any publishers saw potential.

I am also enormously grateful to my current literary agent, Harry Illingworth. He stepped up and fought for this book, at one of the most turbulent points in my career so far. Without that intervention, I'm not sure where we would be right now.

No acknowledgments would be complete without heartfelt thanks to my long-suffering partner, Lee Muncaster, who has spent much of the past five years listening to me tear my hair out over this novel (and the two other books I wrote during the same time span, though those ones likely won't get published). I feel very lucky to have him and to share my life with him.

And finally, I must thank the city of Hong Kong itself for being the most fascinating place a girl could grow up. In the present day, Hong Kong's democracy has sadly been eroded, and I wish to acknowledge the many individuals and organizations who are still fighting desperately for Hong Kong's future, even now.

Credits

So many awesome people go into the creation of a book, all of them integral in different ways. Below, I have listed the names of those whose hard work was instrumental in bringing *The Girl with a Thousand Faces* to life. Some (like the lovely Charlotte Trumble) joined the team only recently, but everyone has been so kind and enthusiastic, and I'm grateful to all.

Tor Team

- Copy editor: Erin Wilcox
- Cover designer: Shreya Gupta
- Cover artist: Lindsey Carr
- Sensitivity reader: Zhui Ning Chang
- Publicity: Giselle Gonzalez
- Marketing: Tyrinne Lewis, Lauren Moye, and Emily Mlynek

Harper Team

- British editor: Charlotte Trumble
- Desk editor: Catherine Perks
- Editorial assistant: Sam Willis
- Cover design: Toby James
- Publicity: Angelica Bowden-Jones
- Marketing: Amy Ruffhead
- Sales: Leah Wood, Rosie Hawkins, Holly Martin, and Ruth Burrow

Early Readers

- Essa Hansen, best of friends and otherworldly SF author
- Scott Drakeford, friend and fantastic fellow Tor author
- Todd Jordan, friend and excellent horror author
- Ariel, friend and excellent SF writer
- Keshe Chow, friend and brilliant YA author
- Ben from Aldi, local superfan and a totally lovely young man

About the Author

Mark Hillyer, True North Studio

SUNYI DEAN (sun-yee deen) is a biracial fantasy author who was born in Texas, grew up in Hong Kong, and now resides in North England. She writes speculative fiction with a weird slant, and her debut novel, *The Book Eaters*, was a *USA Today* bestseller.

Back in the day, her high school was a former seminary built on the edge of the original Walled City, and her grandparents lived in Hong Kong through both world wars. In her spare time, she likes buying whiskey, picking up dumbbells, and dying in jiu-jitsu.